Praise for the novels of Michelle Major

Look for Michelle Major's next novel
available soon from HQN.

For a full list of titles by Michelle Major,
please visit www.michellemajor.com.

MICHELLE MAJOR

The
Wish List

HQN

HQN®

ISBN-13: 978-1-335-43064-9

The Wish List
Copyright © 2022 by Michelle Major

A Lot Like Christmas
Copyright © 2022 by Michelle Major

Recycling programs
for this product may
not exist in your area.

For questions and comments about the quality of this book,
please contact us at CustomerService@Harlequin.com.

HQN
22 Adelaide St. West, 41st Floor
Toronto, Ontario M5H 4E3, Canada
www.Harlequin.com

Printed and bound in Barcelona, Spain by CPI Black Print

CONTENTS

THE WISH LIST

For Matt. Everything is better when we're together.

CHAPTER ONE

BETH CARLYLE'S DAY couldn't get any worse.

That's what she told herself as she walked through Magnolia Community Hospital toward the stairwell at the end of the third-floor hallway.

A familiar voice called her name. She turned to see Dr. Greg Madison, chief of staff and her ex-husband, beckoning to her. A frown marred his boyishly handsome features.

Apparently, her day could get worse.

She felt her coworkers watching as she moved toward Greg's small office. When she'd filed for divorce over a year ago, there had been quite a bit of conjecture among the hospital staff. Everyone seemed to relish the demise of Beth's marriage, enthusiastically choosing sides—Team Beth or Team Greg—and placing bets on whether they'd be able to continue working together.

All very *Grey's Anatomy*-type entertainment, except Beth had made sure the drama never materialized. She and Greg remained friendly, if not close, a sore disappointment to the workplace gossip machine.

Beth Carlyle—she'd returned to her maiden name as soon as the papers were signed—didn't do drama.

Not usually. Not on purpose.

Today had been a weak moment. Beth detested weakness, which was why she started explaining before Greg had even shut the door behind her.

"The stress is getting to me," she admitted as she glanced around the familiar space. They used to have lunch there together, but she hadn't entered his office for months. He'd taken down the framed photos of the two of them, and she waited for pain or regret to zap her heart.

Nothing happened. Did that speak more about her current state of agitation or was the message how easily she'd gotten over the demise of their eight-year union?

She'd think about that later with a big glass of wine to keep her company.

Greg moved behind his mahogany desk, the one she'd helped him choose, then stalked toward her again like he couldn't force himself to stay still. "Beth."

"I was out of line, and I'm sorry. I'll apologize to the patient as well. We know each other from—"

"Beth, this isn't about you."

She took a breath and studied her ex, noticing the tension lines that bracketed his mouth and the way his warm brown eyes were as wide as chocolate saucers.

"Is it my mom?" Her hands clenched into fists at her side. "I talked to the charge nurse from the rehab center this morning. She said—"

"Your mom is okay, at least as far as I know." Greg ran a hand through his hair, a similar shade of brown as his eyes. His hair had been thick and wavy when they'd met during his final year of med school, but recently it had gone fine on the top. Was that a tiny paunch around his middle?

Beth had too much on her plate to pay close attention to her ex-husband, although it was a hard habit to break. She guessed he'd reverted to his preferred diet of microwave meals and processed snacks instead of the healthy food she'd prepared for both of them while they were married.

Stop, she silently commanded herself. Greg wasn't her

problem anymore, not his diet or his hair or any number of things she'd taken care of during their decade together. If Beth had a love language, it would be acts of service. Too often that service felt more like a burden than a function of love. Sometimes it was hard for her to tell the difference.

"Greg, this isn't a good time," she said, imagining he wanted help buying Christmas gifts for his parents or staff.

They'd been newly separated last holiday season, so Beth had automatically handled his purchases. She had a trusty app on her phone that took care of lists and links—easy enough. But she'd forced herself to delete that app over the summer when she found herself mentally adding items for her ex-husband.

It was a good thing he wasn't on her docket of people to care for because due to her mother's stroke a week ago, she was dealing with way more than she could handle, and Beth was known for dealing with a lot.

She made a move to step around him, but his hand on her arm stopped her. How long had it been since his touch had affected her? Beth sometimes wondered if she was still capable of reacting to a man.

"Lucy is pregnant."

Beth stilled, and it felt like the place where his skin touched hers had turned to stone. Not exactly the reaction she wanted. "I don't understand," she murmured, only realizing she'd said the words out loud when Greg answered.

"She's having a baby."

"I know what pregnant means."

"I'm going to be a father," he continued as if she still needed the clarification. "It wasn't exactly the plan, but you know how much I want to be a father."

Those words struck like a blow. Of course she'd known he wanted a baby of his own. She was the one who'd spent the last five years dealing with fertility treatments—hormones and shots and sex dictated by her cycle and the calendar.

Beth was thirty-three. No spring chicken when it came to her ovaries. Even when she'd been younger, motherhood had eluded her. Getting pregnant she could manage. Staying pregnant, not so much.

A sad, secret part of her wondered if it was because she'd never felt truly enthusiastic about becoming a mom. The lion's share of responsibility for raising her two younger sisters had been foisted on her a few weeks after her thirteenth birthday. As an adult, she'd never felt the hard pull toward motherhood the way so many of the women she knew did.

She'd tried. Tirelessly. Religiously. Without thought to the toll her consistent failure took on her body or heart. And when she couldn't take it anymore, she'd let her husband go. Released him from their vows with a few comforting words about how she wanted his dreams to come true.

She'd believed that would release her to focus on her own dreams, even though she had little experience with that. But it wasn't supposed to go like this.

"I didn't realize you and Lucy had gotten serious." She'd only seen Greg and the young medical assistant around town a couple of times.

"We weren't exactly serious," he said, having the good grace to look slightly abashed. "This changes things, doesn't it?"

Beth knew he was asking the question for real and not in a rhetorical sense. He wanted her permission or for Beth to insist he do the right thing by the woman he'd knocked up. The sad part was that he clearly didn't trust himself to do the right thing on his own.

"You want to be a father." She repeated his words, surprised there wasn't any pain associated with them. Only a strange sense of disconnected disbelief. Emotionally disconnected seemed to be her go-to right now. Her heart was encased in ice, whether to keep herself safe or because she didn't have the genetic makeup for something more, Beth wasn't sure.

The phone on the desk rang. "I need to go," she repeated.

"So you're okay with this?" Greg ran another hand through his hair. Was it thinning on its own or because he couldn't stop tugging at the ends? "I asked her to marry me. I want to do this the right way."

Beth didn't bother to mention cart before the horse and all that. "I wish you nothing but the best," she told him. It was true if not enthusiastic.

"I'm sure you'll make right whatever happened with the patient. You're a good nurse, Beth."

"Thanks."

"And a good daughter." He gave a soft chuckle. "Plus a great ex-wife."

One positive about being divorced was she didn't have to worry about laughing at her ex's feeble attempts at humor.

"Happy Thanksgiving, Greg," she said and took a step toward the door.

"Oh, by the way. That reminds me. Any chance you'd send over your sweet potato casserole recipe? Lucy and I are going to her mom's for Thanksgiving. We're going to tell her family about…you know." He made a face. "I want to impress them, and your sweet potato casserole is the best ever."

"I'll email it," she said, ignoring the pang of resentment. She was a real pro at ignoring negative emotions.

"I don't suppose you've bought the ingredients and have enough to double the recipe?" Greg flashed his best puppy-dog smile, the one she used to find appealing. Now it affected her the same way a rock stuck in her shoe might.

"Right, Greg. A surefire way to impress your potential new in-laws would be to have your ex-wife cook for them on Thanksgiving. Freya is handling the meal this year since she's in town and staying at Mom's house. We're going to bring it to the rehab facility unless they give Mom a day pass."

Greg grimaced. "I didn't know either of your sisters could cook. You might want to—"

"We'll manage. You're on your own," she told him and walked out.

The words felt right, but her glimmer of satisfaction managed to be short-lived. Was she mistaken or were more people staring at her as she started down the hall again? Did they already know about Lucy and Greg or did they assume her ex had reprimanded her for her earlier behavior with a patient?

Beth had mastered the art of the poker face. She kept hers intact until the heavy fire door of the stairwell slammed shut behind her then let loose with a slew of curses and a few halfhearted kicks to the wall.

"Stupid idiot," she muttered, unsure whether she was talking about Greg or herself. She drew back her foot and kicked the wall with more force then yelped in pain.

"Unless those clogs are steel-toed, you'd better give the wall a break before you fracture something."

Beth whirled with a gasp, shocked to see a man sitting on the stairs heading down to the lower floors. She'd been so angry and distracted that she hadn't noticed him when she'd first entered the stairwell.

It was a testament to the crappiness of her day and her muddled mental state because the man staring at her was hard to ignore. Although he didn't stand, she could tell he would be tall—well over six feet. His shoulders were broad underneath the battered leather jacket he wore with faded jeans and a dark shirt.

She'd bet her last cent he drove a motorcycle. He looked like the motorcycle type.

He looked like the type of guy who could bring a woman or twelve to their knees with longing. His sandy blond hair was thick and curled slightly at his collar. He had eyes the color of the ocean after a storm and she could almost read the upheaval in them. Why was that upheaval so appealing?

"I thought I was alone."

He nodded but didn't smile. His gaze darkened. Beth had lived in Magnolia most of her life but didn't make a habit of going to the beach. She knew what the waves looked like in winter though, and this man would be right at home there.

"I gathered that. You aren't somebody who makes an awareness of your surroundings a priority."

"What's that supposed to mean?" Beth narrowed her eyes. She was hyperaware of her surroundings and the people in them to a fault. To the point where she often forgot to eat or go to the bathroom because she was so focused on her patients and coworkers and—

"I was in the room when you were rude to Shauna. You didn't notice me. I'm going to give you the benefit of the doubt and say you also didn't notice the effect your words had on her. Otherwise, you should pick a new line of work. She's a good person and a fantastic mom. She didn't deserve you roasting her like that."

Embarrassment crashed over Beth like an icy wave, almost stealing her breath with its force. She squared her shoulders and opened her mouth to issue a sharp retort, to defend herself and rationalize her behavior.

Then she shook her head. Why bother? The stranger was right. He'd pegged her in one decisive judgment.

"I'm going to apologize to Shauna," she said quietly.

"Will you mean it or is it just a way to keep yourself out of trouble with your supervisor?"

"Mothers have a responsibility to be careful," she said, responding to the question without directly answering it.

"Accidents can happen anywhere."

"She's a single mother of six-year-old twins and went skydiving," Beth said, crossing her arms over her chest.

His full lips thinned and he glanced at the floor before meeting Beth's gaze again. "She's a fantastic mother," he repeated.

"How well do you know her?" Beth asked, then regretted the question. "Don't answer that. It's none of my business."

"I know her better than anyone in her life." The man rose, and Beth had been right about his height. What she hadn't counted on was the force of his presence. Hadn't she just been mentally lamenting the fact that she didn't react to men in the way a woman should?

It must be some sick cosmic joke that the man who made her knees wobbly just by looking at her was also one who clearly thought she was a rude bitch.

He moved up a step, and Beth instinctively inched toward the door. "What would the people closest to you say about your character?" he challenged.

Okay, she'd been wrong to lecture Shauna Myer about her free-time activities, but this guy had no right to level a barrage of criticism at Beth.

She licked her dry lips, trying not to gape when his gaze lowered to her mouth. "My ex-husband would probably tell you I'm too controlling and need to loosen up a bit. On the other hand, he just requested my permission to ask a woman he barely knows to marry him since she's having his baby." She held out her hands. "And since I wasn't able to carry a pregnancy to term during all the years we tried, what could I do but give my blessing?"

The stranger's nostrils flared although his expression stayed neutral. "That sucks."

"Pretty much," Beth agreed, but she wasn't finished. "My two sisters would tell you I liked to boss them around too much back in the day, but my mom kind of turned over raising them to me when I was barely a teenager. So I got a little bossy. Sue me. Since they both got to leave town while I stuck around to take care of our mom, they might want to thank me instead."

She cupped one hand around her mouth like she was sharing a secret. "Mom has never been a big fan of pesky details like paying the electricity bill or regular medical care. Those are still my responsibilities, as is her care now that she's had a stroke. All fun things to deal with while I'm doing my level best to find a way to leave this town, you know?"

He held up his hands, palms out, a look of abject panic dulling the storm in his gray eyes. "I get it. Not an easy time for you right now."

"Exactly." She jabbed a finger in the man's direction even as she commanded herself to ease off the verbal diarrhea. "Maybe you could cut me some slack."

"Maybe you could cut Shauna some?"

Beth spit out a laugh. She'd just unburdened her soul to a stranger—for the life of her she had no idea why. In response, he reminded her that his loyalty did not lie with her. She didn't know who he was to Shauna. A friend. A lover. It didn't matter, and she had no explanation for the slight pinch in her chest.

His words reminded her that she was alone in the world, the only one in her corner. Beth had never been much of a fighter.

Yes, she had her mom and sisters, although the baby of the family, Trinity, had yet to arrive. Did Freya and Trinity even count when neither of them particularly liked Beth? If this reunion followed the pattern of their childhood, it would be the two of them in one corner and her in the other.

Their mother, May, hadn't been emotionally present for any of them in years, and Beth didn't see how her recent health crisis would change that.

She was alone.

And like it or not, she owed Shauna Myer an apology.

"I'll go talk to her now," Beth said, digging her finger-nails into her palms until the pain dulled the ache in her chest.

He moved up another step.

"Preferably in private," she clarified, "unless you don't trust me for that."

The stranger studied her for a long moment before nodding. "I trust you."

Emotion clogged her throat at the simple statement. She was worse off than she'd imagined.

"Thanks." She gestured to the empty stairwell. "I'll leave you to it then. Enjoy."

The metal fire door shut behind her with a satisfying creak and bang, leaving the enigmatic stranger behind.

CHAPTER TWO

TRINITY CARLYLE WENT stock-still at the sound of a branch cracking nearby. She knew squatting in the woods on the side of a two-lane highway at dusk wasn't the smartest choice for a pit stop but these were desperate times.

She'd gotten pretty efficient over the past several days driving from the Rocky Mountains to her hometown of Magnolia, North Carolina, and managed to slot in her bathroom breaks so that she'd made decent time on the trip even though she had to stop every few hours.

When she'd left for the West the morning after her high school graduation almost nine years ago, she'd made it to Colorado—over fifteen hundred miles away—in a day and a half. At that point, she'd been fueled by energy drinks and cheap chocolate. Neither of which she'd continued to rely on once she'd decided to stay in the mountain time zone. Okay, she still appreciated a daily cup of coffee and the occasional candy bar, but who didn't?

However, things were different now and mainlining caffeine while binging on chocolate wasn't an option in her condition. So the drive had taken longer. She knew her sisters were irritated with her, and neither of them understood why she couldn't hop on a plane and arrive in North Carolina a few hours later.

It wasn't a discussion Trinity was willing to have over the phone, but she was here now, the night before Thanksgiving. She'd made it back for the start of the holiday season, which her oldest sister, Beth, had told her was non-negotiable.

Although Trinity was dead tired, she was driving directly to the rehab center where her mother was staying as she recovered from the stroke that had shocked all of them. As much as Trinity didn't relish returning to her mother's house, right now she'd pay good money for the lumpy twin-size bed of her childhood and a soft blanket.

Leaves crunched, snapping her mind back to the present, and she started to hum her favorite Dolly Parton Christmas song. Darkness was quickly taking over the shadowy woods. Trinity shouldn't be scared. She'd hiked the back-country of the Rockies and Bitterroot mountains for years. Why did the forest surrounding Magnolia feel so ominous?

She was projecting her anxiety and gave herself a mental headshake when a deer made its way across the clearing in front of her. She had nothing to worry about, she reminded herself. Not here.

Nothing bad had ever happened to her in Magnolia, at least in comparison to what she'd experienced after leaving town. But those experiences were behind her for the moment. She finished pulling up her black leggings and carefully made her way back to her car, now singing loudly, only to find she was no longer alone on the side of the road.

A dark SUV with blue-and-red lights flashing from the roof had parked behind her. Trinity gave a mental eye roll. She must have been passed by a couple of dozen speed racers on the various interstates she traveled and not one had been pulled over that she'd seen. She'd parked on the shoulder for five minutes, and a cop had managed to find her. Just her luck.

"Can I help you, Officer?" she called as she approached

her car, making her voice sound confident, like it was no big deal.

A uniformed man appeared from the front of her hatchback. "I was going to ask you the same question, ma'am."

Trinity nearly smiled at that. Ma'am. Had she ever been called ma'am? "I just needed a potty break," she said with what she hoped was a charming shrug.

As the man drew closer, her breath hitched and she tugged on the oversized sweatshirt she wore to hide her belly.

Not that her sisters would be fooled, but she didn't want to advertise her condition to every Tom, Dick and Johnny Law she encountered on the trip. Especially not one who looked like something out of a Hollywood Western. Broad-shouldered, square-jawed with warm brown eyes that glittered even in the strange glow from his vehicle's light bar.

She reminded herself she wasn't embarrassed about her pregnancy, just private. There was a difference.

"We recommend using rest stops for that sort of thing around here." His gaze raked over her like he was searching for something.

Trinity couldn't imagine what or that he'd find it with her. Maybe once upon a time she would have wanted to turn this moment into some kind of meet cute. To flirt and laugh with a respectable stranger. Trinity used to laugh all the time, easily finding the joy and adventure in even life's tiniest moments.

Not so much these days. Safety and security were priorities, although she hadn't done a bang-up job of attracting either into her world.

The officer's gaze moved away from her to the broken wine bottle on the gravel behind her car. She sighed. Apparently, today was not the day her luck would change.

"Sorry," she said automatically. "I was planning to clean up the mess. The bottle fell out when I opened the back to grab a wad of toilet paper."

"Have you been drinking, ma'am?"

She laughed then shut her mouth when it was clear the cop wasn't joking. "No, sir. I'm heading to my mom's house for the holidays. I picked up wine to bring for my sisters. I'm not drinking. I haven't been drinking."

A car whooshed by, and he lifted his gaze to follow it. Another speeder was getting away with her stuck here explaining an innocent mistake but feeling guilty, nonetheless.

"I'd like to see your license and registration. Would you mind taking a field sobriety test?" he asked conversationally.

This wasn't a conversation Trinity relished. "Yes," she answered then immediately amended her response. "I mean, no. I don't have a problem with the test, but I told my sisters I'd be at the rehab facility by five. They're going to wonder where I am."

"Rehab?" One thick brow rose.

"Shoreline Rehabilitation Center," she clarified. "My mother is there recovering from a stroke, not that it's any of your business."

She shouldn't have added the last bit. She needed to channel her former sunny self, but her back hurt, her eyelids practically needed toothpicks to keep them open, and she already felt the urge to pee again. A gentle kick to her middle reminded Trinity of why it would not serve her to get on the wrong side of a cop.

Not that she expected protection. Still, no sense tempting fate more than she already had by leaving her former life and all that went with it without a backward glance.

"Are you talking about May Carlyle?" the cop asked, his voice gentler.

Trinity blinked. "How do you know my mother? You're not exactly the right demographic to be a fan."

The ghost of a smile touched his pouty lips and darn if she didn't want more. The full grin Monty, so to speak. She was past due having an attractive man smile at her for any reason.

Get a grip on yourself, she commanded. Frequent potty breaks weren't the only unwelcome urge she had these days. Her hormones were all over the place—fat lot of good it did her.

"May is my neighbor." He cleared his throat. "My daughter was the one who found her."

"How old is your daughter?"

"Eleven. She stopped by the house selling wrapping paper for a school fundraiser. Mr. Jingles was going crazy inside, so Michaela peeked in the window. She could see your mother at the bottom of the staircase."

Trinity's brain reeled as she tried to process the man's words. "Who is Mr. Jingles?" It seemed like the most benign place to start.

"Your mom's cat."

"My mom has a cat?"

"You didn't know? She adores that thing even though he's surly and massively overweight."

It was hard for Trinity to visualize her mom adoring anything but herself, let alone an animal that relied on her.

She didn't like how the officer was staring at her like she was somehow deficient as a daughter for not knowing about her mom's pet. Or maybe she was lacking because she'd taken off to have her own life and never looked back.

Either way, she didn't appreciate the scrutiny. "I promise

I'm not drinking and driving or drinking at all at the moment." She tugged at the ends of her shoulder-length hair, about two months past due for a trim. "The wine is for my sisters, obviously not my mom." She swallowed, blaming the emotions bubbling up inside her on fatigue and nothing deeper. "Do you still need my license?"

"You can go. I hope your mom is doing okay."

"Me, too," she said and looked toward the darkening forest, afraid to continue holding the officer's maple-hued gaze. Afraid of what her blue eyes might reveal. She gestured toward the wine bottle. "I'll clean this up first."

"I'll take care of it." The man offered his hand. "I'm Asher Davis. My friends call me Ash. I'm the police chief here in Magnolia. We're all sending good thoughts to your mom. As you can imagine, everyone in the neighborhood cares a lot about her."

Actually, Trinity couldn't. She figured Beth would clue her in as to the changes in their mother's social life. Her sister had told her that their mom had a long recovery in front of her, and the doctors weren't sure she'd ever regain full speech function.

Trinity didn't believe it. May always had so much to say. She couldn't fathom a world where her mother remained quiet for any length of time. She realized the man—Ash— still held out a hand and she took it, registering both the warmth of him and the calluses that covered his palm.

She used to have a thing about work-roughened hands back when she'd been young and stupid. She'd made jokes with her girlfriends about how a man who did hard work was probably good with his hands in other ways as well. That was before she learned the hard way that hands could be used to hurt as well as to fix things.

She released Ash and tried to tamp down the urge to wipe her palm on her sweatshirt.

"May has three daughters," he said. "I've met Beth, of course."

"I'm Trinity," she told him.

He nodded. "The one who lives out West. Your mom talks about you."

Another shock. May wasn't known to talk about anyone but herself, and Trinity couldn't imagine what her mom even knew of her life. The truth certainly wouldn't sit well.

"Thank you," she said, gesturing to the broken wine bottle. "I appreciate it."

"Let me know if there's anything you need while you're in town. We're just next door."

"The Amermans don't live there anymore?"

Emotion flashed in his dark eyes and then was gone before she could decide what might have put it there.

"They do. Well, Helena does. Chuck passed away a few years back. They're my in-laws."

Trinity tugged at her hair again. The hot police chief was Stacy Amerman's husband. They'd been friends back in high school, although Stacy had been more popular than Trinity. Another car sped by, and she smiled as Asher shook his head slightly.

"I'm sure we'll be fine," she told him. "I bet Beth has everything under control."

He stepped toward the road so Trinity could pass in front of him. It was an inherently gentlemanly thing to do. By the look on his face, Asher Davis didn't even register the minor consideration.

Trinity did, and the gesture helped her make up her mind that she would keep her distance from Magnolia's police chief this holiday season and beyond. The last thing she needed was the reminder that there were good men in the world when she only seemed to pick the bad.

CHAPTER THREE

FREYA CARLYLE SAT in the quiet, private room at the rehabilitation facility. She watched over her mother, who slept peacefully in the twin bed, chest rising and falling in a gentle rhythm.

Although Freya had been back in her hometown for the better part of a week, she hadn't grown accustomed to her mother being still. In all of Freya's childhood memories, May was a whirlwind of energy and spontaneity, fun and chaos.

The fun had come to an abrupt halt once May had published her runaway bestseller on rediscovering the wild woman within after divorce.

She'd become the poster single mom for rebirth and renewal after heartbreak, somehow making her singular brand of narcissism seem desirable. Something to strive for according to a generation of discontented divorcees and unhappy homemakers. May had been the original proponent of self-care, long before it became a buzzword.

Freya hadn't realized it consciously as a child, but her mother cared for herself at the expense of her three daughters' emotional well-being. They were a millstone around her neck, weighing her down.

Beth had taken on the role of the responsible one, and it still chafed how much she'd relished bossing around Freya and Trinity. With her sunny disposition and natural peacemaker tendencies, Trin had only noticed when Freya pointed it out. Freya had never liked anyone telling her what to do and certainly not her older sister.

She hadn't rebelled in the obvious ways with drinking or drug experimentation, although as an adult, she'd made plenty of lousy choices in men. As a teenager, Freya had acted out in a way that would hurt her mother the most.

She'd become an amateur beauty queen, relying on her looks and charm to slide through school and part-time jobs. She'd even managed to wrangle herself a spot at the University of North Carolina journalism school, more due to the promise of her potential than any actual broadcast talent.

May had suddenly approved because her middle daughter was making something of herself. Freya couldn't have that, so she'd dropped out of college after a semester.

That had been close to the straw that broke her mother's back, and they'd basically cut off all communication other than a perfunctory call on Christmas each year. It suited Freya and her lifestyle. She'd never relinquished the desire to disappoint her mom.

May had about suffered a coronary when Freya took a role on a reality dating show. For her mother, who was "a woman needs a man like a fish needs a bicycle" type of feminist, it had been the actual last straw. Which meant, of course, that Freya had built her entire career—such as it was—on a variety of reality show appearances with the occasional stint as arm candy for a not-so-famous or failing Hollywood star.

When Beth had called to tell Freya about their mother's stroke, it shamed Freya to admit she'd almost wanted to ignore the summons home.

Her sister, Magnolia's answer to Florence Nightingale, could certainly handle May's recovery on her own.

Yet Freya had come when Beth called. At the end of the day, she had been conditioned to do what her sister said.

Plus, she cared about her mother, even if she didn't want to admit it. Even if she was afraid that being home would expose her to judgment from both Beth and her mom. So far, Beth had been quiet about anything except May's recovery and the fact that their mom wasn't herself.

She'd only had a few moments of lucidity since Freya arrived. She smiled, and tears had filled her eyes when Freya leaned over her frail frame in the bed. She'd tried to speak, although the words came out garbled.

To Freya, it sounded like a rudimentary *I love you*. Three words she hadn't heard spoken by her mother in years. She didn't know what to make of it and was embarrassed that her first reaction was anger and mistrust. Was this simply May manipulating them again for some unknown goal?

Beth had seemed as shaken as Freya, and they hadn't talked about it. Maybe when Trinity finally got there, the tension would ease. Their sweet and carefree baby sister always made things better.

The door to May's room opened. Freya expected to see Beth or Trin. Instead, a man poked his head into the room. He looked familiar, although she didn't think they'd met. She would have remembered a man who looked like him.

Tall, dark and handsome didn't nearly do him justice although he was all those things.

"Freya," he said, clearly not at a loss for her identity. "Is it okay if I come in?"

Recognition dawned as she nodded. When she'd first arrived at her mother's house, she'd noticed a corkboard in the kitchen with photos pinned to it. Several of the three sisters when they were younger but more recent ones as well.

The man now entering the room was in a few of them,

May's slender arm around him as if they were close. A younger boyfriend, Freya assumed. It would be just like her mother to embrace her inner cougar.

She hadn't thought to ask Beth about the stranger's identity, but now he was here. Even more gorgeous than in the photographs, with his chestnut-colored hair cropped short and a shadow of fashionable stubble darkening his chiseled jaw. Her stomach tripped and dipped as he approached the foot of the bed. Oh, lord. She was lusting after her mother's boyfriend.

"It's strange to see her so still," he said, echoing Freya's earlier thought. She didn't like this stranger possessing any sort of insight into her mother's personality.

"My sisters will be here any minute," she told him, letting tacit dismissal flood her tone.

"How are you all holding up?" he asked, turning toward her. He wore dark trousers and a gray sweater in some kind of expensive-looking wool. A chunky silver timepiece encircled his wrist. Freya had a decent sense of designer accessories from her time in LA, and she guessed the value of the man's watch would be upwards of five figures. She doubted it was a knockoff, like the one she'd bought on a New York City street last summer.

This guy didn't seem like her mother's type, especially since he appeared to be only a few years older than Freya. She'd never pictured her mom as the type to go for a younger man. But what did Freya know at this point?

Well, she knew this moment felt too intimate for her taste.

"We're fine," she said, her voice clipped. "You can come back—"

"Greer, you're here."

They both looked toward the door as Beth entered. To Freya's shock, her sister offered the stranger a quick hug. Freya hadn't gotten a hug when she'd arrived home, not that she'd admit she wanted one.

"I got in this afternoon," the man called Greer told Beth. "Any change?"

"No, which might be a good thing at this point. She's resting and her body needs time to heal. You and Freya met?"

Freya felt her shoulders go rigid as the man's inscrutable gaze moved over her. "Not officially," he said. Was there a trace of a Boston accent in his voice?

"Trinity should be here soon," Freya told her sister. "She called from a gas station about two hours ago."

"We need to get her a cell phone," Beth said to herself. "Why doesn't she have one?" Freya could almost see the task being added to the mental list always running in her sister's brain.

She stood. "It will be better if just family is here tonight."

Beth blinked as if Freya were speaking a foreign language. So what if the three sisters hadn't been close for years? She didn't want her mother's boyfriend as a witness to the uncomfortable reunion.

"Greer is like family." Beth laughed without humor. "At this point, he's closer to Mom than any of us."

The man continued to study Freya.

"This is going to change the plans for her book tour and any sort of media appearances for the special," Beth told Greer.

"What book tour?" Freya demanded.

"It's the twentieth anniversary of the book," Beth explained. "Mom updated it and wrote a new introduction."

She bit down on her lower lip. "Apparently, she added a couple of chapters. Didn't she call and tell you about it?"

Freya shook her head, feeling heat rise to her face even as ice enveloped her heart. "Why would she?"

Beth glanced at Greer. His mouth thinned. "We can discuss that later."

Why the hell would Freya want to talk to the boyfriend about *A Woman's Odyssey*, her mother's long-ago best-seller? What did it have to do with her other than fielding more annoying questions at her paid appearances?

But she didn't have a chance to argue because the door opened again. Trinity rushed in, breathing hard like she'd just summited a mountain.

A wave of love for her little sister spilled over Freya. She and Trin didn't see each other often, but they kept in touch via text and social media.

At least they had until Trinity called a few months ago to say she was deleting her online accounts and ditching her cell. Focusing on what matters was how she'd described the change, and Freya had worked not to take offense that she wasn't part of what mattered to her sister.

Trinity's wavy blond hair was fashioned into two braids that fell over her shoulders. Her summer sky blue eyes looked tired, her ordinarily rosy complexion a little wan. It made sense, Freya figured. Driving cross-country would tire out anyone.

Then her gaze dropped lower and she gasped, darting a glance toward Beth, who was also staring in disbelief at their baby sister's stomach. Trinity was the shortest of the three of them, barely grazing five foot four in shoes. She had their mother's delicate bone structure, so the baggy sweatshirt couldn't quite hide the bump.

The baby of the family was having a baby.

"Sorry it took me so long to get here," Trinity said, tugging on the hem of her sweatshirt. Freya noticed that Beth didn't offer Trin a hug either.

In fact, it was difficult to say which one of her sisters looked more uncomfortable at the moment.

She knew Beth had tried for years to have a baby, and she could only imagine the shock of seeing Trinity…well…for lack of a better phrase…looking like she was ready to pop.

"I'm Christopher Greer," the boy-toy said, stepping forward to offer Trinity a hand. "Your mom's literary agent. My friends call me Greer. You must be tired. Can I get you water or something to eat?"

Literary agent? Why did May have photos tacked up of her literary agent like they were friends? Why did she even employ an agent at this point?

Freya had an agent in California, an older man specializing in deals for reality stars. But they weren't friends of any sort.

"I'm fine," Trinity said quietly. She looked between Beth and Freya before tracking to May, still peacefully sleeping. "How's Mom? I found those gross caramel cream candies she likes at a gas station in Kentucky, so I bought a few packs." She dug through the tote bag on her shoulder. "I must have left them in the car. I can get them and—"

"When are you due?" Beth asked, taking Trinity's hand. "You look…"

"Like a beached whale?" Trinity gave a nervous laugh. "I'm seven and a half months along. January baby." She smiled at Beth. "Just like you."

"Are you having twins?" Freya blurted as she stood, still reeling at her sister's condition and the fact that Trinity hadn't bothered to share it with her.

The question earned a snort from Beth and a raised brow from May's too-handsome agent.

"Congratulations," Beth said, finally wrapping Trinity in the hug their sister clearly needed. Trin sagged against Beth. "You are going to be an amazing mother."

With a glance toward May, Freya moved across the small room, ignoring the weight of Christopher Greer's gaze, and joined Beth and Trinity in the hug.

"Super sister power activate," Trinity said, her voice muffled in Beth's jacket. It was a game they used to play when they were young, before their dad left the family and May became famous for putting her own happiness above anyone else's. When they'd just been the Carlyle sisters, spending long weekends lost in their imaginations and the simple joy of being together.

Freya didn't know if they could recapture any of that. So much had happened to drive them apart. But this moment felt oddly right, even with a virtual stranger as a witness and the uncertainty of their mother's condition.

Some bonds could bend and twist in layers of knots but still never break.

A noise from the bed caused them to separate with a start. They turned in unison toward their mother. Her eyes were open and her gaze focused on the three of them.

"Mom?" Beth moved toward the head of the bed with Freya and Trinity following.

"Do you want me to call a nurse?" Greer asked, and Freya noticed that he stepped back to give the sisters center stage.

"I am a nurse," Beth said as she took May's hand. "Mom, can you hear me? Trinity is here now, too. We're all home."

"Ho," their mother said slowly, like it was difficult to form the syllable.

"That's right," Freya confirmed. "We're all here, and we're going to bring Thanksgiving dinner to you tomorrow. I bet you still use double the whipped cream on your pumpkin pie."

Was it Freya's imagination or did one side of her mother's mouth curve up at that comment?

May shook her head and glanced around the room, her eyes going a little wild like those of a caged animal. "Ho," she repeated. "May ho."

"She wants to go home," Trinity translated and May nodded.

"Goo grl." May patted the sheet with her free hand, and Trinity hurried around the bed to grasp it. "May goo grls," May said, looking between the three sisters. "Ho."

Freya could only describe her mother's expression as filled with love. So much overt love it made Freya's heart pinch.

Beth cleared her throat. "Mom, you had a stroke. You're in a rehabilitation center, where they can help you get better. It's a long road—"

"We'll take you home for Thanksgiving," Freya promised, elbowing her sister. "I'm sure Greg has the connections to help us work something out."

Beth shot a glare over her shoulder, but May's gaze had tracked to Christopher Greer. There was no mistaking the smile she offered him, even though it was uneven.

"Ho," she told him.

"Mom, please," Beth pleaded.

Greer's unreadable gaze met Freya's, and her stomach pitched again. She expected him to side with her practical sister, the nursing professional who would never make a promise she wasn't sure she could keep. At this moment, Freya would promise her mom the moon if it meant May

would continue looking at her with love instead of the dis-
approval Freya remembered.

She shouldn't care. She'd spent an embarrassing amount
of time and money trying to prove that her mother's opinion of her life didn't matter.

An obvious crock if this moment was any indication.

Without glancing at Beth, which surprised Freya since
most people automatically deferred to her older sister,
Christopher Greer gripped the end of the bed and nodded.
"We'll find a way to get you home," he told her mother.

At that moment, Freya felt her heart begin to thaw the
tiniest bit. She rubbed two fingers against her chest, unfamiliar with that kind of ache.

May let out an obvious sigh of relief, clearly trusting
her agent to make good on the promise her middle daughter had made.

Beth tsked as Trinity leaned in and hugged their mom.
"You're going to be home tomorrow and home for Christmas," the baby of the family declared.

Okay, that was more than Freya had promised. But as
Trinity pulled back, tears spilled from their mother's eyes.
May looked at each of them and then whispered, "I lo ew."

"I love you," Trinity translated, unnecessarily.

Because there were no mistaking May's words, garbled
as they might be.

Freya's heart was pounding at that point. Over a decade of discontent, anger and years of estrangement and for
what? Three mangled words, and she was suddenly fully
committed to her mother once again.

Maybe that was the power of the maternal bond, or perhaps it was just years of unconsciously craving a way to
connect to her mom again. May had been narcissistic, but
she'd also been a bright and brilliant beacon, the sun her

daughters orbited around. Freya had been living in the shadows for too long, and she realized how much she wanted to walk out into the light.

CHAPTER FOUR

BETH SAT IN her car at the curb in front of her mother's house the following morning. Her heart pounded as much as her head. She'd barely slept the previous night with the emotions swirling through her.

May had drifted back to sleep shortly after eliciting the promise to bring her home from her daughters. Freya and Trinity had seemed almost giddy with the prospect, but Beth couldn't manage to release the resentment and mistrust.

To her surprise, the doctor overseeing her mother's care had supported the idea of May going home for Thanksgiving Day and then in a few weeks returning to her house on a permanent basis to continue her rehabilitation with the help of a private nurse.

Beth didn't want to think about the cost of that because it made her feel like a bad daughter. Depending on how they arranged things and how long Freya was willing to stay, it wouldn't necessarily be more than having her mother in the rehabilitation center for the holidays. But the price was more than Beth could pay unless she used the money she'd saved for school to cover it. And she didn't think either of her sisters had that kind of savings available.

The cost of these developments felt different, at least for her. She hadn't been in her childhood home for nearly five years. She had regular phone calls with her mom, but during the infrequent times they saw each other, it was for dinner or coffee in town or when May would pop by Beth's house, generally around dinner time.

She climbed out of her car and heard children's voices shouting at each other. Looking up, she saw Zach and Timmy, Shauna's six-year-old twins, arguing as they made their way toward the driveway.

"I get to sit in the back with her."

"No, I do."

One of the twins pushed the other, who retaliated by jumping on his brother.

"I do, Zach."

They went rolling across the front yard as Beth watched, strangely fascinated. She and her sisters had never been much for physical roughhousing or altercations, although there'd been plenty of sass thrown back and forth between them.

Once their mother had become a bestselling author and in-demand speaker, Beth had put a stop to any playfulness she might have had with Freya and Trinity. Her entire focus had been making sure things ran smoothly without drawing the attention of anyone who could have possibly separated the sisters or called out May on her negligence.

Beth didn't feel the least bit confident that her mother would have chosen to make her daughters a priority if she'd been pushed into a corner. And there was no way Beth would allow any of them to end up sent to live with their father or a random relative somewhere.

She was still staring at Shauna's house as Declan emerged. When she'd apologized to Shauna at the hospital, the woman had explained she was May's neighbor. So seeing Declan shouldn't surprise Beth, but it did.

"Get off the ground," he bellowed, which made Beth's lips twitch.

"I get to sit with Mommy in the back seat," the boy wearing the red jacket yelled. He was on top of his brother now. Although at first glance they were identical, Beth could see that the red-jacketed kid was huskier, and by the looks of it, stronger than the one in the blue jacket so had the advantage.

"Both of you are going to sit in the back," Declan said, hauling the two boys to their feet by their collars. "Your mother has already made it extremely clear that you have to be in your booster seats buckled at all times. It's the law," he said as if that explained everything.

"I want to sit by Mommy," the kid in the blue jacket said, his voice a plaintive whine.

"We need to get her from the hospital first. Your mommy will be doing plenty of sitting when she gets to the house. You two are lucky I don't leave you here with how you're acting."

"You can't leave us," Red jacket, who Beth thought was Timmy, told Declan with a look of wide-eyed shock. "That's child abuse."

Declan glanced up at that point and noticed Beth. There was an instantaneous sizzle in the air between them before he gave a small shake of his head and looked past her. He lifted his hand in a wave. Beth turned to see Freya on the front porch of their mother's house.

"Happy Thanksgiving," her sister called to Declan and the boys. She didn't bother to greet Beth.

"We're going to pick up Mommy from the hospital," one of the boys called.

Freya walked down the steps. "It's so nice she can be home for Thanksgiving. Our mom is coming home, too."

Now she did glance at Beth. "Despite the objections of certain people."

"I'm worried about her recovery," Beth said under her breath.

Freya narrowed her eyes then continued forward. "Are you guys cooking a big Thanksgiving feast?"

The two boys looked up at Declan. He ran a hand over his jaw, and although Beth couldn't hear the sound of stubble scraping his palm, the sight still sent a shiver through her.

"I'll pick up some food at the grocery after I get Shauna settled."

"What if they don't have any pumpkin pie left?" Zach asked, sounding alarmed.

Freya grimaced. "Is the store even open on Thanksgiving?"

"You have to get extra whipped cream." Timmy tugged on the sleeve of Declan's leather jacket. "Zach always eats the whipped cream right out of the tub. Mommy only lets us because it's a holiday."

Beth almost laughed at that. She didn't know Shauna well but couldn't deny that she'd judged the woman for the kind of mother she assumed her to be. The young single mom reminded Beth of May with her flowing skirts and music always coming from the house.

She could guess the kind of lackadaisical rules that had led to her injury. What kind of mother went skydiving? Probably not the type who worried over whipped cream, whether it was a holiday or not.

"You should join us for Thanksgiving dinner," Freya said.

Beth felt her jaw go slack. She couldn't imagine sharing a meal already destined to be fraught with tension with Shauna, her unruly sons and most of all, Declan.

The first time Beth had gotten pregnant, before the miscarriage at nine weeks, she'd already started reading books and blogs about routines for a baby.

She wasn't going to make the mistakes her mother had. The ones she assumed Shauna might make. Nonexistent rules ended with kids running wild and mothers breaking their legs doing stupid stunts like going skydiving.

"I'm sure Mom would enjoy seeing Zach, Timmy and Shauna," Freya continued. "I'm in charge of the food, so we'll have plenty."

Beth did her best not to gape. What in the world was her sister thinking to invite Declan and their neighbors to Thanksgiving dinner?

One glance at Declan's expressionless features told Beth that he thought the invitation as strange as she did. She nearly breathed out a sigh of relief that he would reject the offer. Instead, he shocked her by nodding. "I'm sure Shauna would appreciate that."

"Will you have extra whipped cream?" Zach asked. "Mommy makes it homemade because she said the tub is full of chemicals."

At Declan's choked snort, Freya gave a soft chuckle, open and appealing.

Maybe there was already something going on between her beautiful, sensual sister and Shauna's guy.

Freya had been the demise of several high school couples when they were younger thanks to her constant flirting. Beth couldn't say for certain that her sister understood her own appeal.

"The whipped cream tonight is going to come from a

canister, but I'll spray it into your mouth." Even Beth smiled as both boys went wide-eyed.

"Cool," Timmy murmured.

"Let's go get your mom," Declan said, ruffling both boys' hair in unison.

He'd gone from irritation to affection in the blink of an eye like it was natural. Beth wished she could manage a trick like that.

When both boys were loaded in the car, he backed out of the driveway. Beth moved toward her sister. "You shouldn't have invited them."

"Why? Shauna was nice when I first got here. I think she and Mom are friendly."

"Birds of a feather," Beth muttered. "We're going to have our hands full today."

"That could be the understatement of the century," her sister told her. "When was the last time you were inside Mom's house?"

"Years. Why?"

"It's pretty bad in there."

Beth blinked. "What are you talking about?"

Freya nodded her head toward their mother's two-story home. It had been built in the sixties in a Cape Cod style. It was a three-bedroom, which meant Beth and Freya had their own rooms until Trinity was born.

Their parents moved Beth and Freya in together to give the baby more space. But Trinity had wanted to sleep with May when their father left, so Beth kicked Freya out of their room. That's how the arrangement had stayed until Freya left town after high school.

At the time she'd forced the change, Beth hadn't figured Freya would care. She and Trinity had always been closer but looking back she wished she hadn't insisted that, as the older sister, she deserved her own space. At this point, she couldn't remember what had been so awful about sharing a room with her sister in the first place.

"Mom and I meet in town or she comes to my place," she told Freya. "Seriously, what's wrong with the house?"

Freya grimaced. "You can see for yourself. She's not exactly a candidate for *Hoarders*, but it's going to take a lot of cleaning to get the first floor ready for her to move back."

Beth glanced at her watch. "Is it going to be okay for today? We don't have much time until I'm scheduled to pick her up."

"It's under control," Freya said, wrapping her cashmere sweater more tightly around herself as she started back toward the house. "I've been working all morning. You're not the only one who can handle important tasks. Trinity and I are both functional adults."

"Is she functional enough to handle being a mother?" Beth asked quietly. "I still don't understand why she didn't tell us."

Freya's shoulders seemed to deflate slightly. "I'm sure she didn't want to upset you, but why wouldn't she have told me?"

"What do you mean upset me?" Beth demanded.

Freya glanced over her shoulder. "Everyone knows how much you wanted to have a baby. I'm sure Trin is sensitive to that."

"My infertility issues don't prevent me from being happy for her. What kind of person do you think I am?"

"I think you're the kind of person who's been through a lot of loss, and you should let yourself feel that."

Beth hadn't anticipated those words of kindness from Freya and mentally chided herself for always expecting the worst from people, especially her sisters.

"I want what's best for Trinity." She followed Freya toward the front door. "Has she said anything about the baby's father?"

"No." Freya's voice was gentler than Beth could have imagined from her sharp-tongued sister. "She climbed into bed as soon as we were both back at the house last night, and she's still sleeping. It seems like the drive took a lot out of her."

"I imagine it did. I hate that she didn't tell us. Did she say anything about how long she's going to stay?"

Freya stopped at the door. "I told you, she went to bed when we got home. I didn't give her the third degree."

"That's not what I'm suggesting. I just don't understand, and I have questions about her medical care and her living situation and her job and what support she has to raise this baby out West. I thought she was in Montana, but she said last night that she drove from Colorado. When did she move?"

"Trinity is an adult. She isn't a problem for you to solve. Neither of us is."

Beth swallowed against the emotion that her sister's words produced. They were the words she wanted to hear. She didn't want responsibility for anyone other than herself right now.

Even though she hadn't told her mom about the nurse practitioner program, she'd already rented an apartment near the Vanderbilt campus and registered for classes. Her tuition deposit was due before Christmas and she'd lose her housing deposit if she didn't show up.

Was there any way she'd be able to leave with her mother's current condition?

It was difficult to envision a world where Freya or Trinity stepped in to help. Her attention was brought back to the present as her brain registered the state of her mother's house.

"How did it get like this?"

Freya turned, hands on hips. "Why are you asking me when you're the one who lives in Magnolia?"

The windows and doors were still accessible, yet piles of books, mail and magazines were strewn throughout the entry, dining room, family room and kitchen. Bookshelves overflowed with knickknacks and collectibles in all shapes and sizes, although Beth could see no tangible worth to any of the overabundance of personal belongings. It was simply a mess.

"Is the upstairs the same way?"

Freya's mouth thinned. "The bedrooms are exactly as they were when we moved out. Mom's is messy but yours and ours are perfect, right down to the horse posters above Trinity's bed."

"I don't understand."

"Me neither." Freya blew out a small laugh. "She's put more time and attention into taking care of our old bedrooms than she did to mothering us when we were kids. I thought you might have some insight."

"Honestly, I feel like I don't know Mom at all at this point. A lot of that is on me, I guess. I was consumed with my own issues after the divorce. Before that, the rounds of infertility treatments took a toll on my body and my emotions. It's been a long road back. She seemed like herself, so I didn't dig any deeper."

"It's not your fault," Freya said, surprising Beth again. "I know how much you gave up when we were younger. I didn't appreciate it then, but I do now. I've seen a lot of messed-up stuff in California. Messed-up people. Believe it or not, I'm fairly well-adjusted compared to a lot of them."

Beth's heart gave a little tug. "Freya, you are one of the strongest people I know. You always have been. It drove me crazy, and obviously, it drove Mom crazy, but there was no denying it. You were always going to manage for yourself."

"You made sure things didn't go totally off the rails when Mom checked out. I don't know what would've happened to Trinity and me if you hadn't taken over. Yes, you were way too bossy, but I appreciate it now in a way I couldn't when we were younger. I've seen some real dysfunction, Beth. And I've made the most of Mom's fame in my own way. I should have given you more credit."

"Thank you. I wish none of us had been put in that position. That we just could have been sisters."

Freya's tentative smile looked out of place on her normally self-assured features. "Maybe we can start now."

The tightness in Beth's chest loosened ever so slightly. "I'd like that."

CHAPTER FIVE

"THE STARS ARE out in full force tonight."

Trinity gasped at the sound of the deep male voice in the darkness and took an instinctive step back only to trip over one of the lawn ornaments strewn about her mother's backyard.

She landed on the grass with a yelp as pain lanced through her ankle.

"The hell…" the same voice muttered. "Are you okay?"

Glancing up at the shadow of a man looming over, she scrambled back, the grass damp under her palms. The cold seeped into her bones, and she mentally commanded herself to get a grip. Her gaze remained focused on the man who'd spoken, his identity becoming clear as her eyes adjusted to the dim light. Asher Davis, Magnolia's police chief.

He was her mother's neighbor, she remembered. An innocent coincidence, not a threat. Not her ex-boyfriend. Dave had no idea where she was and no way to track her. Trinity had been careful since leaving Montana months ago. She'd drained her meager savings in Colorado and only used cash on the drive to North Carolina.

Dave had no idea about her mother's stroke and no reason to believe she'd ever return to her hometown. Her sisters and mom hadn't even known about the pregnancy before Trinity showed up here. In truth, she wouldn't have thought to use her childhood home as a refuge if Beth hadn't tracked her down.

"I'm fine," she told Asher now. "You shouldn't sneak up on people."

"I was standing in the yard." He pointed to the house behind him. "I figured you saw me when you came out."

She ignored his offered hand and rose on her own, then hissed out a breath when pain radiated up her leg as she tried to put weight on her right foot.

Asher placed a gentle hand on her arm, but even that was too much for Trinity's frayed nerves. She flinched away then felt heat rise to her cheeks. Now that her eyes were adjusting to the darkness, she could read the way Asher's features softened in understanding.

He was in law enforcement and had probably seen plenty of women who couldn't tell the difference between a man who used his hands for violence and those who didn't. She was just one more pathetic example of an idiot who'd let a boyfriend turn her into someone she'd never imagined becoming—small and scared.

She placed a hand on her belly, needing the reminder of what was at stake for her future. Of why she had to be stronger. Of why she'd left.

"Let me help you," Asher said quietly, and Trinity wasn't sure whether he was referring to her injured ankle or the more significant circumstances of her life.

She went with the straightforward response. "I just twisted it." She rotated her ankle in a circle, gritting her teeth against the sting as she lowered herself onto one of the wrought-iron chairs at the edge of the patio. "I'm fine."

That was clearly a lie, but Asher didn't call her on it.

"Sorry I scared you. I didn't mean to."

"I know. It's fine." Fine, fine, fine.

She'd lost count of how many times she'd used the word

fine to describe herself or her circumstances. Who was she fooling?

Not Ash by the look he leveled at her.

Trinity wondered why it seemed so easy for other women to pick stand-up guys but not her. It was as if she was a homing device for every deadbeat and loser within a hundred-mile radius of wherever she was at the moment.

None of her previous boyfriends had been as bad as Dave. She'd outdone herself with her most recent relationship. But that was over. She wasn't going back, and she wasn't going to let him threaten or control her in any way. Not with her baby's future on the line.

Maybe Trinity hadn't found a way to be strong for herself, but she would for her child. She shifted away from Ash when the impulsive desire to draw closer enveloped her.

Trinity kept her distance from the cops. Law enforcement was good at protecting upstanding citizens like her sister Beth. People who didn't have dangerous problems believed in the authorities.

Others, like her, knew there was nothing that could truly protect them.

She'd done a poor job of taking care of herself up until now, but the baby she was carrying changed things. Even though it was unexpected, pregnancy had changed her. Unexpected wasn't the same as unknown, and Trinity knew she would love and protect her unborn daughter with every fiber of her being.

She assumed her odd behavior would encourage Ash to walk back to his mother-in-law's house, but he didn't move. "How is your mom doing? I'm sure she's glad to be home for Thanksgiving."

Trinity nodded and glanced over her shoulder at the house. It had been an odd day with all of them together, but also kind of wonderful. She knew better than to trust wonderful. "Beth left a few minutes ago to drive her back to the rehab center. May was happy and emotional and strangely kind for someone struggling to regain her speech. I'm not sure any of us knows how to handle this new version of our mother."

"She's always been kind to my daughter," Ash said with a frown. "I assumed that was her go-to."

Trinity swallowed back a laugh. "Hardly. My mother's go-to has always been her own brand of narcissism. She has a larger-than-life personality, but she also wants to be the center of attention. That didn't mix too well with motherhood, especially being a single parent."

Ash ran a hand through his thick hair. "That is very true. I don't think I have time to be selfish. I'm too busy trying to keep up with life."

"I'm sorry about Stacy," Trinity told him. "We hadn't talked in years, but we were friends as kids."

Trinity had casually asked Beth about her childhood friend moving back with her parents. Beth explained that Stacy had been killed in a car accident two years earlier, and her widowed husband had moved from Raleigh to Magnolia so their daughter could be close to her grandparents. Shortly after arriving, Stacy's father had passed away, so Ash and Michaela had continued to live with Helena.

Ash Davis was a prince among men. Even before knowing his story, that much had been apparent. She might attract losers, but she knew a good man when he was staring her in the face. The fact that he supported his late wife's mother told her even more.

"Thank you," he said, his full lips pressing together. "We're fine."

That word again. *Fine.* Trinity believed Ash as much as

she did herself. She might have the word on repeat in her mind, but no matter how many times she said it to herself or out loud to the people in her life, fine was a lie. An obvious one to anyone who took a hard look at her. She and Ash shared that lie, and the connection of it felt like a blanket wrapped around her shoulders.

This man would suss out her secrets if she let him. Even in the pale light coming from her mother's kitchen window, she could feel Ash studying her.

"Pumpkin or pecan?" he asked.

Trinity blinked.

"Pie," he clarified.

"Pumpkin," she said with a genuine smile. "Buried in whipped cream."

"Homemade whipped cream?"

She shook her head. "My sister Freya and I have a long-standing tradition of spraying it in each other's mouths. It used to make Beth crazy. She wanted to pretend like we were a normal family when we were anything but after our mom published her book."

Ash inclined his head. "You were famous by proxy?"

"We were invisible to her." Trinity blew out a breath as she realized the words didn't elicit the same emotions they had in the past. "Mom loved the spotlight and was in demand as a speaker and on the daytime talk show circuit. She left for long stretches and didn't seem to give much thought to us."

"You were kids. Who took care of the three of you?" Ash asked, disbelief obvious in his tone.

"We took care of ourselves for the most part," Trinity admitted. "Beth did most of the heavy lifting. Our dad wasn't in the picture, and we didn't have any other family to step in. Somehow we all understood that if people found out how often Mom left, the situation would end badly."

"Your mother wouldn't have let you be put into foster care."

"You're probably right," Trinity said with a shrug. "But we didn't feel confident of that when we were younger. She loved the fame that came from being a bestselling author. The whole premise of the book and the subsequent workshops she did was practicing purposeful selfishness. Making it acceptable for a wife and mother to go after her own dreams. Three young girls weren't a part of that image."

"But you were her responsibility."

"She didn't abandon us completely." Trinity glanced again at the house, unsure why she felt compelled to defend her mother now. "And when she came back after a media tour or being a guest lecturer, she was brighter than the sun. When my dad left, Mom was so sad and unhappy. I can't speak for my sisters, but I liked the happy version of her better. I didn't want to be the reason she couldn't have that."

Ash rocked back on his heels as he seemed to digest what she was saying. It had been a long time—possibly forever—since Trinity had shared so much with anyone, let alone a man she barely knew. One who a couple of nights earlier had been on the verge of arresting her when he'd thought she was driving drunk.

There was something about his quiet solidness that made her feel safe. When was the last time Trinity had felt safe?

"What about you?" she asked as the Christmas lights decorating a house across the street flicked off. Trinity liked it when people kept their holiday lights on all night long. "Why are you hanging out in the cold night instead of in the warm house?" She leaned forward. "Tell me you're a closet smoker. I love when upstanding people have secret vices. I always imagined Beth hiding a whole host of wickedness, but sadly she's genuinely perfect."

Ash didn't smile again, but his eyes crinkled ever so slightly at the corners. Trinity's mom used to have a huge crush on Jimmy Stewart, insisting they watch *It's a Wonderful Life* every Christmas Eve. Stewart's character from that movie, George Bailey, had been a stand-up guy and he'd had crinkly eyes. Her stomach did a funny flip that had nothing to do with her pregnancy. Ash could almost make her believe in Christmas magic.

"I'm not a smoker, but I'm also far from perfect." His chest rose and fell as he looked over his shoulder at his mother-in-law's house. "Helena and Michaela are watching some Hallmark movie. Not exactly my style, and I wanted a bit of fresh air."

"And to admire the stars," Trinity added, surprised when she sounded breathless.

He tipped up his face to the night sky. "They're impressive on a clear night like this. It's supposed to rain starting next week, and Michaela is hoping the temperature drops enough to get a dusting of snow."

"I've been living out West for the past few years," Trinity told him. "A bit in Colorado but mostly Montana."

"Big sky country."

"It lives up to the name, but I got used to it, you know? When all of that rugged beauty is in your face every day, it stops feeling special. That's the norm." She tugged on the end of one braid. "Sleeping in my childhood bedroom and being surrounded by family makes me appreciate the quiet and the stars more than I have in a long time."

"I like talking to you," Ash answered. There went her stomach swooping again. "If you're back in town for a while, maybe we could—"

"I'm pregnant," she blurted, pulling back the oversized coat she wore and sticking out her belly.

She registered the shock in his gaze even as her cheeks seemed to catch fire with embarrassment. But she couldn't allow a man like Ash to ask her out. It would be too much of a temptation. Too potentially good. Trinity wrecked things when they got too good.

"I didn't notice the other night," he said, regaining his composure well before she had hers under control. "How far along?"

"Seven months."

He sputtered. "You're barely showing."

"The bump is there. It's my first pregnancy and I'm small to begin with so…"

"Congratulations," he said, still sounding stunned while Trinity felt more like a fool every moment. "To your husband as well. Is he joining—"

"No husband," she said quietly. "No anyone. It's me and the baby."

"So you could go out to dinner with me?"

"I'm due in late January." Why was he still looking at her like dinner was an option?

"Would next week work for you? Tuesday or Wednesday would be great with my schedule."

"You can't possibly want to take me to dinner," she told him even as something fizzy and light bubbled up inside her. She knew better than to trust her reaction to a man. It was just that Ash Davis was appealing on so many levels. Handsome and kind and obviously a dedicated father. Heck, he even liked her mother.

"Yet here I am asking you out." He arched a brow. "Repeatedly."

"I can't." She lifted her gaze to her mother's house. Did

Mom still have the old Christmas lights from years ago? "It wouldn't be fair to you."

"Don't you think I should be the judge of that?"

If her reluctance were just about going on a date while pregnant, then maybe that would be the case. She couldn't possibly get involved with the town's police chief given her history.

Trinity wanted to believe Dave would let her go, but a part of her knew that was wishful thinking. Plus she wasn't going to stay in Magnolia long-term. She'd probably be gone before her baby was even born. No sense getting close with a man who could never be part of her future. She was simply too damaged for a healthy relationship.

Being back in her home with a pile of stuffed animals in the corner and the memories of happy moments was such a sharp contrast to the bleak turn her life had taken. She didn't want Ash to know this current version of her. Maybe once she got her life together, she could come back to Magnolia for a visit and they could try then. She had nothing to give him now.

"I appreciate the offer." She smiled, hoping he didn't notice that it wobbled at the corners. "I'm going to have my hands full helping with my mom's care while I'm in town. I don't think it would be a good idea."

He nodded. "I'm around if you change your mind. How's your ankle?"

Touching a hand to it, she realized it didn't hurt nearly as much as it had after the fall. "I think it's okay."

She went to stand, and he offered his hand again. This time she allowed herself to take it as a way to prove to them both that she wasn't affected by him. It was no big deal. Huge mistake. Ash's hand was warm and steady, and an almost forgotten part of Trinity wanted to lean into his touch.

She shouldn't have turned down his invitation to dinner, but now wasn't the time to change her mind, no matter how much she wanted to. "I need to get back into the house. Beth is coming back to help clean up after dropping off Mom. She and Freya don't always get along. My job is the peacemaker."

Ash grimaced. "That sounds exhausting."

"Sometimes."

"If you ever need a break, you know where to find me."

"I'll remember that," she said quietly then turned and walked up the stairs. There was no way she'd forget this moment. It felt like a wish come true to know she was still capable of feeling the hopeful hum of attraction, even if she wasn't going to do a thing about it.

CHAPTER SIX

CHRISTMAS CHEER EXPLODED all over Magnolia the weekend after Thanksgiving.

At least, that's how it appeared to Freya as she made her way toward the hardware store on Saturday afternoon to meet her sisters.

Maybe she simply hadn't noticed the shopkeepers getting ready for the holiday season when she'd arrived in town last week, her mind consumed with thoughts of her mother's health.

Downtown and the surrounding neighborhoods had become engulfed in holiday decorations. There were boughs of pine encircling every lamppost and twinkle lights strewn across Main Street. Each business had its own unique theme, from snowmen to Santa's toy shop to a vintage display at the florist.

She ducked into Sunnyside Bakery, enticed by the selection of holiday cookies displayed in the front window. Breathing in the scent of coffee and sugar—one of her favorite combinations—she approached the counter.

Like many businesses in Magnolia, the bakery hadn't changed much from what she remembered as a kid, although her memories were somewhat fuzzy. She and her sisters had avoided the local shops and restaurants per Beth's instructions.

First off, their mother often forgot to leave cash when she

went on one of her frequent trips out of town, so it wasn't as if the girls had a lot of spending money. Beth did her best to keep their fridge and pantry stocked.

The grocery store was only a few blocks from their house, and they could stop on the way from school. At first, none of them minded the steady diet of boxed mac and cheese or packets of ramen noodles.

Freya had eventually come to detest ramen noodles.

According to a teenage Beth, too many people in town knew about May and her publishing success. Her sister feared they might ask questions or make inquiries into May's whereabouts if the girls were seen without her. Everything Beth did was to ensure that no one discovered how often May left her daughters on their own.

By the time she was a teenager, Freya had stopped caring what anyone thought of their living situation, although she still hadn't gone into town often. Magnolia had felt too close-knit for her, and they lived on the outskirts anyway. Plus, she understood the need to protect Trinity.

At this point, she felt like a stranger in her own hometown. There had to be people she'd gone to high school with who still lived in the area, but she hadn't kept in touch with any of her former friends.

They'd met with May's care team that morning, including Beth's tool of an ex-husband, Greg. The hospital and rehab staff had explained the recovery process for stroke patients, which could take weeks, months or even years.

Freya learned the term for May's difficulties speaking was aphasia, and the speech-language therapy she was already undergoing would, hopefully, help her regain some function in that area. But no one had concrete answers on whether their mom would fully recover.

The facility's director encouraged the girls to convince

their mother to sell the house so she could move into a smaller, newer place that would take less maintenance.

The three of them had been silent as they walked out of the meeting, and Freya'd had no idea what her sister thought about the suggestion until they were halfway back to town.

At that point, Beth had pulled her car to the side of the road and thrown it into Park.

"She won't agree to sell the house," Beth had announced as Christmas music played in the car's stuffy interior.

"Of course not," Freya agreed. "Do we force the issue?"

"Mom isn't the same as she used to be," Trinity had said from the back seat. "Who knows what she'd say since she can't speak."

That little mic drop from the baby of the family had given them all something to think about.

"Either way, the house needs some updating if she's going to stay there," Beth told them. "We should focus on that."

They'd all agreed because focusing on the house seemed easier than worrying over their mother's future. They headed downtown to the hardware store to start gathering supplies for renovation projects. Beth had offered to stop in at a local realty office to ask about the process for selling if they decided to go that route. Trinity was tasked with ordering takeout from Il Rigatone, the popular Italian restaurant, because no one wanted leftovers again or to be in charge of cooking.

The Freya of a few years ago would have been satisfied to drink her dinner—lunch as well. To numb the emotions that bubbled up inside her, trying to take center stage like the holiday decorations in town, only more fierce and fiery than festive in nature.

But she rarely drank and had given up any other vices

after seeing a particularly unflattering picture of herself in a tabloid at the grocery store.

"Oh, my gosh, can I have your autograph or a selfie?" Freya turned to find a group of teenage girls staring at her, cell phones at the ready. She tried to turn her grimace into a smile.

She hadn't given much thought to being recognized in Magnolia. Her hometown felt like it was a world away from Hollywood and the type of fame she'd courted partly as a middle finger to her mother, whose book was, in many ways, a manifesto that claimed women didn't need men for their happiness.

Freya had made the rounds of reality dating shows as well as a frivolous dancing competition and a slew of paid endorsements. But she'd grown weary of the constant need to feel like she was on.

Still, she posed for selfies with the girls and encouraged them to tag the brand of sweater she wore. She needed that money coming in, especially if she was going to make the career change she planned for the New Year. She ordered her complicated coffee concoction, omitting a cookie order, suddenly losing her desire for the indulgence.

The woman at the counter gave her a strange look. "Are you famous?" She inclined her head toward the teenagers walking out of the shop as they furiously thumbed captions into their phones.

"Not for anything worthwhile," Freya answered. "Do you watch much reality TV?"

The woman shook her head. "I don't own a TV. It messes with the brain cells."

"Indeed it does," Freya agreed.

The woman leaned in like she was sharing a secret then asked, "Was it a sex tape?"

Freya sputtered out a laugh and took the coffee drink she'd ordered. "No. Not a sex tape."

"This is May Carlyle's daughter."

Freya glanced over to see an older woman approaching. She recognized her as the bakeshop owner, although Freya couldn't remember her name.

"We love your mother," the hippie barista said. "Sometimes she brings her tarot cards into the store and does readings for us."

Freya blinked. Tarot card readings. That was a new one for May.

"How's she doing?" the owner asked as she followed Freya to the end of the counter.

"It's going to be a long recovery, but we were able to bring her home for Thanksgiving Day." For some reason, Freya felt proud to share that fact. She'd never been interested in the role of dutiful daughter, but she appreciated the flash of approval in the bakery owner's eyes.

"I'm Mary Ellen Winkler," the woman said, holding out a hand. "You might not remember me from when you were younger."

"I remember you," Freya answered. She and Trinity had liked to play the game of I-wish-she-were-my-mother, and the bakery owner had always been on the top of Freya's list.

"I've been following your career."

"I'm sorry. You must have too much time on your hands." Freya laughed, but Mary Ellen didn't seem to clue in on the joke.

"Your mom is proud of your success."

"Now I know you're being nice. My mother never approved of one thing I did. Thank you for the coffee." Freya started for the door.

The woman plucked a holiday cookie out of the case,

put it in a paper bag and shoved it into Freya's hand. "Of course she was proud, although she wasn't happy when that guy on the survival dating show sent you home."

Freya felt her eyes widen. She would never have guessed that her mother had watched *True Love Island* or any of the shows on which she'd appeared. "Robbie cheated on the winner with a flight attendant he met on the way back to the States. I dodged a bullet with that one." Too bad she couldn't say the same for all of her appearances.

"Well, that's something." Mary Ellen laughed. "I'd like to come by and see your mom sometime if you think she's up for visitors?"

Freya didn't know how to answer. Her mom hadn't really had friends when Freya was younger. Did she actually have connections in the community now or did people just want to get close so they'd have the latest gossip to share at the various holiday events scheduled in town? "She needs her rest now, but I'm sure we could set something up eventually."

The bakery owner studied her as if she knew Freya was putting her off but didn't call her out on it. "That would be lovely. If there's anything we can do to support you and your sisters, let us know. Magnolia takes care of our own."

That was funny. No one had taken care of the Carlyle girls when they'd needed it most. Maybe the people in town would have surprised them if they'd reached out. More likely, they would have ended up shipped off to some relative they didn't know, or May would have hired a stranger to look after them.

In hindsight, the decision they'd made to hide their mother's negligence probably hadn't been the smartest one. At the time, it felt like the only option.

"How long are you staying in town?" Mary Ellen asked.

"We have lots of great events planned this year for the Christmas on the Coast festival."

"I don't know what that is." Freya shook her head.

"It's the town's holiday celebration. Things have changed around here in the past couple of years. There's lots of new growth and people moving to the area. This town is seeing a resurgence. But all publicity is good publicity, and I'm sure the festival coordinator would appreciate your involvement. Having a bona fide star in town would liven things up, if you know what I mean?"

Freya knew exactly what the woman meant. The majority of her income last year had been paid endorsements or events. But even if she was so inclined as far as donating her time, it certainly wouldn't be to this town. It was not her home.

"I'm just here for my mom." The genuine conviction she managed to convey made her thankful for that year of acting classes she'd taken when she'd first moved to California.

"Talk to Avery Atwell if you change your mind." They were at the door to the bakery now, and Mary Ellen reached out for an awkward hug. Awkward because Freya didn't particularly like being hugged. She pulled back quickly.

"Thanks for the cookie," she said and headed out the door.

Trinity was nowhere to be seen. How long did it take to order some ravioli and lasagna? Freya pulled dark sunglasses from her knockoff Birkin bag as she moved toward the hardware store and kept her gaze on the sidewalk in front of her. She wished she'd thought to wear a hat today. Somehow she hadn't given much thought to the idea of being recognized in Magnolia, but the streets were teeming with shoppers.

The media had labeled this day "Small Business Saturday," and it was clear the local shops in Magnolia were doing big sales. Freya had seen plenty of power shopping on the swanky streets of Beverly Hills, but this had a different vibe entirely. It was crafty and quaint, which Freya would normally mock but found oddly appealing.

Beth had yet to emerge from the realty office, so Freya entered the hardware store, shocked at how cheery and welcoming it felt. The scent of cinnamon and cloves along with sawdust filled the open space, and there seemed to be just as many aisles of home goods and gift merchandise as tools and construction supplies.

A thin redhead called out a greeting from behind the register then went back to helping another customer.

Freya slowly moved down one aisle, charmed despite herself by the rows of merchandise. Freya didn't cook, but she'd always wanted to learn, and kitchen gadgets fascinated her with their potential. She reached out a hand to touch a set of stainless-steel mixing bowls that reminded her of the set her mother had when she was younger. Were those bowls still somewhere hiding in the bowels of May's overcrowded kitchen?

"Everything old is new again," a voice said next to her. She glanced up to see a handsome man with chestnut-hued hair and matching eyes smiling at her. "My grandma had that exact type of bowl and probably her grandma before that back in Oklahoma. The retro look is popular nowadays."

"Why change a classic?" Freya asked and the man nodded. His name tag said Garrett, and she noticed the ring on his left hand. No surprise someone had snapped him right up. At first glance, he seemed like a keeper, which made him not her type anyway.

"Can I help you find something?" he asked.

"My sister," Freya answered as she slowly removed her sunglasses. It felt ridiculous to be wearing them in the store, and she didn't think this man would recognize her.

"I'm guessing you mean Beth?"

Freya blinked, but the man just grinned. "You two have the same eyes."

She wanted to shove her sunglasses back on her face but took a drink of coffee instead to keep from having to answer.

A moment later, her sister walked around the corner, followed by Christopher Greer. Freya's gaze instinctively narrowed. What was it about the man that had that visceral effect on her?

He gave Garrett a long once-over, his grin broadening. "I see my best client is focusing on his favorite side hustle once again."

Best client? Why would a hardware store clerk be his best client? "Whatever it takes to keep Lily happy. With the store this busy, it's all hands on deck. You know what they say. Happy wife, happy..." Garrett cringed as Beth raised a brow and Greer snorted. "Sorry, bad analogy."

To Freya's surprise, Beth fist bumped Greer like they were old friends. "Some of us are happier on the other side of marriage."

"Good point." Garrett nodded. "Although I might kill off your stupid ex-spouse just for good measure." With a wink at Freya, he moved off in the direction of a woman clearly struggling to reach something from one of the top shelves.

"Great news," Beth said as she walked toward Freya. "Greer is going to help us get the house fixed up before the holidays. If we can renovate the first floor, it will be easier to stay there. She's going to push for that either way."

"I wish I would have known what shape it was in," Greer

offered. He wore faded jeans and a flannel shirt that almost made him look like he belonged in the store. Certainly more than Freya. "I would have forced her to let me make some updates sooner."

"No one forces May to do anything," Freya reminded them both.

Beth snorted. "You haven't seen her with Greer. Putty in the man's hands."

Freya bristled as the agent lifted the hands in question, large with long, elegant fingers that seemed more appropriate for holding a martini glass than doing any kind of manual labor. "Why is Garrett from the hardware store your best client?" she demanded.

"That's not just Garrett from the hardware store," Beth told her. "It's Garrett Dawes, the thriller author."

"He's the one who introduced me to your mom," Greer explained, not appearing bothered by her churlish tone. "I've only been working with her for a couple of years now. Garrett's wife, Lily, runs the store. It's been in her family for generations. Once they moved to Magnolia, I came for a visit and—"

"And you decided to take advantage of our mother," Freya said with a sniff.

"What's wrong with you?" Beth demanded.

"I've seen plenty of unscrupulous agents milk aging, once-famous actors. I imagine it's the same thing with Mom and *A Woman's Odyssey*. Why would she need a new agent now?"

"Next year is the twentieth anniversary of the book's original publication." Greer said the words as if they explained everything.

"You mentioned that. So what?" Freya countered then

moved out of the way as a father with two young sons walked past.

"Nice snowman," Greer told the boy, who was pushing a cart that held an enormous figure made of vines woven on a wire frame.

"This is Frosty," the boy said proudly. "He's going in our front yard."

Greer smiled. "Lucky snowman."

Freya had no idea why she resented the man's easy way with everyone from her mother to strangers in the hardware store. He was as much of an outsider in Magnolia as her, more so because at least she'd grown up there. Somehow he seemed to effortlessly fit in while Freya struggled to gain her equilibrium.

"The publisher is releasing an updated version of the book." Beth glanced at Greer. "It's a new and expanded version. She's added a couple of chapters. From the little she's told me, those chapters included her more recent thoughts on what it means to be a successful and empowered woman."

Freya noticed Greer shift his gaze to the floor. Suddenly he looked as out of place as she felt. "Her editor and I are the only ones who have read it."

"And you're sworn to secrecy," Beth muttered.

"You know that I am."

"Yeah, but I don't like it, especially with the current situation."

"Have her thoughts changed all that much?" Freya asked, finding it hard to believe.

Greer inclined his head, although his features remained neutral. "Let's just say they've evolved."

Freya thought about the manuscript currently tucked in the nightstand drawer of her childhood bedroom. The one she'd printed out old-school because that made it seem more real.

It was real.

She'd written the domestic thriller in her time off between bookings but hadn't yet had the nerve to send it to any agents or editors. As much as she yearned to be a published author, it felt too vulnerable to put her work out there.

If she wasn't offering the world a backstabbing tell-all or insider secrets to the world of reality TV, why would anyone care? She wasn't confident she could take the rejection of a project that meant the world to her.

To hear that her mother had another book coming out made her feel like her dream was even more out of reach. Her mom was the author in the family, and Freya doubted May would appreciate any competition in that area, especially from her middle daughter.

She placed her coffee on a nearby shelf, pulled the cookie out of the small bag inside her purse, and bit the gingerbread man's head off.

Greer barked out a laugh, and Beth looked shocked then turned to the agent. "That's what Freya thinks about evolution."

"Good to know," he answered. "Good to know."

CHAPTER SEVEN

TWO DAYS LATER, Beth sat next to her mother's bed at the rehab center, lost in her own thoughts about the future.

Freya and Trinity completely supported the idea of May moving back to the house in time for Christmas, and May's care team seemed cautiously optimistic that they could make it happen.

Her mother let out a soft laugh as Will Farrell gobbled up spaghetti covered in maple syrup. May had been watching a steady stream of holiday movies, from black-and-white classics to more modern comedies to sweet romances in which all the heroes wore flannel shirts.

The sisters took shifts at the rehab center so their mother wasn't often left alone.

May dutifully did her physical therapy every day, and although her speech was slowly improving, she seemed content to watch and listen to what was going on around her, which was a complete shift from the mother Beth knew.

"Would you like something to eat, Mom?" Beth asked. "They brought by some vanilla pudding earlier."

May scrunched up her nose then lifted a shaky hand to point at the television. "Spagti," she said, making Beth smile.

"There's leftover ravioli from the other night in the fridge down the hall. Would you like me to heat a bowl for you?"

May grinned and nodded. "Lo u," she said, patting her hand against the sheet as if beckoning Beth forward.

Beth rose from the chair to sit next to her mom on the bed. She still couldn't resign herself to May's current affectionate nature. The sisters had quickly realized that their mother was most interested in communicating how much she cared for and appreciated each of them, her halted words of "lo u" telling them she loved them.

"I love you too, Mom," Beth answered as she took her mother's hand. "I'll get you something to eat, and then we can play some games on your iPad." The occupational therapist had given her mother the device to use for speech and cognitive therapy exercises.

"Ho." Her mother breathed out the one syllable.

May hadn't been an interested participant in therapy at first, content to watch movies and the game show network. Beth had finally gotten her to understand that in order to reach her goal of being home for Christmas, she would have to hit certain milestones in her rehabilitation. Once May understood what was at stake, she became much more willing to take part in her own healing.

There was still no definitive answer as to whether May would be able to live on her own again. Beth felt selfish for wondering what that would mean for the future.

Trinity and Freya likely expected Beth to be the one to take care of their mother. She understood that reasoning because she was the one who'd stayed in town, but she hated the thought of giving up her dream to finally leave Magnolia.

Freya was worried about what their mother had written in her updated and expanded anniversary edition of the book that made her famous. Beth didn't know, and she didn't care. The book meant that her mother would have something to keep her busy and occupied in the months ahead, which helped lessen Beth's guilt. She was a grown woman who'd spent her life taking care of other people. She shouldn't have to feel guilty but couldn't quite shake the emotion.

The future she so desperately craved was in jeopardy. And she didn't know how to handle that. The door to the room opened. Shauna Myer, her twin sons and Declan walked in. Beth was at a loss for words.

"I hope it's okay that we stopped by," Shauna said with a bright smile, looking adorable in overalls with a long-sleeve red T-shirt underneath and her hair pulled back in a messy bun. She moved slowly on her crutches, and Beth couldn't help but notice that Declan did his best to avoid making eye contact with Beth.

"I called the room earlier when your sister was here," Shauna explained. "She said your mom would be up for visitors. Zach and Timmy have been anxious to see her."

May made a noise of assent, clearly excited to see the two boys, who ran toward the bed.

"Hi, Miss May," Timmy said, pressing a kiss to her mother's cheek.

"Hi, Miss May." Zach patted her arm, not as much the kissing type as his brother. "We brought Christmas stories to read to you."

Her mother grinned as the boys took turns pulling books out of the tote bag they'd placed at the foot of the bed. Beth's instinct was to warn them to be careful, which would make her look like more of a wet blanket than she already appeared to be.

"I have way too many," Shauna said, hitching a thumb toward the overflowing box of decorations Declan held. "I noticed the room didn't have much in the way of holiday cheer when I was here yesterday."

May's neighbor had also visited yesterday? Beth hadn't made it over because she'd had to work a twelve-hour shift so one of her coworkers could stay home with her sick daughter.

As someone without kids or a husband, Beth often picked up shifts from other nurses who had family responsibilities. Normally, she didn't mind, but it did get old sometimes, mostly because she'd wanted to be someone with those sorts of obligations.

"That was nice of you," she told Shauna.

The woman gave her a strange look, like she was waiting for Beth to add some sort of dig at the end of the compliment. Declan seemed to be enthralled with the pattern of the carpet. Coward.

"I was just about to heat some food for Mom." Beth's smile was genuine as she watched the boys snuggle up on either side of May. "I'll leave her in your capable hands for a few minutes if that's okay?"

Shauna nodded. "Take all the time you need."

Beth swallowed. She needed hours or weeks or months or a lifetime to figure out her life and her conflicted feelings about her mother.

Instead, she went to the small communal kitchen at the end of the hall. It felt stupid to have tears in her eyes as she took out the carton of leftovers from Il Rigatone. She didn't want to let emotion get the best of her.

"You holding up okay?" Her breath caught at the sound of Declan's voice.

"I'm fine."

"Liar."

"You don't have to keep me company. I'm sure you'd rather be with Shauna and the boys."

He shrugged. "We have plenty of time together. They're happy visiting your mom. She doesn't know me other than I'm the random guy who showed up to Thanksgiving dinner. I figured I'd give them space."

"I'm sure she'd be happy to get to know you. I didn't realize how close she was to your girlfriend." She sighed. "There are a lot of things about my mom I didn't realize, even though I live only a mile away. I guess I was too wrapped up in my own life and problems to pay close attention to her. Badly done on my part."

"I think that's how it's supposed to be with kids, even grown-up ones. For the record, Shauna isn't my girlfriend."

Beth hit the button to start the microwave as she turned to face him fully. "Really? Those two boys look like you. I just figured…"

"No." The word was spoken with a significant amount of force. "They aren't mine. She and I have been friends since we were kids, but we never…it isn't like that between us."

"Okay." Beth suddenly had the feeling she needed to offer him some comfort as if Declan Murphy were a wild animal she wanted to calm. "I did apologize, by the way."

"Shauna told me."

"She's too nice for her own good," Beth said. "I was out of line that day at the hospital. She could've gotten me in big trouble. Instead, the nursing director told me Shauna went out of her way to praise me when she was discharged. Why would she have done that?"

A smile touched the corner of Declan's mouth. "Because that's the type of person she is, although I agree with you. I hope she learns some better self-preservation instincts."

"Were you two family friends?"

"We didn't have families in the way you think of them. Shauna and I met in foster care. It was my second placement, and the first time child protective services separated me from my older brother. I was not handling it well, and Shauna made it bearable."

"That must have been awful," Beth murmured. "My biggest fear was that my sisters and I would somehow be separated when we were younger."

His thick brows drew together. "Why would that have happened? You had a mom."

"I don't know that we would have been put into foster care, but it was my fear. There came a point when my mom checked out on parenting and my dad had left. He'd moved to Vegas to pursue his dream of becoming a famous magician."

"That's an odd dream for somebody with three kids."

"Especially considering he had both three kids and marginal talent. Although I'm pretty handy with the card tricks when I'm on the peds floor. I get that from my dad. We didn't have any living grandparents. There were a few distant relatives who possibly would have taken one of my younger sisters during the times when my mom went on book tours or the personal development lecture and workshop circuit. She did a lot of that on the West Coast, so she was gone for extended periods of time. I did my best to keep us together. Freya and Trinity kind of hate me for it."

"That's because they don't know what it's like to be torn apart." His stormy eyes were intense on hers. "If they understood, your sisters would thank you every day."

She smiled through the ache in her chest that his kindness put there. "I don't know. I was a bossy know-it-all back then."

It felt easier to make a joke than to reveal how much his

words meant to her. No one had ever told her she'd done the right thing by her family, and she hadn't realized how much she needed to hear it until now.

He made a face. "Has that changed?"

Beth would typically take offense, and she'd gotten off to the wrong start with Declan in that stairwell. But like Shauna, he didn't seem to hold a grudge, and Beth could use some more levity in her life.

"I like to think I'm more subtle about it these days."

The microwave dinged at the same time Declan let out a gentle peal of laughter. The sound zipped through her, putting all of her nerve endings on high alert. She busied herself with stirring the ravioli, then placed it back in the microwave for another thirty seconds.

"So you and Shauna are just friends," she said, glancing over her shoulder. "Are you staying in town for a while?"

Did her voice sound breathy as she asked the question? How embarrassing.

"She's non-weight bearing for three more weeks, so I'll be here through the holidays to help. I'm taking over some of her more pressing jobs so she doesn't lose business."

"That's nice of you." Beth knew from her mother that Shauna was a painter, both residential projects as well as murals commissioned by clients around town.

Declan must have registered the question in her gaze because he flashed a sheepish smile. "I don't have an artistic bone in my body, so I'm just handling walls and trim at this point. The people who have hired Shauna for decorative projects are stuck. She has a couple of nurseries booked, but it sounds like those people are willing to wait for her."

Maybe Beth would've hired her if she'd actually needed a nursery wall painted. "And you're able to take time off from your regular job and family?"

"My clients will wait for me. Most of them are desperate."

Beth was intrigued. "What kind of clients are so desperate for you?" She half imagined him telling her he had some sort of Magic Mike review. She could certainly understand feeling desperate if somebody was waiting for him on that front.

"I'm a fixer."

"What's a fixer?" She took the ravioli out of the microwave and put it on a tray, along with a carton of Jell-O from the refrigerator and a glass of lemonade.

"I work with bars and pubs, although a few family-owned restaurants have hired me over the years. I help them turn things around in their businesses."

"Like Gordon Ramsay?"

"Something like that without the swearing. Foul language is cheap. I can get my message across in a better way."

Beth agreed about the language. She'd never been much for swear words. Freya could curse a sailor under the table. Beth wondered if her sister's early penchant for swearing had been more about making Beth mad than caring about how she spoke. She'd watched a couple of Freya's reality shows, and her sister wasn't the type of contestant to rely on vulgarity to make a point.

Maybe Beth had influenced her strong-willed sister after all. "Do you travel a lot for that job?" Declan took the tray from her, a small but gentlemanly gesture that she appreciated. They headed back toward her mother's room.

"Mostly the Eastern Seaboard and Midwest. I typically spend a month or two with each business and then follow up with them over the next year. Sometimes they want the change to save their business. They need to turn things around to make a profitable sale in other cases."

"Do you have your own show?"

He chuckled. "This face wasn't made for television."

Beth could have argued that point. She knew a lot of women at the hospital who would probably pay a pretty subscription penny to watch Declan work his magic.

"Isn't that hard on your family?" she asked, unable to resist. She shouldn't want to know more about him, but she did.

"Shauna is the closest thing to family I have." His voice was several degrees cooler than it had been a few moments earlier. "Nobody's waiting for me."

"You're lucky," she said before she thought better of it. "I wish I didn't have so many people depending on me."

"Maybe we both could appreciate a new perspective this holiday season." One thick brow rose in challenge. "A little Christmas magic and all of that?"

Beth felt her smile grow tight. "I don't really celebrate the holidays, but I guess I could take a fresh perspective minus the magic."

She opened the door to her mother's room and stifled a gasp. If she had been interested in Christmas magic, this would be the place to find it. As May looked on in delight, reindeer ears perched on her head, Shauna and her boys finished putting out the last of the decorations they'd brought.

It was as if the magic from Christmas past, present and future had all converged on this one small room. A mini tree on the dresser was decorated with tiny ornaments and surrounded by a Christmas village display. A colorful wreath hung on the window along with felt garland. Her mother's muted comforter had been replaced with one that showed a winter forest scene, and a couple of overstuffed pillows brightened the chairs in the room.

"You did all this in the time it took me to microwave

ravioli?" Beth went to her mother's neighbor, and without overthinking it, gave Shauna a quick hug. "Thank you."

She turned to May. "You like it, Mom?"

"Yay," her mother answered, nodding.

Beth's eyes stung at her mother's wide smile. When she tried to grin so broadly, it became apparent how her face gently sagged on one side. It was still difficult to tell whether her mom had any concept of the damage the stroke had done. Had the part of May's brain that recognized her former self been wiped away like a sandcastle toppled by a strong wave?

There was no denying the happiness May currently displayed. Beth remembered one particular Christmas when May had sat the girls down and given them a lecture about the objectification of Mrs. Claus being left behind at the North Pole and the misogyny of so many of the classic holiday stories.

That severe stance on the holidays seemed forgotten by her mother. Beth wished she could also put aside what had come before. Maybe this was a new beginning for all of them.

When she met Declan's warm gaze, filled with understanding and humor, she desperately wished for something new.

CHAPTER EIGHT

FREYA STARED AT the front door of her mother's house like Lucifer himself might be standing on the other side.

"Why aren't you answering it?" Trinity asked as she moved past Freya.

"Don't," Freya whispered urgently.

Trin paused with her hand on the door. "It's Greer. You know, Mom's agent."

"I know."

"He's here to work on the first floor."

"I know."

"Is there a reason you don't want to let him in?"

"Yes. No. I don't know why he needs to be here." Trinity gave Freya a look clearly communicating that Freya was acting irrational. Something she knew without her sister pointing it out.

"He's here because he is willing to help and—"

"Do you think he's going to be that big a help? He wears a watch that retails for around twelve grand. How many home improvement, do-it-yourself projects do you think he's handled in his life?"

"Quite a few." Greer's baritone voice carried from the other side of the door. Trinity snorted out a laugh then marched forward.

"Well, this is embarrassing," she said as she opened the door to Greer, who stood smiling on the other side. He wore faded jeans that hung low on his lean hips and a soft flannel shirt.

"You look like something out of a Hallmark movie," Freya complained as he entered.

"That's a compliment," Trinity explained.

Freya sniffed. "It was not a compliment."

"You look helpful and handy is what she meant to say." Trinity patted his arm.

"I said what I meant." Freya pointed at him. "What are you doing here?"

"We went over this at the hardware store. You want to convert the powder room to a full bath on the first floor and make the library into a bedroom. It's a good idea. Whether or not your mom returns home or you decide to sell, a first-floor master suite is always a smart renovation. You'll increase the house's value no matter what."

"What do you know about renovations?" Freya demanded, "and what's in it for you? I do not understand why you're being so nice."

Trinity turned to her, hands on hips, blue eyes flashing. "I do not understand why you're being so rude to our free labor." She glanced over her shoulder toward Greer, who watched her from just inside the door. "I assume you're working for free?"

"That was the plan."

"Agents don't do things for free," Freya insisted. "I may not know a lot, but I can guarantee that's a fact."

"Not everyone in the world behaves like the people you seem to know in California," Trinity told her. "There are plenty of places where folks are nice for the sake of being nice. Where are you from, Greer?"

"Kansas originally, but I'm based in Boston now."

"See." Trinity nodded. "Good old midwestern values. And people from Beantown are nice. I'm sure of it."

"Agents expect to get paid," Freya said with more force. "One way or another."

Greer shrugged, and an emotion she couldn't quite place flashed in his gaze. "I consider your mom a friend, not just a client."

"But you aren't dating?"

"Stop being rude," Trinity commanded. It was a new experience to be taken to task by her baby sister. Despite the novelty of it, Freya continued to glare at Greer.

"We aren't dating, and we never have."

There was more to the story with this man. Freya believed that all the way to her bones. But he wasn't going to spell it out, and she knew she was being unfair given the fact that he'd offered to help and they needed all the help they could get. The amount the sisters collectively knew about renovations could fit in a thimble.

"You can't post anything about my mom and her condition on social media."

His shoulders went rigid. It was interesting because she'd been rude to his face, and he hadn't seemed to mind. But cast aspersions at his motivations where her mother was concerned, and he bristled.

"I wouldn't do that." His voice had taken on a hard edge.

"Let me show you the sketches Freya did for the new space," Trinity told him, her voice almost aggressively agreeable. "She's really talented with design."

"Not really," Freya countered. "I like to draw." She met Greer's gaze, and he lifted a brow.

"You had a good run on *Love with the Carpenter*," he commented casually.

"You watched that?"

He shrugged. "Yeah. I watched a lot of reality television at one point."

Trinity put a hand on her stomach. "Oops, you guys are going to have to excuse me. I know people talk about morning sickness in the first trimester, but this baby seems to be giving me a run for my money until the end."

"Do you want to show me those drawings?" Greer asked when he and Freya were alone.

She studied him. "Why do you watch reality TV? You don't look like the type."

"Can I see the drawings?" His dark eyes had gone almost obsidian.

"Are you a grifter? Are you taking advantage of my mom and making me a part of it?"

"I doubt anyone could take advantage of May, even if they wanted to. She's tough, and I imagine you're a lot like her."

They'd made it to the kitchen. Freya looked around at the worn walls and scuffed counters. They'd gotten most of the piles of dishes and gadgets put away, and she suddenly remembered admiring the kitchen accessories in the hardware store. "I'm nothing like her," she said with more force than was probably necessary. "I don't trust you."

"I get that loud and clear."

Once again, he didn't seem bothered by her feelings about him. It was only when she called his honor into question regarding his professionalism that he took umbrage.

He reached for the drawing she'd done on a pad of paper, but she yanked it away before he could take it. "I don't believe for a minute that you're a reality television fan. What's the deal?"

He glanced at the doorway to the kitchen like he would

rather bolt than answer her question. His reaction only made her more suspicious.

"Shortly after Garrett moved to Magnolia, my mother was diagnosed with lung cancer. Stage four. She was a lifelong closet smoker, although she would have denied it. She was living in Kansas City at the time. She told me all she wanted as her last wish was to spend the summer at the beach. I thought about taking her to Florida. Magnolia seemed like a logical choice since Garrett was here. His longtime agent had just retired, and the agency had given him to me. He was going through a bit of a dry spell, and I was naive enough to think I could kill two birds with one stone. Take care of my mom and schmooze my best client."

He ran a hand through his hair. "It's laughable now. I had no clue what caring for a cancer patient in the last months of her life would involve. I didn't know your mom lived in this town, but we saw her at the bakery one morning before mine got too bad. My mom recognized her because she'd read the book when I was younger. It gave her the courage to walk away from my dad. That action made a huge difference to us both."

He paused to draw in a deep breath. Freya didn't want to hear any more. Her gut churned with embarrassment over how she'd misjudged Greer. She hated herself at this moment, which was why she didn't force him to stop. He deserved her attention on whatever history he wanted to share.

"We owed your mom," he continued, his gaze lowered to the table. "When she found out I worked for the agency that repped her back in the height of her career, she talked to me about her thoughts on the twentieth anniversary. It was a win-win. She'd been with the agency for years, but nobody was looking after her, and her original agent had also retired. She was kind to my mom. They were friends of a sort. Then May and I became friends. Only friends," he emphasized. "I am not your mother's boy-toy or whatever other crap you want to think about me. I respect her. When she mentioned that you were on a reality show, my mom wanted to check it out. She became a huge fan. She liked your moxie, she said, and when things got bad enough that she couldn't leave the house, we watched a lot of TV. We watched a lot of your TV. Maybe that's why I feel like I know you. I understand it's not all real, but I know a lot about you, Freya."

Freya couldn't begin to name all the levels at which that terrified her. She liked to think of her life and career in LA as something separate from her hometown.

She knew that was ridiculous. She'd already been recognized by the group of teenage girls in the bakery. But teenagers obsessed with reality TV felt different than knowing that this attractive, enigmatic man had watched her open herself up to millions of viewers over the years.

She'd grown tired of it, which was why she'd been so excited to pursue the idea for a novel inspired by her time on the fringes of Hollywood. It had made her feel so good to have something that seemed real to occupy her time.

Maybe that explained her visceral reaction to Greer. He was an agent. If she had the nerve to talk to him, he might be willing to read her work or at least recommend someone who could. Yeah, she had reality friends who'd gotten book deals for their memoirs or a random cookbook, but she hadn't yet been willing to put herself out there for something that truly mattered.

At this point, she wouldn't try with her mom's agent, although she owed him the courtesy of stopping the spoiled brat routine.

"If you watched the shows, you know everything there

is to know about me." She offered a genuine smile. "I'm sorry I've been a jerk to you."

"No, you're not." The gleam was back in his eyes.

"I said I was."

"You're willing to make me an ally right now, but it's all part of the gameplay."

"This isn't a game," she insisted. "It's my life."

"It's a game."

He really did know her well. The realization appealed to her, although she couldn't explain why. Not many people understood what made her tick or could offer her much of a challenge.

She had a great track record for winning the reality contests she'd participated in, and most of the ones she'd lost had been on purpose. She wondered if Greer realized that as well. Probably.

"Then you know I always find a way to win."

"What's the prize at the end of this one?" he asked, his rumbly voice doing funny things to her insides.

"I'll let you know when I figure it out." She handed him the drawing. "At the very least, one of the small wins is you being my slave for the next several weeks. You're like my personal elf."

That earned a belly laugh. "Your elf, huh?"

"Pretty much."

As he took the drawing from her, his finger brushed hers, sending sparks trailing across her skin. "For the record, I don't like to lose either."

She swallowed but kept her features neutral. "Then let the games begin."

CHAPTER NINE

TRINITY CLIMBED THE three-rung stepladder at the end of the week, cursing the strand of twinkle lights that had just flickered out as she started to wrap them around a tree in her mom's front yard.

"What's the problem now?" she demanded of the Christmas lights.

"I don't think pregnant people are supposed to be on ladders. That could be a problem."

She glanced toward the house next door to see a girl walking up the path that led to the front porch.

"It's not that high," Trinity called. "Are you Michaela?"

The girl nodded. Michaela had light brown hair that fell to the middle of her back and a skinny build that reminded Trinity of herself at that age. She dropped her backpack on the ground and started across the lawn. "Do you want help?"

Trinity wasn't great at accepting help but nodded. Things were different in Magnolia. Maybe it was just because her sisters were in town, but she didn't feel so alone here. She'd made friends in Montana but lost touch with many of them as her relationship with Dave got more difficult. Lost touch with herself as well. And she'd been too anxious to try making friends when she'd moved to Colorado after leaving him.

"I swear they were all lit just a few seconds ago."

As she got closer, Michaela pointed to the ladder's bottom rung. "You stepped on one of them."

Trinity groaned as she stared at the pieces of smashed bulb. "I didn't even notice." She cradled a hand around her belly. "I don't have the best spatial awareness at the moment."

"Is your mom going to be okay?" Michaela asked as she took the string of lights from Trinity.

"It's nice of you to ask about her." Trinity remembered now that Ash told her his daughter had been the one to discover May when she stopped by selling wrapping paper for a school fundraiser. "Walk with me to the garage," she told the girl. "I'd like a chance to thank you for what you did to help my mom."

"I didn't do that much," the girl countered, "other than yell for my dad. And Beth thanked me. She bought all my wrapping paper."

Trinity smiled. Of course her sister had taken care of things. That was Beth's way. "Well, I'd like to thank you as well. I'm Trinity."

"Is Miss May going to be okay? You didn't answer the question. When adults don't answer questions, it's because they think a kid isn't going to like the answer, and they hope maybe we'll forget asking it."

"Wise beyond your years," Trinity murmured. She'd left the garage door open and glanced around at the chaos inside, hoping a broom and dustpan would magically appear. "We hope our mom is going to make a full recovery. She's got a lot of work to do, almost as much work as we have on this house to get her home. But everyone wants her back here."

Was that actually true? It was hard for Trinity to know what Beth wanted. There was something her sister wasn't telling the rest of them, or perhaps Beth felt uncomfortable with Trinity and her pregnancy.

She knew it had to be difficult since Beth had tried for so long to have a baby of her own. Trinity hadn't even been certain she wanted to be a mom, although she was sure she loved her unborn child.

"Are you ready for Christmas?"

The girl brushed a limp strand of hair away from her face. "Christmas makes my grandma sad because she misses my mom. I miss her, too, but I don't know how a holiday makes any difference."

Trinity nodded. "I imagine you miss her every day."

The girl bit down on her lip and looked away. "Is that a broom in the corner?" She pointed to the far side of the garage.

"Thanks," Trinity murmured and moved forward. "Were you selling wrapping paper for a class?"

"My choir group. We have a field trip to Washington, DC, in the spring."

"That's great. I always wanted to be able to sing. My sister Beth has a gorgeous voice. I thought about taking lessons before the baby's born. I'm worried that I'll start singing and even my baby will beg me to stop. The only creatures that like my voice are alley cats."

Michaela laughed as she followed Trinity back into the yard. "How's Mr. Jingles?"

Trinity handed the girl the dustpan, but Michaela also took the broom. "I can bend down easier than you," she explained.

Ash Davis was raising a lovely daughter, Trinity decided at that moment.

"Mr. Jingles is ornery. He pooped in my empty suitcase yesterday."

The girl wrinkled her nose. "That's disgusting. Are you giving him his special food?"

"What special food?"

"Miss May keeps cans of wet food in the hutch in the dining room. She gives him a little bowl every morning. I know because when she goes out of town, I cat sit for her. He likes the soft food."

"Probably too much," Trinity agreed. "He's fat."

"I don't think Miss May cares." Michaela's smile was gentle. "She wants him to be happy."

It still was difficult for Trinity to imagine her mom caring about anyone's happiness other than her own. The more time she spent in Magnolia, the more she understood that either her mother had changed or the years of Trinity's absence had brought a change to May that her daughters never would've expected.

"If I had a cat, I'd make sure he only pooped in his litter box," Michaela said. "My dad promised I could get a dog or a cat for Christmas, but Nana said she's allergic. I don't think she's allergic. She doesn't want an animal in the house. A cute little doggy or kitty might make her smile, and she doesn't like to smile."

"That must be rough on you."

"She says it's because she misses Mom, but Dad and I miss her, and we still smile."

"I'm sure that's what your mom would want," Trinity said. She plucked out one of the extra bulbs she'd put into her pocket and replaced the one she'd smashed. "Did you know I was friends with your mom growing up since we lived next door?"

"Mom always acted like she had so many friends in Magnolia, but not many people around here have nice things to say about her."

Trinity inwardly winced. She thought the same thing about Stacy but would never act that way toward her daughter.

"Do you like living in Magnolia?" Trinity asked as she handed the string of lights to Michaela, who'd moved to the stepladder.

"It's okay. I like the beach and stuff. Plus walking from school to downtown for ice cream is cool."

She looked past Trinity as Ash's SUV pulled into the Amermans' driveway. "Kids sometimes act weird because my dad is the police chief."

"What grade are you in?"

"Sixth."

"Why on earth would sixth graders feel weird about a cop? That's not supposed to happen until you're sneaking beer from your parents."

"Why is it that when I asked you for help with lights you said you were too busy?" Ash called to his daughter as he approached. He wore a canvas jacket over his uniform shirt and trousers. Trinity had never thought herself a sucker for a man in uniform, but her heart raced inside her chest and her body felt like it hummed its awareness of the police chief.

Michaela grinned. "I was too busy."

"You were making a TikTok," her dad complained.

"That was still busy."

"I love TikTok." Trinity pressed a hand to her stomach when the baby kicked. "My favorites are the talking dog accounts. I can't get enough of them."

"Have you seen the one with the talking hippos at the zoo?" Michaela asked.

Trinity shook her head. "Oh, I missed that."

The girl held out a hand. "Let me have your phone, and I'll find it for you. It's the best."

"Maybe I should get an account," Ash said as he moved closer.

"Oh my gosh. Dad, no way. That would be so embarrassing."

"You might go viral," Trinity told him. "Come up with some kind of cop-shtick. Freya might be able to help you with that. She's kind of a big deal on social media."

"Miss May told me about all the shows she was on. But she and Dad said I couldn't watch most of them because there's too much bad language and kissing and drinking."

Trinity laughed. "I get the picture. To be honest, I haven't watched them either. Reality TV isn't my thing."

"But she's your sister," Michaela said. She handed her dad the string of lights. He walked around the tree, placing them just so in the branches. "Aren't you supposed to watch to support her?"

Trinity felt guilt ping through her. "That's a good point," she told the girl. "Maybe I'll watch them while I'm here in Magnolia."

"How long are you staying?" Michaela asked. Trinity felt Ash's gaze on her.

"At least through Christmas."

"You should stay until the baby is born," Michaela insisted. "It would make your mom happy. She loves babies."

Trinity could not reconcile the mom she knew with the woman described by her neighbors.

"Hey, do you want to make a TikTok together?" The girl grinned. "We could do one where we make your belly pretend talk."

Trinity laughed. "Um, sure."

"Awesome. I'll stop by later." Michaela jumped off the

stepladder. "Also, would it be okay if I went to visit Miss May with you sometime? I heard Shauna and the twins decorated her room. I could ride along when—"

"Mic, honey." Ash put a hand on his daughter's shoulder. "You can't invite yourself along."

"Sure she can," Trinity told him. She smiled at the girl. "If it's okay with your dad then you're welcome to come. I'm heading over in about an hour. One of us has dinner with her every night."

"Can I go, Daddy?" Michaela gave Ash the sweetest puppy-dog eyes Trinity had ever seen. "It's leftover night, so Gram won't mind."

"Are you sure?" Ash asked Trinity.

"Absolutely."

"If you get your homework finished," he told his daughter.

"Going right now," she shouted, then rushed back to her grandmother's yard, picked up her backpack and ran for the house.

"How did you manage that?" Ash asked, picking up another set of lights from the lawn. "You've connected more with my daughter in the five minutes I was with the two of you than I have in the past six months."

An unexpected heat exploded through Trinity as Ash studied her. "I cut hair for a living. It's part of my job to connect with people."

He ran a hand over the top of his thick head of hair. "Maybe you could cut mine sometime?"

Trinity had been a stylist for years. Although she loved the tactile feeling of her work, she'd never considered it something sensual. Right now, the thought of putting her hands on Ash felt downright dirty. "I'm not sure your reg-

ular stylist would appreciate that. We're a pretty territo-
rial lot."

He gave her an abashed smile. "I don't think you have to
worry. My mother-in-law cuts my hair with one of those…"

Trinity put her hands over her ears in mock horror. "If
you say a Flowbee, we're going to have an issue."

"You said it. I'm only agreeing with you."

"Oh, my word, Chief." She stepped forward and gave
in to the urge to touch him. His hair was softer than she
could have imagined. She tugged on the ends as she moved
around him. "Yes, you're in desperate need." She tried to
make the words a joke, but when their eyes met, her voice
trailed off.

"Of you," he said softly.

"Of a haircut," she corrected.

One side of his mouth curved. "My daughter is going to
want in on the action. Helena does hers, too."

"Haircuts for you both." She glanced up at her mother's
house. "I could take care of you in my mom's kitchen some
night when I don't have dinner duty with her."

"I'll pay you."

Trinity laughed. "No, you won't. I miss my job. It's not
something important like what you or my sister do, but I
love it."

"I could pay you with dinner," he amended. A blush rose
to his cheeks. Adorable and out of place on such a strong
and capable man.

The reminder of his physical strength had a flash of
terror shooting through her. Ash was nothing like her ex-
boyfriend, but he was a man. He could overpower her in
a second.

She had no reason to believe he would, yet fear wasn't
rational when it took hold.

Ash stepped away as if he sensed the change in her. "I get it. I don't want you to think I can't take no for an answer. I just…" He scrubbed a hand over his face. "It's been a long time since… I haven't gone on a first date since before Stacy. I'm out of practice with women. I'm sorry if I made you feel uncomfortable. You have every right to say no, and I respect that. No matter how much I like you or at least think I could like you."

His words softened the sharp edge of anxiety inside Trinity. They helped her remember that some men were considerate with women and honored their boundaries. There were men who used their hands in kindness and healing instead of to hurt and humiliate.

"Are you and Michaela going to the parade Friday night?"

She'd read about the holiday light parade downtown this coming weekend. When Trinity had been younger, Magnolia hadn't been much to speak of, even around the holidays. Sagging storefronts with businesses doing their best to eke out a living and little else downtown. A few of the local shop owners, like the lady who ran the bakery, had tried to drum up community spirit, but it had never really taken.

The town was different now, vibrant and alive with crowds of people and a sense of vitality and hope. She'd seen a help wanted sign in one of the local salons, and for a second, she'd considered the possibility she might stay. Beth could help her with the baby, and in turn, Trinity would pitch in with their mother.

Even with her stomach growing bigger every day and the baby's regular movements as a reminder that life would soon change dramatically, Trinity had trouble envisioning her future with any sort of clarity. One day at a time had been her motto for so long she wasn't sure how to change.

"It's one of our traditions," Ash said with a nod. "Well, this is our second Christmas in town. If you can count two years as a tradition, then it's one of ours. Are you going? Do you want to go together?"

"I have plans to go with Freya and Beth, but I read on a sign for it that there'll be a funnel cake booth in the park after. Maybe you could buy me a funnel cake?"

A slow grin spread across his face. "I could definitely buy you a funnel cake."

"Great." She wasn't sure what to do about the fizzy feeling that whooshed through her. It wasn't like the indigestion she'd gotten so used to in the last trimester of pregnancy. The sensation was light and airy, as if she'd swallowed champagne bubbles. She liked it, maybe too much. "I think we've gotten all the lights up. Thanks for your help."

"I can carry the ladder back to the garage for you?"

"I've got it, but thanks. I'll see you on Friday night."

"It's a da—" Ash stopped himself. "It's a plan."

Trinity nodded, then picked up the ladder and started toward the garage before he could see the smile she couldn't quite hide. A new plan might be exactly what she needed.

CHAPTER TEN

As BETH STOOD between her sisters watching the cars and makeshift floats roll by on Friday night, she poked around her heart for lingering sadness or resentment. To her surprise, she found nothing.

The first person she, Freya and Trinity had seen when they'd arrived downtown to find a spot along the parade route had been her ex-husband and his brand-spanking-new fiancée, based on the sparkling diamond the younger woman wore on her left hand. Lucy's doe eyes had widened, and she'd moved closer to Greg like she expected Beth to start a catfight in the middle of one of the Christmas on the Coast town events.

Public displays of any sort of emotion had never been Beth's thing.

In fact, she'd been about to offer the couple her best wishes when Freya had yanked on her hand and pulled her away.

"Not today, Satan," Freya muttered as they walked away, eliciting a giggle from Trinity and a shocked gasp from Beth.

"Did you learn how to make an exit on the reality show circuit?" Trinity had asked with a laugh.

"Of course. One of the few useful skills my career has given me." Freya had turned to Beth at that point. "You don't have to be nice or polite, and you damn sure better not buy them a wedding present or a baby shower gift."

Beth had felt her face heat with embarrassment. She'd been planning to send over an arrangement from In Bloom, the local florist, as a way to show she wasn't fazed by her ex moving on.

"Greg and I are divorced, but we're still friends," she'd told her sister. "No hard feelings."

"Sure, sure," Freya had agreed. "Let me be clear, Beth. He is no longer your responsibility. You get to move on. I'd advise you to pretend he doesn't exist. Whatever works for you is all that matters."

"He's still one of Mom's doctors."

Freya's glossy mouth thinned. "Despite Greg helping with Mom's care, you don't owe him anything. He's a well-paid doctor. That's his job."

"We'll deal with him," Trinity had added. "We've got your back."

Beth thought about those words and the fiercely protective look in Freya's eyes as Greg and Lucy had walked by. How long had it been since someone had taken Beth's side? Maybe never. That was the problem with being hyper-competent. She was always in the role of caregiver.

She would have expected pain from seeing her ex-husband and his new fiancée together, knowing he was going to have the family with Lucy that Beth had tried so hard to give him.

She felt only a vague sense of relief, plus a healthy dose of gratitude for her sisters. It felt good to be reminded that they were all adults and that Freya and Trin were plenty capable of offering support. Beth needed to work on taking it.

"Oh, my gosh, is that Mrs. Jessup?" Freya's voice was hushed as a float passed with a jolly Santa and a very sexy

Mrs. Claus waving from atop it. "She didn't look like that back when I had her for World History in high school."

"Her husband left her for another man a few years ago. She reinvented herself."

"Reinvention in the form of dropping fifty or so pounds," Freya clarified.

"She didn't drop any weight in her chest." Trinity whistled appreciatively. "She looks like she could be a geriatric Rockette with that short skirt and low-cut sweater. She's going to catch her death of cold in that outfit. Who's her Santa?"

Beth shook her head. "I don't recognize him with the beard and stuffing."

"Bill Williams," Declan offered as he came to stand next to Trinity along with Shauna's twins. "He owns Champions."

"The old bar down the street?" Trinity asked.

"Yup. I'm helping him update things while I'm in town."

"Cool. We need to go for a drink," Freya said, making space for Timmy and Zach to move to the front of the sidewalk. "It was the one place that wouldn't take my fake ID in high school."

"What's a fake ID?" Zach asked as he waved to the next float rolling by. Several teenagers dressed as elves tossed candy at the crowd.

Freya glanced at Beth and mouthed *help me*.

"You're on your own," Beth told her sister with a wink.

"Not fair," Freya complained. "I just gave a verbal smackdown to your jerk-face ex. Boys, look." She pointed toward the sky. "I saw a shooting star, or maybe it's Santa making a trial run so he could check out the parade."

"Did your ex-husband give you trouble tonight?"

Beth could feel Declan's powerful gaze on her.

"No, but we saw him with his new girlfriend, now fian-cée, based on the hardware she was sporting."

"Soon to be baby mama," Declan supplied, surprising Beth with the humor in his tone.

"Pretty much. Freya reminded me that Greg no longer has any meaning in my life."

"Is that true?" Something in Declan's tone gave Beth pause.

"Yeah," she answered, turning to look at him. "It is."

"Good."

Was it possible that one word—one syllable—could con-vey an entire world of meaning? Beth felt tingly all the way to her toes.

"It's colder tonight than I expected," she said to explain the shiver that passed through her.

"Are you joking?" Trinity placed her hands on her belly. "It's practically balmy compared to Montana, and anyway, this little girl is like my own personal space heater. I'm al-ways roasting with…" She paused. "Does it bother you to hear me talk about being pregnant?" She flashed an apolo-getic smile. "I can—"

"It's fine, Trin." Beth gave her a small hug. She wasn't much of a hugger but was trying to become more comfort-able with physical affection. "I can't wait to be an auntie."

"You're going to be the best," Trinity answered.

"I'll spoil her more," Freya offered. "Speaking of spoil-ing…" She patted both Timmy and Zach on the head. "The parade's almost over. How about we head over to the hot cocoa station after this?"

The offer elicited cheers from both boys.

"Okay with you if I steal these two little elves for a few minutes?" she asked Declan, who gave an almost audible sigh of relief.

"Works for me. Be good, boys. You know your mom will ask later."

Zach and Timmy promised, clearly not wanting to disappoint their mother.

"I'll walk with you," Trinity offered as Freya took each of the boys' hands in hers. "I'm meeting some people at the funnel cake booth."

"Meet up in front of the hardware store in an hour." Freya winked and slid a not-so-subtle glance between Beth and Declan.

"Your sisters are fun," Declan said when they were alone. Alone as they could be with half the town surrounding them. "I like them."

Beth laughed softly. "Me, too, although I could do with a bit more nuance. What's the point of leaving the two of us together?"

"Maybe we could come up with something," he said, raising one thick brow as he swayed closer.

Was he flirting with her? Impossible. He barely even liked her. He'd seen her at pretty much her worst at the hospital, and she wasn't certain Thanksgiving or their interaction on the street before that had been much better. Maybe they'd shared a moment the other night, but it didn't mean anything. Did it?

"How's Shauna feeling?" she asked, needing a neutral topic as her body continued to tingle. She rubbed her hands against her arms then smiled at a collection of dogs in festive sweaters that matched their handlers walking by in the parade. Two of the women held a sign for a local animal rescue. It was an adorable display.

"Bored and healing," he said as he shrugged out of the oversize flannel jacket he wore. "She didn't want to navigate tonight on crutches so stayed home to do some early gift wrapping. Thank God for online shopping, otherwise, she'd be sending me to the toy aisle. She appreciated the magazines and brownies you dropped off. You didn't have to."

"I wanted to thank her for decorating Mom's room. I owe you something, too. She loves the lights and the tree."

Beth sucked in a breath as Declan moved to drape his jacket over her shoulders. "I'm fine," she protested automatically.

"You're freezing, and I don't know a lot of people in town. Nor am I much of an extrovert. You can hang out with me while your sister entertains the twins. That's all the thanks I need."

"Easy enough."

Easy but not uncomplicated. If Beth were going to pick a man to have lustful feelings toward, the object of her affection would not be Declan Murphy. Yet here she was wrapped in his jacket, the scent of him tickling her senses until she felt almost woozy from it.

"Do you want hot chocolate or a funnel cake? Have any shopping to do?"

She smiled because it was cute that he looked unsure of what to do next. Maybe she wasn't the only one overwhelmed by this unexpected connection.

"Let's just walk. You said you're doing work for Bill Williams at Champions? Is that part of the bar fixing business?"

"Sort of. It's a smaller project, and in theory, I'm there because he hired Shauna to do some painting in the office and the bar's underused kitchen."

"That place needs way more than a fresh coat of paint." Beth scrunched her nose. "I think it was old and run-down back in the nineties, and there have been no improvements made that I can see."

"Right. Bill's getting ready to retire, and he wants to sell the bar. To get the right price, there need to be some updates. The place has a lot of potential, especially with how the town is growing. I'm here so figured I could lend a hand."

"Work your magic?"

"Something like that."

Beth could just imagine the type of magic Declan might be capable of working. She cleared her throat. "Does he stock Pinot Grigio?"

"I think so, but I can't vouch for the quality of it."

"I'm not picky."

He flashed a grin so wide and disarming, it caught her off guard. "I find that hard to believe."

"I can choose not to be picky when it suits me. I'd like a glass of wine. How about you show me your plans for the bar?"

"I can do that and buy you a drink."

She knew this wasn't a date, but her heart didn't get the message. "I'm the one who should be treating you."

"We can argue about the tab when it comes. I bet you're fun in a debate."

They walked toward the bar with Beth greeting people she knew along the way. She answered several questions about her mom, and her heart stuttered again. May was doing better, but it was still questionable whether she'd be able to come home permanently before Christmas. And her mom was still so sweet and kind every time Beth or her sisters visited.

The neurologist believed the change in personality resulted from the stroke. He couldn't tell them when things might change again or go back to normal or if this was how their mom would be on a permanent basis.

Beth couldn't help imagining how her childhood would have been different if she'd had this version of her mom growing up. She knew better than to focus on things she couldn't change from the past.

"What do you normally do for Christmas?" she asked Declan.

"I work. Things aren't always as Norman Rockwell as they appear in Magnolia. Bars are crowded around the holidays and not just because of office parties. Plenty of people don't have the greatest memories surrounding Christmas past. They want to drown their sorrows and forget."

"Are you one of those?"

He shrugged. "I'm not a fan of memory lane, but I gave up drowning my sorrows several years ago. Turns out getting so plastered that you forget the night before doesn't make for a great coping mechanism."

"Yet you've carved out a career working in bars?"

"It's what I know and what I'm good at."

"Have you thought about settling down?"

"I've never found anything worth settling for."

She swallowed. "Good to know."

He held open the door, and the smell of roasted peanuts and the sound of voices almost made Beth turn around and tell him she'd changed her mind. She wasn't very good at being casually social. Most people in town knew her as either May's uptight daughter or one of the nurses who ordered them around when they had a sick family member.

Freya was the fun sister and Trinity the sweet sister, leaving Beth as neither.

Declan put a hand on her back, the barest hint of a touch,

but it propelled her forward like she belonged because she was at his side.

Bill was still doing his Santa duties, but Declan waved to the current bartender like an old friend. Several of the patrons called out to him.

"Exactly how long have you been in Magnolia?" Beth asked.

"A couple of weeks now."

"I think you have more friends than I do."

He chuckled, and it reverberated through her. "That's not true. You don't give yourself enough credit. You need to get to know people or let them get to know you."

She shook her head as she followed him through the crowd. "I don't think the issue is that I don't know people. I think the issue is they don't like me."

"I like you," he said, turning to face her like they were the only two people in the world. "Does that count for anything?"

"Yes," she whispered, her mouth suddenly bone dry. "Yes, it does." Her gaze snagged on a movement behind him. "Ugh. Greg is here."

Declan continued to watch Beth. "Does that bother you? Do you want to leave?"

She drew in another deep breath, then released it with the sensation she was pushing out more than just air. "I want to stay." She hoped he understood that the part she didn't say out loud but meant from the bottom of her heart was that she wanted to stay because of him.

Whatever was between them couldn't lead anywhere, but she would enjoy the moment just the same.

CHAPTER ELEVEN

BETH WOKE WITH a start later that night and glanced at the clock on her nightstand. One fifteen. What had woken her from the amazing—if shockingly intimate—dream she'd been having about Declan?

For a moment, she wondered if her nocturnal fantasy might be real, but a glance at the empty side of the bed confirmed she was indeed alone.

She still couldn't believe how easy she'd found it to ignore her ex-husband in favor of Declan, even though Greg had tried to get her attention in a number of ways while loudly carousing with a couple of the young scrub techs from the hospital.

She and Declan had left Champions after one drink—a soda for him, she'd noticed—so that he could collect Timmy and Zach from her sister. Of course, Trinity and Freya had taken great enjoyment in teasing about her new potential love life, although she assured them that they were making something out of nothing.

Beth had never been a fan of make-believe fantasies before tonight.

The sound of voices brought her back to the present moment with a gasp. There was somebody in her house. What was she supposed to do now?

She quickly got out of bed and grabbed a hardcover book

off her nightstand, the first thing she could get her hands on that might act as a weapon.

She'd gotten in the habit of charging her phone in the kitchen overnight because she wanted her bedroom to be a device-free zone. Stupid health-conscious habits.

Adrenaline and panic whirled within her. Where could she hide?

Her midcentury bungalow didn't have walk-in closets, although she'd thought about converting one of the guest bedrooms into one now that she was in the house by herself.

Closet size hadn't mattered when she and Greg bought the place. To Beth, it had felt like a house that would be good for a family.

She glanced toward the window. She was on the first floor, so maybe she could escape into the backyard and...

She paused at the sound of a crash followed by a muffled curse then laughter. She recognized one of the voices speaking. Her panic immediately transformed to anger. She stalked into the living room to find her ex-husband struggling to take off his loafers as he stumbled around the living room, knocking into furniture.

Even more than having Greg back in her house, Beth was shocked by the sight of Declan standing in the doorway watching him.

"What is going on?" she demanded.

Greg gave her the lopsided grin she no longer found cute. "Hey, Elizabeth who's not Elizabeth. How's it hanging?"

"Greg, what are you doing here?" She looked at Declan, who seemed to be as stunned as she felt. "What are the two of you doing here?"

He scrubbed a hand over his face. "I headed back to the bar to help out after the twins went to bed. Champions was slammed tonight. It was closing time and this guy..." He

hitched a thumb toward Greg. "Was in no shape to make
it home on his own, so I offered him a ride."

"You brought him here?"

"He told me this was his house."

"It *is* my house," Greg said. He'd given up on the shoes
and had lowered himself to the couch. He stared at the
floor, his hands cradling his head like it was too heavy to
stay up on its own.

"It is *not* your house," Beth reminded him. "I don't understand why you still have a key. If I had known you were
going to break in, I would have changed the stupid locks,
Greg."

"Beth, come on. Don't be that way."

"You scared me half to death."

"Let's go, Doc." Declan stepped toward the couch. By
the set of his jaw and rigid shoulders, Beth could tell he
was not pleased with this development. "We're going to get
you to where you belong."

Beth felt her jaw drop as Greg burst into loud, sloppy
sobs. "I don't know where I belong. I don't know what I'm
doing. Beth, I don't know how to be a father. Not without
you. I mean I'm happy about it, and Lucy is great. Also really, really hot."

Beth rolled her eyes.

"Which doesn't change the fact that I don't know what
I'm doing." He listed to one side and curled up into a ball,
yanking the quilt that always rested on the back of the
couch over him.

"Greg." Beth moved forward, shaking her head at Declan when he stepped closer. "You're going to be a great
dad with Lucy. This is what you wanted. You need to pull
it together, both for Lucy and the baby."

"It came so easy," he said, covering his eyes with his

forearm. "After how hard things were for us. For you. Everything you went through. How can it be so easy now?"

Once again, Beth searched inside herself for pain. Surely, she was due a little self-pity indulgence in this situation, but she couldn't find any desire for it. She didn't wish Greg and Lucy anything but happiness.

Maybe things would have been different in her marriage without the infertility struggles, but there was no way to know that now.

Revisiting the past would only lead to unhappiness in the present. If her mother's situation and the return of her sisters had taught Beth anything over the past few weeks, it was that she wanted a chance to be happy. She didn't know whether she'd find that in Magnolia or in Nashville pursuing her dreams, but she wanted to find a way.

"You're going to be a great dad, Greg," she repeated.

Greg blew out a sniffly breath. "You promise?"

"I promise."

"Thanks, Beth. You're the best."

"Now you need to go home," she said.

Greg shifted, and she thought he was going to stand, but instead, he turned on his side, wrapped the blanket more tightly around himself, and almost immediately began to snore.

Declan let out a disgusted grunt. "Years of working in bars, and I still can't tolerate a sloppy drunk. I'll get him out of here if I have to carry him over my shoulder."

Beth appreciated the offer but shook her head. "It's fine. Let him sleep it off."

"You're not responsible for your ex-husband."

"I know." She did know. Her sisters had told her the same thing. Heck, even her mom had said it before the stroke changed things. As much as Beth didn't feel responsible, she continued to care about Greg.

Declan gestured to the book she held in her hand. It was her mother's. "Were you going to try to bore a potential burglar to death?"

Beth grinned and placed the hardcover on the coffee table. "That thing has been on my nightstand for almost a decade. I still haven't brought myself to read it. Too many unwanted associations from when we were kids." She sighed. "Now she's coming out with the twentieth anniversary updated and revised edition. I guess I should wait for that."

He quirked a brow. "Or you could read something for pleasure."

There were a lot of things Beth wanted to do for pleasure. Most of them involved Declan. Then her ex-husband let out an audible fart, and Beth pressed her fingers to her mouth when a giggle threatened to escape. She was afraid it might sound hysterical.

"Thank you for getting him home safely."

"This isn't his home anymore," Declan reminded her.

"You're right. Looks like a trip to the hardware store for new locks is in my future."

He nodded. "I can help with that."

She shrugged. "I'm not your responsibility." She didn't like how the words felt on her lips, but they were true enough.

"I can help."

Who was she to look a gift hunk in the mouth? "Thank you."

"You're welcome."

Greg turned over in his sleep.

"I *will* take him out of here," Declan offered again.

"He's fine." Beth didn't even spare a glance for her ex. "I'll use earplugs when I go back to sleep."

Declan nodded. "Which I should let you do now. Nice pajamas, by the way."

Beth crossed her arms over her chest, thinking about how she must look wearing no bra under her comfy flannel PJ set with the bright peony pattern splashed across them. "They're my favorite," she admitted because she had trouble hiding anything from this enigmatic man.

"Mine, too," Declan said quietly, and her body immediately responded to the deep timbre of his voice.

He moved toward the door, and she followed.

"Thanks for taking care of him."

One big shoulder shrugged. "I'd do it for any customer. Drinking and driving is a nonstarter as far as I'm concerned."

"You're a smart man."

He turned with his hand on the doorknob. "Unlike your ex-husband."

"It's…" She wrinkled her nose. "I won't say fine because that's not true. A failed marriage wasn't part of my plan, but I'm over it—him—now."

"Really?"

Once again, she did a gut check. "Really."

"I'm glad to hear that." He leaned in and brushed his lips over hers, a whisper of contact that sent desire rushing through her like a raging stream.

Was that a moan that bubbled up in her throat? If Declan heard it, he must have approved because his free hand lifted to cup her cheek, angling her head to deepen the kiss.

Their tongues met in a sensual dance that was at once deliciously familiar and yet different than anything she'd experienced. Declan Murphy kissed like a man who wanted to savor every bit of her. He was tender and demanding, and Beth barely recognized the version of herself who met his carnal need with her own.

All too soon, he pulled away. "I knew it would be like that," he told her with a wicked half smile.

"I had no idea it could be." She was stunned at the way her body continued to tingle.

Her words drew a wider smile from him, and he dropped a gentle kiss on her forehead. "Good night, Beth. Sweet dreams."

As she closed the door behind him, Beth felt as though her life had just turned into one massive, confusing question. One thing she knew for certain was that any dreams involving Declan were bound to be sweet.

CHAPTER TWELVE

"You guys, I can do this on my own. I'm sure you have better places to be than at the doctor." Trinity leveled a meaningful glance at Beth. "You can't possibly want to be here."

"Of course I can," her oldest sister said, and it was hard for Trinity to know whether Beth was telling the truth.

For more years than she cared to admit, Trinity had taken for granted Beth's engagement in every aspect of her life. Trinity had been seven when their mother burst onto the book scene with *A Woman's Odyssey*. Young enough not to realize it was a big deal that Beth, who was also still a child, had been thrust into the role of caring for her younger sisters.

She'd understood eventually and missed her mother, but it had seemed as simple as that. Once she'd grown up and had friends with older siblings and regular parents who hadn't emotionally abandoned their kids during their formative years, Trinity had realized what a burden it must have been for Beth.

Now Beth was at Trinity's side after pulling strings to get her seen by a local obstetrician, the one who had helped Beth with her fertility treatments. Freya was here, too, the reality show diva who could have cared less about her family. At least that was what Trinity assumed until these past couple of weeks showed her a different side to her glamorous sister.

Freya had stopped wearing makeup or doing anything to her hair but running a brush through it, but the biggest change was her energy. The first couple of days after Trinity's return, she'd noticed her sister had trouble sitting still for even a few minutes. She compulsively checked her phone and glanced around as if she expected a paparazzo to pop up at any moment. Trinity knew what it felt like to live with a sort of underlying panic ruling her life, but it had been a shock to understand she and Freya might have that in common now.

They'd been close as kids, united in resenting Beth, but they'd lost touch in recent years. Trinity had wanted to blame that on Freya's career. In truth, it was more because of Trinity's life choices than Freya's.

"We've been over this. I'm excited to be an aunt," Beth said, and Trinity no longer had a problem believing that.

"Me, too," Freya added. "I'm going to spoil your little girl so rotten."

Trinity smiled even as tears filled her eyes. She didn't want to think about being alone again.

"What's wrong, Trinny-bug?" Freya asked, using the childhood nickname she'd given the baby of the family. "We've had enough strife and sadness recently. This is a happy moment."

"They're happy tears. I promise." Trinity lay on the exam table, waiting for the ultrasound technician. "I don't know how I thought I was going to raise a child on my own."

"You're not on your own now," Beth said. "You're not on your own ever. We're your sisters."

Trinity nodded. "I'm grateful for you both."

The technician entered the room at that point, and her eyes went wide as she recognized Beth.

"What are you doing here?"

"This is my little sister," Beth said brightly, patting Trinity's arm. "She's come back to town to help with our mom, and she's having a baby. I'm here to support her."

"Great," the technician said, quickly schooling her features. "How far along are you?" She eyed Trinity's belly. "I'm guessing five or six months?"

"Seven," Trinity told her and felt a little embarrassed when the woman looked shocked. "I'm taking good care of myself. I just didn't pop until recently."

"Must be nice." The woman appeared to be in her early forties with dark hair piled high on her head. "I have three teenage boys. During each pregnancy, I got asked questions about whether I was having twins. No twins—I simply grew big healthy boys, one at a time."

"I'm having a girl," Trinity told her. "Maybe that's part of it."

The woman smiled. "Let's take a look at her then." Trinity gasped as the woman squirted gel under her belly. "Sorry, I know it's cold."

"That's okay."

The monitor began to make noise, and Trinity heard the swish of her baby's heartbeat. It comforted her to listen to the rhythmic sound.

"I assume this isn't your first ultrasound?"

Trinity shook her head. "I had one at fourteen weeks."

Beth squeezed her hand. "Doctor Brennan ordered another one since Trinity is new to the practice."

The technician smiled. "You've moved back to Magnolia to help your mom?"

Trinity kept her eyes on the monitor. "I was thinking I might stay awhile."

She sensed both Freya and Beth's surprise but didn't make eye contact with either of them. She couldn't explain how and why she had left behind her life out West. Not without having to talk about Dave.

"However long you're here, Dr. B will take good care of you. Plus, you're in great hands with your sister."

"Both of her sisters," Beth clarified. "The three of us are taking care of each other now." It was a huge thing for Beth to offer.

The technician pointed out the feet, hands and the chambers of the heart, then she paused. Or at least it seemed to Trinity that she paused. Was there a problem?

Beth leaned forward, squinting at the monitor. "Trinity, did you say you thought you were having a girl?"

"I'm definitely having a girl." Trinity nodded, trying not to sound as panicked as she suddenly felt. "I had an ultrasound at a clinic when I first moved to Colorado. They said it was a girl."

The technician gave her a tight smile. "They were wrong."

"No, they weren't. It's a girl. I have to be having a girl."

Freya squeezed her hand more firmly. "Listen to Beth, Trinny-bug. And me. I'm not an expert at reading ultrasounds, but that's a penis."

"Nope. You must have a bug on your machine."

The technician sniffed. "Honey, a fly and a penis don't look the same."

Freya smiled, although Trinity had trouble focusing on it through the tears that sprang to her eyes. "I'm going to spoil my nephew so hard he'll give a royal prince a run for his money."

"No," Trinity whispered. "Not a boy. Boys grow into men. I can't…" She jerked the wand off her belly, and it slipped out of the technician's hands and clattered to the floor.

"Marlene, would you give us a minute?" Beth asked.

The technician placed the wand back in its holder without looking at Trinity. "That's a good idea."

As the woman shut the exam room behind her, Trinity looked down at her belly, the gel still covering it, and felt a wave of nausea roll through her. "I'm going to be sick."

Freya immediately stood and reached for... There was nothing to reach for in the sterile exam room.

Beth put a hand on Trinity's forehead. "Lean back. You aren't going to be sick." She grabbed a wad of tissues from the nearby counter and wiped clean Trinity's stomach. "I think it's time you tell us what's going on."

"I want to have a girl baby."

"Yeah." Freya came to stand next to Beth. "I think we are all clear on that, sweetheart."

"Why?" Beth asked.

There was something in her tone that made Trinity realize Beth had already guessed the answer. She forced herself to look at her sisters. They knew. They both knew. Her most shameful secret wasn't a secret to two of the people who mattered most in the world to her.

"I left him. I want you to know that. As soon as I found out I was pregnant, I left. He doesn't even know about the baby."

"How long were you with him?" Beth asked gently.

"How many times did he hit you?" Freya demanded. "Because that's how many times I'm going to kill him. Over and over again."

"It was only once that he actually put a hand on me," Trinity told them.

"He hit you," Beth said through clenched teeth. "You're sure it was only once?"

"Maybe twice, but it wasn't a lot. I promise."

"There are other ways to abuse people than physically," Freya said.

Trinity told herself that she was not going to break down. She was going to be strong in front of her sisters. "Yes," she agreed. "He wasn't kind."

"I'm guessing that's an understatement," Freya muttered.

They heard voices outside the door.

"We can discuss this in more detail later." Beth studied her. "He doesn't know about the baby. Does he know where you went?"

Trinity looked away. "I didn't want him to follow me."

"And you're sure he didn't realize you were pregnant?"

"I'm sure."

"We're going to take care of you, Trin," Beth told her. "We will figure this out, which includes you having a boy."

Freya nodded. "We are going to raise the best man the world has ever seen. There's a girl out there—maybe she hasn't even been born yet, maybe she isn't even a twinkle in her mother's eye, but she's going to thank you someday. Or maybe there's another boy out there who will thank you. Who knows? But what I do know is he's not going to turn into your ex-boyfriend."

Trinity sucked in a shaky breath. "That's what I'm afraid of. What if my baby takes after his father?"

"Nope." Freya held up her hand. "We're not even going to honor that scumbag by calling him a father. We can refer to him as the blessed sperm donor."

Beth's eyes gleamed as she met Trinity's gaze. "I don't care if I was raised in the South, I won't even bless that jerk's heart."

Trinity smiled and the heavy weight that had been sitting on her chest felt a touch lighter. "I wouldn't bless his heart if he was the last man on earth."

Beth nodded and leaned in to kiss her cheek. Another unexpected, if appreciated, bit of affection from her normally standoffish sister.

"I'm going to talk to Dr. Brennan for a minute," Beth said. "You're going to be okay, Trin, and your son is going to be more than okay. He's going to be loved by all of us."

Trinity kept it together until the door closed. Then she couldn't hold back her tears any longer. Freya gave her a little nudge and climbed on the exam table next to her.

"I don't think there's room," Trinity protested with a laugh.

"We'll make room." Her sister smelled of expensive perfume.

Trinity guessed that the stylish wrap dress Freya wore cost more than Trinity made in a month of styling hair at the little salon in the tiny speck of a town she'd moved to in northern Colorado. She'd left Montana with nothing but the stuff she could fit in the back of her car. Most of her possessions were still shoved in her trunk in black garbage bags.

She was about to bring a baby into the world, and the sum total of her worldly belongings amounted to a couple of bags of trash. Certainly not enough to build a life for a child. But now her sisters knew the truth. Maybe not all of it. Maybe not the details that were too embarrassing for her to say out loud.

But they knew she was in trouble. As much as she wanted to believe she could take care of herself, the thought that they would protect her gave her no small amount of comfort.

"It's going to be okay," Freya promised. She placed a hand on Trinity's stomach.

"How do you know?" Trinity asked.

"I'm not sure," Freya admitted, "but I do."

Trinity closed her eyes and dashed a hand across each cheek. "It's going to be okay." She repeated Freya's words, hoping if she said them often enough, that she could eventually believe them.

CHAPTER THIRTEEN

FREYA REALIZED SHE had a severe problem two days later. She liked Christopher Greer. Not just in the way of appreciating that he was an undeniably attractive man and it had been far too long since her lady parts had seen any action.

She enjoyed him as a person. The two of them had taken over most of the work on the main floor of her mother's house while Trinity did what she could to clean and make room upstairs for things that would no longer fit on the first floor. There was plenty of work for everyone, and they'd quickly fallen into a routine. Freya also had plenty of ways to stay busy with her affiliate and endorsement deals.

She didn't love capitalizing on her time in Magnolia to make money, but unless she got brave enough to send out her manuscript and someone offered her a book contract, it was the career she had.

Things had changed in her mind and heart with Trinity's revelations at the doctor. How did she not know her sister was in trouble? How had she allowed distance and life excuses to pull them so far apart?

At least Beth had been as unaware as her. Freya wasn't sure if she could have taken it if Trinity had confided in Beth. She occupied herself with wiping imaginary dirt from the kitchen counters she'd cleaned earlier that morning and tried to ignore the sound of Greer setting up for his day of work.

She liked to tease him about spending so much time at her mother's house instead of brokering deals for clients and doing whatever else it was agents did with their time.

He'd only smiled and assured her he could handle both. The man was annoyingly unflappable.

Freya considered getting under people's skin one of her superpowers. She'd honed it to a sharp edge during her time in California, and it was one of the tactics she used to help her stand out among a crowded field of reality stars.

She did her best to affect her mother's agent. Affecting people made her feel special—she was a typical middle child in that way.

But Greer could have cared less about Freya, and it bothered her. She heard the whir of the saw, and when it stopped, the soft hum of his baritone. He liked to listen to music while working, although she noticed that he took out his earbuds when Trinity was around.

She noticed he had no problem conversing with her sister but mostly ignored Freya unless he had a specific question for her. She wasn't the type of woman to be ignored.

She touched the hem of the dress she wore, which barely covered the important bits, and with a final fluff of her silky hair, walked into the family room. She wanted to surprise him and figured her best chance of sneaking up on him was to catch him while he was listening to music.

As usual, the infuriating man had some sort of sixth sense where she was concerned. He stopped and turned as she came toward him, although he didn't remove his earbuds. His eyes roamed over her, and she had a small measure of satisfaction when his nostrils flared. That was the only outward sign he gave that she was basically wearing the equivalent of a slip.

"Business meeting today?" he asked conversationally as

he pulled the earbud out of his right ear. The tinny sound of classic rock echoed in the silence between them.

She would have made a fabulous eighties video vixen and had the sudden urge to pose on the back of the couch like it was a classic Chevy Camaro.

Only that would make her look like she was trying too hard, and she was already bordering on desperate.

"I was interviewed for an entertainment show this morning. They're doing a segment on celebrities and their favorite holiday traditions. We each had to share ours."

He studied her. "Did your tradition involve downing eggnog shots at a trashy Vegas nightclub?"

Direct hit.

Was she mistaken or were the tips of Greer's ears turning pink? Maybe he wasn't as unaffected by her as she'd first believed. She didn't bother mentioning that she'd put on a conservative red blazer over her nude mini dress for the interview. It was none of his business that Freya had given up dressing provocatively several years ago.

To each her own, but she felt more comfortable without revealing much skin. She'd retained a few key pieces from her more outlandish wardrobe. They came in handy for certain types of events.

"Are you slut shaming me?" she asked. She pushed one hip forward, posing like she would on the red carpet.

"I don't think you're a slut," he answered with an earnestness that made it hard to swallow around the emotion in her throat. "You have nothing to be ashamed about."

She frowned. It wasn't true. There were plenty of things she could think of that brought down the weight of shame on her. She wasn't going to admit it to Greer. "Do you need a hand?"

He stared at her for several seconds then inclined his

head. "You could hold the end of this board while I measure it."

Freya blinked. She'd expected him to dismiss her offer. Her plan was to make a bit of a scene then retreat upstairs to put on some comfortable clothes before starting on her projects for the day.

Of course she hadn't thought that he'd want help. He never seemed to want her anywhere near him. She certainly wasn't prepared to go there in a skintight sheath. If she were going to help Greer, it would be with layers of denim and flannel between them.

He had the denim part down but wore a short-sleeve T-shirt like the cool morning air didn't affect him. Because she knew he couldn't be wearing short sleeves because he wanted to show off his muscles to her, impressive as they were.

"Unless you'd like to slip into something more comfortable," he suggested.

"I can help you in this," she said. There was no way she would let him fluster her.

She started to approach cautiously, feeling a bit like a deer in the crosshairs of a hungry wolf.

Then she gave herself a mental headshake. Freya had never been a baby deer in her life. She would say she'd never been afraid of anything, but that wasn't true. She just knew how to hide the fear and would do that with Greer as well.

Not that she thought he would take advantage of her or try anything funny the way plenty of men had in the past. He was way too honorable, and there was the pesky uncertainty whether he even found her attractive.

No. Greer wouldn't put the moves on her because he was a stand-up guy. Somehow her mother had found an agent who cared about her. In Hollywood, Freya had started to believe those types of people were as rare as unicorns, which was to say nonexistent.

He scared her. She'd never made good men a priority in her life, but he made her want to. This town made her want to, which was why she couldn't stay here, even for Trinity.

She sashayed over and lifted her arms wide, knowing the stance would put her breasts on full display. What she was doing was wrong, using her body like a weapon. She hated that part of Hollywood and chided herself for now stooping so low.

But it didn't make her stop.

He chuckled at her movements like she was an entertaining toddler. She would eventually find a way to make this man treat her like a woman.

"Keep the end steady while I measure."

She grabbed the piece of wood, letting her mind wander to the edits she was doing on her manuscript. There was no point in toying with Greer anymore today. She'd just end up embarrassing herself. But she'd gotten to a problematic point in plotting the mystery thread and had woken up early with her mind churning through ways to fix it.

Now she let her brain go back there. Maybe she could add another red herring or draw out the clues. She was so involved in thoughts about her book that she didn't notice how close Greer stood. Then, like a rush of warm water, his scent cascaded over her until she felt like she was drowning in it.

Suddenly, Freya wished she had fewer clothes on. She would have preferred Greer to be buck naked. She could imagine how his skin would feel against hers. Even though the spicy, wild, yet somehow restrained scent of him was all around her, she wanted to lean closer and breathe him in more deeply.

He seemed so gentle, and she knew without a doubt that

instead of taking advantage, he would protect her. Except Freya didn't need protecting. Trinity needed protecting. Beth probably needed protecting from herself because she was undoubtedly still doing her routine of taking on the whole world like it was her responsibility.

What Freya needed was an excuse to let go.

Not the fake explosions that happened with the camera rolling but really feeling free. Greer made her feel free.

They stood together for several seconds as if they were caught up in the swirling connection looping between them. It made her heart happy that he seemed just as reluctant to let go as she was.

She heard the sound of Trinity singing as she came down the stairs. A moment later, the heat of Greer was gone as if it had never been there. Freya shouldn't miss it as much as she did, but he'd managed to move a few feet away at lightning speed.

"Are we filming a lingerie ad in the construction zone and no one bothered to mention it to me?" her sister asked as she took in Freya, who was now standing by herself on one side of the two-by-four. "Because I have to tell you, the look is weirdly empowering."

Greer chuckled. "Your mom would be so proud," he told Freya.

She gave him an enthusiastic one-fingered salute.

"My mom has never been proud of me."

"We've been over this," he said with the patience she'd come to expect from him. "She's proud of all three of you."

Freya stared at him, unsure of how to answer, wanting to believe him with every fiber of her being.

"She likes to touch my stomach," Trinity said into the silence.

Freya stared at her sister. "Mom does?"

"Yeah. Every time I'm alone in her room, she has me climb up in bed with her and puts her hands on my stomach until the baby kicks. I haven't had the heart to tell her I'm having a boy."

"You think that's going to upset her?" Greer frowned. "Your mom loves the twins."

Trinity's rosebud mouth opened slightly, and the pucker that marred her forehead smoothed. "She might be happy I'm having a boy. She was never all that interested in her girl children. Maybe a boy grandchild will be different."

"It will be. Your mom is different from how the three of you describe her. From how she used to be."

"You're right," Trinity said, and Freya had to agree.

Once again, she wasn't sure how she felt about Greer being so able and willing to point out her mother's new and improved personality. Perhaps the change wasn't fully a result of the brain damage from the stroke.

Beth admitted she wasn't close to Mom despite living in Magnolia. Freya hadn't given May much of a chance over the past few years. If she'd come to visit or spent longer with her mom on the phone, there was a chance she wouldn't have so much trouble believing this loving mother persona would last.

"They're doing a holiday concert at the school this afternoon," Greer told the two of them. "I wanted to ask if it was okay if I bring your mom to it? I know she's still weak and it would be a shorter outing, but I thought she might enjoy it. She loves holiday music."

"Mom loves Christmas songs?" Freya bit back a snort. "You must be joking."

Greer shook his head. "Come on. That can't possibly be something new. Does anybody acquire a midlife taste for Mariah Carey and Bing Crosby?"

"I can remember Mom singing 'White Christmas' in the kitchen when I was little," Trinity said with a grin. "Not once the book was published because then she was always doing special events around the holidays but before that. Freya, you remember, right?"

Freya searched her brain. It felt like she'd buried all of the positive memories she had of her mother. It was too easy to focus on the negative and keep her heart hardened. If she overthought the good times, it only made her sad. It made her remember all the things she'd lost after her parents split up and her mom started on her new path.

Their lives hadn't been perfect before that, but they'd been better than they were after.

"I remember," she admitted now. "She made thumb-print cookies. That was back when she still liked to cook, or at least pretended she liked to cook. We'd bake cookies, and she'd dance around the kitchen singing at the top of her lungs."

Greer grimaced. "That must have been horrifying. Your mom has a terrible voice even though she loves to sing."

Trinity laughed. It might have been the first time since the doctor's appointment, and it warmed Freya. It warmed her heart toward Greer as well, which was the last thing she needed.

"Freya takes after her. Dogs hide when she starts singing."

"Rude," Freya muttered. "I'll have you know I was singing in the shower the other morning and Mr. Jingles poked his head in."

"He probably thought you were Mom," Trinity said without a trace of sarcasm. "I think he really does miss her."

CHAPTER FOURTEEN

BETH STILL COULDN'T believe she'd allowed her sisters to convince her to attend a holiday concert at the local elementary school. Although they hadn't exactly worked hard at convincing her.

Freya and Trinity had simply told her that they, along with Greer, were taking their mom to see the show. Both of them seemed surprised she wanted to join them, and she didn't blame them. In the past couple of days, she'd made it clear that while they were in town, she was tapping out as much as she could on their mother's care.

She had no doubt they both figured it was because she would be taking on the brunt in the long months of rehabilitation. But she still hadn't mentioned Nashville and nurse practitioner school to either of them. She wanted to have a plan first.

She wasn't ready to give up on her dream if she could figure out a way to make it work and still care for her mom. Whenever she decided on the plan, she'd present it to Freya and Trinity as a done deal.

It was a trick she'd learned when she'd first taken responsibility for running the house as a kid. She'd been terrified of screwing up or doing something wrong or the pipes freezing when they had a cold spell along the coast. But she'd learned that if she didn't show her doubt, nobody understood how pervasive it was.

She'd done the same thing in her marriage. She refused to let Greg see her pain, either as a result of the difficulty conceiving or the three miscarriages she'd endured.

She'd focused all of her energy on supporting him and then resented him for it, which wasn't fair.

At least Beth could admit it now. She checked her reflection in the rearview mirror and wished she'd had enough time to go home and change out of her scrubs before the concert. But one of the nurses on shift after her had come in late. It was a typical occurrence.

Her coworkers knew Beth rarely minded staying. She'd pick up extra shifts and was always available if someone needed off, but today her constant pressure to be indispensable felt like it was taking a toll.

As she walked across the parking lot, she thought about her ex-husband and the night he'd spent on her couch. Greg woke the next morning with a pounding headache, embarrassed at his behavior and ready to convince her of his love and devotion for Lucy and his readiness to be a father.

At first, Beth had let him ramble on, but after a few minutes, she'd stopped him, motivated by Declan's claim that she could choose not to take responsibility for every single person in her life. What a novel idea.

When Declan kissed her, it felt good to allow him to be in control. To give up the burden of responsibility and savor the moment. She'd enjoyed it way more than she expected.

It was funny because she'd thought he might ask her out or give some indication he wanted more than just a kiss, but he left it at that. In doing so, he'd made Beth desperate for more and unsure how to go about getting it. Beth was inexperienced in asking for what she wanted, but Declan made her yearn to change that.

Shaking off her thoughts about Declan Murphy, Beth

hurried toward the school's entrance. She hadn't been inside since Trinity was a student, although it seemed not much had changed.

The school even smelled the same, like crayons and sweat. She'd had her first miscarriage a year and a half into her marriage and being in this place made her think about how old her child would have been. What grade and whether he or she would have been athletic or artsy or a bit of both. Beth had been a soccer player, which she'd loved but had given up when looking after her sisters and hiding their mother's negligence took up too much time.

She entered the auditorium, which also doubled as the school's gymnasium. Neither Freya nor Trinity had been interested in sports, which at the time Beth thought was a blessing. One less thing for her to manage. It was hard enough keeping their situation hidden at the school.

From what she knew of her colleagues who had kids in activities now, sports parents were way too involved. She figured somebody would have realized things weren't right in the Carlyle home. In retrospect, it probably wouldn't have been the worst thing that could have happened for any of them. But it was too late now.

She easily spotted her mom and sisters. May's wheelchair was situated at the end of one aisle. Trinity saw Beth first, and the broad smile her baby sister flashed made Beth's heart pinch. Her sister—her sunny, often irresponsible sister—was going to be a mother. Beth still felt sad that Trinity worried about her reaction.

But she didn't blame her. Beth had long ago stopped resenting or doing what-ifs on the future and families other people had that she didn't. Maybe Trinity would decide to stay in Magnolia to raise the baby. She could even continue living with Mom as long as May's personality stayed the way it was now.

Beth didn't like to think about what it said about her that she didn't want her mom's brain to heal. It wasn't exactly true. She was happy for it to heal. She simply hoped it recovered in a way that would leave May still loving toward them all.

Her mother's face brightened as Beth arrived at the end of the aisle.

"Hewwo," May said. "Ew so pretty."

Beth blinked. She was the opposite of pretty right now, coming off a twelve-hour shift.

While May usually dressed like the aging hippie she was in flowing skirts and brightly colored silk blouses, Beth's style, if it could be categorized as such, was more efficient than anything else. In the past few years, May had several times suggested they go shopping. Often the timing coincided with a setback in Beth's fertility journey.

At the time, she'd taken it as a slight. Her mom kicking her when she was down, making it clear that if Beth had dressed different—been different—then maybe she'd have more luck getting pregnant.

It sounded so ridiculous, she wondered if she'd been unfairly judging her mom while May had been offering to spend time together for the sake of being supportive. She still had trouble associating the concept of support and her mom together.

May lifted her right hand and gestured Beth closer for a hug. Her left side was still mostly limp, although she'd been making solid progress with her exercises. At this rate, May was on target to be home for Christmas, while Freya and Greer were determined to have the main floor ready for her.

She leaned in and hugged her mother, tears springing

to her eyes at the whispered "I love you" that was now becoming familiar with May.

"Have a seat," Trinity said. She made room so Beth would be sitting between their mom and Greer. Freya looked nearly apoplectic that suddenly she was next to the handsome agent.

Beth didn't think she imagined the sparks between her sister and Christopher Greer, although she didn't understand the connection for either of them.

Before she could spend too much time contemplating whether her glamorous sister was on the cusp of a burgeoning romance during her time in town, the teacher in charge of the production took the stage.

Her mother made a noise of pleasure. Instinctively, Beth reached out and enfolded May's small hand in hers.

Her mom leaned closer, resting her head on Beth's shoulder as they watched the children file out onto the stage.

The woman who introduced herself as the school's art teacher seemed to be in charge of the event. She explained this year's theme was "a light in the darkness."

Beth dabbed her eyes as the first song started. She held tightly to her mother's hand and smiled at Trinity. She hadn't even realized she was living in darkness and regretted that her mother's brush with death precipitated her slow passage into the light.

She couldn't deny that despite all the ways her life wasn't going as expected, the past couple weeks of reconnecting with her sisters—as awkward as it was at times—made her heart feel less troubled.

She mouthed the words to one of her favorite Christmas songs and glanced around the audience to see Declan sitting with Shauna a few aisles in front of them.

To her shock, he turned like he'd been waiting for her to notice him and smiled.

"Lord, he's handsome," Trinity murmured around their mother.

Beth felt the heat of his smile down to her toes and couldn't deny her sister's words. "He and Shauna aren't dating," she said, wondering why she felt the need to clarify that.

"Good to know." Trinity laughed softly. "Although bad boys aren't my type these days."

"I don't think he's a bad boy. I think he looks like one, or maybe he's reformed. What kind of a bad boy agrees to take care of six-year-old twins of a woman he's not even dating?"

"Are you trying to convince yourself or me?" Trinity asked as the first number came to an end and the audience applauded.

"Neither. But speaking of handsome men who aren't in the bad-boy category, do you have any thoughts on why Police Chief Davis keeps looking at us—or more specifically you?"

Beth nodded her head toward May's neighbor, who sat across the aisle with his mother-in-law. His daughter was in sixth grade at the school, so her class would perform next according to the program.

Trinity cradled her baby bump like a security blanket. "I have no idea," she said, but Beth caught the breathy edge to her voice.

"He's a good guy, Trin."

"I'm going to pop out a baby in a month and a half. I'm not interested in men."

Freya leaned around Greer to shush the two of them as the next song began. Beth and Trinity shared a smile when Greer reached out to pat Freya's hand like he was calming an agitated child.

Instead of smacking him away as Beth would've expected, Freya's features gentled. She gave an eye roll that felt more perfunctory than filled with real annoyance and sat back.

The rest of the show was lively and entertaining. Beth was surprised at how much she enjoyed every second of it. Even the parents and grandparents waving to their kids didn't elicit the sorrow she would have anticipated.

So much so that she was the one who suggested they take their mother to the reception in the school's cafeteria for her to visit with Timmy, Zach and Michaela. May meant a lot to the kids in the neighborhood and seeing them made her happy.

Freya and Greer were tasked with collecting cookies and drinks for the group while Beth and Trinity wheeled their mother to a table.

Ash and Helena joined them almost immediately. As Helena sat down with May, Trinity drifted toward Ash. The two were quickly engaged in conversation like it was the most natural thing in the world.

Her little sister had a crush on their neighbor. There was no doubt in Beth's mind.

"Your mom had the right idea with the wheelchair," Shauna said as she hobbled forward on her crutches, Declan a solid figure at her side.

"You're doing great," Beth told her. "You haven't been taken out by a kid on a sugar high or an overexcited relative. That's a win."

"She tripped a dad back in the hall," Declan muttered. "I thought the guy was going to try to fight me."

Shauna snorted. "We're at an elementary school Christmas concert, Dec, not a seedy dive bar. Nobody is going to fight you, especially when you're dressed like an extra for some motorcycle gang movie."

Beth had gotten used to Declan's typical outfit of jeans, a dark shirt and leather jacket. He ran a hand through his hair as he and Shauna glared at each other. It was an uncharacteristically tense dynamic between them, and Beth didn't like it.

"What's going on?" Beth focused all her attention on Shauna. She didn't need to look at Declan to feel the frustration radiating off him but wasn't sure where it came from. Did a Christmas concert set him off?

The twins had been fidgety during their grade's performance, but they held it together, unlike one little girl in their class who burst into tears mid-song and had to be escorted off by one of the teachers.

"It's all going to be fine, Shauna."

"Don't make me take you out with this crutch like that dad," the single mother muttered.

Beth felt her eyes widen. She'd never seen Shauna be anything but bright and sunny, although she was still inclined to put her in the same category as May with regards to mothering. A little flighty and not a lot of rules.

"I don't need it to be fine," Shauna said and closed her eyes as if she were trying to pull herself together. "Christmas needs to be perfect, and I can't manage that right now."

She shook her head as she attempted a smile. "Dec's right, of course." She gave him a little nudge with her arm. "He's annoyingly right."

"I told you I'll bake some crap if you want me to."

"You bought prepackaged dough."

"Sugar and chocolate chip cookies," he countered. "They fit the bill."

Shauna gave up attempting to smile. It wasn't convincing anyway. "You probably think I'm crazy," she said to Beth. "But I have a thing about Christmas. The holidays can be uncertain when you spend time in foster care, like Dec and I did. It meant a lot when a family included me in their holiday traditions. I remember those times, and I want my boys to have only positive associations with Christmas."

Declan leaned forward. "She also still sends homemade gifts to the families who weren't jerks to her."

"I want them to know they made a difference in my life." Shauna nodded. "Some of those families still foster kids. I keep in touch and try to support them where I can."

"That's great." Beth realized she'd misjudged Shauna in every way. Shame sliced through her as she knew better than to rely on outward appearances as a measure of what was going on.

After all, maybe if someone had looked closely at the situation with her family and stepped in to help, things could have gotten better sooner. Or she would have ended up separated from her sisters. There was truly no telling.

"I tried to help decorate the tree," Shauna lamented, "and I knocked it over. Two of Timmy's ornaments from preschool broke. I can never get them back."

"He can make new ornaments."

Shauna shook her head. "It's not the same."

Declan threw up his hands, clearly at a loss for what to do to help his friend. Beth admired the fact that he cared enough to try.

"We got the damn tree set up again. It's fine."

"All the ornaments are clumped together in front," Shauna whispered.

Beth had to smile. She understood how perfectionism could drive somebody crazy.

"I make homemade hot fudge for my clients," Shauna told her. "And I'm supposed to help with the class holiday party."

"You were in a horrible accident," Declan reminded her. "People will understand."

"I should never have gone skydiving. It was stupid and reckless." She pointed at Beth. "You were right to call me out."

"No, I wasn't." Beth held up her hands. "I was way out of line."

"I wish you'd been there to talk me out of it in the first place."

"You're a good mom," Beth told the other woman. "I don't offer that as a compliment lightly."

"I imagine you don't," Shauna agreed.

"Which means you have to listen to me. I'm off work tomorrow at four. How about I come over and help with the fudge or gift wrapping or whatever else you need. I can bring paper and bags and bows. We'll get everything together for your clients, and Declan can deliver them over the weekend." She pulled up the calendar app on her phone. "What date and time is the holiday party? I have so much vacation time banked, it's not even funny. If you want, I can help out there as well."

Declan inclined his head as he met Beth's gaze. She couldn't quite decipher the look in his eyes, but it felt like something close to gratitude. "I've got the holiday party covered."

Shauna took another awkward step toward Beth and tried to hug her. It didn't work well with the crutches. Most people got used to maneuvering on crutches within a few days, but it was apparent Shauna needed more time.

"That would be great on both of your parts. It always feels like my boys stick out because they don't have a father."

Declan growled low in his throat "They have a father."

"No." Shauna glared at him. "They don't."

"They would if you told him."

"Let's focus on Christmas," Beth interrupted, placing a hand on Declan's arm and trying to ignore the way his muscles bunched under her palm. "You can save your paternity revelation lectures for after the New Year. Okay, bud?"

He looked shocked at the admonishment. "How did I become the bad guy in this situation?"

"You're not the bad guy," Shauna assured him with another clumsy attempt at a hug. "I couldn't have made it these past few weeks without you. But…"

She broke off then turned to Beth. "I don't think I realized how much I needed a friend. Thank you."

Beth nodded. "I'm happy to be there for you." She was surprised to find she meant the statement.

The students entered the cafeteria at that point, and the focus shifted to snacks and the performance as the kids ran forward for hugs from their families.

She drifted to one side of the room to get her emotions in check. How was it that she'd spent most of her life in this town, and it was only now that she was starting to feel a connection to the community?

"I have it under control," Declan said as he came to stand next to her.

"I'm sure you do. But you can't know what the holidays do to the mom brain." She waited for him to argue or remind her that she couldn't be an expert on mom brain, having never been one herself.

Instead, he nodded. "My brother and I got in a lot more fights around the holidays. It was like we had to act out to prove why we didn't deserve any of the love and attention the kids around us received. We were in some dark situations. It wasn't until the foster family where I met Shauna that I understood how special this time of year could be with a good family." He sighed. "Flynn never got the chance to experience that."

"Is Flynn your brother?"

Declan nodded. "He's a couple of years older, so he was already on his own when I met Shauna."

"So he doesn't know her?"

Declan laughed without humor. "They know each other."

"He's the father," Beth whispered. "Are you two close? Is he involved in Timmy and Zach's lives? The way she talks—"

"The answer to pretty much any question involving my brother is no. Flynn and I haven't spoken for a couple of years. He's in the military—or he was. I'm not in contact with him anymore. He and Shauna had one night together a few years ago. That was all it took."

Beth breathed out a laugh. "For some people, that's all it takes."

Declan's mouth went hard at the edges. "Flynn doesn't know about the twins. She doesn't want to tell him because then maybe he would have felt obligated to be involved. He's not exactly the paternal type."

"Don't you think he should have gotten that choice?" Beth held up a hand when he would have answered. "Never mind. I don't know the background. I'm not judging. I made that mistake once with Shauna, and I won't do it again. She's not who I thought she was, and it's none of my business in the first place."

"She gives of herself to a lot of people," Declan said quietly. "The two of you have that in common, but it isn't easy for her to trust or to accept help. How we were raised doesn't make it easy to trust. It's nice of you to offer to help her. The fact that she's willing to let you is a big deal.

As long as you're doing it without reservation. As much as I care about Shauna, she's also not your responsibility."

Beth wasn't sure how to describe the emotion that bloomed in her chest at his words but managed to smile. "I know. I offered because I want to. Help feels different when it's given freely. Even though I've lived here most of my life, I don't have a lot of close friends. I also have some issues with trusting people or letting them in that have been hard to overcome."

"I can imagine the issues." Declan nodded. "Although not the part about friends."

"It's true. I think Shauna and I are alike in enough ways that maybe we could become better friends. Real friends. I'd like to have more friends."

The look he leveled at her could only be described as scorching. "Am I supposed to forget that I told you I'd like to be your friend?"

Heat poured through Beth, and it felt like her knees might melt. But she was distracted as Freya waved and called her name. "Beth, come here. I need you to settle a debate."

"I've got to go," she told Declan.

"I'm sure you do."

She walked away, but in a move that was completely out of character for her, she turned back and met his heated gaze. "I'd like to be your friend as well," she said before she lost her nerve and maybe even more.

She started walking toward her sister again before he could answer, but something made her glance over her shoulder one last time. The emotion banked in his stormy sea-colored eyes made her glad she had.

CHAPTER FIFTEEN

"OH, MY, I LOVE IT. I love it so much. I couldn't love it any more than I do."

Trinity grinned as Michaela Davis beamed at her reflection in the mirror she held. Trinity had taken about three inches off the girl's long hair and added a few layers to frame her face. It wasn't a huge change but enough to take Michaela's style from girlish to a more mature look.

"So you like the haircut?" Ash asked his daughter, grinning just as broadly at the joke. He lifted his hands in mock question as he caught and held Trinity's gaze. "I think she likes it, but I'm not quite sure."

"I don't like it. I love it." Michaela turned her head from side to side. "It makes me look so much older."

Trinity caught the flash of panic in Ash's eyes.

"Not that much older," she said quickly. It was just the three of them in her mother's kitchen, as Freya had gone to the rehab facility to have dinner and watch a movie with May.

Michaela sat in one of the old oak kitchen chairs that had belonged to Trinity's great-great-grandmother, according to family folklore.

She'd brought her supplies to Magnolia and had used her favorite floral-patterned cape to cover the girl after washing Michaela's hair in the kitchen sink. The scissors she'd splurged on after graduating cosmetology school felt right in her hand. It made her more certain about the decision she'd made to stop into the salon around the corner from the bakery downtown earlier that afternoon.

She'd introduced herself to the owner, explaining her history as a Magnolia native and her plan to potentially move back. She understood that someone about to have a baby didn't make the most sense as a hire. Still, she told the woman that she'd be willing to fill in over the holidays if anyone needed a day off and had offered photos of some of her clients out West as well as the letters of reference from the two previous salons where she'd worked.

At least she'd had the forethought to get those. When the salon owner had asked if she could call Trinity's former bosses, Trinity asked her not to. She'd done her best to explain that she needed a fresh start without anyone from her past knowing where she'd landed.

Although she hadn't explicitly mentioned abuse, the knowing flare of understanding in the woman's eyes made it clear she knew exactly why Trinity needed her location to stay a secret.

But she was done letting fear or shame rule her life. She had more important things to think about, like her baby boy. Now that she'd gotten used to the idea of having a son, she liked it. She would be a mother who raised an amazing man. It was both a challenge and a mission to reclaim her life and pride for both of their sakes.

"I think I look like I'm sixteen." Michaela was still admiring herself in the mirror. "I could probably borrow Gran's car, and I wouldn't even get pulled over."

Ash looked absolutely stunned before he snatched the mirror from her hands and put it on the counter. "No, you can't drive your grandmother's car because you are eleven, not sixteen. You don't know how to drive, and every police officer in Magnolia would recognize you."

"Well, yeah, but I still think if I was driving really fast, they might not know it was me as I sped by."

Ash threw up his hands and looked so discombobulated it made Trinity smile. "If you were speeding by, they would pull you over. Also, you are eleven."

"And you look lovely," Trinity said. "I'm happy you like the cut."

"Next time, can we do highlights?" Michaela glanced hopefully toward her dad. "Please."

"Your hair has natural highlights," Trinity assured her. "I have clients who pay for hair like yours."

That seemed to satisfy the girl, at least for the moment.

She got up and took off the smock, handing it to Trinity. "Thank you so much. It's the best Christmas gift ever. Unless Daddy gets me a puppy."

"No puppy," Ash said, making an apparent effort to retain his patience with his daughter's exuberance.

"I think your father is the one to thank," Trinity reminded Michaela. "This was his idea."

The girl gave Ash a huge hug, and Trinity could almost feel him melting. "Thanks, Daddy. I'm gonna go show Gran. She can drive me to Cameron's house for the sleepover on her way to book club."

"I'll pick you up tomorrow morning. Use your good manners and stuff," Ash counseled his daughter. "Winter break is coming soon, and you don't want to spend it in your room grounded."

She nodded and after a quick hug for Trinity, ran out the back door.

"And stuff?" Trinity asked with a laugh. "That sounds like it encompasses a lot."

"I hope so." Ash ran a hand over his jaw.

Normally, he was clean-shaven, but end-of-day stubble shadowed his jaw in a way that appealed to her. She found everything about him appealing.

"I hope it's enough when she's an actual teenager. I have a feeling I'm going to need all the help I can get."

"I have a feeling you'll do a great job." She quickly swept the hair trimmings into a pile. Before she could bend over to gather it in the dustpan, Ash took the broom from her hand.

"Let me. You shouldn't be bending over in your condition."

"I'm pregnant. It's not a back injury." But she did appreciate the assistance, even if she didn't want to need it.

"It's okay to accept help," he said gently. "It doesn't mean you can't handle it on your own."

Trinity gave a reluctant nod. "I know and thank you."

She grabbed a clean smock from the box of supplies sitting near the refrigerator. "I'm ready for my next customer."

"I appreciate you doing this. I'm not sure why it's so hard to find time to make it to the salon."

"You've got a lot going on."

As he sat back in the kitchen chair, she stepped closer and tucked his collar under the cape. It shouldn't come as a surprise that the skin on the nape of his neck was warm. It wasn't as if he were a vampire.

But that slight touch made her want more. Wanting more was dangerous to a woman in Trinity's situation.

"It's not just my schedule. The last time I got my hair cut, it felt like everyone was staring. Like they'd been waiting for me to walk in the door."

She could imagine they had been. There were a couple of single cowboys who'd come into the shop she'd worked

at the longest. It was always a big event for the female hair-
dressers. Several of the male ones as well.

"Your virtue is safe with me."

He chuckled. "That's disappointing."

Heat rushed through her. "Just a trim?" she asked, needing to remind them both why he was here.

"You're the expert. Whatever you think it needs."

She liked when clients had faith in her, and Ash's confidence felt more poignant. Maybe because he was strong and
capable in real life. For him to relinquish control to her felt
like it meant something. Something she liked very much.

She handed him a small towel. "Cover your face with
this while I wet your hair. I'm sorry we don't have the setup
for me to give you the full treatment. Michaela fit on the
counter, but I think you're a bit too tall. I can't imagine
what my mom would think about me cutting hair in the
middle of her kitchen."

"Maybe she'd surprise you and get in line."

"Maybe," Trinity agreed, although she couldn't imagine that being true.

Ash was the kind of client she liked. He kept his chin
level and looked straight ahead as she moved around him.
He didn't even react when her stomach accidentally bumped
him several times.

"Sorry," she murmured. "I'm not quite used to the new
dimensions of my body."

"How are you feeling?"

"Sometimes tired but mainly good. As long as I have
access to a bathroom every five minutes, things are going
well."

"You've proven a clump of trees works," he said with
a laugh. It seemed so long ago since the night they'd met.

"You thought I was up to no good," she said, smoothing the hair away from his face.

"I thought you might need assistance," he countered.

"Rescuing," she murmured. "I bet you see a lot of damsels in distress." She'd meant the comment as a joke but color bloomed in Ash's cheeks. Trinity had a feeling that he would have ducked away if she wasn't wielding scissors.

"Not exactly."

"Oh, my gosh. You do. Do single women in this town speed on purpose so you'll pull them over?" She snipped and asked the question, then pulled back to gauge his reaction.

"That only happened once," he muttered. "Maybe twice."

She grinned, but her amusement was quickly followed by disappointment. Ash probably had every available woman in Magnolia lusting after him. Despite his dinner invitation, there was no way he'd be interested in a soon-to-be single mom who'd lost her way in the world.

"Not every woman in town is impressed by me." Ash gave her a meaningful look, and it was Trinity's turn to blush.

"You're impressive." She was pregnant, not dead. She could appreciate a handsome man, especially one who was also kind and a good father.

"The dinner invitation still stands," he told her.

She sifted her fingers through his thick hair. "I don't understand why you'd even ask me out. I'm not easy, Ash."

He looked horrified. "I never thought you were."

She laughed despite herself. "I don't mean that kind of easy. I'm complicated. My life right now is complicated."

"I'm the single father of a soon-to-be teenage girl," he reminded her. "One who is talking about trying her hand behind the wheel despite being nowhere near old enough for a license. Let's not forget the fact that I live with my late wife's mother. What would make you think that I'm afraid of complications?"

"You should be." Trinity suddenly felt much older than her twenty-seven years. "You should be finding excuses to let your hair down a little, hypothetically speaking. You're a stand-up guy. That much is crystal clear. You deserve something in your life that's easy."

He reached out and touched her elbow, then moved his hand slowly until his fingers circled her wrist. Somehow she understood he was making the touch measured and gentle because that's what she needed. His thoughtfulness made her silly heart fling itself against her rib cage.

"I keep telling you, Trin. My feelings for you are simple. I like you. Easy enough. I'm not asking for anything but dinner. Just dinner."

It was on the tip of her tongue to refuse again, but she didn't want to. She wanted to take for herself the advice she'd given him. Her feelings for Ash might be complicated, but they also came without having to make an effort. She yearned to explore them more deeply.

"Dinner," she said. "One dinner. Someplace casual."

"Italian? Il Rigatone has a new chef. I've heard everything on the menu is even better than before."

"That was the restaurant we used to go to as kids for family celebrations, at least before my dad left."

He still held her wrist, and she pulled away slightly, telling herself she was only curious as to what his response might be. He released her without hesitation, and she smiled.

"Il Rigatone would be lovely."

His grin was so boyishly charming Trinity realized she didn't have a chance of resisting him.

"I'm off at five on Monday," he said. "Michaela has dance class until seven thirty, and I have to pick her up. Could we time it around her schedule? I know that sounds—"

She pressed a finger to his soft lips. "That sounds perfect." She placed her scissors on the counter and lifted a jar of pomade. "I'm guessing you're not a hair-product guy?"

He grimaced. "Not usually."

"But you're going to trust me, right?"

He nodded. "Yes, I trust you. I hope you'll find a way to trust me as well."

Trinity sucked in a breath. She honestly couldn't imagine a scenario where she would allow herself to trust a man again. It would be a man like Asher Davis who made her take that risk.

CHAPTER SIXTEEN

FREYA YELPED IN satisfaction as she furiously typed the end of the new scene she'd created on her laptop bright and early Sunday morning. Mr. Jingles, who had decided her lap was the perfect napping spot, gave an annoyed meow.

She didn't think the cat could take credit, but the past week had given Freya more creativity than she'd had in the past year. She finally felt like her manuscript was taking shape into the story she wanted it to be.

Maybe she'd start a side hustle as a house remodeler when she returned to LA. There was something about working with her hands that seemed to loosen the pressure around her heart.

Every morning and night, when things quieted, she went back to work on her manuscript. She could give credit to the pace of life in Magnolia.

Although it was different than LA, she had just as many responsibilities in her hometown as she'd had in California. Of course, they were not the same.

Less party hopping and making paid appearances. More helping her mother eat whatever was on the menu at the rehab center and the housework and holiday activities in town.

December meant a rotating door of parties and fake cheer in her other life.

Magnolia was the most authentic place she'd been in

forever. It shocked Freya how much the slower cadence of the small town allowed her to feel more like herself. To rediscover herself as she was now, or maybe for the first time. She wasn't sure she'd ever understood who she was on the inside. She'd never stopped long enough to consider it. That kind of self-reflection felt contrived, her mother's deal but not hers.

She chuckled out loud as she typed a line that felt particularly clever even in her own critical head. Just then, the door to the bedroom burst open. She turned as Beth and Trinity rushed through, both of them with wide eyes. Beth's in alarm and accusation, and Trinity looking guilty as all get-out.

"Did one of you burn the pancakes?" she asked as she closed her laptop and turned. She might not be an award-winning actor, but she thought she did a decent job of not appearing terrified they might have a clue as to her secret.

"I'd just arrived when we heard you shout and then laugh," Beth said as her gaze moved past Freya toward the desk. "We weren't sure what was going on or if you were in trouble."

Freya frowned, unsure she understood the thread of the conversation but confident she wasn't going to like where it ended. "What kind of trouble were you thinking I might be in?"

Beth's mouth tightened at the corners. Freya knew that look. She'd seen it plenty during her teenage years when she'd flouted the rules her sister tried and mostly failed to maintain within the household.

Shortly after the book's publication, they'd endured a particularly rough spring when their mother took off on a month-long trip to Italy with her yoga group.

Beth had been worried someone in town would find

out the girls were alone and that Trinity, who was ten at the time, would be sent to live with whatever relative child protective services could flush out.

Freya hadn't cared at that point. She'd had plans to run away and make her mark in the world. Now she realized how much she owed her sister. Freya hadn't finished college, but the initial acceptance into the UNC J-school had impacted her sense of self.

Sometimes she thought about going back to study creative writing, although she'd probably be laughed out of the classroom by the more serious students given her background. Not only because of her career but due to her love of commercial fiction.

Even she understood enough to know that the kind of books she enjoyed reading and wanted to write weren't respected in the hallowed halls of academia. But Beth didn't know that, and Freya got that her sisters believed she'd been engaging in a less than creative endeavor.

"Do you honestly believe I'm a drug user?" she demanded.

Trinity looked absolutely stricken. "We don't…it's just…"

"You've been sneaky since you got here," Beth finished.

"Sneaky? What does that even mean?"

"You go off by yourself and always seem to be in your own world." Trinity cradled her belly. "We can't figure out what's going on. That's the only reason…"

Beth shrugged. "We want you to be okay, Freya."

"You don't want me to be difficult or hard to handle," Freya shot back, rising from the chair. "I get it. I spent a lot of time being a pain in your butt, Beth. It makes perfect sense that you don't want to deal with me now."

"I didn't say that." Beth shook her head. "Of course I thought you were a pain in my butt. That's what happens with sisters. Only neither of us had a chance to have a normal relationship because of what Mom chose for herself."

Her older sister moved forward. "That's not your fault, Freya, but it's not mine either. I know I screwed up and was overbearing, but I was also a kid. I didn't know what I was doing and didn't want to lose the two of you. We have no idea what's happening now because you won't share anything. Your social media followers know more about you than I do." Beth pointed at Trinity. "Neither of us understands what's going on with you."

Freya focused on Trinity. Her sweet, sunny baby sister. "Do you agree with her?"

"Well, neither one of you made things easy back then," Trinity said. "And Freya isn't the only one keeping secrets now." Beth took a step back like she'd been slapped.

If Freya was going to be raked over the coals, at least she wasn't alone in it.

"Yes, Beth. I know what you've been hiding." Trinity flashed a brittle smile. "I ran into one of your coworkers at the bakery the other day. She said she's going to miss you. Everyone is going to miss you when you move. Where are you going, sis?"

Embarrassment flashed in Beth's eyes, but her chin jutted out. Freya knew the baby of the family couldn't derail their stalwart older sister. "Let's talk about Freya first, and then I'll tell you what's going on with me."

Freya didn't want to talk about herself. She wasn't ready. She needed things to be perfect so that no one would judge her. But it was clear Beth wasn't going to spill her beans until Freya did. Trinity had already shared so much, although she'd skimped on the specific details about how she'd ended up in a relationship with a man who hurt her.

Freya appreciated Trinity's courage. If her little sister

could share something so private, Freya owed it to their relationship to be brave enough to do the same. She wanted to tell her sisters. Writing was a part of her life that actually gave her a feeling of purpose.

"I wrote a book." She opened the drawer of the small desk and pulled out the most recent printed manuscript.

"Like a tell-all memoir?" Beth looked confused.

"No, not like a tell-all. It's a domestic thriller, although the action centers around a reality show set."

"How long have you been working on this?" Trinity stepped forward and took the bound stack of papers from Freya's hands.

"Off and on for a couple of years. I came up with the idea when I did *Manhunt Island*. The premise came to me one night in a dream when we did the isolation challenge. *Manhunt Island* was my fastest elimination because I did my best to lose. I wanted to get home to my laptop."

"Can we read it?" Trinity asked. "Are you going to send it to editors in New York or publish it yourself?"

Beth stared like she was seeing Freya for the first time. Freya didn't know whether to be amused or offended. "I haven't shown it to anyone yet." She snatched the manuscript from Trinity's hands. "You can't read this version because I've done a lot of edits since being back in Magnolia."

She gave Beth a pointed glare. "That's what I'm doing up here in the early mornings and late at night. I haven't turned Mom's house into some sort of den of iniquity if that's what had you worried."

"Always a flair for drama," Beth murmured. "I didn't think you were hosting sunrise raves."

"But you thought I might be doing drugs?"

"Don't blame Beth," Trinity said. "I told her I thought something was wrong."

Another direct hit to Freya's pride. "Or maybe you were projecting onto me to take some of the attention away from how off the rails your life is?"

"Freya." Beth's admonishing tone was unnecessary. Before the words were even out of her mouth, Freya regretted them, especially seeing the way they made Trinity fold in on herself. Going after her little sister was the worst form of kicking the dog.

"I'm sorry, Trin." Freya tugged at the ends of her hair and tried not to fidget. She felt two feet tall. "This is the first thing I've done that felt real, and it's honestly hard for me to talk about it."

"You've made out with more than one man on camera." Beth grimaced. "How can writing a book make you feel more vulnerable than that?"

"Because reality shows aren't really reality. On-screen, I'm a character. Even though this book is fiction, it's me writing it. I've put a piece of myself on every page, and I struggle with the thought of allowing people to judge my talent."

"I'm proud of you, Frey," Trinity said gently, always the peacemaker.

"It's exciting," Beth agreed. "When you weren't raising hell, you always had your nose in a book. Now you're writing one. That's a big deal, Frey. We should go out and celebrate. Even if we can't read the book yet, you can tell us about the plot and the writing process."

Freya's chest burned like tiny sparks were flaming inside her. She would love to talk about writing and appreciated that neither of her sisters were mocking her for even attempting to write a book. She'd given them plenty of reasons to.

"You should talk to Greer," Trinity suggested. "He has clients who—"

"No." Freya held up her hand. "Neither of you are going to tell Greer about this. Not one word to anybody unless I say you can. Anyway, it might be absolute trash."

"I bet it's amazing," Trinity offered.

Beth nodded in apparent agreement. "You were a great writer back in high school. I know college didn't work out, but that doesn't change your natural talent."

Freya looked between her two sisters, afraid to let their faith in her bolster her confidence. The more confident she felt now, the more devastated she'd be if it turned out she was terrible at putting a story together.

"You won't know whether it's good or not," Trinity pointed out, none too helpfully, "until you let somebody read it. Remember what Dad used to say about hiding your light under a bushel?"

"I saw him," Freya blurted, more to distract them than because she'd been planning to share that tidbit.

The tactic worked. "Where?" Beth demanded in a hushed tone.

"I was in Vegas for an event last year, and he's still working as a magician. Someone handed me a random flyer advertising his show. I tracked him down at the casino where he works a couple blocks off the strip. It's a complete dump, which might explain why he never sent money to Mom."

"I think it was all too much for him," Beth said quietly. "A flighty, boisterous wife and three girls who always wanted attention. Maybe if we…"

"No." Trinity held up a hand to interrupt Beth. "We're not going to do this. We are not going to take the blame for the choices he made. Not even a little bit. The three of us were kids. We had nothing to do with it. They chose to have us. They chose to marry each other."

She cradled her stomach. "My pregnancy might have been a surprise, but one thing I know for sure is that this baby boy, unexpected as he was, will be loved and cherished. I will never make him feel less. I will never make him feel like he is a burden by being born. I'm glad Mom is the way she is. Not the stroke or the potential long-term deficits. But I hope whatever happened in her brain lasts, even if that means she needs somebody to care for her for the rest of her life. I'll care for a mom who makes me feel loved."

Freya saw Beth brushing a hand across her cheeks as she looked away. Freya's eyes stung with unshed tears. "We are going to love your baby, too," she told Trinity.

"I got accepted into the nurse practitioner program at Vanderbilt." Beth made the announcement before either of them could say anything else. "I applied after the divorce because I needed something for myself. I didn't consider Mom in my decision. It felt as though she'd barely notice if I left town. I'm a shell of a person and haven't taken care of her the way I should have. Maybe if—"

Freya squeezed her sister's hand. "If we're not feeling guilty about Dad, we are not feeling guilty about Mom. You did way too much for far too long, Beth. If moving to Nashville makes you happy, then that's what you should do."

Trinity looked somewhat alarmed but nodded. "I'll take care of Mom," she offered.

"You will?" Freya could hear the disbelief in Beth's voice and felt it herself, but she also understood that the sisters had misjudged each other for years. The shared childhood trauma had colored their adult relationships to the point they barely had them.

"Or we can hire somebody to help Trinity out when she needs it," Freya suggested.

"I don't know if insurance will pay for that," Beth said. "She'll get some money if she sells the house, but even that…who knows. I haven't sent in my final tuition payment. I could put it off for a semester or two. It might not even make a difference in the kind of work I do. I'm already a nurse. I don't need—"

Freya shook her head. "We'll figure this out." She was the last person who should be making that pledge when her life was at loose ends. But she knew that Beth needed reassurance and the opportunity to pursue her dreams however that looked.

She felt Trinity waiting for Beth to reiterate to them both that she only trusted herself to be responsible for their mom. Instead, their older sister sniffed and let out a small sob before yanking her hand away from Freya's to cover her mouth.

"I'm not going to cry," Beth whispered. "But thank you. Knowing you two are here makes a huge difference."

"When can we read your story?" Trinity asked as she touched the manuscript Freya had placed on the desk.

"More importantly, when are you going to give it to an editor or an agent?" Beth demanded. "Greer is a perfect place to start."

"He represents big authors," Freya muttered.

"You're a big deal," Beth replied.

Freya laughed "I appreciate that, but not Greer. Anyone but Greer."

Beth lifted a brow. "I know you like him."

Freya felt panic rush through her but kept her features neutral. "Do you want to talk about Declan Murphy?"

"I need to get to work," Beth answered. "I picked up an extra weekend shift."

Trinity laughed. "You two. Some things never change."

Freya smiled. Some things did change, which made the struggle that came before worth it.

CHAPTER SEVENTEEN

BETH LOOKED AROUND Shauna's living room on Monday night and smiled. "This makes me almost regret not having Christmas decorations of my own."

"What do you mean you don't have decorations of your own?" Shauna asked, turning on her crutches to study Beth. "Is it because you don't celebrate Christmas? Is there another holiday you—"

"I celebrate, just not with lots of decorations. Or much of any decorations. Even when Greg and I were married, the holidays weren't my thing."

She picked at a strand of ribbon stuck to her leggings and wished she'd worn something nicer. Despite being in a plain white T-shirt and jeans that had been cut off at the knee to accommodate the boot, Shauna looked effortlessly beautiful. Her dark hair fell in soft waves down her back, and she had no need for makeup to enhance her delicate features. Beth figured her under-eye circles had bags at this point.

"Was it because of the fertility issues?" Shauna's voice was achingly gentle. "I can imagine how hard it must be at this time of year."

Beth shook her head. "No. It had more to do with how I grew up. The work to make Christmas special mostly fell on me, and I already had enough to do."

"Really?" Shauna sounded genuinely surprised. "Your

mother seems to love Christmas. She had the boys and Michaela the past two years to bake cookies."

Beth blinked. "My mom bakes?"

"How do you not know your mom bakes? She told us the recipes were handed down from her mom and grandmother."

"Add it to the list of recent May revelations. We never talked about baking. I think Greg appreciated that I didn't like Christmas. It got him off the hook for buying thoughtful or extravagant gifts."

"Your ex-husband sounds like a real tool," Shauna said. "I hope it's okay that Declan told me about dropping Greg at your house."

Beth froze. Had Declan told his friend about the kiss he and Beth had shared? Based on Shauna's relaxed expression, Beth didn't think so.

"He's not a bad guy, but we weren't right for each other. It's a blessing that we didn't end up with children. We probably would have ended in divorce either way. But I still don't understand how I missed so much about the ways my mom has changed. She was so different when we were growing up."

"She was a single mom trying to raise three girls."

"No. I'm not letting her off the hook. You're a single mom, you're injured, and you're still making an effort."

"With help. Maybe your mom didn't feel like she could ask for help. Maybe that's where you get it."

Beth felt her hackles rise but didn't let anger push through to take over the moment. Shauna was right. She was terrible at accepting help. "I'm working on that," she said.

"How is your mom doing?"

"She's good, although none of us want to broach any

difficult topics with her. We're enjoying her new affectionate nature. It's better than the doctors had expected at this
point. She'll be home for Christmas if things keep going
in this direction."

"That's great. Maybe we can do some holiday baking
over here or if you want to check her out for another afternoon?"

Beth laughed. "You should be resting, not trying to host
cookie-baking parties."

Shauna winked. "Yeah, but I have Declan to do the work.
He makes a pretty good slave."

Beth could just imagine Declan as her slave. "You should
get him a costume. Really milk it."

"Oh, he'd look good as a French maid." Shauna and Beth
laughed, then laughed even harder as Declan and the boys
came through the front door.

"You guys are talking about me," Dec said in his deep
voice.

"Wow, don't you have the ego," Shauna teased. "What
makes you think you've factored at all in our conversation?"

"Because you look guilty," Declan said then pointed toward Beth, "and she's blushing."

Beth lifted an automatic hand to her cheek. "I'm not
blushing."

"We were talking about that hot ER doctor who was on
duty when I had my accident."

The boys shed their winter coats, hung them on pegs
near the front door then hurried around the room inspect-
ing the decorations Beth had set out with instructions from
Shauna.

After touching a gentle finger to one of the nutcrackers
on the television stand, Timmy ran over to hug his mom.

"Declan said that Santa's elves were going to come over tonight and help finish decorating the house."

Shauna lowered herself to a chair, propping her crutches against the wall and then ruffled her son's thick hair. "Actually—"

"Clearly, I was right," Declan said, "since one of the things Timmy asked for in his letter to the big guy was some help for you. Santa always listens when little boys have been good."

"And we've been good," Zach said, although Beth couldn't tell whether it was a statement or a question.

Timmy frowned. "I've been especial good 'cause I'm the one who asked for it. You asked for Legos and action figures."

"We didn't both need to ask," Zach said, taking a menacing step toward his brother. Beth wasn't sure if she should laugh or insert herself between the two boys.

"Like I told you…" Dec stepped forward to interrupt the fight that Beth could see brewing. "The two of you getting along is what makes the most difference to Santa because that makes the most difference to your mom."

"You are my best boys." Shauna gestured Zach closer and wrapped an arm around each twin. "A few of Santa's elves did stop by." She winked at Beth. "They helped out a lot and they might have given me a hint about what you're getting for Christmas."

Both boys gasped. "What did they say?" Zach asked.

"I can't tell you because that would give away the surprise. We have more time for you to show that you can be good."

Beth smiled. She'd once tried using Santa as an incentive for Trinity to eat her vegetables. Then Freya had spilled the beans about Santa Claus, and Beth lost that battle. Their mother hadn't cared much about vegetables, even before the divorce.

Even in the rehab center, May made a fuss over every spoonful of green beans or peas the girls tried to coerce her to eat.

"I'm heading to Champions if you've got things under control," Dec told Shauna.

She nodded. "Thanks to the elves, I feel way calmer than I did before. I think we might make it through Christmas with my sanity intact."

"God bless the elves," Declan murmured.

"Do you want me to stay and help with bedtime?" Beth offered. She felt Declan's heated gaze on her but didn't make eye contact. Blushing was one thing, but it would be mortifying to spontaneously combust in front of Shauna and the twins.

"No thanks. I think we're going to watch part of a Christmas movie before bed. I'm ready for some snuggly sofa time. Those elves inspired me. Boys, how about you change into your jammies while I cue up *Elf*?"

Zach and Timmy cheered then headed for the stairs.

Beth smiled as she zipped up her quilted jacket. "I'll talk to my mom's care coordinator about an afternoon that would work for baking."

Zach paused halfway up the staircase. "Baking with Miss May? Awesome."

"Yay," Timmy added.

These boys really did love May, which Beth still had trouble wrapping her mind around. She hugged Shauna and walked out into the night with Declan.

"It was nice of you to help Shauna," he said.

"I had fun." She didn't quite know how to describe it

without admitting that she had work colleagues but no true friends in town.

He nodded and shoved his hands into his pockets. "I'm working until eleven tonight if you want to stop by?"

"You manage twin wrangling and bartending plus helping Bill get the business ready to sell. Is there anything you can't handle?"

"I suck at relationships."

She burst out laughing. "I bet you've never tried at a relationship."

"Because I know I'll suck."

"I'm not looking for a relationship." Her words hung in the cool, quiet air.

Declan nodded. "I'll be there until eleven," he said and walked toward his car.

Beth felt anticipation skitter through her even though she had no intention of going to Champions to meet him.

She thought about returning to her empty house and found the idea held no appeal. Instead, she walked across the street to her mother's house. As she climbed the porch steps, a low-level panic gripped her. What if Trinity and Freya were doing something they wouldn't want her involved in?

Her sisters had always been tight, although she and Freya were closer in age. Even before the divorce and the book, Beth had felt like an outsider, unsure how to deal with Freya's big personality or Trinity's exuberance about even the most minute aspect of life.

Beth had been what her father termed an "old soul." At that point, it sounded like a compliment. As she grew older, she wasn't so sure.

Did she walk in or knock on the door? What if they

were disappointed to see her? Maybe she should just turn around and—

The front door opened, and Trinity yanked her inside. "What are you waiting for—an invitation?"

Beth chose not to answer that specific question. "How did you know I was outside?"

"We saw you talking to Declan on the street," Freya said, closing the buttery cardigan she wore and crossing her arms over her chest.

Trinity looked embarrassed like she'd been caught snooping. "I forgot that I picked up some fresh cookies today, but I left them in my car. I was about to go out when I noticed you and Dec."

"Are you spying on me?" Beth demanded.

"Absolutely," Freya confirmed. "Although it was kind of hard to focus past the blinding chemistry between the two of you. He's a perfect rebound guy."

Beth sniffed. "I've been divorced almost a year now. How do you know I haven't already had my rebound?"

"That's a rhetorical question, right?" Freya grinned. "Because I would hope if you've had a rebound worth anything, you wouldn't still be so tightly wound."

"I am not wound tight."

"I'm going to get the cookies," Trinity said, clearly not wanting to get in the middle of her older sisters. "There's wine in the kitchen if you want it. Freya already has a glass. For the record, I think it's rude for the two of you to drink in front of me."

Freya tipped the stem of her goblet. "I toasted you. Doesn't that count?"

"It was a nice touch," Trinity admitted. "Try not to kill each other while I'm gone."

"It's still weird when she says adult things," Beth said as the front door closed behind her baby sister.

"And shows more maturity than either of us."

"That, too."

"Why did you let Dec leave by himself?"

"He had to work." Before she thought better of it, Beth added, "He asked me to stop by the bar before he gets off. I think that means something."

"It probably means he wants to walk you home, and I am talking about the horizontal walk."

Beth blinked. "You can't walk horizontally."

"You know what I mean."

"I do, and it terrifies me."

"What did I miss?" Trinity asked as she came through the door, already taking a bite of cookie.

To Beth's surprise, Freya didn't immediately blurt out her secret. But she did cock a brow.

"I think I'm going to have sex with Declan Murphy." Beth could hardly draw in a breath for the nerves and anticipation that pulsed through her.

"Wow." Trinity grinned. "That's awesome. Will you give us all the details?"

"No. Rude and not very classy."

Trinity seemed to consider that. "You're right. It would be disrespectful. Maybe we could ask questions, and you could blink once if the answer is yes or twice if it's no. That way, you're not giving anything away, but we'll still know."

"I don't think so." Beth grabbed a cookie out of the box.

"Chocolate chip pairs well with wine," Freya told her. "Can I get you a glass?"

Beth shook her head. "I think I need all my faculties tonight."

Freya made a face. "I think you need to loosen up a little."

"I'm not sure I remember how to be loose if I ever knew."

Trinity leaned forward like she was telling a great secret. "I bet Declan Murphy can show you."

"I just bet he can," Beth agreed and took a massive bite of the cookie.

AT EXACTLY TEN FORTY, she walked into Champions, praying she didn't see anyone she knew, especially not her ex-husband.

Apparently, avoiding people she knew was asking too much at the town's most popular watering hole. She waved to a couple of familiar faces, relieved that at least Greg didn't seem to be among the patrons tonight.

She also didn't see Declan as she took a seat at the bar. Maybe he'd gotten off early and already left. Maybe he'd gone with a woman. He certainly didn't owe Beth a thing.

She ordered a hard cider and tried not to look as out of place as she felt. Lots of people went to bars on their own.

"Last call in ten minutes," the bartender told her. "Do you want anything else right now?"

Beth shook her head. "This is fine."

He didn't seem ready to call her out on how she didn't belong, so Beth took a sip of her drink and tried to look normal instead of terrified. Just then, Declan appeared from the back of the bar with a keg hefted on one shoulder like it was no heavier than a sack of flour.

Even though Beth was bundled up in a quilted purple coat over her sweater, Declan wore only a T-shirt. The muscles of his arms bunched and bulged as he balanced the weight of the keg.

The bartender called out something to him, and Declan rolled his eyes. Suddenly, his gaze tracked to Beth, and his expression changed. His eyes, always wary like he was waiting for someone to hurt him, gentled. The grin he flashed lit up his whole face.

"Damn," a woman standing nearby murmured then poked Beth gently in the back. "You're a lucky girl. I might spontaneously combust if a man looked at me like that."

Beth felt like she could go up in flames at any moment, but the word that struck her was *lucky*. When was the last time anyone had described her as lucky?

She couldn't remember ever feeling like that word fit part of her life. But tonight it did. After finishing his work with the keg, Declan approached.

"I wasn't sure you were going to make it."

She didn't bother trying to smile. Her lips felt far too stiff for that.

"Me neither."

"I'm glad you did."

"Me, too."

Her voice sounded different, somewhere between a squeak and a growl. Declan had to hear the fear in her tone, but he was polite enough not to say anything.

"How's the drink?"

It took a minute for her to catch up with his simple question. "Refreshing. It's pear flavored. A seasonal blend apparently."

He nodded. "I met the guy who owns a local brewery. I worked out a deal with them. The town is having a resurgence so supporting local business is a good thing for the bar business."

"I didn't realize so much thought went into the type of alcohol served."

He shrugged. "It doesn't always, but it should. It will

lend itself to the Champions story when Bill tries to find a buyer."

"You take your job seriously."

He looked almost shocked by her comment. "Yeah, I do."

"And you're good at it. You're good at a lot of things. Except for relationships," she said before he could. "I got that."

"You want to get out of here?"

"Are you going to show me what else you're good at?" she asked and let out a little gasp, surprising herself with her boldness.

Declan gave her that disarming grin again. "Do you want me to?"

"Yes." She breathed out the word like an oath.

Without turning around, his gaze steady on hers, Declan lifted a hand. "I'm taking off, Pete," he called.

Beth quickly dug for her wallet to pay for the drink. She'd only finished half but felt tipsy, which she knew came more from her reaction to Declan than the alcohol.

"On the house," he said.

"Thank you."

"I need to grab my jacket from the back."

He disappeared again, and Beth popped off the stool.

"I would tell you to have a good night," the woman who'd made the earlier comment about being lucky said. She lifted her hand for a fist bump. "But I think you're guaranteed one."

Beth knew there were no guarantees in life. But if anyone could screw up a guaranteed good time, it would be her. She didn't argue.

"I hope you have a good night, too," she told the woman.

The woman tipped her head toward the far end of the bar, where a group of rowdy young men played pool. "I plan to get me some holiday cheer if you know what I mean."

Beth didn't, but she could imagine. Then Declan was there with a light hand on the small of her back, guiding her out of the warm bar into the cold night.

"Didn't take you long to make friends," he said into her hair.

"Is that what I was doing? It's been a long time since I've made a friend. Other than Shauna, I suppose. Is it weird that I consider her my friend too? Would she think I'm a pathetic dork?"

"I doubt it," Declan told her. "Shauna likes you. The woman in the bar seemed to like you as well."

"Does that make me likable? The fact that a woman in a bar struck up a conversation."

"Not necessarily, but I think you're likable anyway."

"She mostly wanted to talk about you and how hot you are."

It was hard to tell in the dim glow of the streetlight illuminating them, but she was pretty sure he blushed.

"Maybe she'd already been overserved."

"You must get hit on a lot."

They got into her car, and she turned to face him.

"Do we have to have this conversation?" he asked.

She nodded. "I think so. Before this goes any further I need to know…" She held up a hand. "It's stupid. You don't do relationships, and I don't necessarily want one. Still, I don't like the idea that I'm signing up as the umpteenth member of the Declan Murphy fan club."

"Are you sure?" He leaned closer. "All the members get a secret decoder ring."

She laughed despite herself. "You know what I mean."

"I do, and I'm trying not to be offended by it. I'm not indiscriminate, Beth. I can't tell you that I'm a monk, but it's been a while. Meaningless sex lost its appeal at the same time hangovers did."

It wasn't fair of her to ask the question. He'd told her he didn't do relationships. She'd told him she didn't want one, so it was none of her business who else he slept with, but she liked that he was willing to answer. She liked the answer he gave.

She placed her hands on the front of his soft leather jacket and brushed her mouth against his. He let out a groan that made her lady parts want to cheer. To think that she could have this kind of effect on a man like Declan was far more intoxicating than any drink.

"What about your car?" she asked.

"I'll get it in the morning," he said against her mouth. He was going to spend the night with her, not just a few hours.

She slipped her tongue into his mouth, deepening the kiss, and he shuddered because of her.

"We should go before I forget my name, let alone how to drive."

He leaned back and grinned at her. "I'd make sure you got home safe, no matter what."

That's exactly how he made her feel. Safe. So safe that when they got to her house, she didn't hesitate. She took his hand and led him through the dark rooms to her bedroom. There was no need to turn on the light. The full moon would appear later that week. The glow from the window gave them all the light they needed.

It had been years since she'd been with a man other than Greg. And for them, sex became mixed up with making a baby. Declan was only about pleasure, and she intended to savor every moment.

CHAPTER EIGHTEEN

"YOUR NAILS ARE so festive and cheery, Mom."

Trinity's heart lurched as her mother studied the manicure she'd just received. "Sparkle red," May said slowly.

"Sparkly," Trinity agreed. "Just like you, Mom." Her visit to the rehab center had been spontaneous, but she was meeting Ash for dinner later and had been a bundle of nerves all day.

Beth was working, and Freya had driven to Raleigh to pick up tile for the new master bath, leaving Trinity alone with her thoughts—worries mainly. So many worries.

She'd received two calls on her prepaid cellphone in as many days with no one on the other end of the line and no caller ID. Most likely they were spam or a telemarketer who couldn't get it together. If Dave was going to track her down, she had a feeling he would have done it by now.

She'd become convinced that her ex-boyfriend, controlling and manipulative as he was, had moved on from their relationship. Dave had never been much for hard work, and Trinity made things easy for him during their time together. She'd made herself small and afraid so he could feel big and strong. There was no strength in a man who was willing to hurt a woman.

It had taken a long time and a backbone she hadn't realized she possessed to come to that realization. She placed a hand on her belly. Going back now wasn't an option, whether Dave found her or not.

A couple of hours in the peace and relative quiet of her mother's room relaxed her. May had been napping when Trinity first arrived, so she'd pulled out Freya's new manuscript. She sat in the lounge chair next to the bed, reading and feeling not so alone.

Although Trinity couldn't understand why, it had taken quite a bit of cajoling to convince Freya to share the updated book. Freya was an amazing writer. Trinity had been immediately sucked into the gritty yet optimistic narrative of an aspiring actress navigating the rough waters of Hollywood. There were twists and turns she hadn't seen coming as the story progressed.

The book needed to be seen by more people than Trinity, although Freya had sworn her to secrecy. Not even Beth had a copy.

"Why you sad?" May asked as she reached out and patted Trinity's arm. "Don't be sad, Trinny."

Trinity sat up straighter, unsure how to respond to her mother's question. May's ability to speak coherently was returning, but it remained odd to hear her express concern about the emotional well-being of any of her daughters. It just wasn't like May.

Trinity remembered how many times as a kid she'd wanted her mother to worry about her or take an active role in her life. Trinity might have been the sunny Carlyle sister, but all of that optimism had come with immense effort. Yes, she chose to look on the bright side, but that didn't mean there were never storm clouds in her life.

"I'm not sad, Mom." Trinity drew in a steadying breath. "I'm… I have a date tonight."

May's eyes widened. She wore a blue sweatshirt and

matching joggers because buttons and zippers were a challenge. Her hair was pulled back into a low bun, and lines fanned out from her eyes and across her forehead.

It wasn't exactly that the stroke had aged May. For Trinity, the changes in her mother made May look more accessible. Less like the aging icon on women's empowerment and more like a regular mom. "Who?" May's lips curved around the one syllable.

"It's with Ash Davis. Your neighbor and the town's police chief." Trinity wasn't sure why she felt it necessary to say those words out loud. Of course her mother knew Ash. He'd been to visit the other day along with Michaela. May had been excited to see them both.

"He nice. Trinny need nice man."

A laugh burst forth from Trinity's throat before she could stop it. "Mom, you wrote the actual book on why a woman doesn't need a man. You can't tell me I need someone nice."

May scrunched her eyes shut like she was concentrating on searching for the word to communicate what she wanted to say. "De-serve," she said finally, clapping her hands. "You de-serve a nice man."

Trinity went still as May's gaze tracked to her stomach. "Trinny not have nice man before."

She hadn't spoken to her mother about any of the loser guys she'd dated over the years, and certainly nothing about Dave or the way he'd treated her. Her mother couldn't have a clue about her history, but what other explanation could there be?

"I haven't made the best choices," she agreed when she felt like she could speak without breaking down. "I'm going to do better for this baby and myself, although I might be reaching above my station with a guy like Ash."

May shook her head. "You de-serve," she said again. "I sor-ry, Trinny. I made lots mis-stakes. You de-serve better."

Wow. Weren't those the words Trinity had longed to hear for so long? May's eyes shined with unshed tears. Trinity knew that her mother still had a long way to go with her recovery, but the apology had been from the heart. Was it the brain damage speaking? Did it even matter?

"I love you, Mom," she whispered and leaned in for a gentle hug then turned at the sound of the door to the room opening.

"I can come back later," Greer said gently from the doorway. "I didn't realize—"

"It's fine," Trinity told him. "Please come in. I'm going to be heading out soon."

"Trinny has date," May announced.

"Mom, geez. Greer isn't interested in my life."

"Sure I am." The movie-star-handsome agent wiggled his eyebrows as he approached. "Tell me more."

"It's dinner," Trinity clarified.

"Wiv Ash." May clapped her hands again. "Nice Ash."

"Ash is very nice," Greer agreed. "Good for you, Trinity."

Trinity felt like she was getting the blessing of her protective older brother. Greer's relationship with her mom was strange, but she appreciated it just the same.

"Give Trin book," May said, her gaze intent on the agent.

His mouth opened and closed a few times. Was it Trinity's imagination or did his gaze stray to Freya's book on the table? She picked it up and shoved it into her purse. She'd never seen Greer appear flustered, even with Freya, so this was quite the turn of events.

"I thought you wanted the girls to read it when it came out," he reminded her mother.

Was this about the new version of *A Woman's Odyssey*, and what did it mean?

May shook her head. "Trin reads now. She give to Bef and Frey."

Greer and her mother stared at each other for several long seconds. Trinity had the impression that the man knew far more about the inner workings of May's brain than even the doctors at this point. He opened the briefcase he carried whenever he visited May and took out a copy of the updated book.

"This is an advance copy," he told Trinity as he handed it to her. "No one but you and your sisters should read it."

She nodded and stared at the cover, which showed the updated title, *A Woman's Odyssey and Return to Her Heart*, in bold red font on a golden background.

"This is not what I expected. What is 'the return to her heart'? How much did you add to the book?" she asked, looking between Greer and her mother. "I thought it was only a new introduction."

May gave a lopsided smile. "It's more. Big change. I change."

"You'll understand when you read it," Greer said. "This isn't how May or I planned things to go, but perhaps it's better this way. You should read the entire book before sharing it with Beth and Freya. You might understand more than they do with regards to what your mother was feeling."

Trinity breathed out a laugh. "That would be a first. You carry this around with you?"

Greer's mouth tightened as he ran a hand through his thick dark hair. "I've been reading it to May when I visit, and she's been reading sections to me as her speech returns. She is adamant about not pushing back the publication date, and I want to give her as many chances as I can to understand what that means as far as the content of the book."

"I know." May pressed a hand to her chest, shiny new nails glinting in the lamplight. "I undstand," she said softly. "My words. I know them."

She looked at Trinity. "I know you. You des-serve nice man. New, strong, Trinny."

Trinity could have burst into tears right there but managed to hold herself together. "Your lips to God's ear, Mama."

She glanced at her watch. "I need to go. I'll read it as soon as I can," she promised Greer, "but you don't get to dictate when or what I can share with Beth and Freya. I'll make that decision."

A look of respect flashed in his gray eyes. "Your mother is right, Trinity. You're stronger than you give yourself credit for."

"I right," May said with a nod.

"Thanks." She dropped a quick kiss on her mother's forehead. With a last nod at Greer, she hurried out of the room, clutching the book to her stomach with one hand and her purse that held Freya's manuscript close to her side with the other.

Once in the parking lot, she took a few cleansing breaths of the evening air and then got in her car. She shoved the book between her seat and the console, not wanting to be distracted at the moment.

It was only a ten-minute drive to downtown, and she found a parking spot in front of the Italian restaurant, which she chose to take as a sign. She could use all the good karma signs she could get.

As she opened the door to Il Rigatone, a young boy rushed around her and into the restaurant.

"Andrew Thomas Guilardi," a feminine voice called from behind her. "Where are your manners?"

The boy stopped and backed up with almost comically slow steps. "Sorry, lady. I'm real hungry. Let me hold the door for you."

"Thank you, kind sir," Trinity said with a smile. "You have lovely manners. Your mother raised you well."

"That's a work in progress," the woman who had called out to the boy said as she followed Trinity into the restaurant. "I see you'll soon be doing the same." The woman gestured to Trinity's stomach.

"With my own son." Trinity felt her heart stutter as she said the words to the dark-haired stranger. They felt more comfortable rolling off her tongue than she would have expected.

"Boys are awesome." The woman stuck out her hand. "I'm Angi Guilardi."

"Trinity Carlyle. I grew up in Magnolia, and I remember when your parents ran this place. It's nice that you've kept it in the family."

Angi rolled her eyes in a good-natured way. "No pressure, right? My family still owns the restaurant, but I've given over most of the daily operations to a new chef and manager. I take care of catering at the Wildflower Inn. Are you familiar with it?"

Trinity shook her head. "I came back to town recently."

"How's your mom doing?"

"Pretty well, all things considered."

Angi nodded. "I get those things. My mom had a heart attack a little over a year ago. Andrew and I moved in with her for a while. It felt like my life was over. But she's doing well now and getting along better than ever. I wish the same for your mom."

"Thank you. Me, too." Trinity smiled. "I won't keep

you, though. I'm meeting someone." Her smile grew as Ash waved from a booth in the back.

Angi followed Trinity's gaze. "I don't think I have to tell you to have a good time."

"It's just dinner."

"Honey, I've seen a lot of couples have dinner over the years. When a man looks at a woman like our police chief is staring at you, he's got more on his mind than a plate of gnocchi."

"I'll remember that." Trinity could feel her face heat as she walked toward the booth. It still felt a bit ridiculous to be dating at seven months pregnant, but there was no denying the butterflies flitting across her stomach as Ash stood and took her hand.

He gave it a gentle squeeze. "You look lovely."

She wanted to deny it. She wasn't used to receiving compliments. Even before Dave's outright cruelty, she hadn't exactly picked men who were known for their sweetness.

"Hello, Chief. Nice to see you out and about for a change." The waitress who approached the table looked to be in her mid to late forties with a short bob and bright red lips. "A few of the ladies around town wondered whether you were in the right line of work. Not that you aren't a great police chief. I appreciate how you got my Michael on the straight and narrow. But there was talk…"

Trinity leaned forward. "What kind of talk?"

"Don't encourage Abigail," Ash warned.

Trinity imagined petty criminals and mischievous teens cowed by that tone, but she was made of sterner stuff.

"Someone suggested that our strapping, virile police chief might be better suited for a monastery." The older woman winked at Trinity. "I can see our fears were unfounded."

"Oh." Trinity wasn't sure how to respond, although the woman's gaze was approving. She sat back and patted her stomach. "I hope I'm an okay dinner companion, but I'm not exactly in the market for virile at this point."

Ash choked out a laugh. "Why are we having this conversation?" he asked, sounding genuinely confused. "Because it's awful."

"I like teasing you, Chief." Abigail chucked him on the shoulder. "What can I bring y'all? Probably not a bottle of wine."

"I'll have water," Trinity told her.

"Same for me," Ash said. "I'm picking up Michaela after this."

"Can I put in an order of calamari as well?"

Trinity nodded. "That sounds delicious."

"It also happens to be the chief's favorite," Abigail said. "I'll be right back with those waters and some fresh bread."

"Did you bring me here so you could show off your fan club?" Trinity asked when they were alone again.

Ash covered his face with his hands. "We should have gone to the next town over. The next state over—someplace where they don't know me."

"I think it's cute. This is how it should be in a small town, but my family never fit in the right way. I guess May does now, but that didn't help us back in the day."

She held up a hand when he would have responded. "I don't want to talk about how things used to be tonight. Not for me anyway. I feel like you know so much about me."

He shook his head. "I think there's a lot I don't know about you, Trinity Carlyle."

She did her best not to squirm under his assessing gaze. "Be that as it may, I'd like to talk about you. Tell me what inspired you to go into law enforcement. Was your father a police officer?"

Ash shook his head, his gaze taking on a hard glint. "My father was a petty criminal who took on jobs for the kingpin in our neighborhood because he always had some gambling debt or another to pay off. Eventually, he was killed during a raid."

He said the words without emotion, but Trinity could feel the anger rolling off him in waves.

"Ash, that's horrible. I'm so sorry." She reached across the table and squeezed his hand. "Your father's difficulties inspired you to become a cop? It's noble."

He ran a hand over the back of his neck. "Thank you, but I feel like I need a do-over on this whole night. One where I'm smart enough not to take you to someplace the staff knows me or to start the conversation with my father's murder. I wanted this to be light and easy, Trinity, a break for both of us."

Abigail returned to the table with two ice waters and a basket of fresh bread that smelled divine. "We have both regular and our homemade garlic butter," she said as she placed two ramekins on the table. "The garlic butter is fantastic as long as you share it."

"Why?" Trinity asked.

"Because then you won't notice if he kisses you good-night and you both have garlic bread breath."

Trinity nodded and tried not to burst out laughing again. "Sound advice."

"Seriously need a do-over," Ash muttered as Abigail moved to a nearby table.

Trinity broke off a piece of bread and held her knife aloft over the two ramekins. "What's it going to be? Do we go regular butter or...?"

Ash picked up his knife and dunked it into the garlic butter. "Garlic all the way," he told her.

This conversation should not resemble flirting or foreplay, but Trinity's body didn't seem to get the memo. A shiver passed through her, and she trembled a little bit as she popped the bread into her mouth.

"Wow," she said on a moan. "They should call this better-than-sex bread. It's unbelievable."

She realized her blunder, and her eyes popped open to find Ash grinning at her. He inclined his head. "It's incredible, but let's hold off on naming it quite yet."

Talk about a flood of heat. Trinity could barely make eye contact with Abigail as she returned to the table with the calamari. "You have two dipping sauces, marinara and a lemon aioli for—"

"My water," Trinity said on a gasp. She went stock-still. This could not be happening. No, no, no.

"I can get you more water, honey," Abigail said. "Is the garlic too spicy?"

Trinity focused on drawing breath in and out of her lungs. Then she sucked in another gasp as pain sliced through her. "My water broke," she said. "I think I'm having contractions."

She felt paralyzed, at a loss for what to do next, but Ash showed no such worry. "We're going to get you to the hospital," he said.

Trinity shook her head. "I'm a mess. I can't…you can't…"

Abigail offered a sympathetic smile. "Honey, you're in good hands."

As if sensing trouble, Angi Guilardi appeared at the table. "What's going on?"

"She's in labor," Ash said, already taking Trinity's elbow to guide her out of the booth.

"No." Trinity shook off his touch. "This isn't how it was supposed to happen. Nobody goes into labor on a first date." She stared straight ahead and did her best not to panic.

Angi pushed Ash aside and scooted into the booth next to Trinity. "It's wet," Trinity whispered. "Sorry."

"You have nothing to apologize for."

Trinity could see Ash looming over them out of her peripheral vision, hands on his hips. "We need to go."

Angi turned and pointed at him. "Pull your car up and call Beth Carlyle. She's going to want to meet you at the hospital. She'll get ahold of the doctor."

"I can help her."

"By getting the car," Angi repeated.

"Please, Ash," Trinity added.

He looked like he wanted to argue but nodded. "Don't dawdle," he told them and stalked away.

"I have to say it's pretty charming that a man who looks like that can use the word *dawdle* so confidently." Angi placed an arm around Trinity's shoulders. "Right now, we're focused on you. I know this wasn't the plan, but your son didn't get that memo. You need to adjust. Trust me, this is the first of about a million adjustments you're going to make as a mother."

"My baby doesn't have a father." Trinity winced when another contraction pulsed through her. "At least he's not in the picture. Why did I think I could do this on my own? I can't. I changed my mind."

Angi tightened her grip, squeezing gently. "You're not going into it thinking you know everything, which works in your favor. You'll be willing to learn and try new things and be creative. Most of all, you are going to love your child. Every parent makes mistakes, Trinity. Some big ones on occasion. Love is what will see you through."

"I can't do this," Trinity repeated. "It's too soon. It's not right."

"I was a single mother, and there was no logical reason on the planet for me to think I could be successful. Do you want this baby? Because you have options even now."

"I do want him."

"Then you'll figure it out. Parenting is a great equalizer. Even moms and dads who think they're prepared are thrown for a loop multiple times a day."

Trinity wasn't sure if it was the words Angi spoke or the conviction in her tone, but she trusted the restaurant owner. "I need to get to the hospital."

Angi nodded. "Ash will get you there. You can trust him."

Trinity bit down on her lower lip. "You don't know how much I want to believe that."

CHAPTER NINETEEN

THREE HOURS LATER, Thomas Michael Carlyle entered the world.

"He's perfect," Freya told Trinity. She and Beth stood on either side of Trinity's hospital bed. Their younger sister looked tired and terrified and so beautiful it made the backs of Freya's eyes sting.

How was it possible that her baby sister was now a mother? The baby was tiny but perfect with a nearly full head of dark hair the color of his mother's. It made him look like an adorable grumpy old man.

Freya would never have expected Trinity to be the first of the three of them to have a child. Somehow even knowing Trinity was pregnant, seeing her belly and feeling the baby move hadn't changed that thought.

Beth picked up a washcloth from the table next to the bed, dipped it in warm water and pressed it to Trinity's forehead. "They're doing a few more tests, but he's good, Trin. His vitals are strong. His oxygen is within the normal range. You should have him back here with us in just a short time."

"Why did he come so early? Was it something I did? Was it because of the drive or… I took all my prenatal vitamins and I went to the doctor and—"

Beth frowned. "It's nothing you did, sweetheart."

"You were perfect and brave," Freya confirmed.

"That can't be right," Trinity insisted. "I had a birth plan." She lifted the sheet and held her hand over her stomach, where the C-section incision stood out, red and angry under the sutures. "They had to take him from me. That has to be my fault."

Beth shook her head. "Is it my fault I couldn't carry a baby to term? Were the miscarriages or months when IVF didn't work my fault, Trinity? Would you blame me for not being able to have a baby?"

Trinity gasped then shook her head. Freya swallowed at the raw emotion she heard in her older sister's tone. Beth did not do that kind of emotion.

"You have a healthy baby, Trin," Freya said, wanting to remind all of them about what was important right now. "That's the grand prize. It doesn't get any better. You did it."

Beth sniffed. "Next time, I'd prefer you didn't scare the holy heck out of all of us, but that little boy is worth it."

"Worth everything. But is it weird that I want Mom here?" Trinity asked as she nodded.

Freya patted Trinity's hand. "It wasn't all bad growing up. We had good times, too."

"She's going to be a fun grandmother," Beth said with a laugh. "Do you remember when we used to do dress-up tea parties in the backyard catching fireflies and drinking apple juice out of Grandma's chipped china? Those were some of my favorite nights. Mom could turn even the most boring activity into an adventure."

Freya nodded. "We're going to have more adventures." She felt the conviction of it all the way to her toes. "No matter how far apart we've been, we're back together at this moment." She didn't dare bring up how long it might last. One day at a time worked better for the sisters.

"We're going to make all kinds of adventures for your boy," Beth said.

Trinity gave them a wobbly smile. "I just want to hold him."

"I'll see if I can't hasten that along," Beth said. "And tomorrow we'll bring Mom over to meet him."

"Thank you," Trinity whispered, leaning back against the pillows as Beth exited the hospital room.

"Can I get you something to eat?" Freya asked. "I've seen you finishing off Mom's pudding at the center. I'll find whatever flavor you want. What about more water? You need to keep up your strength. I don't know much about babies, but it feels like the advice I should be giving to a new mother."

Trinity's smile quivered. "Why do I feel like it's my fault that he needs extra attention? I didn't want him at first," she said in a hushed tone. "When I first found out I was pregnant, my initial reaction was that I didn't want a baby, a boy especially. Women like Beth try so hard, and they get nothing. For me, it came out of nowhere, and I wanted to wish it away. What kind of person makes that sort of wish?"

Freya's heart hurt for the emotion in her sister's voice. "You were scared, honey, and in a tough situation. Nobody is going to fault you for that."

"What if Thomas is paying the price?" Trinity asked. "What if he has to suffer for the wish I made?"

"That's not how it works. We know your heart, Trin. Yes, you may have made a wish because you were scared and shocked, but I don't believe that lasted."

"It didn't," Trinity said. "It wasn't very long until I knew I wanted a baby. He knew I loved him, right? I wished to be a good mom. I wished for him to be healthy but at first…"

"Do you know what I wish?" Freya lowered herself to

the edge of the bed. "I wish you could see yourself the way Beth and I do. You are strong and resilient. When we were kids, I used to wish for your personality. I thought if I could be as kind and happy as you that Mom would stay around. I wanted to be the easy daughter, but it wasn't in my nature."

She shook her head when Trinity would have argued. They both knew Freya told the truth. "You have so much love to give. I can't tell you why certain things happen. Like why Beth doesn't have a baby after trying for so long. Yet I have no doubt you are going to be an amazing mom, Trin."

Trinity swallowed. "I will never make him doubt my love. No matter whether he's easy or causes me endless pain, he will always know I love him."

"He's a lucky kid."

The door opened, and a nurse wheeled in a bassinet as Beth and Christopher Greer followed. Freya felt her eyes widen, although Trinity didn't seem surprised to see the man.

"What do you think, Greer?" Trinity asked, although her gaze stayed on her newborn son as the nurse placed him into her arms.

"He's a handsome boy. Congratulations."

Freya moved toward Greer. "It's late. What are you doing here?"

"I went by the house earlier and saw Ash. He told me what had happened, and I thought I'd stop by and see if I could help in any way."

"Since when do literary agents deliver babies?"

"We don't. I was worried about Trinity."

"She isn't your concern." The spiteful words shamed Freya even as she said them. Why did this man push every one of her buttons?

"Thank you for that reminder," he said. "Are you doing okay?"

"I'm not your concern either."

"He's a handsome lad," Greer said, looking over Freya's shoulder. "A bit of an abrupt arrival, eh? Is everything okay with Trinity? Was there something specific that triggered—"

"We are not focusing on why it happened," she said matter-of-factly. "We are focused on a healthy baby."

"Of course," he agreed. "I was just wondering…"

"Stop wondering."

"Would you like to try feeding him?" Beth asked Trinity, who continued to stare in wonder at Thomas.

Freya darted a side glance at Greer.

"I'll give you all some privacy," he said immediately. "Congratulations, Trinity. If there's anything you need, please reach out. I'll get as much as I can done before you come home."

"Thanks." Trinity was already tugging at her hospital gown.

Greer turned for the door, like someone had just lit a fire under his tailored slacks.

Freya followed him into the hallway. "What is your angle?"

"I don't know what you're talking about. I wanted to congratulate your sister and make sure she was doing okay."

"There's more to it. Something you aren't telling me."

"Suddenly you're such an expert on my behavior?"

"I don't trust agents."

"I get that, Freya." He leaned in. "You can trust me."

"We'll see," she said. He opened his mouth to say more, then closed it again. "If you need anything…"

"Visiting hours are over." The nurse who'd helped with

the bassinet walked past. "Each patient gets one overnight guest."

Greer stared at Freya as she nodded at the nurse. "I'm sure Beth could pull some strings so you can both stay."

Freya shook her head. "We've already decided Beth is going to stay tonight, and I'll stay tomorrow night. If everything goes well, Trinity should be released after that. I'm just going to say goodbye," she said to the nurse.

"Do you need a ride?" Greer asked.

"I can take Beth's car and bring it back in the morning."

He looked up to the ceiling as if he could draw patience from the faded tiles. "I'm here, Freya. I can give you a ride home."

She wasn't sure why her instinct told her to refuse other than her emotions felt wild and fierce right now. She was too vulnerable as the adrenaline rush she'd had when Beth called her wore off. Her sister had been across the street at Shauna's helping to assemble gifts for the woman's clients.

Beth and Shauna were becoming friends, and Freya had no one. She shouldn't feel jealous of a single mother who was struggling to keep things afloat after such an intense injury but couldn't quite help it.

Beth had offered to drive both of them to the hospital, so Freya's car was still at the house. She reentered the room, and her eyes filled with tears at the sight of Thomas latched onto his mother. Trinity and Beth both watched the baby, and Freya's ovaries did the strangest sort of squeeze when the tiny baby made soft grunts of satisfaction.

She quietly said goodbye then slipped back out of the room.

"What's wrong?" Greer asked immediately.

"Other than you all up in my business?" Freya shook her head. "Nothing."

"You're crying or about to."

Freya laughed despite herself. "I'm a little emotional. Cut me some slack."

She deserved an argument or snide comment after her behavior, but he simply nodded and fell into step beside her as they exited the hospital. Sleet came down in icy ribbons, about as close to snowfall as Magnolia got on a regular basis.

"They're forecasting a white Christmas," Greer said as he opened the door to the Audi sedan. "It would be the first white Christmas in Magnolia in nearly a decade."

Freya waited for him to climb into the driver's side. "How are you an expert on the meteorological history of this town?"

He flashed a boyish smile. "I spend time at the hardware store. I know a lot about the weather and high school sports around here."

She felt the urge to challenge him, but what was the point? "Does it make me a terrible person that I hate that you fit in Magnolia more than I do?"

He looked almost embarrassed by her comment. "I'm not sure I belong, but I like this town. I never knew anything like it growing up. It was just my mom and me. She did her best, but it was hard to make ends meet a lot of months. Nondescript apartment in a nondescript suburb."

"You had school friends?"

It took him a moment longer than it should have to reply. "I know the divorce rate in the country is fifty percent, or at least that's what they would have us believe. Growing up, everyone I knew either had an intact family, or if their parents were divorced, they got along. I didn't fit in there. Sure I had friends, but it wasn't..."

He gestured at the houses they passed with their cheery

Christmas decorations. Lights and inflatables, like a Clark Griswold fantasy come to life. "It wasn't like this."

"If it makes you feel better, Magnolia wasn't exactly like this when I was growing up either. A lot has changed. In fact…"

She glanced out the window at her mother's house as Greer pulled into the driveway. He didn't rush her, just waited patiently until she completed her thought.

The man possessed an infinite amount of patience, at least where Freya was concerned. She found it disconcerting because it made her want to talk to him, to spill her secrets. Perhaps even to mention her writing aspirations even though she'd promised herself she wouldn't.

"I posted some pictures from downtown on social media. The producers of *That Special Someone* want me to be part of a reality star special where we share real-life footage of our holiday celebrations. They think Magnolia is the perfect town. Viewers will love the juxtaposition of me with my heels and designer clothes against the backdrop of the down-home charm of where I came from."

He touched a gentle finger to the bulky cable-knit sweater she wore. "I haven't seen you in heels or designer clothes in a while."

"They don't fit who I am."

She wanted to end the sentence there. It was true. Away from California, the things that had mattered to her for so long seemed insignificant.

"Who I am when I'm here," she forced herself to clarify. How could she admit that she wanted to be someone different when she had no idea how to make that happen?

"I like who you are," he said softly. She waited for him to add a qualifier to the compliment, but he didn't.

"Do you want to come in for a minute?"

"Sure," he answered, and she appreciated that he didn't make it weird. Freya couldn't deal with any more emotional weirdness right now.

"Do you like ice cream?" she asked as they walked toward the house.

"More than anything."

Freya grinned. "I bet mint chocolate chip is your favorite flavor."

"Is that what you have in the freezer?"

"Yep."

"Then it's my favorite."

Freya knew she didn't deserve his kindness, but she soaked it in just the same. She scooped them each a cup of ice cream. "How do you feel about Rudolph? Because I'm in the mood for a horrible holiday movie."

"Nope."

Freya blinked. He'd been so agreeable and was going to take a stand on a red-nosed reindeer?

"What do you want to watch?"

"Love Actually," he said without a hint of sarcasm.

"You're joking?"

"You don't like that movie?"

"I love it. But I can't believe that would be your choice. What's your backup? *Little Women*?"

"I guess that would depend on which version you're talking about. In my opinion, Katharine Hepburn is the ultimate Jo."

"You aren't for real. Men who look like you don't watch movies like that. They aren't nice or kind. They want something," she said around a big bite of ice cream. "They have an ulterior motive."

"Men who look like me?"

She plopped down onto one of the chairs at the kitchen

table and jabbed her spoon into the ice cream again. "Like you should be sailing on a yacht in the Hamptons or ordering martinis shaken, not stirred. Not fixing up some middle-aged woman's dilapidated house and helping her to re-release her dated feminist manifesto."

"California has made you jaded, Freya." He sat next to her and used one of those elegant fingers to tuck a strand of hair behind her ear. She resisted the urge to shiver. "I might have an ulterior motive where you're concerned, but it isn't what you think."

She didn't need to ask what it was because the way his gaze strayed to her mouth told her everything she needed to know. "What's your favorite scene in *Love Actually*?" she demanded, shaking the spoon in his face. "If you tell me it's the scene where Emma Thompson unwraps the Joni Mitchell CD, I'm going to punch you. Figuratively, but I'll really want to in my heart."

His mouth curved up at one end. "It's the part where the little kid plays drums in the band." He shrugged. "You can blame or thank my mom once again. Sappy movies and television shows, reality TV and baking competitions made her happy. She didn't like home improvement so much. Felt like people should be content with what they had and not constantly want more. If you want a different movie, pick it. I'm easy."

Wasn't that just the problem for Freya? Christopher Greer was far too easy. Easy to like. Easy to laugh with. Easy to want to kiss. Easy to fall for.

She should send him away, but she didn't want to be alone. More than that, she wanted to be with him.

"Die Hard," she said just to get a reaction.

"Yippee-ki-yay."

Without thinking about the consequences, she leaned

in and kissed him. He lifted his big, callused palms to her cheeks, cradling her like she was precious to him.

Like he thought she might pull away and wanted to keep her close.

She wanted to be closer.

"More," she demanded and turned to face him in her chair. She moved her hands under the wool sweater he wore. Suddenly it felt imperative that she touch his skin. She needed the heat of him against her.

A shudder ran through him and he muttered, "tickles" against her lips, but he didn't stop her. He tasted like mint and sugar and continued to kiss her like it was his life's mission to turn her knees to jelly. His mouth was the perfect combination of tender and insistent, and somehow Freya could feel an undercurrent of admiration in his kiss.

How could a kiss that melted her bones also be described as respectful? She didn't know, but it added to her desire, fueling it to almost inferno levels.

"No movie," she said, standing from the table to tug on his hand. "You and me, upstairs."

He started to follow then stopped but didn't release her hand. His chest rose and fell in uneven breaths and color spiked his ruddy cheeks, but he stood his ground. "Is that a good idea?"

"The best one I've had in a while," she confirmed, but he still didn't move. "Greer, please."

His eyes drifted shut as if it were painful to hear his name on her lips. "I don't want to take advantage of you when you're in a vulnerable spot."

Lord save her from this man and his sense of chivalry. "What if I want to take advantage of you?"

"Is that what this is?" He didn't seem put off by the thought.

"Maybe," she admitted. "I don't want to be alone to-night." She shook her head, knowing that if nothing else, she owed him honesty at this moment. "That's not true. I don't want to be alone, but mostly I want to be with you. Not just a random guy to take the edge off. You, Greer. I'm choosing, against my better judgment, to have this moment with you. Because I trust you."

His eyes turned even more molten if that were possible. "I choose you as well." He squeezed her hand. "And I want you more than you could possibly know."

Those words were exactly what she needed to hear, and she led him up the stairs.

CHAPTER TWENTY

THE CURSOR ON Beth's laptop hovered over the submit button on the email to the Family Nurse Practitioner Specialty director. Tonight was the deadline for submitting her final acceptance for the program.

What had seemed like an easy decision a month ago now felt rife with potential drama. Could she truly leave Magnolia when her mom and sisters' lives were in such upheaval?

Freya and Trinity had told her they would manage things, but that was before Thomas had made an early arrival in the world. The baby was remarkably healthy, all things considered, but to Trinity's dismay, he was going to have to stay in the NICU for a few days, according to the doctors, to continue his physical development. Beth's baby sister had been heartbroken to return home without her son, and Beth knew Trinity would have her hands more than full when Thomas finally came home.

How could she expect Trin to take care of May as well? Yes, their mom continued to improve, and thanks to Greer and Freya, the house's first floor was almost ready, but May would still need help.

More help than Trinity or Freya were used to giving. That kind of care was second nature to Beth. But she couldn't provide it from nine hours away in Nashville.

She was slowly coming to understand that part of her discontent was caused by taking on too much, often without being asked, and refusing to allow the people she cared about to help shoulder the burden.

It felt exhausting.

The potential of taking care of only herself felt exhilarating.

And terrifying.

She'd never understand if she could genuinely release control unless she tried. Holding her breath, she tapped her finger on the mouse to hit the submit button, then let out a little yelp.

She was committed.

Committed to something just for herself.

At that moment, the doorbell rang, and she popped up off the sofa like she'd been caught with her hand in the cookie jar.

She hurried forward and threw open the door like she expected the disobedient daughter police to be on the other side.

Instead, Declan stood there in all his broad-shouldered, stormy-sea gaze glory.

"Is this a bad time?" he asked, thick brows drawing low over his eyes.

Beth shook her head. "No, why?"

He frowned. "You're flushed and panting. Did I interrupt something?" He took an almost imperceptible step back. "If you tell me the ex-husband is here then—"

Beth stepped forward and kissed him, delighted when he let out a soft groan. "No one is here. I'm glad it's you at the door."

Well, anyone but her conscience calling, but he didn't need to know that.

His strong hands cupped her elbows. "So you're good?"

She took a quick internal inventory. "I'm good."

"Anything you want to share?"

"Not at the moment."

He looked vaguely disappointed, which was strange because she hadn't told anyone but her sisters and her boss at the hospital about her plan for leaving. After a moment, his features gentled. "I brought Christmas."

"Christmas cookies?" she asked hopefully.

"No," he said with a grin. "I'll remember that for next time."

Next time. She liked the sound of that coming from this man. Since their first time together, he'd spent several nights at her house, but he only ever came over late, after a shift at the bar.

She wondered if that was because he wanted to keep their relationship—or whatever it might be called—from Shauna. Beth didn't like being anyone's secret, but she understood the sentiment. It wasn't as if she were yearning to step out on Declan's arm around town.

Or was she?

He bent to retrieve one of several large plastic tubs she hadn't noticed sitting on her front porch. "You have no decorations, so I brought Christmas." He wiggled his brows. "I even have the perfect Charlie Brown tree. I thought we could put up a few things so the town doesn't call you out as the local grinch."

Ouch. Okay, he'd probably meant the words as a joke, but the holidays typically made Beth feel like her heart might be a few sizes too small.

Right now, though, it seemed to be slamming against her ribs like an animal intent on escaping its cage. Whether that was from the adrenaline rush of making the actual commitment for school—taking a step toward life on her own— or from the way Declan made her feel when he looked at her like she was the most beautiful woman in the world, she couldn't say.

"Where did you get the decorations?"

His eyes took on a hard glint. "I didn't steal them if that's what you're thinking."

She laughed. "Of course I wasn't thinking you stole them." Her smile faded as she realized he was serious. "Declan, I didn't think you stole them. I just… It's well… It's very nice and unexpected."

He ran a hand through his hair. "I'd like a do-over on this conversation, please. Let's start again. Shauna has lots of decorations. More than she could use in one season. I know you're not a big fan of the holidays, but you do so much for everyone else. I'd like to help you find the fun in the season."

Beth smiled and nodded. "Come on in. I'm going to let you in on a little-known fact about me. When I was younger, my best friend from school had a tiny tree of her own that she decorated in her bedroom with wee ornaments her dad had made. I thought it was the coolest thing I'd ever seen. All I wanted was a tree of my own. Everything I had when I was younger was shared with Freya and then Trinity. Trin got things, including her own bedroom, because she was the baby. Mom figured it was easier for Freya and me to be together. Because we were so close in age and Freya was always taller, she got the new clothes. Plus, she always made such a fuss. I was never much of a fusser."

"That doesn't surprise me." Declan placed one of the tubs on her dining room table.

"I sound petty," Beth said with a nervous laugh. "Forget it."

"Beth, it isn't petty for a kid to want their own things. I spent a good portion of my childhood in foster care or trying to keep my mom's junkie boyfriends from selling every possession we owned. Flynn and I were close in age, too, so we shared almost everything. When he aged out and I stayed in foster care, he gave me a baseball. It was his prized possession. I don't know where he got it, but it was signed by Wade Boggs. In Boston, that's a big deal. I guarded that ball with my life. It cost me a lot, but it meant the world that he shared it with me."

Beth smiled. "Do you still have it?"

A shadow crossed his face. "No."

It surprised her, given the reverence with which he spoke about the ball.

"And you never got a tree of your own."

"I suppose I could have bought one as an adult, but I moved out of my mom's house and in with Greg, so it still wouldn't have been mine."

"The two of you didn't have a tree?"

She grimaced. "We did. His mom gave it to us our first Christmas together, and it belonged to his grandmother. Or at least that's how the story went. It was so ugly. I couldn't imagine anybody wanting to decorate that tree, and it smelled like mothballs. I think his mom gave it to us so she wouldn't have to put it up. But I didn't speak up for myself or get my own tree. I was a grown woman, and I couldn't even find the nerve to buy my own Christmas tree."

He put a hand on her shoulder. "Now I got one for you. I feel like I should take it back so you can buy your own. You admired the one in the florist shop, so I talked to the owner, and he ordered one just like it."

"I thought you got this stuff from Shauna's leftovers?"

"Right," he agreed almost too quickly. "Most of it came from her, but she didn't have an extra tree. It was no big deal to get one. We can take it back and you can order your own."

"Can I see it?" she asked, trying not to burst into sentimental tears right there.

He opened one of those tubs and pulled out the small tree. The size would easily fit on a tabletop.

"I got ornaments, too. Again, you don't have to use them."

"I love it," she whispered and threw her arms around his neck. "All of it. Thank you."

She connected her phone to the speaker on the entertainment center and chose a holiday playlist as they began to adorn her family room with Christmas cheer. To her surprise, Declan sang along with the words to every festive song.

"Will you see your brother for Christmas or New Year's?"

Declan shook his head. "Flynn and I don't speak anymore. It's better that way."

Beth placed one of the tiny ornaments onto the tree and stepped back to admire it. "Normally, I would agree with you, but the recent time with my sisters has changed the way I see family. Maybe not completely, but at least somewhat. I wish I wouldn't have let so much time go by without trying to mend those relationships. I wish I hadn't let them get so bad in the first place, but I guess you can't change the past."

"You can't change it," Declan agreed. "That's how things are with Flynn and me. Too much bad stuff went down when we were younger. I don't think either of us would know how to move beyond what came before."

"The first step is trying," Beth told him.

"We should do more decorating and less talking," Declan said.

Beth's head snapped back at the ferocity of his words, even though they were spoken in a quiet growl. She felt like she'd been well and truly chastised and didn't care for it.

If someone—a coworker or her ex-husband or her mother—made her feel as if she were speaking out of turn, her instinct would be to immediately back off. She knew her place, and it was not to make waves.

But that didn't ring true with Declan. He'd seemed to appreciate when she was uncharacteristically outspoken, and his acceptance had lit a spark she didn't want to snuff out. Even if things were more difficult, Beth wanted to speak her mind. She craved meaningful conversations with the people in her life instead of just going through the motions of making everyone happy other than herself.

"If you're just here for the sex, there was no need to bring decorations. I'm not sure you've noticed, but where you're concerned, Dec, I'm kind of a sure thing."

He looked shocked and affronted. Beth almost smiled. She felt as if she'd just offended somebody's conservative grandmother.

"Do you think that's why I'm here?" He held up a hand. "Not that it isn't great, because it is."

"You were great," she couldn't help but point out. "I'm mostly along for the ride."

His eyes went dark, molten and seductive. "Not that I don't enjoy the ride, as you call it," he said, "but it's the two of us together. It's the combination that makes what happens between us so good."

She mulled that over, and satisfaction swelled inside her. "Don't think for a minute that you're going to distract me."

"Why would I bring you a Christmas tree as foreplay?"

"Maybe they were out of sex toys online."

"What in the hell are you talking about?" he demanded.

How could she explain something to him that she didn't understand? She'd never had someone treat her like she was special, and it was hard to know how to accept his kindness without feeling too vulnerable. "I don't know why you'd bring me Christmas decorations in the first place if…"

"Because I thought they would make you happy."

Wasn't that just a punch to the heart? "They do make me happy, but it's like having sex with you."

"You're comparing sex to a Christmas tree?" He looked even more baffled, not that she could blame him.

"It's not only the tree that makes me happy, although it's lovely. It's the fact that you brought it to me. And you're here now. But I refuse to open up to you and not have you trust me in return. It goes both ways, Declan."

"Sometimes, it's just a tree."

She hitched a thumb at the tiny, perfect symbol of Christmas given pride of place on her entry table. "Is that what this is?"

He stared at the tree as if searching for answers, then switched his heated gaze to Beth. "Shauna and Flynn have…or at least had a relationship. But it's…" He ran a hand over his jaw. "Flynn is complicated. For the record, he makes me look like a ray of sunshine."

A snort escaped Beth's mouth before she could stop it.

"Exactly." Declan nodded. "Flynn met Shauna when I was in foster care with her. I'm not sure if you could call it love at first sight, I'd never experienced anything like their connection. I don't think any of us knew what to do about it. He certainly didn't and…"

His eyes took on a grim cast. "The place we were in wasn't good. Our foster mom and dad tried, but their college-age daughter had a new live-in boyfriend child protective services didn't know about. The boyfriend came after Shauna, and I tried to intervene. I was still scrawny and used to my older brother fighting my battles. I wasn't as strong as I should have been. So it was Shauna who stepped in to save me. If she hadn't, the guy likely would have beaten me to death. She…"

He shook his head like he couldn't say the words. A sour pit opened in Beth's stomach, and it felt like her head was stuffed with cotton. She could hear the song in the background. "White Christmas" by Bing Crosby.

She'd never hear that song again without feeling nauseous. She stepped forward and took Declan's hand. She was so used to the heat of his touch. His cold fingers shocked her.

She wrapped one of his big hands in both of hers. "I'm sorry. You don't have to tell me more."

Declan lowered himself to the ottoman that was right behind him like he was afraid his legs might give out. "Flynn burst in before it was over," he said, his voice devoid of all emotion. "He would have killed the guy if our foster parents hadn't arrived home at that time. Somehow they managed to get him away from the boyfriend. Or maybe Shauna did. It's all a blur. The foster dad was a bailiff at the local courthouse, and he called the judge he worked for that night before he called the cops. The daughter's boyfriend was taken away in an ambulance. I don't know what happened to him. If Shauna does, she's never talked about it. But Flynn was given a choice—an arrest or the army. He enlisted the next morning. I was in bad shape, so I didn't even get a chance to say goodbye. A few months later, I got a letter from him saying it was better that way. For all of us."

Beth stepped between his legs and hugged his broad, stiff shoulders. "Was that the last time you saw your brother?"

Declan let out a humorless laugh. "No. Every couple of

years, he shows up. I don't know how he tracks me down. I haven't had a permanent address beyond a PO box in nearly a decade. He only came back for Shauna that one time."

He shook his head. "One time was enough for those two."

"Why did she keep it from him?"

"It isn't my story to tell, but something happened when they were together." His eyes were so stark, it took her breath away. "I can guess what it was, but she won't talk about it. All I know is she was well and truly broken after he left. Then she found out she was pregnant and pulled herself together. She didn't want him to know."

"He was able to find you so easily…"

"She put some measures into place to fly under the radar. I don't think she has reason to believe he'll come looking for her. It's hard to say with Flynn. I don't think he would have stuck around even if he had known. Neither one of us is cut out for long-term or white picket fences or any of that crap."

Beth traced a finger over his brow, wanting to gentle the lines that bracketed his eyes. He'd brought her happiness tonight, and she wanted to give him peace.

"You don't give yourself enough credit, Declan Murphy. You could do anything you set your mind to, including making a home."

He shook his head even as he buried his face into the front of her pajama top. "I wish that were true, Beth." He pulled back. "I have a question for you."

She swallowed. "I'll answer anything at this point."

"When your dope of an ex was here, he called you Elizabeth who's not Elizabeth. What kind of jacked-up nickname is that?"

Of all the things he could have asked her, Beth wished

it wasn't that simple question. One more petty weakness to reveal to him.

"My name is Beth. It isn't short for Elizabeth or Bethany. Just one simple syllable. My sisters are Freya and Trinity. They have exotic, exciting names, and I'm just Beth. I made the mistake of sharing that with Greg in a moment of weakness. I'd always wanted to be an Elizabeth. His idea of a joke was that nickname."

"Greg has a jackass sense of humor, and he can't hold his liquor. It's a pathetic combination. We should come up with a nickname for him. Greg the Goober."

Beth laughed and hugged Declan closer. Oh, she was in trouble with this man. He refused to believe he was worth loving, and she remained committed to putting herself before anyone else.

Atrocious timing, but there was no denying her feelings for him, which grew stronger every moment. She might not be able to deny them, but she could at the very least hide them.

"Goober works for me," she said and held him tight. He worked for her. Somehow Beth knew if she was with a man like Declan, nothing would prevent her from getting everything she wanted in the world. If it was a baby, he'd move heaven and earth to make her a mother, and it wouldn't matter whether the child was biological or one they adopted.

Something fluttered inside her heart. Maybe it wasn't that she didn't have the desire to be a mother because of all those years of taking care of her sisters. Perhaps it had been Greg and the fact that she knew their marriage wasn't built for the long haul.

No matter what Declan told her about not being a long-haul sort of guy and everything she said to him about not wanting commitment, there was that flutter again. Precious and dangerous. She clenched her hand into a fist and locked the secret yearning away deep inside her, safe from anything that could cause it or her harm.

If nothing else, she'd learned that keeping her heart safe was both the most difficult and important task she would face.

CHAPTER TWENTY-ONE

TRINITY WALKED INTO her mother's room two days later, hoping that May would be asleep or at an activity. She cradled her stomach as if there were a baby still in there instead of alone in a hospital bassinet.

She was frustrated and still sore, her body struggling to recover when her heart hurt so badly, although she couldn't fault anyone on the NICU staff. The nurses were caring and conscientious. Thomas was gaining weight, and if things continued to go well, he could be released soon, which both relieved and terrified Trinity.

The reality of having a baby was so much different than what she'd expected. Already, the thought of keeping that tiny, adorable, helpless bundle alive on her own felt like a daunting task. Just pumping enough breast milk to keep him going when she wasn't at the hospital was overwhelming.

What would happen when he was home, and she didn't have the nurses to rely on if something went wrong?

She knew she wasn't alone. Freya would be staying through the New Year, and Beth had offered to spend the first few nights with them. Trinity would make this work no matter what.

To her surprise, May was standing at the window framed by holiday garland when Trinity walked into the room, her walker pushed to one side.

"Mom, should you be out of bed on your own?" Trinity hurried forward like her mother might stumble and fall if she didn't reach her quickly enough.

"Fine," May said with the lopsided smile that was becoming familiar. "I fine, Trinny. Where you been?"

May searched her face then her eyes widened as she looked down at Trinity's stomach, which wasn't exactly flat but clearly had changed shape since the last time she'd visited.

"Baby," she whispered.

"Yeah, Mom." Trinity did her best to blink back the tears that threatened to overflow. "You have a grandson. His name is Thomas Michael."

"Trinny, so happy." May lifted her right arm to envelop Trinity in a tight hug. Her left side was still stiff, although she was beginning to get some mobility back in her hand and wrist. "Where…" May pulled back and searched her daughter's face. "Why you cry?"

"He's still in the hospital," Trinity said, trying to keep her voice steady. "He's doing well, but because he was born so early, they wanted to keep him."

"Baby healt…" May swallowed. Certain words and sounds continued to be difficult for her to form, although sometimes it was difficult to know whether her brain or her motor skills were causing the issue. "Healthy?"

"Yes." Trinity pulled her phone from her purse. "Would you like to see him, Mom?"

May nodded and squeezed Trinity's arm. Trinity still found it difficult to believe that her mother was so excited about a baby, but she was learning to appreciate May's now typical enthusiasm for the tiny details of her daughters' lives.

Not that a baby was tiny in anything but size.

They sat on the bed together, and Trinity scrolled through the dozens of pictures she'd taken of Thomas.

May cooed over each one and leaned in to press kisses against the screen. It was exactly the response Trinity would have hoped for, and it triggered a tidal wave of emotion.

"Mom, I hate that he's in the hospital. He was born too early, and I can't stop thinking I did something wrong. This is somehow my fault. What if I messed things up from the very start?"

"Trinny, no." May tried to lift her left hand to grab Trinity's then placed it on her thigh. "Thms perfect." She cupped Trinity's chin in her right hand until Trinity met her gaze. Then she said slowly, "You are good mama. I know tis."

"I want to be." Trinity nodded. "I don't think I know how."

"You learn."

"What if I make mistakes? What if I fail? I've failed at so much in my life."

May seemed to contemplate this or else she was lost in thought for another reason. It was hard to tell what was going on in her brain sometimes. "I messed up," she said after a moment. "Real bad. My daughters still perfec."

Trinity laughed. "We're hardly perfect, Mom, even Beth."

May patted Trinity's cheek with her soft palm. "To me, you perfect. I sorry for being bad mama. I love girls."

"Oh, Mom." Trinity leaned into May's touch. "You weren't bad."

"I bad." May patted her chest. "I know bad. I angry and not good. I wad not good, but you will be good mama, Trinny. I know."

"I wish I had your confidence."

"You stay here with me. I help. Will be good gramma."

"I want to stay," Trinity admitted, the tightness in her chest releasing a bit at finally saying the words out loud to her mother. "But I don't want to be a burden to you, Mom. You have to focus on your recovery and the book."

"You read book?"

Trinity gasped. "The book. I totally forgot. I'm so sorry. I went into labor the night Greer gave it to me. I haven't read it. It's still in my car."

May smiled again. "You read. Then you understand. This your home, and you stay."

"I'll bring Thomas to see you," Trinity promised. "As soon as he's healthy enough to come home." She smoothed a hand over her mother's hair. "And soon you'll be coming home. I'm going to take care of you for as long as you need it, Mom. Both you and Thomas."

"You safe, Trinny," May said, and Trinity almost lost it. Her mother couldn't possibly know what had happened unless Beth or Freya had said something.

"Did one of them tell you?" she demanded.

So much for sisterly loyalty. May only smiled. "You safe," she repeated.

Trinity held onto her anger so that no other emotion could take over. She looked away from her mother to the Christmas decorations making the room look cheery and bright.

She wanted to believe she was safe. She needed to know that her son was safe but wasn't sure how to release the fear that had become her closest companion in the past year.

"I'm fine," she lied. "They shouldn't have worried you. He's part of my past now."

May continued to smile that tranquil smile. "Safe. Show me more granson."

Trinity nodded and snuggled in closer to her mother,

bringing up photos of her precious baby once again. They gazed at the phone together until May drifted off to sleep. Trinity gave her mother a soft kiss on the forehead and then left the rehab facility and headed to the hospital.

Freya and Greer were at the house today painting trim. After they finished, the downstairs would be ready for May to come home.

Trinity had planned to help them, but Thomas's arrival had changed all of her plans. She didn't mind. Nothing was more important to her than her son, and she would be a good mother even if she didn't know how. Nothing else would take precedence over him.

Her romance with Ash had ended before it started. Even that was a casualty she could handle, although the thought of him still made her heart pine for another chance.

He and Michaela had come to the hospital the day after Thomas was born, but the visit had been short and awkward. Trinity couldn't shake the feeling that something negative in her behavior had caused her to go into labor so early.

Even her mother had managed to give birth to three full-term babies. No C-section scars for May. Each of the girls had been born naturally, with no epidural. The way her mom had told their birth stories, the sound of ocean waves played in the background and ambient lighting had facilitated their transition from the womb to the world.

It was one of the things she knew her mother to be most proud of based on how often she told the story. Trinity hadn't even gotten around to putting together a labor playlist, not that it would have mattered. Thomas had entered the world in a brilliant, sterile operating room with his mom puking on Beth's shoes because she was so nauseous from the anesthesia.

Her sisters might agree that May had been a bad mother, but Trinity didn't feel so strongly. Yes, May had been selfish and self-centered, but she'd loved her daughters in her own narcissistic way. Two days into motherhood, Trinity felt that she could be a little more generous with her judgments.

May had been left with three girls on her own when their dad took off for Vegas. May had been completely alone.

The book and the subsequent fame and tour and workshops and new life for their mother had hurt the girls but they'd always had a roof over their heads. Occasionally May had forgotten to pay the electric bill, but at least she'd found a way to make money to support them all.

Trinity wasn't sure how she was going to manage that feat at this point. How was she supposed to take a shift at a salon with a newborn baby? Could she find a good day care for him or would her mother really be both well enough and willing to help?

Part of her still feared once May recovered and her brain went back to normal, she'd get on with her life again. A life that certainly wouldn't include childcare for her youngest daughter. Freya and likely Beth would eventually leave. In her deepest heart, Trinity wanted to ask Beth to stay. She knew if her responsible older sister was in town that Beth would take over.

But she couldn't keep relying on other people. Her pregnancy might have been a surprise, but Trinity was an adult and now a mother. She owed it to herself and her baby to make it work.

Her phone rang as she entered the lobby of the local hospital. "Is everything okay, Beth?" Trinity asked, not bothering with a greeting since she knew Beth was just finishing her shift on the fourth floor. "I just walked in, and I'm on my way up to feed Thomas."

"That's perfect." She heard her sister's voice in stereo and turned to find Beth striding toward her from the bank of elevators. "He's being released today."

Trinity blinked. "No, he's being released next week at the earliest. That's what they told me."

"His vitals are good and he's gained another two ounces. They're sending him home early, Trin."

Trinity felt her heart start to slam against her rib cage. "I'm not ready. I don't know... What if I can't..."

She clenched her hands into fists, digging her nails into her palms to try to distract herself with pain. A different kind of pain. She would carve herself bloody if it meant she didn't have to feel the trembling fright surging through her at the thought of leaving the hospital with her baby. She should be happy but only felt fear.

"I don't know what I'm doing," she whispered. Beth immediately took her hand and ushered her into a nearby restroom.

"What's going on, Trin?"

"I'm alone. I have no business trying to raise a baby by myself."

Beth tried to take her hand, but Trinity shrugged off the touch. She could not unclench her fists. Somehow she knew if she gave up that tight grip, then she would lose even her hold on her sanity.

"Honey, you can do this. You're already doing it. They haven't even had to supplement your breast milk. You're giving him all the nutrition he needs. That's excellent."

"Which makes me more like a cow than a mother," Trinity blurted. "What if he needs something in the middle of the night, and the nurses aren't there to help? What if he cries, and I don't know what he wants? I'm not like you. I'm not competent. I'm fun and happy and travel a lot. A baby doesn't need travel. He needs a mom who knows what the hell she's doing."

"Where is this coming from?"

"It's coming from me. I didn't realize how much work this would be before he was born. How stupid am I? People know babies are a huge responsibility."

"Of course you didn't know. You're a first-time mom."

"You would have known," Trinity insisted. "You should be his mother."

Beth's head snapped back. "Don't say that. If I was meant to be a baby's mother right now, I would be. Thomas is yours, Trin. I know you love him."

"I love him. It's not a question of love. Mom loved us. How much comfort was that to you when she left? Dad told me he loved me every night before I went to bed. It didn't make him stay."

Trinity's breath came out in harsh gasps. What was wrong with her? She'd felt so sure and confident. Now in a moment when she should be happy, all she could feel was terror.

"You aren't Mom or Dad," Beth said simply.

Trinity nodded. It was one small fact, but she wasn't sure she could handle anything more than one small fact at a time right now.

"Do you want to look at other options?" Beth asked. "Because—"

"No." Trinity shook her head. "I want to feel confident."

"One moment at a time," Beth said. "You'll get there, and we'll all be here to support you."

"Not you. You'll be in Nashville."

Beth's mouth thinned. "If you want me to stay, I will."

"You've already given up so much for both Freya and

me. More than I realized when I was younger. I want you to go and be happy."

"I'll come visit as often as I can and call every day if that helps."

"I'm tired of being afraid," Trinity said as if she were revealing some huge secret. "Can you help me not be afraid?"

Beth shook her head. "I wish that was an option. Here's what I can tell you. I think fear is part of life. Sometimes it's healthy and helpful and sometimes not so much, but you have a choice. Fear can come along for the ride, Trinity. But don't let it drive. You are in control. It may not always feel that way, but you are. It's a lesson I'm learning at the same time as you."

Trinity sniffed. "You've always been powerful."

Beth laughed softly. "I let fear run the show for years. First, my anxiety about letting down Mom. Then the fear of what our neighbors and friends would think about the situation. Then Greg, my coworkers, bosses, doctors. I let my concern about what people would think about me rule the day. I missed out on a lot of things because of it, and I don't just mean as a kid when I was trying to take care of things. I have no excuse for how I've let it take over as an adult. My fear of what other people think about me. Your fear about what you believe about yourself. Two sides of the same coin in a lot of ways."

Trinity thought about that. "Do you think Freya is ever afraid?"

"I don't know for sure, but my guess is yes. I think everybody is afraid some of the time and that's okay."

"I wish it felt okay."

"Me, too, but I think it gets easier with practice."

Trinity drew in a deep, cleansing breath. "I know you're right. I've done things I didn't think I could or should or other people didn't believe I could despite the fear. I guess being a mom is no exception."

"Know that until you completely believe in yourself," Beth said, squeezing Trinity's shoulder, her eyes shining with a faith Trinity wished she could have in herself. "I believe in you. I know you can do it. Listen to me if you can't listen to yourself."

In her heart, Trinity knew Beth was telling the truth. Her smart, capable sister believed in her. It was a start. "Let's go get my baby," she said, and when the fear rolled through her, she breathed it in and then out again.

You can ride along, she mentally told it, *but you can't drive. I am in the driver's seat.* She waited for the terror to grow until it overpowered her. To her surprise she waited a few moments and the fear seemed to settle. It didn't leave completely but she could manage it.

She reminded herself she would do anything for her baby and followed Beth into the hall.

CHAPTER TWENTY-TWO

FREYA WALKED ALONG the cheery streets of Magnolia a little over a week before Christmas, mentally choosing shots that she would use when the crew came in a couple of days to film her. She had initially planned to say no to being part of the reality franchise's holiday special.

This time in her hometown felt too precious to share or commercialize. But something happened when Trinity came home with Thomas. Freya couldn't explain the effect having a newborn in the house had on her. Suddenly all of the ways her life had no purpose and meaning became crystal clear, and she had no idea how to change it. She couldn't even find the inspiration to work on her book again, although Trinity told her over and over how good it was.

Freya still hadn't given the manuscript to Beth. Sharing it with her baby sister was one thing but showing it to her big sister felt like quite another. How was she supposed to consider having a career as an author if she couldn't even share her work with more than one person? The fear that ruled her life felt ridiculous and embarrassing, but she couldn't let it go.

So she'd done what she knew how to do to bring in a paycheck and had her agent work out a deal for her involvement in the holiday special.

Of course she wasn't going to share her real life in Magnolia. She planned to give the crew a tour of the town. She hadn't yet explained that she wasn't going to introduce them to her family but doubted it would come as a complete shock. Let somebody else mine the girl-next-door America's sweetheart vibe. That was never Freya's shtick anyway.

She looked at the perky swaths of pine boughs and window dressings that typically raised her spirits. Today her mood remained stubbornly in the toilet, and there seemed to be no amount of Christmas cheer that could change that.

If only she had Trinity's optimistic outlook on life. Freya wished for so many things that seemed destined not to come true. Then something in a window just off Main Street caught her eye.

A woman was arranging a scarf on a mannequin that wore a colorful fit-and-flare dress with a frill neckline. The deep magenta fabric looked like a cotton-blend with the most intriguing pattern of eye-popping gardenias splashed across it. It wasn't Freya's style, far too conservative and schoolmarmish. Not one ounce of cleavage would show with that high collar. But she moved toward the shop anyway. In bold letters, the sign above the door read *A Second Chance*.

She'd noticed the shop on earlier excursions into town but ignored it until now. Freya had plenty of clothes and had been convinced that nothing offered by a boutique in her sleepy hometown would interest her.

Still, shopping nearly always lifted her mood so she figured it was worth a shot, especially as she prepared for the camera crew to arrive. It wasn't as if anyone would notice her in her ubiquitous black leggings and oversized sweatshirt.

Welcoming bells chimed as she entered the shop, and a woman called out a greeting. Freya wasn't sure what she envisioned for the store's aesthetic, but it was nothing like the bounty of stylish apparel items and adorable gifts she found on the racks and rows of display tables.

They weren't her usual style. No sleek lines or body-conscious silhouettes. The clothes managed to be both trendy and timeless, the kind of style she imagined the author version of herself embodying.

She couldn't deny the appeal.

"Are you looking for something in particular?" a woman asked.

Freya glanced up, ready to dismiss the shopgirl but felt her eyes widen. "I know you," she said.

The stunning blonde, less shopgirl and more thirty-something fashion icon, nodded. "I know you, too, Freya Carlyle. I heard you were in town." The woman stuck out an elegant hand. "I'm Mariella—"

"Mariella Jacob, the wedding dress designer. Several of the *Married on A Dare* brides have worn your creations."

Mariella wrinkled her pert nose. "Let's be clear. They have worn creations of my former label, Belle Vie. The new management team made the deal with the reality show after I was gone. I would never design a dress for a bride who agreed to be married on a dare."

"I can't blame you," Freya said. "Those unions don't have a great track record for lasting much beyond when the cameras stop rolling."

Mariella snorted. "Go figure. Were you ever part of that franchise?"

"No," Freya said with a grimace. "I can't resist a dare, which seemed like a bad combination. Not that I haven't on occasion sold my soul for ratings."

"A lot of people sell their soul for suspect reasons," Mariella agreed, tucking a lock of golden hair behind one ear. A petite diamond stud winked from her earlobe. "It's easy to get caught up in the fame and fortune. I'm not sure I sold mine, but I certainly rented it out to the highest bidder on occasion. I once designed a silk casing around a gown because the bride wanted to look like a beautiful butterfly emerging from the chrysalis as she got to the altar. Unfortunately, a woman shrouded in a white cocoon looks like a life-size tampon. It wasn't pretty, but I was all about the money."

"That's something I would have paid to see."

"Do an internet search for 'worst wedding dresses.' We made more than one list."

"Now you live in Magnolia?"

"I do."

"And you own this shop?"

"Yes. I'm also a partner in a local boutique hotel, the Wildflower Inn. We host weddings, so I've started working with brides again. Designing gowns, but on my terms."

Freya mulled over that information, trying to reconcile the transformation with what she'd known about Mariella and her reputation as the go-to wedding dress designer to the rich and famous. "That seems so—"

"Boring?" Mariella asked with a smile.

"Normal," Freya supplied.

"You're right. It's a far more common existence than I ever expected for myself and boring by the standards of my former life. I love it."

Freya was intrigued despite herself. "Do you ever miss the excitement of how things used to be?"

"Not often. It would be interesting to return to that life as the person I am now. I like to think I would use the power I had to do more good in the world. But I'm managing it on a smaller scale. My fiancé runs a clothing company, The Fit Collective."

Freya nodded. "I heard they moved their corporate headquarters to Magnolia. Things have changed since I was a kid growing up here."

"I hope for the better. I'm helping Alex and his team with some design work along with my other projects. I'm now busy in ways that mean something to me."

Mariella pointed a finger at Freya. "I can tell I piqued your interest with that statement. You want more than reality show notoriety."

"I have more," Freya said automatically. "I have endorsements and affiliations."

"You want a life that means something," Mariella told her as if she were some sort of well-dressed fortune teller. "I know that look. I *had* that look. Although to be honest, I dulled it for a lot of years with alcohol and pills."

"I don't do drugs," Freya quickly clarified.

"Then you are several steps ahead of me, friend."

"I'm also not your friend."

"I think you could be," Mariella said, undaunted by Freya's rudeness. "The Fit Collective has an ongoing campaign where we use real-life women and not just professional models. We're trying to tell a story with the brand. You're in the entertainment industry, but there's more to you. Maybe you'd like to be part of it?"

Freya scoffed. "My real life is a pretend world. I don't think I'm the kind of woman you want in your campaign."

Mariella didn't look convinced. "I think you have a story to tell. Consider it, at least while you're in town. We could brainstorm an angle that would work for both the brand and you. In the meantime, I have a dress that would be perfect for you."

To Freya's shock, Mariella went straight to the window

display and pulled down the mannequin wearing the dress she'd first noticed.

"What makes you think that's my style?" She did her best to sound dismissive. "If you know anything about me, you know that I'm about boobs and butt. That grandma frock is going to hide my best assets."

"Humor me. Try it on."

Freya glanced at the door, feeling like an animal about to be ensnared in some kind of trap with only one shot at breaking free. But what was the big deal about trying on the dress? It wouldn't mean anything. It wouldn't change her soul, and she had noticed it after all. She plucked it out of Mariella's hands after the shop owner took it off the mannequin. "Where are your fitting rooms?"

Mariella gestured to the back of the shop. "I'll leave some boots and a necklace on the hook outside the dressing room."

"I don't need help accessorizing," Freya said through clenched teeth.

"Humor me," Mariella repeated with a laugh, then moved forward to greet a pair of women who'd just entered the shop.

Freya pulled off her clothes, examining her body in the wide dressing room mirror. It was the first time she'd really looked at herself since coming to Magnolia. What she saw shocked her.

She'd never had to worry much about her weight. She'd inherited her height and her fast metabolism from her father, but now her arms had definition. Compared to the bevy of uber-fit people with bulging muscles she knew in California, they were tiny, but represented a strength Freya had never associated with herself. She hadn't gotten this way by hours in a gym or being berated by a personal trainer. It had happened naturally thanks to hard work and made her appreciate her body all the more.

Uh-oh. Appreciating her body. She really wasn't going to fit in when she returned to her old life if she started down the road of genuine self-acceptance.

She opened the fitting room curtain after slipping into the dress to grab the boots and accessories, then pressed a shocked hand to her chest at the sight of Christopher Greer standing in front of her.

"I'm sorry," he said immediately, hands lifted and palms out in apology. "I didn't realize anyone was in the dressing room."

His gaze traveled down her body. "Wow. You look amazing."

Freya felt a blush creep up to her cheeks. She still didn't know how to define her relationship with Greer, if you could call it that. After the night they'd spent together, which had been spectacular, he'd left in the early hours of the morning and then showed back up later acting like nothing out of the ordinary had taken place between them. Which made her feel like ten kinds of an idiot for being affected by just one night.

She couldn't deny she liked hanging out with him, even minus the physical aspect. But what had she expected after great sex—Greer professing his undying devotion? She imagined that being with her was as much about scratching an unwanted itch for him as she wanted to believe the same thing for herself.

She'd spent too much time being kicked in the teeth by romance to believe in real-life fairy tale princes. In the case of Greer, her heart refused to get the message.

"This isn't my style," she muttered even as she snatched up the boots and tossed them behind her.

"I think it looks perfect," he said. He leaned in and seemed to shock them both by pressing a quick kiss to her lips as if he couldn't resist, which made her smile.

"Are you stalking me?" she asked, cupping his jaw with one hand. "What are you doing in a women's clothing and gift boutique?"

He held up the hammer she hadn't noticed him holding. "We're installing a new closet system in the storeroom for Mariella."

"We?"

At that moment, Garrett Dawes appeared from the door that led to the shop's storeroom and private office. "I think we can make do without ordering more lumber," he said to Greer then noticed Freya. "I'm sorry. I didn't realize there was anybody back here. Don't meant to be in the way."

Greer let out an almost resigned-sounding breath. "Freya, you remember Garrett Dawes."

"The author," she murmured and realized he was holding a drill. She frowned. "I understood you helping your wife at the hardware store, but since when do famous authors slash screenwriters moonlight as handymen?"

Garrett's grin widened. "My wife is a friend of Mariella's. Crews in the area are slammed, and Mariella had an easy job so..."

Greer snorted. "Garrett's on deadline, so he's procrastinating."

"I call it productive procrastination," Garrett clarified. "I would like to tell you that every day the words just fall out of the sky like rain in the Amazon, but lately it's been more like the Sahara where my muse is concerned. I'm glad to see you again, Freya." He patted Greer's arm. "This one talks all about—"

"Your mom," Greer said quickly.

Freya frowned as she felt Greer tense but kept her attention on his client. She was pretty sure Garrett hadn't been talking about her mother. "I'm a big fan of your work," she told the author. "I have to admit I prefer the books to movie adaptations, even the one starring Brad Pitt."

Garrett tipped the drill toward her as if in salute. "I appreciate that, and I imagine someone with your obvious natural talent would be a fair judge."

Freya darted a glance toward Greer. What kind of natural talent was Garrett talking about? She couldn't imagine a world where he was a fan of reality television, although she wouldn't have guessed that about Greer either.

"I'm not sure—"

"He's watching *Dating on Site*," Greer supplied. "In the latest installment of his series, Garrett has a subplot involving a home improvement show and a suspicious host. I suggested he study parts of your oeuvre for tips on how to handle."

"My oeuvre?" Freya asked at the same time Garrett murmured, "What tips?"

A muscle ticked in Greer's jaw despite his blinding smile. He shoved the hammer toward the author. "I'll grab the lumber and meet you in back."

"Sure, buddy." He smiled again at Freya. "It was a pleasure. I hope we can talk in more detail. In fact, Lily and I are having a post-holiday open house the day after Christmas." He glanced at Greer. "Our strange friend will also be there. I hope you'll stop by, Freya."

Invited to a party with a famous author. Could she spin that for social media? Immediately, she chided herself for even considering it. That was exactly why she didn't want her California life to interfere with her time in Magnolia. It made her into a person she didn't like all that much.

"I'd love to. Thanks for the invite." She plucked the necklace off the hook. "I'm going to finish here."

"The dress is lovely on you," Garrett said without a trace of sarcasm. "See you in a minute, Greer."

A few seconds later, Freya gasped as Greer slid into the dressing room, coming to stand directly behind her as she gazed at her reflection in the mirror.

"So damn beautiful." With one finger, he pulled the hair away from her neck.

A shudder ran through her as he placed a lingering kiss on the sensitive skin just under her ear.

"You must have some sort of librarian fetish," she told him, trying to play off the way her body reacted to his attention.

"Not exactly. I have a you fetish. Only you."

"How's it look?" Mariella's voice called out before Freya could react to Greer's statement.

"You were right," Freya said hoping he didn't hear the tremble in her voice. "I actually like it."

"I love it," he whispered.

"That's great," Mariella answered. "I have to ring up a customer, then I can grab a couple more pieces if you want to try on anything else. Now that you understand my taste is impeccable."

"I'll just take this one for now," Freya said as Greer ran his hands along the soft fabric that clung to her hips.

"Sounds like a plan."

As soon as she heard Mariella move away, Freya rounded on Greer. "The plan is not to get caught being groped in a public dressing room."

"I wouldn't call this groping." He took a step back, giving her space she both needed and didn't want. "I can get there if you'd like. I've been wanting to touch you again since the moment I left your bed."

She splayed her hands on his chest. "But you haven't. You didn't say anything. You didn't even act like it happened. It was as if it didn't mean anything."

He blinked. "Freya, do you think I'm the type of man who would sleep with a woman who didn't mean anything to me?"

How could she admit she wasn't the kind of woman who was worth caring about?

"You didn't say anything," she repeated, plucking an invisible hair off of his shirt collar.

"I didn't want to scare you off, but now I'm even more sorry if I hurt your feelings."

She pressed her lips together. Admitting she was upset by his behavior would make her seem weak and vulnerable. It would give him power.

"We had fun, Greer. Let's do it again sometime." She forced a relaxed tone when that was the exact opposite of how she felt. "But you need to get out of this dressing room so I can change."

"Can I take you to dinner?"

"That horse left the barn. You don't need to wine and dine me."

"I'd like to talk to you." There was a note in his voice that gave her pause.

"I think we should stick to hanging out and not talking. You might annoy me too much over dinner."

His full mouth, the one she knew he could use so expertly, tipped up at one corner. "I'll say okay for now, but not for long." Then he kissed the top of her head and slipped out of the dressing room.

Freya quickly changed back into regular clothes. She

wanted to walk out without buying the dress despite how much she loved it. She'd never be able to wear it without thinking of the way Greer looked at her in the dressing room mirror.

But she wasn't going to admit that it had that effect on her, so she scooped it up, along with the boots and necklace. After stopping to pick up bottles of lotion to use as stocking stuffers for each of her sisters and her mother, she approached the counter. Mariella was just finishing up with another customer.

"Does this place really satisfy you?" Freya asked, unsure whether she was speaking of the shop or the town in general.

Mariella smiled as if she understood exactly what Freya wanted to know. "It does. You should stop by the inn sometime and take a look. The weddings we host might give you a different impression about romance than you get on those dating shows with all the rose petals and complicated maneuvering. Sometimes love is simpler than we think. We're the ones that make it harder than it needs to be."

Freya wrinkled her nose. "Rose petals aren't my favorite anyway," she admitted.

She pulled her wallet out of her purse then frowned as Mariella told her the total. "That can't be right," Freya said. "That sounds like what I owe for the lotion. I don't think you included the outfit."

Mariella shook her head. "You have a secret Santa who took care of the outfit," she said as she began to fold the dress. "Would you like me to gift wrap it? Better than rose petals."

"He shouldn't have done that," Freya said quietly.

Mariella's gaze lit with a gentle understanding. "Nice

guys are hard to come by and sometimes even harder to appreciate."

"That's the thing." Freya wasn't sure why she felt she could be honest with this virtual stranger, but she did. "Greer has no reason to be nice to me that I can figure out. It makes me suspicious like there's something he wants from my mother or me. I want to know what it is."

Mariella inclined her head. "Is it possible that he wants to make you happy?"

"You truly have gone all-in with small-town life if you believe that. Also, I have some land in the Everglades I'd like to sell you."

Mariella let out a throaty laugh. She picked up a business card from the small stack next to the cash register. "I'm going to write my cell phone number on here. I'm serious about a potential collaboration between you and The Fit Collective. Consider it and give me a call if you're interested."

Freya didn't bother to tell the woman there was no way she would be calling. She knew enough to never say never.

The producers might not be excited about her idea for a tour of the town that didn't include her family home, but maybe the promise of a behind-the-scenes look at a company like The Fit Collective would be an appealing carrot to dangle. Besides, she wasn't sure how long she'd have the muscles she'd gained during her time in Magnolia. Might as well put those things on display.

It was easy enough to share her body with people. Her heart was another story, even though every day she felt more certain she was missing something important.

CHAPTER TWENTY-THREE

"WHAT DO YOU think is going on?" Freya asked as she leaned closer to Beth. "And why do I feel so nervous about it?"

Beth pressed a hand to her stomach, where it felt as though a thousand butterflies were gearing up to take flight. "I'm not sure. Whatever it is…" She lowered her voice as she looked toward her youngest sister, standing near the window across the conference room with Thomas in her arms. "I hope it doesn't upset Trinity. She's adjusted to being a mom so well and doesn't need more stress."

The director of the rehab facility had called Beth that morning and asked that she and her sisters meet but hadn't offered any details—at May's request, she'd explained.

"Greg couldn't find out anything?"

Beth felt Freya's gaze on her. "I didn't talk to him," she admitted. "I need to leave that relationship in the past to move forward." She wasn't sure why, but she expected her sister to admonish her for her selfishness.

Certainly her ex-husband could access the information for them, but it felt wrong to ask. It felt like pimping herself or opening the door to him calling on her for a return favor. She didn't want that or to explain to Declan that she continued to have ties to her ex.

Even though her relationship with Declan was undefined, it felt somehow disloyal.

"That makes sense," Freya said simply. "We'll discover

what's going on soon enough. We don't need anything from Greg. No matter what they tell us about Mom, we'll make sure that Trinity stays on a good path."

"Yes," Beth agreed. "We can. We will."

Why did it still feel she had to single-handedly take on life's challenges when she wasn't, in fact, alone? It was a lesson she needed to learn one way or the other. The door opened, and the facility's director walked in.

"Thank you for coming today," she said as she moved to the other side of the conference table. Jennifer Hoffman was in her late fifties, a stout woman with severe features and a short, utilitarian bobbed hairstyle. "The doctor rounding at the center today had hoped to be here but was called to the hospital on an emergency. I think we can handle this meeting on our own."

Beth couldn't decide whether the purpose of the meeting was as serious as the director's expression would lead them to believe or if the woman just needed to learn how to fix her face when talking to families.

"We see many roads to recovery, especially with stroke patients," she began. Beth surprised herself by slipping a hand into Freya's.

Something else that had changed for Beth since Declan had come into her life was the desire for physical touch. It hadn't previously been part of her makeup. If Freya was surprised by it, she didn't show it. She simply squeezed Beth's hand.

Trinity moved from where she'd been standing and lowered herself into the chair on Freya's other side. "Is our mom okay?" she asked.

"Because all these covert ops and metaphorical talking around the issue is freaking us out," Freya added.

Beth appreciated her sister's directness. She could learn from that. She *would* learn from that.

"Your mom is good," a familiar voice said from the doorway. Beth drew in a breath as May walked in, using a cane instead of her walker, to join Jennifer on the other side of the table. "I am good," she repeated. "I woke up today with a better brain." She paused to breathe, as if speaking slowly made the words come more easily. "They say I'm a miracle."

"Those were the neurologist's exact words this morning," Jennifer Hoffman confirmed. "It's an astounding recovery. Your mother has defied all expectations."

"It no longer feels like my brain and body fluttering in different directions," May explained. "I feel like me again. Mostly me."

Beth felt Freya's hand go slack. She could imagine her sister having a similar reaction to her own. Relief mixed with panic. Of course, she wanted her mother to recover. It was a huge, miraculous development. The droop in their mom's face had mostly disappeared. While she spoke slowly with an occasional missed word, May barely slurred.

But a return to normal—who May had been before the stroke—wasn't something any of them would necessarily celebrate, even though the past few weeks of watching their mother struggle had been difficult.

This time had also been its own kind of miracle, a do-over on the loving mother Beth had always wanted.

May looked at each of them expectantly, and Beth tried to calm her reeling thoughts and jumbled emotions. She latched onto the words Freya had spoken earlier. They would get each other through this. While they'd been worried about Trinity, it was their baby sister who reacted first.

"Mom, this *is* a miracle." She stood, baby in her arms. "It's exactly what we wished for."

Not exactly, Beth thought, then immediately felt guilt pound through her. May nodded and reached a hand across the table. Her left hand, Beth noticed.

The left side of her mother's body had stayed stubbornly resistant to therapy. Her movement now was jerky, but she'd clearly regained an incredible amount of mobility on her weaker side.

The brain was an amazing mystery, and this was beyond any outcome Beth had allowed herself to imagine. Even now, she couldn't quite fathom what it might mean for all of them.

"What does this mean?" Freya's words echoed Beth's chaotic thoughts.

Jennifer nodded, her face still stern while her tone was gentle. "First, it means your mom can go home right away. She might have some lingering physical and cognitive issues. It's hard to say with this kind of swift recovery. The fact that you've converted a bedroom on the first floor so she doesn't have to use the stairs will still be a benefit. She's going to continue her therapy on an outpatient basis. She won't be cleared to drive yet, but at this rate, we hope her recovery will continue to move ahead at warp speed."

Hope. Beth's heart clenched. Wishes coming true. She forced her mouth into a smile. "This is wonderful."

"I talked to Greer." May made this statement like her daughters should know why or what that meant, although Beth wasn't following. "We talked about the book tour," May said in clarification. "I will go."

Jennifer's eyes pinched at the corners. "This is where your mother and I disagree, but she is stubborn when she wants to be."

That could be the understatement of the year as far as Beth was concerned. She leaned forward and made sure her smile stayed in place. "Mom, it's amazing that you've had this…well… I don't know what else to call it but a miracle. Don't you want to take it easy for a little while?"

Out of the corner of her eye, Beth saw Freya nod in agreement. "I'm sure Greer can come up with a lighter schedule or some virtual events that wouldn't be so taxing."

May pointed at Beth, her nails still the cherry-red hue Trinity had painted them weeks ago. A lifetime at this juncture. "You can come with me," she said.

Beth blinked. Her mother was looking at her, but certainly she didn't mean that Beth should accompany her on a book tour. Not once in all the years May had been doing publicity, speaking engagements, and leading workshops had she asked any of her daughters to come with her.

"I can't," Beth stammered. She tugged her hand away from Freya's grasp because she felt her world tilting on its axis and she needed to be alone for the fall. She would not take down her sister with her. This could not be happening. "I have commitments here and…"

May's smile was understanding. "I talked to Greg this morning. He talk to your boss."

"Excuse me?"

"You have time off. Personal hours in the bank," May said. "I take you with me. We spend time and you there if I need help."

"Mom, slow down." Freya's voice had taken on a flustered edge. "Beth can't go with you on tour. You know that—"

"Family is most important," May said, patting her chest. "I had lots of time to think. I want to be closer to my girls. We are family."

Right. A family where May was most important.

"We have Christmas at home," May told them. "I like

Christmas now the way I should have when you were kids. We can make up for lost time, and after Freya will stay with Trinity to help. Beth come with me. We are family," she said again.

"I can handle things on my own," Trinity offered. "Thomas is an easy baby. If Freya has to go back—"

"Trinny, you sweet mama." May's gaze softened as she smiled at the baby her youngest daughter held. "Babies are hard. I know. I needed help and didn't have any. You have your sisters."

Beth wasn't sure what to say. Was she an ungrateful horrible daughter for wishing for the version of her mother who had been so docile and nearly nonverbal? This should be a happy moment.

"Tell her about Nashville," Freya said under her breath.

Beth couldn't speak. It was as if history and the familiar weight of responsibility robbed her of her voice. She glanced past her mom to the window, which was now being pelted with icy raindrops. The perfect weather accompaniment to her mood.

Why had she ever thought it could be different? She didn't know how to deny her mom anything.

"I'm so happy you're coming home," she said to May, which was at least the truth. Then she pushed back from the table. "I need to go. I'll see you later."

"We have more to discuss," Jennifer called even as Beth took a step toward the door.

She couldn't make eye contact with either of her sisters. They must be so disappointed in her. The oldest child who had no ability to stand up for herself or show any sort of a backbone. Unsure of where she was even going, she hurried out the door despite hearing her mom call her name.

Her body felt like it was both frozen and burning as she

drove away from the rehab center. Her breath came out in ragged puffs and she gripped the steering wheel like it was the only thing tethering her to the present moment.

She should have known not to grasp for a future that she controlled. Beth couldn't remember a moment when she'd done something for herself that had turned out right.

Other than being with Declan.

It was still hard to believe he found her appealing, with her uptight personality and complicated history and family. For a man who professed to want simple and straightforward, she was anything but either of those.

Yet he'd brought her Christmas decorations and made her feel things—want things—she thought she'd given up with the demise of her marriage.

Things she'd never expected from her ex-husband, like respect and the feeling of being cherished. Wanted for who she was instead of who she pretended to be.

At the intersection to turn right to her house, she took a left instead. Within a few minutes, she was parking in front of Champions downtown. The rain had stopped, and even the bar was decorated for the holidays with kitschy golden garland draped around the windows and a bedazzled wreath encircling the bar's illuminated sign.

It was early afternoon, and she didn't know if Declan would be inside. He'd told her he was finishing up some renovations at the bar in addition to completing a few of Shauna's simpler painting jobs.

The single mom would be cleared to walk in a boot just after the New Year. Declan would no doubt leave at that point, just like Beth had expected to be going as well. Maybe that was why she felt comfortable getting close to

him. Their relationship, or however he thought of it, had a
built-in end date.

They were more than friends with benefits, at least to
her. In fact, she'd never allowed herself to fall so hard, so
quickly. While it would hurt to her core when they separated, it was for the best.

Declan could talk all he wanted about not being the kind
of man who settled down or made commitments. There
was a family guy inside him waiting to emerge, and Beth
could never give him what she knew he'd eventually want.

Still, she walked into Champions, hoping to see him.
His solid presence had the ability to transcend her fears
and doubts. He allowed her to just be.

As soon as her gaze caught on his tall, broad-shouldered
form behind the bar, her breathing seemed to calm. He
straightened and turned, immediately moving toward her.
He wore black jeans, boots and a gray Henley, looking intimidating and wild. To Beth, he was a safe harbor in the
maelstrom of her emotions.

It was a preposterous notion, but she believed in her
heart that nothing could harm her when Declan was around.

Which made it even more difficult to know he wasn't
going to stay.

"What happened?" he asked, searching her face as he
stood in front of her.

She shook her head. How could she explain that something so positive made her feel like her future had transformed into a puff of smoke, vanishing out of her grasp?

"My mom is…" She sniffed and dashed a hand over her
cheek, refusing to cry about this. "She's better."

He continued to stare at her, his gaze unreadable. His
lack of reaction—and more importantly, judgment—gave
her the courage to continue.

"Something happened, and so many of the deficits caused by the stroke have been lessened, maybe even eliminated. She appears to be back to her old self." She forced a brittle smile. "It's a good thing. Everyone will be so glad. Shauna and the boys will—"

"What happened to you?" he clarified.

Beth drew in a shaky mouthful of air. "She wants me to go on the book tour with her. She talked to Greg, who spoke with my supervisor at the hospital. I had planned to…" Beth swallowed, realizing she'd never discussed her plans for school with Declan. "It doesn't matter what I had planned. My mom needs me."

"Give me five seconds. Don't move." Declan stalked across the empty bar. "Bill, I'm heading out," he called. Although Beth couldn't see the bar's owner, he shouted an answer from the back of the bar.

Declan grabbed a canvas jacket from a hook near the door to the office and returned to her.

"You don't have to leave work," she told him as he approached. "I don't want to get you in trouble."

"You aren't getting me in trouble for leaving the bar." He sounded amused. "Let's go."

She nearly sighed when he pressed a gentle hand to the small of her back, just below the waistband of her dark jeans. They emerged from the relatively dim light of the bar into the bright winter sunshine and the bustle of downtown holiday traffic.

Beth hadn't noticed the crowds earlier, but now it felt like the happy shoppers, locals and visitors, were gaping at her like they could see that she was a horrible person for her conflicting feelings about her mom's recovery.

Declan might not have reacted either way, but he didn't need to say it explicitly for her to trust he wouldn't judge her.

"My truck is across the street," he said, taking her hand as he led her past her parked car.

She didn't argue. Without knowing it, he was giving her what she wanted and needed. A break from thinking.

Beth spent so much of her life being responsible and in control. It felt good to be able to relinquish it to someone else.

His thumb traced circles against the center of her palm, but he didn't speak or ask her questions or try to parse out her feelings about the situation with her mother.

She wasn't sure if she could have answered without bursting into tears, and maybe he understood that.

Declan, with his brooding stare and unrelenting lack of faith in himself, understood her in the way she needed.

He opened the passenger side door then moved around the front of the truck to climb into the driver's side.

"It smells like clean laundry." She glanced around at the dark interior of the truck's cab.

He smirked. "Shauna made me put an air freshener in here—said the combination scent of twin boys and bar wasn't doing it."

"She's a good friend," Beth murmured. "You'll miss her and the boys when you leave."

He opened his mouth as if to answer then shook his head. "How do you feel about the beach?"

"I like it, although I rarely have time for sunbathing."

"Would you believe it's one of my new favorite places?"

She wondered if he understood how well he did at distracting her from her worries. "You don't exactly give off sun-kissed vibes, and the shore isn't popular this time of year."

"I could surprise you," he said with a wink. "Maybe I'm a surfer dude at heart. Hang ten. Shred the gnar."

"You can't say those things in real life unless you own a surfboard."

"I just did."

"You're a goofball."

A laugh escaped his mouth. "That's a novel description of me. Let's roll up our pants and go for a walk on the sand."

"The beach works, but I'm not putting my feet in the Atlantic Ocean right now. Do you know how cold the water gets?"

"I'll keep you warm," he promised. Once again, Beth believed him.

"The bar looks great," she said as he drove east toward the beach. "The changes you've made have improved things more than I would have thought. I'm no expert on bar decor, but I imagine Bill will have no problem finding a buyer."

Declan nodded. "He might already have one."

"Impressive, Mr. Murphy."

"I still have a few more things on the punch list, but I'm happy to have helped Bill. I like Magnolia more than I expected. I like it a lot, actually."

"That's nice. It's a nice town."

Declan must have heard the catch in her voice because he fell silent until they pulled to a stop in the empty parking lot near the boardwalk that led to the shore. He turned off the ignition and shifted to face her.

"Do you want to talk about your mom?"

Beth bit down on the inside of her cheek. "She needs me."

"What about what you need?"

"What I need is not to think right now. Can you help me with that?"

He brushed his mouth over hers. Was it possible to become addicted to the taste of a man's kiss?

His tongue danced with hers, and desire swirled through Beth, drowning out everything except this moment with Declan.

"I'm not having sex at the beach when it's cold outside," she told him with a hoarse laugh.

She felt his grin. "I wasn't thinking of having sex."

"Really?" She pulled away to gape at him. "Because that's about all I can think about when we're together."

"Are you using me for my body?"

She nodded solemnly. "Certain parts of it anyway."

"I'm yours for as long as you need me."

It was difficult to hide her shock and pleasure, but she didn't want him to know how much his words affected her.

"Shall we brave the elements and go for a walk?" She mock shivered. "I must really like you because this is insanity."

"Have you ever been to Chicago?" he asked.

"Um…no."

"I'm going to take you sometime in the winter so you can truly appreciate what cold and windy feel like." He glanced out the front window. "The Magnolia beach in December is a balmy spring day in comparison."

"It's legit cold for us locals." She grinned at him.

They held hands as they walked down the empty boardwalk. It was approaching low tide, so a wide swath of pristine sand greeted them along with the waves crashing against the shore.

Beth had never been much of a swimmer, but she liked the beach, although not in the same way summer tourists appreciated it.

For her, the crowded beach was a reminder of family vacations that she'd never gone on. Moms with coolers packed full of sandwiches and sodas while the dads situated the umbrellas and gaggles of kids ran into the waves or built sandcastles.

Plenty of locals spent time at the beach. The popular kids in high school had hung out near the pier on summer nights after slathering themselves with coconut-scented lotion all day.

Beth had never joined them. She hadn't hung out with cool kids, or really any kids. She'd been too busy keeping her sisters in line.

Stepping onto the soft sand with Declan's steady presence next to her, she wished she'd allowed herself to cut loose on occasion when she was younger. So many wishes never brought to fruition.

Heck, she wished she could find a way to relax more now.

"Bare feet," he said, reaching out to tuck a strand of hair behind one ear when it blew into her face. "It's the only way to experience it."

She didn't argue, although that was her first inclination. Instead she toed off her clogs, embarrassingly utilitarian for long days on her feet at the hospital, and then peeled off her socks.

When she looked up, Declan, who'd divested himself of boots and socks far more efficiently than she had, was grinning broadly. "Are your feet shy?" he asked with a twinkle in his eye.

"You're a regular comedian," she told him, rolling her eyes toward the pale blue sky. The sun was already beginning its slow descent to the horizon, and she sucked in a breath as a gust of wind swept up, making her breath catch. "Are you sure distracting me with your naked body wouldn't have been a better idea?"

"Later," he promised and took her hand. "I want to show you something."

They started down the beach, and Beth had to admit the cool, soft sand felt good on her bare feet. The air smelled briny and crisp, the ocean relatively calm for this time of year. The gray-blue water reminded her of the changing color of Declan's eyes, not that she was going to mention that to him.

But she matched the cadence of her breath to the roll of the waves, feeling her tension recede as if sucked away by the turbulent water. Her problems didn't exactly disappear, but there was something about the ocean that reminded her—in a good way—that she was nothing more than a pinprick in the greater spinning of the world.

Yes, her world might be turned on its side at the moment, but she would right it again one way or the other, even if that meant releasing her dreams or finding new ones to go after.

Declan's legs were longer than hers, but he shortened his stride so that their steps seemed to rhyme like the stanzas of a poem.

"It gives you perspective," he said as if reading her thoughts.

"I've heard that bartenders are like psychologists without the degree," she answered. "It's true in your case."

He laughed. "I don't pretend to know more than I do, but I'm glad this works for you."

It was working. All of it. The vast expanse of water, the solitary shore and the man holding her hand. His arm brushed hers with every step.

"Look at that." He pointed to a spot near the seagrass where someone had erected an artificial Christmas tree, complete with bright ornaments, garland and a sea star on top.

"I can't believe it doesn't blow away." A grin split Beth's face.

"Whoever put it up has taken great care to make sure it's secure."

"Do you come here a lot?"

He shrugged. "Sometimes when I need a break from life. My brother and I always said we were going to swim in the ocean together. We never got the chance as kids, and who knows what he's doing now."

Beth could hear the tension in his voice and automatically moved closer to wrap her arms around his middle. They were in front of the tree, and she turned her head to gaze at the colorful ornaments. "It probably makes me a horrible person, but I like hearing about your imperfect relationship with your brother. I feel not so alone."

"You aren't alone, Beth." He dropped a kiss on the top of her head. "I believe you'll find a way to work things out with your mom. She'll understand that you have reasons that prevent you from going with her on tour."

Should she explain about Nashville? Somehow she knew this moment wasn't the right time to mention leaving, not when being with Declan made her want to find a way to convince him to stay.

She held on and wished for a solution for her problems. If this little tree could hold up against the whipping wind and pounding surf, maybe Beth could find a way to remain steadfast in her dreams as well.

CHAPTER TWENTY-FOUR

IT WAS NEARLY midnight when Trinity's phone pinged with an incoming text.

I have leftover dessert. Want to come over for a late-night snack?

Trinity's gaze shot to the kitchen window that faced the neighbor's property. Across the lawn, silhouetted by the glow of the light behind him, Ash waved from a window on the first floor of his mother-in-law's house.

I have a baby with me, she typed and cringed a second after hitting the send button.

He's invited, too, came the immediate replay. But I'm only sharing my treat with you.

Butterflies danced across her stomach.

What kind of dessert?

Peppermint bark cheesecake.

Sounds like my new favorite.

Come over. You and Thomas.

Trinity hadn't been alone with Ash since he'd driven her to the hospital. Honestly, having a newborn took up way more time than she would have expected, which showed how unprepared she'd been.

Ever since Thomas had been discharged from the hospital, it felt as though she spent every waking moment caring for him. Not that she'd change anything.

She thought about saying no. Looking down at her fleece pajama pants and oversized sweatshirt, she wasn't exactly feeling pretty or witty or like any sort of decent company.

But the first evening with May home had been strangely tense. Trinity would have liked to talk about things with Freya or Beth, but both of her sisters seemed closed off, just like she remembered from the past.

Their mom had been happy with the updates to the house and definitely seemed like a kinder, gentler version of herself. Unfortunately, she didn't seem to realize or acknowledge that her daughters might have plans other than devoting their current lives to her care.

So the house that had been a refuge in the past few weeks suddenly felt confining. Trinity looked down at her phone to see three dots appear then vanish several times. Had Ash come to his senses and realized he could find a far better late-night companion than a new mom and her baby?

I have whipped cream.

She grinned when that message finally showed up on her screen, then wrapped the blanket more tightly around Thomas and headed out the door.

It was strange to walk across the lawn with only the glow of the moon lighting her way.

Ash opened the back door as she approached. "Fancy meeting you here," he said, his voice deep and kind.

"What are you doing up so late?" she asked, then noticed he still wore his uniform. "Work," she murmured.

He nodded, his eyes dimming a little. "We had a fatal traffic crash out on the state route, so I just got home." He stepped back to let her into the house. It was warm and cozy and smelled like sugar.

"That's so sad and right before Christmas," she said, suddenly feeling nervous. He was strong and capable and dealt with more serious issues than lack of sleep from around-the-clock breastfeeding.

He shrugged. "Even in a town like Magnolia, bad things happen. I'm here to make sure we minimize the damage."

"Serve and protect." She repeated the words she'd seen emblazoned on the department SUV he sometimes drove.

"Yeah." His smile widened again as he looked at the baby in her arms whose eyes were wide and bright. "Sometimes I have a hard time sleeping after a late night—too much adrenaline. It seems like I'm not the only one who's wide awake."

"He has his days and nights mixed up," Trinity said with a sigh. "The pediatrician says it's normal, but I'm hoping we get it worked out soon."

"Can I hold him?" Ash held up his hands, palms out. "Freshly washed in anticipation."

She transferred the baby into his arms, trying not to notice how good Ash smelled. Greer had held Thomas earlier, but it didn't have the same effect on Trinity as seeing her son cradled in the police chief's arms.

Thomas's little mouth worked for a moment, and then he sighed and stared quietly up at the new person holding him.

Ash bounced him gently, clearly remembering the move from when Michaela was a baby.

"Help yourself to the cheesecake." Ash nodded toward

the counter. "I hope you don't think I'm a creep texting you. I was getting water from the tap and saw you pacing in the kitchen."

"My days and nights are a bit jumbled at the moment as well."

"How's it going overall?" he asked, and the intensity in his gaze made Trinity's heart seem to skip a beat. Such a simple question but no easy way to answer.

She laughed, trying to play off her reaction, and touched a hand to the messy topknot she wore. "I'm not sure I've combed my hair in the past two days, but questionable personal hygiene and sleep schedules aside, I love everything about being a mother."

"You look beautiful," Ash said with grave sincerity.

Trinity flushed. "Thanks." She busied herself with cutting a slice of cheesecake. "Do you want one?"

"Not yet," he told her.

"My mom came home today."

"That's wonderful."

"Yeah," she murmured as she plated the cheesecake and took a spoon from the drawer.

"Not a convincing response," Ash told her.

"She had some kind of a brain breakthrough," Trinity told him, wondering how to explain the situation without sounding ungrateful. "In less than twenty-four hours, she's made a miraculous recovery. Her processing is slower', and her speech isn't quite the same, but she's more like the person she used to be before the stroke."

"Which isn't necessarily a good thing for you and your sisters?"

"My mom has a strong personality."

"She's a force to be reckoned with," Ash agreed with a smile.

"That hasn't always been a boon for my sisters and me." Seeing that Thomas was still content in Ash's arms, she sat at the kitchen table and took a bite of cheesecake. It was sweet and velvety with the perfect amount of minty tang that balanced the richness of the cream cheese.

For the first time all day, Trinity felt completely relaxed. She appreciated that. She appreciated Ash and being able to talk to him.

"My mom wants Beth to accompany her on the book tour for the new edition of *A Woman's Odyssey*. She expects me to remain at the house with Thomas and Freya to help."

"Were you planning to stay in Magnolia?" Ash asked, sounding shocked.

"Would that be a bad thing?"

He shook his head. "Not as far as I'm concerned. But are you willing to give up your life out West?"

"I'm willing to do anything to keep my baby safe," she said as she took another bite. "Does cheesecake taste this good during daytime hours or is it a special trick—the indulgence of eating something so decadent at midnight?"

She looked at her plate as she asked the question like the dessert might be able to answer.

Then she realized something had changed in the atmosphere of the kitchen, and her gaze darted to Ash's. "What's wrong?"

His arms tightened around Thomas. "You said safe."

She blinked as panic shot through her. "You know what I mean. I want to give Thomas a good life."

"Who do you need to keep him safe from?" Ash demanded quietly. "I've had my suspicions. Were you not safe in Montana, Trinity?"

She pushed the plate away from her and pressed her

palms to the table. "It's late, and I'm tired. Maybe I used the wrong word."

"I don't think so. Tell me what you meant."

She thought about getting up from the table, taking her baby and walking back to her mother's house. She didn't owe this man an explanation or a window into her weakness or the stupid choices she'd previously made.

He took a step closer. "I will keep you safe. Both you and Thomas."

A nearly irresistible offer. But part of starting fresh was learning to stand on her own two feet. To take care of herself, no matter what that entailed.

And she knew that to do that, she had to stop blaming herself for what happened with Dave. Ash continued to study her, his gaze unreadable in the soft light of the kitchen.

"I left my ex-boyfriend because he..." She swallowed against the bile rising in her throat. "He was abusive, and I wouldn't allow Thomas to be raised by someone like that."

"Do you think he'll come after you?" Ash asked, his tone deceptively gentle. Trinity could see by his rigid posture and the muscle ticking in his jaw that there was nothing gentle about this man at the moment, but it didn't scare her.

"He doesn't know where I am," she explained. "He also doesn't know about Thomas. I'm sure he's moved on from me at this point. I was never truly important to him."

"I doubt that," Ash muttered.

"It doesn't matter. He's my past."

"What if he comes looking for you?"

"I'll leave," she said automatically.

"Running isn't an option forever, Trinity. Not for you or Thomas."

"I don't think it will come to that," she said, trying to

sound more confident than she felt. "I was in Colorado for most of the summer and fall, and he didn't come after me."

"Did he know where you were or have a way to reach you?"

She shook her head. "But there's no reason to think he would track me down in Magnolia."

"I need you to text me his full name, birth date, address, any information you have on him."

"Ash, this isn't your fight."

"To serve and protect," he said, repeating the words she'd spoken earlier. "That's the vow I took. Even if it wasn't, I would take care of you. I can't explain it, Trinity, but you mean..." He blew out a soft laugh. "I'm going to embarrass myself if I say anything more."

"I'm not weak and helpless."

"I don't think you are."

"My mom does. That's why she wants Beth to go with her and Freya to stay with me. She doesn't think I can handle being on my own with Thomas."

"A baby is a lot of work no matter what. Wanting or needing help isn't a bad thing."

"I know." She sighed. "In my rational mind, I understand that, but it feels like it means something about me. When I thought about staying in Magnolia, it was to raise my son and help my mom. I was going to be the strong one in my family. I don't know what to do if she's like before. She's nice to you and Michaela and to Shauna and her boys. But she's different with my sisters and me."

"Maybe there's a middle ground," he suggested.

"I find that hard to believe with May, but I hope so. Because suddenly I feel needy and weak, like I came crawling back to my mother's house to hide."

"You're talking to the guy who lives with his late wife's mom."

"I think it's clear that you are supporting her."

He looked down at Thomas, who was beginning to drift off to sleep in his arms. "That's true to an extent. It's also true that I was overwhelmed at the idea of being on my own with Michaela after Stacy died. She'd made it clear that the dedication to my career hurt my ability to be a good father. Suddenly, I'm a single dad with only that career to support my daughter. Helena and I have a mutually beneficial relationship, although Michaela and I will be moving to our own house after the first of the year. It's time for all of us."

"How do you feel about being on your own during the teenage years?"

He chuckled. "Nervous as hell. But it's the right thing. It's not as if Helena won't still be there for Michaela."

Trinity lifted a brow as she dug the spoon into the cheesecake's graham cracker crust. "I'm also sure you could find plenty of women willing to step in and offer a helping hand or a sympathetic shoulder for you."

His lips twitched. "Are you volunteering?"

She laughed despite the nerves that fluttered through her. "My shoulder's going to be caked with baby spit-up for the foreseeable future. I don't think I'm going to have time to support anybody but that little man in your arms."

"Maybe you could use some support, and not because you're weak, Trinity. You can be strong and not handle everything on your own."

"I wish I could believe you." She popped the last bite into her mouth and rose from the table. "Now that you've worked your baby-calming magic, I should get him back to the house and take advantage of possibly sleeping for a couple of hours. Thank you for the dessert."

She placed her empty plate and spoon in the dishwasher. "Thanks for the words of encouragement as well. I appreciate…"

Her throat clogged with emotion, which she wanted to blame on hormones and exhaustion. But she had a feeling they were just her reaction to Ash. "I appreciate you," she finished.

"Enough to eventually go out with me on a second date?"

"I didn't figure you'd want one," she admitted as she stepped closer to take the baby into her arms. "Is there any worse potential romance killer than going into labor on a first date?"

"That's one way to look at it. You could also decide it's going to be a great story to tell down the road."

She swallowed at the intensity in his dark eyes as he looked at her. Without allowing herself to worry about what she was doing, Trinity leaned in and brushed a kiss across his mouth. "I like how you think," she said.

Ash grinned like she'd just given him the best gift in the world. "I like how you kiss."

"I'll agree to a second date." She laughed when he pumped his fist after transferring Thomas to her. "Good night, Ash."

"Best night ever," he told her.

In this moment, she couldn't help but agree.

CHAPTER TWENTY-FIVE

"YOU NEED TO RELAX." Freya kept her smile in place as she and Trinity walked along the downtown sidewalk later that week.

"How can I relax? There's a guy with a camera filming me."

"Pretend the crew isn't there." Freya smiled and waved at a random stranger across the street like she was greeting an old friend. Because this was Magnolia, the somewhat befuddled woman waved back in the same manner, and the reality-show crew caught the whole exchange. "I do it all the time."

"I'm not a movie star," Trinity said, sounding exasperated.

Freya laughed out loud. "Honey, neither am I. Far from it. Have you ever faked anything? Gratitude…your qualifications for a job…an orgasm?"

Trinity snorted. "On occasion, but I'm not going to tell you what I've faked."

"You don't have to." Freya noticed her sister's death grip on the stroller handles loosen slightly. "Just channel your inner faker."

Trinity seemed to think about that. "From the moment I held Thomas in my arms, I've been faking that I know how to be a mother. I might even have Mom convinced, although I'm pretty sure Thomas is well aware that I have no idea what I'm doing."

Freya grabbed hold of the stroller and stepped in front of Trinity, blocking the crew's view of the two sisters. "You're doing fine, Trin. I don't know why you can't see that."

"Maybe it's because I'm too exhausted to have any type of perspective. It will get better."

Freya made a face. "Of course. In the meantime, you could let Mom or me help more. I think she'd like helping you."

"I think she'd like reading your book," Trinity countered and glanced over Freya's shoulder at the camera crew. "I think your fans would like to read your book. You're an excellent writer, Freya."

Freya felt panic begin to squeeze her lungs. "You haven't shown anyone, right? That manuscript was for your eyes only. Although I'm glad you like it. What did you think of the ending?"

"I haven't quite made it to the ending." Trinity looked at the ground. "I have another book I'm trying to finish."

Freya tried not to be hurt by that. She couldn't imagine what would take precedence over hers. Trinity continued to avoid eye contact and made a show of rearranging the blanket to cover Thomas.

"Greer gave you Mom's book," Freya said as realization dawned on her.

"Freya, could you face the camera? Any chance of stopping at the bakery? We could use some footage inside one of the stores."

For a moment, Freya had forgotten about the camera crew. They hadn't gone for the idea of her touring solo around the streets of Magnolia for Christmas, so she'd convinced Trinity to join her for an outing. The producers had tried to persuade her to include her mother in some of the footage, but she'd flat-out refused.

She would do a lot of things for a paycheck but not give airtime to her once-famous mother. She figured it would give May too much satisfaction. Plus, Freya struggled to get a read on her mother now that May had returned home, monumentally improved both physically and mentally from where she'd been weeks earlier. Leave it to Mom to keep them on their toes.

"Sure," she said with a fake smile that would easily fool the cameraman. "I could go for a coffee and afternoon treat."

"I knew it!" Jennie, the assistant producer handling Freya's shoot, jabbed a finger in the air. "You've gained weight since you've been home, haven't you?"

Freya blinked and heard Trinity let out a soft snort of disbelief. Topics that were off-limits in normal conversation were run-of-the-mill in the industry. "I don't think so. Why?"

Jennie looked perplexed. "I can't come up with another reason for you to be dressed the way you are. I figured you were trying to hide something. Either an unfortunate spray tan or a few extra pounds. It's not the end of the world, Freya. Once the holidays are over, you'll come back to California for preproduction on Love at the Five and Dime. A few weeks in the gym plus a round or two of colonics. You'll be right back where you need to be."

Back where she needed to be, Freya thought. How was that possible when she had no idea? She'd worn the dress from Mariella's shop and felt more comfortable—both in it and her own skin—than she had in years. So much for adopting a new look going forward.

"You look beautiful," Trinity told her with a gentle arm squeeze. The new mother faced the cameraman and producer. "She could eat a half-dozen bear claws a day and would still look beautiful. Did you all not get the memo on the body positivity movement?"

Freya glanced with alarm at the green light flashing on top of the camera. "They're recording," she said under her breath.

Trinity shrugged, her earlier nerves forgotten. "Let them. It was a rude statement that needed to be called out. You are beautiful and talented in many ways."

Go, little sister. "Let's get that bear claw." Freya offered the camera a conspiratorial wink, knowing she had to keep the potential audience in her corner during the clip. "When I'm in my hometown, calories do not count."

Smile in place as they entered Sunnyside Bakery, she greeted Mary Ellen with a cheery wave.

She wished she would have warned some of the business owners about filming but had felt like that was trying too hard. Plus, she didn't want to admit she was nervous about how the locals might respond.

She and Trinity ordered pastries and hot drinks while the two baristas working the counter gaped at the camera. Freya's cheeks were beginning to ache as she did her best to look like she belonged in Magnolia. That this was truly her home.

Suddenly she felt as nervous as Trinity. Would the camera pick up on how out of place she was in the town where she was raised? Once again, she wished she had done more prep instead of letting nerves dissuade her from reaching out.

Mary Ellen caught her eye, winked and stepped forward to coo over Thomas. "He looks just like you when you were a baby," she told Trinity and smiled at Freya.

The presence of the plump woman with the rosy cheeks and her graying hair up in a rhinestone clip did more to relax Freya than an entire row of drinks. "You were so excited to be a big sister," Mary Ellen revealed.

Freya had no idea if she told the truth or if the woman had missed her calling as an actress. "That's a bit far in the past for my memory, but I'm going to spoil my nephew like nobody's business. I don't even care that he's too young to appreciate the joys of holiday shopping. I'll make sure he appreciates the finer things."

"He'll appreciate having you to look after him," Mary Ellen said. For some reason, the words made Freya's throat clog with emotion.

"I'm going to take a load off," Trinity said, hands gripping the stroller again. "Don't forget the napkins, Freya."

As Trinity moved away with the stroller, Mary Ellen stepped closer to Freya, darting a glance at the camera out of the corner of her eye. "We're all looking forward to you announcing the winners of the holiday art contest. The kids have been working diligently on their projects. We can't wait to celebrate them tonight."

Freya blinked, well aware the camera was still rolling. She nodded even though she had no idea what the bakery owner was talking about. "I'm so happy to be a part of it."

Mary Ellen beamed, her smile bordering on conniving. "Avery is at her sister's art gallery right now. Weren't you going to stop by to work out the details of your involvement? I can give her a call so she knows you're coming."

"I guess I was." The barista handed her two drinks, and she held up one mock salute to the camera then gave the signal for them to stop filming.

"You didn't mention you were taking place in a public event." The producer nodded. "It'll be a perfect final few moments to your segment. We were planning to head out after this bit, but we'll stick around and get some footage from tonight. Local girl comes home famous and gives back to the community."

"Perfect," Freya repeated. "I'll text you the details once I confirm everything. Right now, I'm going to bring this decaf to my sister. We've had the baby out long enough."

"The baby and all that sisterly bonding was a nice touch," Jennie told her. "Your sister is funny with the mama bear routine." She waved a hand up and down in front of Freya. "I guess the new look fits for this town, but you can leave that dress behind when you return to California."

"Right," Freya agreed automatically. She loved the gardenia dress.

"We're going to start editing your footage back at the hotel," the producer said, then pointed at Freya. "Nice tip on the Wildflower Inn. It's exactly the kind of place we wanted to stay during filming."

"You bet." Freya cleared her throat, not wanting to admit she'd never actually visited the inn. "You can see why I love coming home."

The cameraman moved closer. "Any chance I could get a bear claw for the road?" he asked. "They smell incredible."

"Of course." Mary Ellen went behind the counter and did the honors herself, packing up a bag of mouthwatering pastries for the two-person crew.

Freya brought the drinks and the cinnamon roll Trinity had ordered to the table. "Will you text Beth to pick up you and Thomas?" she asked Trinity. They'd installed a car seat in both Beth and May's vehicles as well as Trinity's. "I can tell you need a rest. I'm going to stay in town and apparently go over a few things before doing MC duties at the Christmas on the Coast art award show tonight."

Trinity yawned then took a bite of the cinnamon roll. "Sounds good," she said like it was no big deal for Freya to be headlining a town activity. "I didn't realize you were involved."

"Me neither," Freya admitted. She stiffened as Mary Ellen put a hand on her shoulder.

"Isn't it wonderful?" the older woman asked. "Everyone will get such a kick out of seeing our little town on TV. It's great of you to volunteer to lend a hand in this way."

"Volun-told is more like it."

Mary Ellen's smile remained steady and sincere. "We appreciate you, Freya."

How was it that the woman knew exactly what to say to warm Freya's cynical Hollywood heart? She'd gotten so used to the notion of doing nice things quid pro quo that the idea of being valued for who she was meant more than it should.

"It's not a big deal. I'm benefiting as much as the town. Otherwise, I wouldn't have gone along with it."

"Sure," Mary Ellen agreed far too readily.

"You aren't fooling anyone, Frey," Trinity said as she stood. "You're a big softie. You always have been. The hardest part about tonight is that you can't announce that every kid is a winner."

"Not everyone wins in life," Freya muttered. "It's better to learn that sooner than later."

Trinity frowned. "I want Thomas to win," she said quietly. "It's just too hard to imagine him disappointed."

"Then we'll make sure he's one of the lucky ones," Freya promised her baby sister. And to her amazement, Trinity seemed to believe her.

"Love you, Frey." She gave Freya a quick hug then pushed the stroller toward the exit.

"I bet you would have pitched in even without the cameras," Mary Ellen said, lifting a hand when Freya would have protested. "Either way, you're doing a good thing for the town."

"And myself," Freya felt it necessary to add.

"I'll call Avery while you walk down." Mary Ellen didn't bother responding to Freya's words. "She'll be thrilled to have your help."

"Slim pickings in Magnolia." Freya sniffed. "If you consider me a big draw."

"We consider you one of us," Mary Ellen said, her smile gentle. "Have fun tonight, Freya." The older woman took a phone out of the front pocket of her apron as she turned away.

One of us. The thought reverberated through Freya as she left the bakery. She'd never felt like she belonged anywhere, not in Hollywood or her family. Her mother had made it abundantly clear in a myriad of ways that Freya didn't act the way May wanted or expected. While flouting her mother's expectations was the only way Freya had found to assert her independence, the constant effort cost her. And she wasn't sure she was willing to continue to pay.

Did she have to?

A shiver passed through her as she walked along the sidewalk toward The Reed Gallery, which had been the artistic home of the painter Niall Reed, Magnolia's most famous resident for several decades.

Now his daughter, Carrie, a well-respected artist whose reputation was quickly eclipsing that of her male-chauvinist father, had taken over running the gallery. It not only featured her paintings but offerings from a wide range of artists from around the region.

Obviously, Carrie also gave back to the community since the gallery had sponsored the prize for the holiday art contest. The winner would have their creation featured as the primary graphic for next year's holiday celebration and be given a two-hundred-dollar cash prize.

Tonight's celebration was the culmination of a month of holiday activities in town, but Freya hadn't considered being a part of it.

What business did she have celebrating the town she'd left behind?

But touring Magnolia with the crew had made her see the town in a brighter light than before. She knew hers wasn't the only small town in America working to revitalize its community.

Would her segment highlighting the town bring new visitors who might want to experience the charm for themselves? And how many other places could benefit from a bit of national attention?

There were food network shows that made hotspot destinations of local eateries around the country. Renovation programs that could turn a sleepy town into a modern mecca. What about a show that focused on local perspectives on small towns?

With Freya as the host.

What if she could parlay her D-list fame into something that felt purposeful? If people saw her as more than a reality show star, would she feel comfortable also going after her dream of becoming a published author? She would be legitimate. Heck, her mother might finally see her as worthy of respect and love.

Mary Ellen had said May was proud, but Freya still had difficulty believing it.

What if she had options beyond the reality circuit that no longer held any appeal?

She entered the gallery, her entire body tingling with

possibility, only to come up short as she practically ran smack into Christopher Greer.

"You're here," she announced as if he didn't realize it.

His eyes lit in the special way that seemed directed only at her. "I had a meeting with Carrie."

"During which I convinced him to help me with a book proposal," a sweet voice announced. A tall woman, lean with caramel-colored hair and delicate—almost ethereal—features, came forward. "You must be Freya. I'm Carrie. I see you already know the most generous agent in all of publishing."

"Flattery will get you everywhere," Greer said with a laugh. "I'll let Avery know Freya is here."

"My mom works with Greer," Freya said, trying to ignore the pang of jealousy she had at the apparent affection between Greer and Carrie.

"Oh, yes. We're so happy to hear that May is doing better." Carrie offered a genuine smile. "She's a treasure. I'm not sure how we didn't know each other growing up."

Freya tried to return the smile, although her buoyant mood from minutes earlier had started to sag. "My sisters and I went to school in the next district over for a year. Mom had an issue with the Magnolia schools at some point, so she moved us." More like the Magnolia schools paid attention to attendance and parental involvement, which did not sit well with free-spirited, rule-defying May. "But then we transferred back because it was a headache for her to drive us across town."

"That makes sense." Carrie wrinkled her adorable nose. "I've read your mom's book. I have a feeling she wouldn't have been besties with my dad. He had the misogyny thing down to an art." She raised her arms to the open, airy space surrounding them. There were framed paintings in several different styles on the walls, along with shelving at one end with various sculptures and blown glass items. "I do understand the irony of that statement."

Freya felt her mouth relax into a real smile. "Oh, May would have showed him the error of his ways. I am certain of that. You mentioned a book. Are you an author as well as an artist?"

Carrie looked almost embarrassed. "I'm writing and illustrating a children's book. It's a lesson about the value of individuality and creative expression. Let's just say I'm working out some childhood issues on the page. I'm not sure I would have had the courage to send it out to publishing houses without Greer's support. I wish we could get him to stay in town year-round." She chuckled. "Several single women I know wish the same thing."

Once again, Freya tried to tamp down the jealousy that stabbed her lungs, making it hard to breathe. She had no claim on Christopher Greer. "Are you sure you can trust him? I don't have much experience with literary agents, but the film and talent agents I know in Hollywood aren't exactly well known for their honor and commitment to doing the right thing."

"Hollywood isn't a place I'd want to spend any time," Carrie said. "You must be extremely strong to have navigated the entertainment business and remain down-to-earth and true to your roots."

Freya blinked. "What makes you think I'm those things? You don't know me."

"Greer speaks highly of you. Beth, too, although I've only met your sister once or twice. But it's clear that Greer thinks you're the bee's knees."

Freya was saved from responding to that shocking bit of news when Greer and a cool blonde, who she assumed must be Avery Atwell, entered the gallery from a room in the back.

Her hackles immediately went up as she took in Avery's slim-cut silk suit. She didn't look half as kind and generous as Carrie, and Freya couldn't imagine the woman needing help with anything.

Once again, Freya was mistaken in her snap judgment.

Avery approached and threw her arms around Freya. "You are a godsend. It's going to be such an opportunity for the kids to have their artwork featured on national television."

"It's a reality show, and not exactly a well-respected one," Freya pointed out. "I'm not really a celebrity."

Avery tsked like a schoolteacher. "How many Instagram followers do you have?"

Freya shrugged. "A couple hundred thousand."

"Will you post about tonight to those followers?"

"Sure."

"Would you be willing to post a link to the site we have set up for donations toward the community art program?" Avery's eyes twinkled, and Freya realized she'd underestimated this woman's understanding of how Freya could benefit her initiative.

"Of course."

"Then you are officially my new best friend."

Freya's heart thumped in a happy rhythm at the idea of more friends. True friends. Ones who mattered and added to this unfamiliar sense of belonging that she wanted more than she would have thought possible.

She drew a deep breath and held it for a moment as if it would allow the feeling to stick. Then she nodded with a sincere smile. "I'd like that."

CHAPTER TWENTY-SIX

BETH SAT IN her car at the curb of her mother's house on Christmas Eve, just like she had a month earlier at the start of the holiday season, staring straight ahead as she hummed along with Mariah Carey.

All Beth wanted for Christmas was the weight of expectations and obligations to be lifted from her shoulders. Could she make a wish list for Santa and put that at the top of it?

The worst part was that so much of her worry and anxiety were self-imposed. Her sisters had already given her permission to leave, ostensibly taking up the torch of maternal responsibility so that she could be free to go after her dreams.

Only she couldn't seem to allow herself to relinquish control. May wasn't even to blame at this point. Yes, her mother had assumed Beth would help on the book tour without asking first, but that was to be expected. Beth had always made herself available to her mother without question.

Why would May assume things should be any different if Beth didn't advocate for herself?

She could readily counsel Freya on reinventing herself into the person she wanted to be and give Trinity the advice to claim the life she wanted for herself and her son. When it came to her own wants and needs, she still didn't know how to press for them.

A knock at the window made her startle, and she whipped

around to find Declan stepping back, hands up like she was pointing a gun at him.

Doing her best not to look as freaked out as she felt, Beth opened the car door and stepped into the cold night. This part of the coast typically stayed temperate, even in winter, but a low-pressure system had stalled over the town, causing temperatures to drop to just below freezing.

The humidity made it feel at least ten degrees colder, and tiny ice crystals floated in the air. The forecast called for snow, and despite Beth's tumbling emotions, she was excited about the prospect of a white Christmas.

"You good?" Declan asked, searching her face.

"More than you could ever know," she sang with fake cheer.

"So not at all," he said with a gruff laugh and pulled her close.

She went willingly, burying her face in his canvas jacket and breathing in the now-familiar scent of him—spicy, fresh and all male. "Christmas makes a lot of people feel weird. It's not just me."

"Until this year, I've done my best to ignore the fact that Christmas even existed. No judgment here."

She appreciated that about him, the fact that she could say anything—be herself in a way she couldn't even with her sisters—and still feel confident that he wouldn't judge her for it. Maybe it was because she didn't mean enough to him to worry over, but it still helped calm her nerves.

"It's hard to ignore the holidays in a town like Magnolia." She spoke into his jacket. "We kind of go all out."

"You know the best part about this Christmas season for me?"

She leaned back and looked up at him. "Shauna's baking ability?"

"Spending time with you. Making things special for you. I wasn't expecting this, Beth. I never anticipated how you would change—"

"Beth!"

She looked over her shoulder to find her mother waving from the front porch. "We ready to decorate cookies," May called.

"If I didn't know better," Declan said with a laugh as he released her, "I would say your mother was cock blocking me."

Beth felt her shoulders shake with laughter. "May has never had healthy boundaries."

"I'll let you get to your cookies," he told her. "Text me later."

She grimaced. "I'm spending the night here. We thought it would be nice for Mom to have us all wake up together on Christmas morning." She expected Declan to seem put out by her being unavailable. Greg certainly would have been when they were together.

But Dec nodded, taking it in stride as he did everything. "I know Shauna wants to stop by tomorrow with a gift for your mother. So let's leave it at I'll see you later."

"Merry Christmas." She rose on her tiptoes to kiss him. She didn't know if Declan realized how much his soothing presence did for her, but she walked up the steps to her mother's house with far less trepidation than she would have imagined thanks to those minutes with him.

May wrapped her in a tight hug as she entered. Even Mr. Jingles meandered over to rub against her ankles. "I love you, Bethy," she said. Her mother had continued to be effusively affectionate even after the astonishing strides she'd made in her recovery.

Beth had wondered if her mother's demonstrative nature resulted from the stroke and would disappear with a return to health. But May continued to offer hugs and words of love—a strange amalgamation of her bullish pre-stroke personality and the caring mom she'd become since the incident.

"That boy likes you," May said. She wore an embroidered skirt that fell nearly to her ankles and a peasant blouse with a chunky necklace. "He has good taste."

Color rose to Beth's cheeks that could not be blamed on the cold air. She'd never had the kind of relationship with her mother where they could discuss her boyfriends, not that there had been many before Greg. "He'll be leaving town soon," she said, trying to sound as though it didn't matter. "Once Shauna is weight-bearing again, he's getting on with his life."

May didn't look convinced but led Beth into the house. "He likes you. You like him, too."

Beth was saved from answering when Freya gestured to them from the kitchen. "We can't figure out how to get the stupid spritzer to dispense cookies. We need a spritz expert on the job."

Beth smiled, and her heart warmed when May took her hand. "Beth the expert," May confirmed as they walked forward.

It was true, if mildly embarrassing. Beth's eighth-grade teacher had encouraged students to bake cookies for the class holiday party. May had been out of town speaking at a women's empowerment retreat that week, which meant Beth had been on her own with baking.

The domestic arts didn't come naturally to any Carlyle woman, and she'd forgotten to add baking soda to her dough. The cookies she'd baked had ended up flat as pancakes but bringing them in got her extra credit, so she'd slathered them with frosting, ignored the sloppy mess and plated them for school.

The other girls, none of whom were her friends to begin with, had made fun of her sad attempt. The girl who had won the contest did so with neat rows of adorable spritz cookies in the shapes of trees and stars and perfectly symmetrical angels. It was the kind of order that Beth craved in her life but had never come close to achieving in their chaotic household.

By some strange coincidence, her mother had called that night to check in on the girls. May often didn't bother to communicate while she was away for work, needing to focus on her audience and assuming Beth had things under control. In a move that was just as out of character, Beth burst into tears at the sound of her mother's voice and cried about her awful cookies and insisted that the only thing on her wish list for Christmas was a cookie spritzer.

May had laughed off her request, but on Christmas morning, a colorfully wrapped box had appeared under the tree with a cookie spritzer inside. May had even splurged for an expansion pack of various shapes. For the next six months, Beth had made cookies to celebrate every holiday on the calendar. Mostly a celebration that her mother had made an effort to do something thoughtful.

Beth never had an issue directing her sisters, and tonight's cookie baking activity was no different. However, their mother taking part was a huge change. May willingly pitched in with the tasks Beth assigned her, and then transitioned to holding Thomas when he woke from his nap.

Maybe things really had changed with their mother.

Normally, May engaged with a light that was brighter than the sun, her daughters left to orbit around her. Tonight she seemed content to let each of them take the spotlight in turn.

They baked cookies, then heated up and ate frozen pizza. Grocery-store pizza might not seem like traditional Christmas Eve fare, but it's what they'd had every year growing up.

Beth wasn't sure how it started. Even during her marriage, when they'd gone to his parents' for a big Christmas Eve family get-together, she always made pizza, either before or after. The familiarity of it gave her a curious, comforting feeling of home. Greg had made fun of her, and she'd told herself every year that she was not going to bother. She always did.

Now she understood that traditions didn't have to be elaborate or formal. They just needed to be cherished. Pizza crust that tasted like cardboard with stringy cheese and bland tomato sauce was good enough for her.

She might even make a Jell-O salad tomorrow as a dinner side dish, the way her grandmother used to when she was very young.

"I have gifts," May announced as they cleared the dinner plates.

"I thought we were going to open gifts tomorrow," Freya protested immediately. "On Christmas morning. That's what we do."

Beth laughed. "You don't have yours wrapped yet."

"Because I thought I'd have time tonight," her sister countered.

Freya had always waited to the last minute.

"One from me tonight," their mother said. Without waiting for agreement, she carried Thomas into the living room.

Beth had initially balked at the idea of fussing with a real tree while their mom was in the rehabilitation facility. But Trinity insisted, so Greer had gotten a Douglas fir for them.

And they'd used the vintage decoupage ornaments and colored glass balls plus colored lights to make it look festive.

Butterflies danced along Beth's spine as she took the seat along with her sisters on the chintz couch in the living room. Maybe they should think of getting her mom one of those motorized recliners that would help her get up and down more easily.

It was difficult to think of May as a mere mortal even after the stroke. Beth wouldn't be surprised to learn her mother had somehow willed her brain to heal with miraculous speed from the sheer force of her personality.

She reminded herself that that wasn't such a bad thing, and maybe she'd inherited some of her mom's determination.

May looked lovely in the soft glow of the lights hanging from the tree. She bent forward, her movements slow but steady, and picked up three matching gift bags.

"For you," she said as she turned and held up the bags. She gave one to each of the girls then stepped back to watch them open the packages.

Without saying a word, Beth, Freya and Trinity coordinated their timing.

Beth wasn't sure what to think as she unfolded the piece of paper inside the bag. Perhaps May planned to take the three of them on a girls' trip or treat them to an afternoon of pampering at a local day spa. She felt her eyes widen as she read what turned out to be an article from a fancy New York lifestyle magazine. One particular quote stood out to Beth: "The updated edition of *A Woman's Odyssey* demonstrates that, once again, May Carlyle is the mother we all wish we could have. She shows insight and compassion as she tackles the issues her grown daughters have faced and discusses her dreams for them—and for every woman who needs a champion."

"What the hell is this?" Freya demanded, her voice a low growl. "Does this mean you talked about us in your book?" Freya clenched her fist around the now-empty bag in her lap. The paper crackled in the silence that had fallen over their group. "Mom, you had no right. We are not fodder for your publishing ambitions."

May's smile faded. "I thought you'd appreciate it the most. You should be happy, Freya. This will benefit you. I have contacts. Can introduce you to people who help with your book. You good, Frey."

"You read my book?" Freya turned her back on Beth to glare at Trinity. "You gave her my book?"

"I didn't give it to her." Trinity's knuckles went white as she held the article's edges in a death grip. "She saw me reading it and, well, it's hard to say no to Mom."

"You gave Trinity a copy of your book and not me?" Beth reached out and shoved Freya's shoulder. "Why didn't you trust me to read it?"

"You know why." Freya's voice sounded defensive and sharp, a tone Beth had heard a thousand times when they were younger.

"If I knew why I wouldn't ask."

"By the way, I'd like to know why Trinity didn't tell us she was also reading Mom's book."

"Excuse me?" Beth sputtered. "Trin, you had them both?"

"This isn't my fault," Trinity whispered, clearly miserable.

Freya snorted. "Maybe this universal mother garbage makes more sense to Trinity, and that's why—"

"It's not garbage," May interrupted, but Beth didn't spare her a glance. Not yet.

It felt like she'd suffered a one-two punch from her baby sister.

"You had both books and didn't share?" she asked again, still unable to believe it.

"I was going to, but I've been busy. You know that."

"Too busy to even mention it?"

"Yes," her sister said even as she refused to meet Beth's gaze. "Excuse me for not being able to handle motherhood like it's a walk in the park. I'm sure you would do a much better job."

"That's not what I said or implied." Beth spoke through clenched teeth. "Don't try to make this about me."

"Isn't it about you?" Trinity countered. "And the fact that you don't have control over this. You aren't the boss of who people share their work with. Maybe you would have been invited to read them if you weren't so judgmental."

Beth tossed the article to the coffee table and rose. "I'm not judgmental." She took a step toward Trinity only to have Freya stretch out a leg, effectively blocking her. The two of them against her, just like it used to be. Rage rushed through her, fiery and destructive like molten lava.

"Don't put that on me, Trin. Have I judged you for coming back here with no plan for yours or your baby's future, no clue how to provide a life for him? Or have I supported you?"

Trinity grimaced. She also rose and inched toward Thomas's bassinet. "I thought it was the latter," she said quietly. "Now, I'm not so sure."

"This isn't about me," Beth repeated.

"Why are you acting like this?" May held out her arms like she could embrace all of them at once. She sounded genuinely mystified. "You should be happy. I spoke my heart in those pages, beautiful words about each of you."

Beth shook her head and finally turned her attention to her mother. To the confrontation that she could no longer avoid. "Did you ever stop to consider that we don't want your words? We want you to be our mom—for that to be enough. It's never been enough. We've never been—"

"You don't know how I feel," May said. "How I felt for those weeks with my brain whirling."

"I know that you were kind and loving," Beth told her, unable to avoid the truth. "I know that you cared about us."

"I care. I always cared. I want to help you. Let me—"

"We don't need your help anymore," Freya said slowly. "We needed you when we were kids, and you weren't there. Literally." She held up her hands. "You weren't here. That's why frozen pizza is our tradition on Christmas Eve. Frozen dinners and packaged food. Simply getting by has always been our tradition. It's what you gave us."

"I'm proud of each of you."

Beth could see the tears in her mother's eyes but didn't understand why this was such a shock to May.

"How could I done such a bad job when you all turned out so good?" May challenged.

"We raised ourselves." As quickly as Beth's anger had come, it disappeared. Instead, she felt nothing. The emptiness burned far more than the anger ever had.

"Congratulations on your new book, Mom. I want no part of it. Merry Christmas." She grabbed her coat from the hook in the hallway and walked out into the cold, silent night.

CHAPTER TWENTY-SEVEN

BETH DROVE AROUND FOR…it was hard to say how long. She went past her high school, which seemed a little run-down and far less intimidating than it had when she was younger.

She wished she'd handled things differently, not just tonight but when back when she, Freya and Trinity were trying to navigate their lives around their narcissistic, sometimes negligent mother. Why had she thought May's personality changes were sustainable?

Hope was a fruitless endeavor when it came to her mother.

Still, she couldn't help wishing she might reach a point where she could appreciate the mom she'd had for those couple of weeks. She would not feel guilty for loving that mom more than her healthy one.

Her feelings might not be the most admirable, but she was entitled to them. At least she could give herself that grace. Once again, the one person she wanted to lean on for comfort was Declan. How long could she fool herself into thinking it was merely a fleeting connection between them? Nothing about her feelings for Dec was casual.

She loved him.

Beth drew in a shaky breath as she allowed the truth to wash over her—a truth her heart already understood.

Tonight's family debacle made her more certain about her decision to leave Magnolia. What choice did she have and what should she do about her feelings for Declan?

Yet even after quarreling, it still hurt to think about leaving her mom and sisters. She liked the closeness of the past weeks, but Beth didn't know how to set boundaries or advocate for her own needs and still maintain those relationships. Old patterns were too tempting when things got hard.

What if she didn't have to lose everyone? Once Shauna didn't need him, Declan had no fixed ties to this town.

Perhaps the reason he hadn't set down roots was because no one had ever asked him to before. No one had chosen him. Beth wanted to change that.

Fingers trembling, she texted him that her plans for the evening had changed and was he available?

Christmas was a time for wishes and miracles coming true. Beth wanted hers to be the miracle of finally trusting she was worthy and deserving of love and the happiness it could bring into her life.

His response was almost immediate. Instead of agreeing to come to her house, Declan asked her to meet him at Champions.

She checked her watch because she knew the bar was closing early on Christmas Eve and messaged him that she could be there in ten minutes.

Arriving before him, she parked at the curb. It was late enough that the whole of the town had rolled up the sidewalks for the evening, although each shop had left lights glowing in the windows. The street had a magical quality as a result, and it didn't surprise Beth when a few chunky flurries landed on the front window of her car.

It felt like a sign. What could be better than a white Christmas to renew her waning hope?

Even her thoughts about her mom and tonight's argument lessened in severity as snow continued to fall like it was settling her difficult emotions into something gentler.

Declan parked his truck next to her car, and she waited under a nearby streetlight, then greeted him with a lingering kiss.

"It's a white Christmas." She tipped back her head and opened her mouth to catch the puffy flakes.

When she'd left her mother's house, it had been in a state of emptiness and regret. Now she felt hope again—both for a new life and love to see her through whatever came her way. With Declan at her side, there was nothing she couldn't overcome.

Once the stranglehold of the past had released its grip on her, she would reunite with her sisters and even her mother—this time on her terms. Declan would help her to define those terms. He would be her rock.

"This means your Christmas wishes will come true," she told him. The tenderness in his eyes as he stared down at her was all the confirmation she needed that this was the right path. "But what are we doing here? The bar's closed."

He kissed her again and drew in a deep breath. "I want to show you something inside." He inclined his head to study her. "Why aren't you with your family?"

She shrugged. Leave it to Declan not to be fooled by her buoyant spirits. He could see to the heart of her.

"Things didn't exactly go as planned tonight."

"How far off the plan?"

She tried for a smile. "A twenty-car pileup on the highway during a blinding snowstorm with a tornado heading in that direction not as planned."

He cringed. "Are you okay?"

"In some ways I am, and in some ways I'm not. Let's not focus on the bad right now. I can get so busy focusing on other people that I forget to care for myself. You've helped me remember that my needs matter, too."

He nodded solemnly. "You matter. You're important to me, Beth. I—"

An SUV pulled around the corner carrying a load of teenagers who'd probably snuck out for a joy ride in the snow. Someone rolled down the window as they sped past, wolf-whistling and calling out Christmas greetings.

Declan blinked as he stared after them. "This is some town. In most places, gangs of teenagers would be stealing yard ornaments and generally wreaking havoc. Here they shout wishes for a Merry Christmas."

He chuckled and took her hand. "Let's go inside. The snow is great, but it's cold."

"Are you going soft on me?" She poked him in the ribs with her free hand. "What happened to your big talk about Chicago winters? I think you've spent too much time in town. It's time for a change."

His fingers squeezed hers. "It's time for a change," he agreed. There was something about the seriousness in his tone that gave her pause.

Maybe this was when he would end things because he was leaving. They'd tacitly agreed to that from the start. How would he react when she suggested he accompany her to Nashville?

Even if he wasn't willing to admit he could settle down, they could still see each other. He traveled, and Nashville was an accessible airport for a connection. Her schedule would be fixed during the program, but they'd find a way to make it work.

Beth wanted so badly to make it work.

He flipped on the lights inside the bar. The place felt almost spookily silent. Even when she'd stopped by during off-hours, there'd been at least one or two customers plus a bartender and always music from the jukebox. Now it was quiet, and a tendril of doubt spiraled through her. She pushed it away.

"It feels strange, like we're doing something illicit by being here when the bar is closed." She flicked a glance at the door. "Can you imagine the trouble a car full of rowdy teenagers could get into if they were in our situation?"

"I can," Declan said. His deep voice sounded different, almost hesitant. "But it's just us."

"Is everything okay?" He was always checking on her, but Beth could tell something was going on.

His Adam's apple bobbed as he swallowed. "I hope so. Damn, I haven't been nervous like this since I planted a kiss on Brandie Knolls under the slide on the playground in fourth grade."

"You had your first kiss in fourth grade?" Beth grinned. "What an overachiever."

As she'd wanted, the teasing seemed to help relax him a bit. "Hardly. We clinked teeth. It was bad."

"You've gotten better," she assured him, turning in a circle to take in the whole space.

Declan moved closer and laced their fingers together. "You make it better," he said, and her heart tumbled.

"I need to talk to you about something." She'd expected to ask him about Nashville curled up together on her sofa in front of the tiny tree he'd brought her, but she didn't want to wait. An empty bar would have to make do.

"Me first." He squeezed her hands and then released one to dig in the pocket of his canvas jacket. "Before I chicken out."

Her heart picked up speed. It didn't feel as though he was going to break up with her, but she'd had enough surprises lately that she knew better than to trust her instincts.

He pulled out a small box wrapped in bright red paper. "Merry Christmas, Beth. I hope you like it."

"Your gift is at my house." She took the box from him and stepped back. "Should I wait, and we can open them at the same time?"

"No waiting."

"Okay. I'm sure I'll love whatever it is, Declan. You don't have to be nervous."

"Just open it."

She ran a finger under the taped seam to reveal a plain brown box. She placed the ribbon and wrapping paper on a nearby table then opened the lid.

"It's a key." She studied the small, gold piece of metal, unsure how this was a gift to her but not wanting to hurt his feelings.

"It's the key to Champions."

She blinked then glanced up at him, even more confused. "I don't understand."

"I bought the bar from Bill," he said proudly. "I'm staying in Magnolia, Beth. For you. For our future."

"No," she whispered, placing the key and the box on the table. "You can't."

His head snapped back like she'd slapped him.

"That didn't come out right." She waved her hands then pressed them to her belly. Her stomach pitched like Declan's announcement was the first giant dip on a roller coaster. Her heart did not want a ticket for this ride and what she saw coming down the track.

"Declan, I'm leaving."

"I don't understand." His gaze flicked to the key in the box on the table and back to her. "This is your home."

"I'm moving to Nashville to go back to school. It's a nurse practitioner program." Her throat felt dry, hands clammy. Why did it feel as though following her plan was going to wreck every other aspect of her life? Was this how goals were supposed to work? "Classes start after the New Year."

"How long have you known?" He pressed two fingers to his temple as if his head had started pounding. She knew the feeling.

"It's been in the works for a while. It was something I decided to do after my divorce. I needed a new path and something for myself—to get away. When my mom had the stroke, I wasn't sure it was going to work. But I enrolled and rented an apartment near the Vanderbilt campus. I'm going to make it work. I have to."

"You didn't think to share any of this with me?" He scrubbed a hand over his face, and when he looked at her again, all of the emotion she'd seen in his gaze was gone. His eyes were flat gray—no storm, no turbulence, no warmth.

"I didn't think it would matter. At first, I was worried about telling my mom and my sisters. You were—"

"Not a priority," he finished.

She shook her head. "You were unexpected. This…" She gestured between the two of them. "We were unexpected. I was going to ask you to go with me."

"To Nashville?" He raised a brow.

"Yes. I wouldn't ask for some big commitment. You travel. We could keep it…light, casual, fun." This was not at all how she'd wanted to broach the subject of them continuing their relationship. She didn't want casual from Declan.

But he seemed to have shut down, so that was all she felt like she could offer without risking total humiliation and heartbreak. Hadn't she been through enough of that? Didn't she deserve something easy?

"You said you didn't do relationships," she reminded him. "If that's what you want, then I…"

"What?" he demanded. "You'll change your plans for me?"

She wanted to tell him she'd changed everything. These past few weeks with him had already changed her. "Magnolia and Nashville aren't that far apart," she offered, the words sounding lame even to her ears. "It's a day's drive. We could have weekends where—"

"I don't want a casual weekend relationship with you, Beth. I made a grand gesture." He held up his hands to indicate the bar.

"But you didn't ask me if it's what I wanted. Do you know how much of my life I've spent with people making choices that I had to work around?"

"You wanted someone to depend on. I'm ready to be that person if you'll let me."

In truth, Beth didn't know what she wanted. Ever since the end of her marriage and even before that, she'd been making choices based on not only other people's criteria but things she thought were right for her without really checking in with herself to know that they were what she wanted.

"I can't." She wished she could give him something else. "Not like this. If you could—"

"I won't change my plans again." Declan's tone was as frigid as the ocean water at the beach in winter. "I thought this would make you happy."

It should, but all of Beth's fears about relinquishing her power to choose a future that worked for her came rushing back. Drowning her with doubt and regret. Why had she thought she could make a go of it with Declan? It wasn't him who was the problem. The past had broken her, and she didn't know how to overcome it.

"I'm sorry," she told him. "I don't think I know how to be happy."

She sucked in a breath as her declaration hung in the air between them. It was the most honest thing she'd ever shared with another person, but it didn't make things different. It couldn't fix what was broken inside her.

"Good luck in Nashville," Declan said, his voice devoid of emotion. "I hope you figure it out."

Me, too, Beth thought but didn't say the words because they might genuinely break her open.

Instead she turned for the door before the tears rising fast and furious to her eyes blinded her.

"Merry Christmas, Declan," she whispered on her way out.

CHAPTER TWENTY-EIGHT

"WOULD YOU DARE to wear this dress if you were me?" Freya glanced from Mr. Jingles to survey herself in the mirror hanging on the closet door in her childhood bedroom the day after Christmas. She did not like the person she saw staring back at her.

Her mother's cat, who was sleeping at the foot of her bed, yawned and began to clean his toe beans, dismissing both Freya and her wardrobe conundrum. She was getting ready to leave for the open house Garrett Dawes had invited her to and wore a skin-tight and ruched black bandage dress that would have made the Kardashian sisters proud.

The sheath didn't reveal much skin but left even less to the imagination. As the producer on the reality show segment noticed, Freya had put on weight during her time in Magnolia, making the dress even more body hugging.

She wasn't ashamed of her curves, but the past few weeks showed her that her body and the image the public wanted her to portray weren't all she had to offer. After the argument with Beth, she'd made the mistake of retreating into her room and checking the reactions to her segment on the reality holiday special.

Some were kind, praising her for showing a more genuine side of herself in her hometown. The ones she couldn't get out of her mind were the harsh comments, from snarky remarks about the modest dress to her weight gain. Armchair critics seemed to have no problem trolling her for being dull without some sort of drama to make her more interesting.

Freya wished she weren't affected by the cruelty, but she couldn't lie—at least to herself.

If she couldn't change her reputation, she might as well lean into it, which had led her to choose the form-fitting dress for the party. She'd likely stick out like a sore thumb with the hardware store crowd, and maybe that's what she needed to remind herself she didn't fit into this close-knit, quaint town. The sooner she stopped trying to, the better.

"You're going to make me cry with jealousy," Trinity said, cradling her son in her arms as Freya descended the steps.

Trin had been almost preternaturally bubbly since the blow-up on Christmas Eve. May had been subdued yesterday and spent most of the day in bed, using the excuse that she needed to rest. Beth hadn't made an appearance other than a text to say she wasn't feeling well and wishing each of them a happy holiday.

It wasn't like their older sister to bail when May expected something, and their mother had certainly wanted all of them together for Christmas. As irritated as Beth made Freya, she respected her sister for standing her ground on something. Freya just wished it hadn't been Christmas and that her manuscript hadn't been part of the incident. She didn't want to fight with Beth any longer.

Freya ran her hands along her hips and flashed Trinity a demure smile. "Just something I found in the back of my closet."

"You look way too big-budget for a town like Magnolia."

The dress might be expensive, yet Freya's smile wobbled because it was hard to deny that she felt cheap in it. She suppressed a groan as her mother came around the corner from the kitchen.

"I thought you were at Shauna's, Mom. Do you want to go to Garrett and Lily's open house with me? I'm sure you're invited."

May shook her head. "I'm tired. Twins are cute but a handful." Her gaze took in Freya from head to toe, and the corners of her mouth drew down.

"Go ahead." Freya lifted her arms in supplication. "Tell me how awful I am for wearing this dress to a party with your friends and neighbors. I'm sure you want to."

"You are beautiful," May said softly. "You live life on your terms, Frey. I'm proud."

Trinity's eyes sparkled, and she gave Freya a definite I-told-you-so nod. "You need to read Mom's book," Trinity said. "You and Beth both. It's not what you think."

May nodded. "Things have changed. I didn't mean to be a bad mom. It's not too late if you give me another chance."

Freya crossed her arms over her chest like she could block out the yearning she had for her mother's love and acceptance. Hadn't she learned not to rely on anyone? "What's going on? Is this because you want Beth to go with you on tour and me to stay with Trinity because—"

"I don't need you to stay," Trinity interrupted. "I'll figure it out."

Freya didn't take her eyes off of May.

"I changed before the stroke, but it made me realize…" May shook her head. "I want to have this conversation with Beth, too. I called her and texted, but she won't answer."

"I think Beth needs a break, Mom." It was strange for Freya to find herself defending her older sister.

"I know," May agreed, which felt even stranger.

Freya glanced at her watch. "I need to go, or I'm going to miss the party. If either of you wants to come with—"

"We can start over," May said, her tone beseeching.

"I can't do this right now, Mom. Get Beth to agree to meet and then we'll all talk."

"Will you at least agree to read the new section of Mom's book?" Trinity asked. "I'm going to drop off a copy to Beth today as well."

Sweet Trinity, lobbying for peace in their family. Freya nodded and tried not to notice her mother's sigh of relief at her acquiescence. Why in the world were a few updated pages of prose so important?

"Don't forget Thomas is being baptized on Sunday," Trinity continued quickly, then dropped a gentle kiss on the baby's head. "We can talk then—all of us together again."

"It will have to be a short conversation. This morning I scheduled a flight to Vegas Sunday night. I've agreed to a paid appearance at one of the clubs on New Year's Eve."

May pressed a hand to her chest like she had trouble catching her breath. "You're leaving?"

"Trinity just said she didn't need help."

"That doesn't mean I don't want you to stay," Trinity countered.

"I can always come back for a visit. There isn't anything for me in this town. I don't belong here." Both her mother and Trinity looked like they wanted to argue, but neither of them did.

"It's your choice," May murmured.

Freya wasn't sure what she expected. If her mother begged anyone to stay, it would be Beth. Beth was always the most dependable daughter, but Freya made herself expendable on purpose. She had no one else to blame.

"Put the book in my bedroom," she told Trinity. "I'll

see you in a bit." She walked out of the house, unsure why she was bothering to go to this party when she'd decided to leave Magnolia.

In her heart, she knew it was because Greer would be there, and she wanted to see him despite knowing she shouldn't.

She hadn't returned his recent texts or answered his calls. He'd stopped by the house yesterday, but Freya had retreated to her bedroom like a coward instead of facing him.

Maybe she wanted to publicly prove to them both that they were not a good fit. Her mother had told her that Greer would be heading back to Boston after the first of the year because Garrett had pushed through his bout of writer's block. All that Christmas cheer and manual labor worked wonders. It had for Freya. She'd polished her manuscript until it glowed like the North Star but still refused to consider submitting it to an editor or allowing her mom to share it with Greer.

The business of putting herself out there as a celebrity was enough of a challenge these days when something as simple as a different type of dress made her a target for social media trolling. The thought of sharing her creativity and being judged for it was more than she could bear.

It took less than ten minutes to reach Garrett and Lily's house on a tree-lined street a few blocks from downtown. There were still patches of snow on the lawns, and icicles had formed at the edges of some of the low-hanging branches.

The temperature was supposed to begin climbing again tomorrow, so Freya appreciated this brief holiday sojourn into winter weather.

The heels of her round-toe pumps clicked on the concrete as she approached the two-story, whitewashed brick house. Cars lined the street on both sides, and the sound of lively conversation and music hit her as soon as she opened the front door.

For a moment, she thought about turning around. Her act of defiance in wearing the bandage dress suddenly felt immature and ridiculous. She didn't need her clothes to prove she didn't fit in. Her insecurity took care of that no matter what she wore.

"Freya," a feminine voice called before she could make her escape.

Mariella Jacob wrapped her in a tight hug. "Don't you just look like a snack and a half. You have to let me introduce you to Alex. We can talk collaborating."

Freya breathed out a laugh. "I stick out like a sore thumb in this dress."

"You own that dress," Mariella argued then frowned as she studied Freya. "You know that, right? You're gorgeous. But the reason I'm so keen to work with you is because of your fierce attitude and inner radiance. That's what sells the outfit."

"Can you record that so I can listen to it as my daily affirmation?" She glanced away when tears pricked the backs of her eyes. "This was a mistake. I'm leaving town after my nephew's baptism, Mariella. A collaboration isn't going to work. You don't want me."

"I do," Mariella said slowly. "And I don't think I'm the only one. Come and meet some of my friends." She leaned closer like she was revealing a secret. "It's a relatively new thing for me to describe people as friends. Did you know I have a daughter, too? She's a teenager and is in town with her adoptive parents for the day."

Freya blinked. "I don't know what to say to all that."

"Do you still feel like you're going to cry?"

"How did you…" Freya shook her head and realized the moment had passed. "No, I don't."

"Verbal diarrhea has its uses. You've made it this far, Freya. Meet a few people. Lily had Angi Guilardi help with the food, so it's amazing. Stay."

She held up her hand when Freya immediately began to decline. "I'm not talking about forever. That's your business. Stay at the party a few minutes."

The shop owner, who felt more like a friend to Freya than women she'd known for years in California, was right, of course. Freya had come this far, and she'd already decided she was leaving town. What did it matter if people judged her at this point?

She followed Mariella into the light-filled kitchen, with honed marble counters, stainless steel appliances and muted white cabinetry. At this point of her stay in Magnolia, she shouldn't be surprised by the friendliness of the residents. Mariella introduced her to her partners at the inn, Emma and Angi, and Freya took a moment to thank the restaurant owner for her help when Trinity went into labor.

No one seemed shocked by her body-conscious dress, and a few people made a point of approaching to say how much they enjoyed seeing Magnolia and its local businesses spotlighted on her tour. Several older folks, who looked like hardware-store regulars, congratulated her on the snippet where she'd interviewed the winner of the youth art contest during the town's final holiday event.

Freya realized how jaded she'd become thanks to living in a world of paid endorsements and sponsored posts. While the home-for-the-holidays segment had been a job, she'd also genuinely enjoyed showing off the town. Authenticity and accessibility were a powerful draw in celebrity marketing.

These locals didn't care that she'd worn something out of character during the tour or that she was practically poured into today's dress. They focused on her, just like Mariella seemed to.

Just like…

"Hey, there." She whirled at Greer's soft greeting to find him standing directly behind her like she'd summoned him with her longing.

"You're here," she whispered then shook her head. "Of course you are. I expected to see you."

"Really?" One thick brow lifted. "Because you've been doing a bang-up job of avoiding me recently."

She glanced around to make sure no one was close enough to overhear their conversation. She didn't want an audience with Greer.

He took her hand and led her through the crowd, then into an empty room that functioned as a small library and Garrett's office by the look of the space.

Expansive bookshelves lined three walls, and a picture window overlooked the house's backyard. There was an antique desk, the kind Freya dreamed of having, situated in front of the window and a small but cozy love seat in one corner.

"Things got difficult with my mom and sisters," she said, facing the window as he shut the door. The quiet felt disconcerting after the revelry of the party. "I didn't mean to blow you off."

He cleared his throat but not before she heard the curse he muttered under his breath.

She straightened her shoulders and turned, prepared to blast him with her bravado. "I'm sorry," she said instead. The apology slipped out before she could stop it. "It's complicated."

"We're not complicated."

She heard the tenderness in his tone underneath his customary good humor and realized she'd hurt him. She didn't want to hurt him.

"You're right," she agreed. "I'm leaving after the baptism, and you're ready to return to Boston. That makes this simple."

"I'm staying in Magnolia."

"You can't."

His lips quirked. "I can. The agency is going remote and downsizing the Boston office. A few people will stay there, but most of us now have a choice. I can advocate for my authors from anywhere."

She snorted derisively, trying to cover her shock. "And you choose Magnolia?"

"I've already told you, Freya. I choose you."

"I'm going back to California."

"Why?" He took a step closer, and she automatically edged back. "You don't want to be there. It's not your home."

"It's where my career is based. I can't be a celebrity in some Podunk coastal town."

"You could be a published author."

Panic, swift and sure, clawed at her lungs, making it difficult to draw in a breath. "What are you talking about?"

He massaged a hand over the back of his neck. "I wasn't supposed to say anything yet."

"Mom gave you my manuscript?" Suddenly the fabric of her dress seemed to cut off her circulation. She reached out a hand and grabbed hold of the corner of Garrett's desk to steady herself. It felt as though she might crumple to the thick rug that covered the hardwood floor.

He shook his head. "Trinity let it slip that you'd written

a book. I convinced her to let me make a copy and take a look."

"You convinced her…" Freya's gaze darted to the door. "Oh, my God. Did you show my work to Garrett Dawes? He said something that day in Mariella's shop. It didn't make sense at the time but now…"

"I didn't show him, but I talked to him about your talent. Garrett struggled with embracing his gift after his debut novel was a runaway success and adapted into a blockbuster movie. I thought he could offer some perspective or potential advice to you."

"You've known for weeks that I had aspirations of becoming a writer." Freya swallowed as her throat felt stuffed with cotton. "You talked about me. You read my book." She felt her eyes widen. "Did you…"

"Send it to editors? No. Not without your permission, of course." He dipped his head then glanced up at her, his dark eyes searching hers. "But I teased it with a few of my contacts."

"No, you didn't."

"They don't know it's you, Freya. But they should. I know this is awkward because…well… I'm in love with you."

Did that soft cry of disbelief come from her?

"It might not be appropriate for me to be your literary agent, but you need one. You have a unique voice and a lyrical style that is almost guaranteed to resonate with both reviewers and readers."

"I'm not going to publish the book," she said slowly. "I signed on for another dating show."

His brows drew together. "I don't understand. I just told you I love you. I thought you felt…something."

"Right now, I feel betrayed," she said quietly. That was

the easiest to pinpoint in the maelstrom of feelings surging through her. Love was in that powerful mix, but she couldn't let herself go there. Not when other, darker sentiments tainted it. "You don't know what's best for me, Greer. People have always assumed I'm not smart or savvy enough to choose for myself. I am the one in control."

"I don't want to take it from you." He squeezed shut his eyes for a few seconds. "I didn't expect this, Freya. Maybe I'm mishandling the whole thing. But…" He opened his eyes and the raw emotions swirling in their depths were like a sharp spike to her heart. "Tell me you don't feel anything for me."

She licked her parched lips and opened her mouth to do just that. The words wouldn't come. Finally, she sighed. "I'm a lot of things but not a liar. The problem isn't what we feel for each other, Greer. It's that the kind of connection you want… I'm not built for it."

She clenched her fists. "I'm made for something less. Just like I have with my mom a thousand times over, I'd only disappoint you in the end."

"Impossible," he whispered.

"Not when I believe it to be inevitable." She moved toward the door. "Would you keep the manuscript to yourself? As much as I appreciate your faith in me…in us…" She clenched her jaw and tried to stem the tide of tears she knew was coming. "I wish I deserved it."

Then she opened the door and walked away from the best man she'd ever met. If Freya had ever questioned whether she was a true master of self-destruction, she had her answer now.

CHAPTER TWENTY-NINE

A BEAD OF sweat rolled between Trinity's shoulder blades even though it wasn't exactly warm in the small office where she waited for the baptism to begin a week later.

She should be out in the vestibule greeting the few guests she'd invited to the service, but for some reason, Thomas refused to stop fussing. It was unlike the baby, who Freya had nicknamed "Little Buddha" because of his serene personality.

He rarely cried in earnest but had been cranky since he awoke this morning, which made Trinity irritable as well.

She didn't like the feeling of not being able to comfort her son.

"You want me to take him?" her mother asked. May sat on the striped damask sofa across the room from Trinity, watching her pace back and forth with Thomas.

"I want him to stop crying before the baptism. He's got a fresh diaper and ate an hour ago. I checked his outfit to make sure nothing was poking or scratching him. Why won't he stop fussing?"

"Babies cry," May said matter-of-factly. "It doesn't mean you're a bad mom, Trinny."

"I didn't think that," Trinity lied, although that was exactly what she feared. Somehow the people closest to her— her mom, sisters and their neighbors plus Greer—everyone attending the baptism would think Thomas was crying in response to something she had or hadn't done.

If only she could figure out what it was.

"Everything okay?" Beth asked as she opened the door.

"Minister says five minutes," Freya added, giving Beth a slight shove to make room inside the office.

"Don't push me." Beth elbowed Freya, and Trinity half expected to see them start rolling around on the floor, pro-wrestling style.

"Would you two knock it off?" she said on a hiss of breath and then grimaced as Thomas's chin began to tremble. "It's okay, sweet boy," she sang in a soft voice, bouncing him as she started to pace again. "Your two aunties are still acting like fools, but they're going to behave so I don't have to kill them."

Freya laughed. "Catchy tune."

"You might have missed your call as a recording artist," Beth said.

"World-class arguers and comedians. I hit the sister jackpot with you two."

There was a moment of awkward silence inside the room because Trinity never snapped at them.

"Come on, Trin." Beth stepped forward. "He's just having a bad day. It happens to everyone."

"Especially Beth." Freya tried to put an arm around Trinity's shoulders as Beth took Thomas from her.

"Maybe Dad needs an opening act," Beth muttered then glanced at May and cringed. "Sorry, too much."

Trinity shrugged out of Freya's grasp and covered her face with her hands. "I don't want us to fight anymore." She looked up and dashed her fingers across her cheeks. "I'm tired and hormonal, and my boobs leak every time I start to cry. Stop making me cry."

"We don't want you to cry," Freya said, sounding appalled.

Beth's eyes widened. "Of course not."

"It makes me sad that you hate each other."

Her two older sisters shared a confused look.

"Trin, we don't hate each other." Beth kissed the top of the baby's head when he gave a little squawk. "Sisters argue."

"It's more than that," Trinity insisted.

"Sometimes." Freya's smile was hesitant. "And sometimes people change. We heal."

"You read the book," May said, rising from the sofa.

Beth and Freya glanced at each other again, and then Beth nodded. "You took responsibility, Mom. We appreciate that." She turned her gaze toward Trinity. "You were right, baby sister. We should have listened to you earlier. I'm sorry we upset you."

Freya sighed and allowed May to pull her close. "I wish the two of you would have just given us the CliffsNotes version. Maybe it would have actually been a Merry Christmas."

Trinity shook her head. "You needed to read it willingly to appreciate what Mom wrote."

"I appreciate it now." Freya placed her head on May's shoulder.

As Beth moved to May's other side, Trinity understood that the rift that had plagued their family for so long might finally heal. In the revised edition of *A Woman's Odyssey*, May had taken responsibility for her narcissistic parenting and given advice on how busy and stressed mothers—both single and married—could make sure they took care of themselves in a way that maintained their capacity for loving their children unconditionally.

She'd discussed each of the sisters but only in the most generous terms, giving them credit for meeting their own emotional needs. And apologizing for her role in their self-doubt and troubles with emotional intimacy.

"I wanted you to read the book before I talked about it with you," May explained, "so that you didn't feel an obligation to accept my offer of amends out of guilt or misplaced loyalty. You are free to define your relationship with me in whatever way works for you."

Trinity nodded, but her sisters didn't look convinced.

"What about the tour?" Beth said.

Freya straightened. "And staying in Magnolia to help?"

May shook her head. "I'm not going on tour. Not yet. I'm staying to be with Trinity and Thomas. I'll do remote interviews, but that's all."

"Are you sure?" Freya looked unconvinced. "You like the limelight even more than me."

May reached out and brushed a strand of hair off Freya's shoulder. "Do you truly like it?" She turned to Beth. "Is the nurse practitioner program what you want, or do you feel compelled to leave town so you can finally have your own life?"

Freya drew in a sharp breath then darted a glance at the door. "The minister and guests are probably waiting for us."

Beth whistled and shook her head. "Yep. Need to go. Right now. I didn't wear enough waterproof mascara to answer that question."

"The answers will come," May said. "You'll figure them out. Trinity and I will be here to help."

"That's right." Trinity smiled as Beth transferred Thomas to her. The baby had returned to his cherubic serenity, contentedly gazing up at his mother. "I've got my life together now, so you two can ask me for advice on yours." She rolled her eyes. "We should probably start with romantic advice because Declan Murphy and Christopher Greer are good men."

"Wow, go, Trin," Freya said with a laugh.

There was a knock at the office door. "We're ready to begin," an older male voice called.

"Coming, Reverend," Trinity answered then wrapped an arm around Freya and leaned her elbow into Beth since she had Thomas in that arm. "Group hug."

Her sisters and mom complied, and a few moments later, Trinity entered the church feeling more at peace than she had in ages.

Unfortunately, that peace only lasted as long as it took to make it to the edge of the chancel.

"Trinity!" Her heart seemed to freeze at the sound of her ex-boyfriend's angry shout. She turned around slowly, hugging Thomas more tightly to her chest as Dave Conklin stalked toward her.

He looked the same as Trinity remembered with his lanky build and close-cropped black hair. But he seemed different somehow, not as intimidating or powerful. Had he lost weight? There were dark circles under his eyes, and he needed a shower.

"Sir, this is a private event," the minister announced, peering from behind rounded glasses at the worst mistake of Trinity's life.

Dave flashed an oily smile and yanked a knife from his back pocket, flipping it open with a flourish. "Got my invitation right here."

"No," Trinity whispered when her two sisters surged forward in the commotion that followed.

"Everybody shut it," Dave hollered and continued up the

aisle until he was a few feet from her. "I'm here to meet my son and talk to my girl."

"I'm not your girl," Trinity said, forcing her voice to remain steady. She held up a hand. "Don't come any closer, Dave. You have no right to be here."

"Au contraire," he said in an exaggerated Southern accent. "Show me the baby, Trin."

She shook her head and held Thomas more tightly. To her relief, he'd fallen asleep and didn't seem to notice the ruckus surrounding them. "How did you find me?"

"Your sister led me to you." He pointed the knife in Freya's direction. "Imagine my surprise when I stopped by a gas station to buy a pack of smokes on Christmas Eve and saw my mousy little Trinity on the TV behind the register."

"No," Freya breathed. "I'm so sorry, Trini—"

"Shut your fancy mouth, too, Hollywood." Dave drew lazy figure eights in the air with the blade of his knife.

"I'm not yours." Trinity squared her shoulders. "And neither is this baby. You need to go, Dave. This is your chance to walk away with no consequences. I don't want anything from you so—"

"I want something from you. I want you and that baby to come home with me."

"I am home."

He growled low in his throat. "Not if I say you aren't."

"You have no power over me." She spoke the words slowly, so he couldn't mistake her meaning. "I won't let you hurt my son or me."

"*My* son." He smacked an open palm against his chest.

"There isn't a chance in hell I will let you near this baby, Dave."

"What happened to you?" Dave inclined his head as he studied her. "Where is the sweet, docile woman I knew?"

She swallowed down the humiliation of her past show-ing up to threaten her future. She could see Shauna holding her boys tight and Ash nudging Michaela nearer her grand-mother as he inched closer to the end of the pew.

The police chief was out of uniform today, and she highly doubted he was carrying a weapon to her baby's baptism. Even if he had a gun, what would he do with in-nocent people on every side?

She tipped her chin as she glared at her ex-boyfriend. "You beat the sweet right out of me, Dave."

May gave a small cry behind Trinity, but she didn't turn around. As much as she wanted to rely on Ash or her sisters or mother to help rescue her, she knew she had to stand up to her abuser if she was going to truly move forward, no matter how this standoff ended.

She also knew it would end with Thomas safe. There was nothing she wouldn't do for her son.

"We can try again, Trin." Dave's tone had turned sickly cloying, the way it used to when he was attempting to whee-dle his way back into her good graces.

She'd left good and grace behind in Montana with her old life.

He mistook her silence for assent and held out a hand, beckoning to her. "Come with me, sweetheart. We'll be a family. You'll see. I'm not leaving here without you, Trin."

It felt as though the entire church held its breath, wait-ing to see what would happen next. She wasn't fooled or tempted but didn't know how to ensure no one got hurt when her answer was sure to enrage her unstable ex.

Out of the corner of her eye, she caught Ash's dark gaze. He gave her a barely imperceptible nod, which was all the encouragement she needed.

Yes, she could do this alone. But she didn't have to.

THE WISH LIST

306

"I don't belong to you, Dave. I'm not your girl or your woman or your victim any longer. I belong to me and to my son. You will not take another thing from me."

His face went mottled with rage, and then everything happened in a blur of motion. Greer, Ash and Declan all seemed to move at the same time. Declan jumped up from his seat and grabbed Dave's arm as Ash rushed toward them.

Greer stepped directly in front of Trinity, blocking her from Dave's line of sight. She felt the arms of both her sisters come around her and willed herself to stay lucid despite the adrenaline rushing to her head. She needed to protect Thomas.

She heard a scuffle, the sound of flesh pounding against flesh and Dave crying out in pain along with a low curse that sounded like Declan.

Shauna and Helena had moved the children to the far side of the aisle, where the minister had joined them. Trinity's heart thumped a little lighter knowing they were safe.

Then she heard Ash reading Dave his rights while her ex-boyfriend moaned an incoherent response, facedown in the aisle.

Greer turned to face Trinity. "You're okay now. It's all okay."

Before she could answer, Freya threw her arms around him. "You big dummy. Literary agents aren't supposed to be heroes."

"Beth," Ash called. "Declan is going to need stitches."

"I'm fine," the new bar owner said when Beth rushed toward him.

Trinity took a step forward then May was at her side. "Let me have Thomas, Trinny. You're squeezing him awful tight."

She relinquished the baby to her mother and watched as her no-nonsense, unemotional oldest sister burst into tears and planted a deep kiss on Declan Murphy.

"If I'd known all it would take was a little blood to turn your head." Declan let out a shaky chuckle. "I would have set something up a lot sooner."

"You turn my head. I love you," Beth said, kissing him again then tugging on his arm. "Now let's go get those stitches." Beth glanced back at Trinity. "You good, Trin?"

Trinity nodded, although her head felt wooden.

A moment later, one of Ash's deputies charged through the church door.

"I need the handcuffs, Jordan," Ash shouted to him.

The young man nodded at Beth and Declan then joined Ash on the floor.

Trinity breathed a sigh of relief when Dave was handcuffed, not that she thought he was any match for Asher Davis.

"Want me to take him in on my own?" the deputy asked his chief.

"Put him in the back of the squad car," Ash commanded. "I'll be there in a second. I'm going to take great pleasure in booking this loser myself."

As the deputy hauled Dave off the floor, Trinity got her first look at his beaten and bloody face. He was only semi-conscious as the deputy led him out of the building. Then she noticed that Ash's knuckles were bleeding.

He followed her gaze and shoved his hands into the pockets of his khaki pants. "Are you really okay?" he asked gently.

She nodded, and he looked past her to his mother-in-law. "Helena," he called, "I'm going to leave the keys on this pew here." He pulled a set of car keys from his pocket. "I'll see you and Michaela at home."

"Way to get the bad guy, Daddy," his daughter called.

"Thanks, honey." He returned his gaze to Trinity. "Way to stand up to the bad guy."

She felt the ghost of a smile curve one side of her mouth. "Thank you for helping me to realize I could."

He looked like he wanted to say more but nodded. "I'll talk to you later," he said and walked down the aisle.

A moment later, Freya and May surrounded her once more, and Trinity knew that no matter what challenges or scary monsters she faced in her life, she'd wouldn't ever again have to do it alone. Somehow that made everything worth it. Though still shaky, she'd never felt stronger than she did in this moment.

EPILOGUE

ON A WET and rainy Friday night in January a month later, Beth clinked a silver fork against her champagne glass to get the attention of the small crowd gathered in the living room of the Wildflower Inn.

She smiled as a hush fell over her family and friends with all eyes turning toward her.

"Thank you all for coming on such short notice," she said, inclining her head toward the bay window that looked out onto the inn's front lawn. "And in less-than-ideal conditions. I'd hoped the temperature might drop enough for Magnolia to receive the same snowfall that blanketed the town at Christmas, but no such luck."

Michaela, who sat on the arm of a chair next to her father, led Timmy and Zach in chanting "snow day" a few times.

"You wish," Beth told the girl with a laugh. "Speaking of wishes, our family has enjoyed a number of them coming true recently."

She saw Trinity squeeze their mother's shoulder, Thomas serenely cradled in his grandma's loving arms.

"Tonight, we're here to celebrate one particular piece of good news for my sister, the soon-to-be-published author."

Freya stood and made an elaborate curtsy, her delicate features alight with so much joy it made Beth's heart pinch with gratitude.

When Freya had texted Beth, Trinity and May earlier

that day to share the news that her debut novel had been acquired by one of the largest and most well-respected New York publishing houses, there had been no question about planning an immediate celebration.

If the incident with Dave Conklin had taught them all one thing, it was that time was both precious and priceless, and they shouldn't waste it when no one had a guarantee what might happen next. It was a lesson that had started with their mother's stroke and the changes it brought to their lives—the best of which was their family reuniting after so many years of estrangement.

Beth and her sisters had what now felt like an unbreakable thread stitched across their hearts, tying them to each other as well as their mom. Unbreakable because the holiday season together had shown them the value of reinforcing their connection to make it grow stronger.

"We're proud of you, Frey," Beth said, clearing her throat when emotion bubbled up inside her. "You deserve every accolade—"

"And advance dollar," Freya added with a brief happy dance.

"Every accolade and that big advance," Beth amended. "I hope this is the first of many opportunities we have to celebrate your new career."

"Look out, Garrett," Greer said from where he stood next to the buffet table. He pointed a mozzarella stick in the direction of the famous author. "My Freya will give you a run for your money on the bestseller list."

"I hope so," Garrett agreed and held up his glass in salute. "To Freya Carlyle's impending chart domination."

Everyone raised a glass to toast Freya, who met Beth's gaze with a mouthed *thank you*.

"This was nice," Declan said as he slipped an arm around Beth's waist. "You did a good job, sweetheart."

"I hate public speaking." Beth turned into his embrace, wondering if the spicy, clean scent of her beloved would ever stop eliciting a tingle along her spine. She hoped not.

"You're a natural," he assured her. "Personally, I don't think there's anything you can't accomplish."

"Definitely nothing we can't manage together," she answered and placed a kiss on the underside of his jaw. "Do you need to get back to the bar?"

He sighed. "Probably. I'll try not to wake you when I come in later."

"Please do wake me," she told him. "It's the one bonus I see to your late nights."

"You have a test on Monday," he said but drew her closer. "You need a good night's rest so you can spend tomorrow cracking the books."

"That's why they invented coffee." She kissed him again. "You're worth losing sleep over, Mr. Murphy."

"Then I'll be sure to make it worth your while." After another lingering kiss, he released her and headed for the door.

"If I weren't so happy for the two of you, I'd be equally nauseous and jealous over your adorableness as a couple."

Beth tried to hide her blissful grin as she turned to Shauna. "You brought us together in a way, so at least you can take credit."

"Ah, yes." Shauna popped a stuffed mushroom into her mouth. "I can live vicariously and all that. How's school going?"

"It's amazing. I don't know why I didn't think about doing the remote program from the start."

"Because you were trying to run away from home," Shauna reminded her.

"Right." Beth wrinkled her nose. "It was a good plan but allowing myself to be happy here is an even better one."

She might have wished she'd had that epiphany before causing both Declan and herself so much pain but at least she could take comfort in the fact that she'd realized it before it was too late.

It had taken a superficial knife wound to give her instant clarity and the understanding that no dream was worth having if it meant losing the man she loved with her whole heart.

"I just wish Trinity's loser ex had been more seriously hurt in the process. Maybe a little knife wound of his own? I admire Ash's sense of honor and all that but…"

"I hear you," Beth agreed. "Still, Dave had some serious charges waiting for him back in Montana in addition to the laundry list of offenses from his stunt in the church. One way or another, he's out of Trinity's life. That's what counts."

"How's she doing?" Shauna asked gently, tilting her head in Trinity's direction. She'd taken Thomas from May and showed him off to Mariella and Angi on the far side of the room.

Ash stood near his mother-in-law talking with Mary Ellen, but his gaze surreptitiously tracked to Trinity when he thought no one was looking.

"It was traumatic, but Trin is stronger than any of us gave her credit for. Standing up to Dave did her confidence a world of good. I think she wanted to believe she'd do anything to protect her son, but now she has no doubt."

"What about her and our handsome police chief? He's got some major longing radiating from those gorgeous honey-colored eyes."

"Maybe that match will happen someday, but Trinity wants to focus on Thomas and building their life here. As great as Ash is, I think she's afraid of letting herself depend on him. She wants to prove she can make it on her own."

"Wow, the stubborn, independent streak runs hard in the Carlyle women," Shauna said with a laugh.

"Yeah." Beth winked at Greer when he caught her eye. She loved seeing the pride in his gaze as he watched Freya bask in the glow of her new success.

The two of them had also recognized they were meant to be after the near tragedy in the church. Although Greer had introduced Freya to a different agent for representation, he was the fledgling author and now-retired reality star's biggest fan.

"Trinity will figure it out, and no matter what she chooses, we'll be here for her."

"It makes your mom happy to have the three of you together again." Shauna crossed her arms over her chest. "I can't imagine my boys and me ever having that kind of falling-out."

"You're a good mom, and the twins clearly adore you and each other."

"Too bad that brotherly love manifests in shouting matches and wrestling bouts more days than not."

"You make them both feel special. And I bet they're going to be each other's best friends for their whole lives. Freya, Trinity and I may have misplaced our connection for a while, but it was never truly lost. We have a bond that can bend, but it won't break."

"You're lucky," Shauna murmured.

"It took me a while to realize it," Beth admitted. "But you're right. I am so very lucky and blessed. For years I wished for a perfect family. Now I know the family I needed was right here all along."

* * * * *

A LOT LIKE CHRISTMAS

CHAPTER ONE

"WHO'S THE PRETTIEST GIRL?"

Carli Connelly smiled as the raggedy-looking mutt gazed up into her eyes then gave a tiny, high-pitched yap, as if to answer her question.

Sitting on the family room floor, she adjusted the red-and-white polka-dot sweater she'd fitted on the small dog and sat back on her heels. Queenie, a canine of indiscriminate breed who looked like a Yorkie-poo mixed with a bedraggled mop head, pranced across the living room floor, her nails clicking on the hardwood.

"You work it, Queen," Carli told the dog, feeling inordinately proud of Queenie's newfound confidence.

When Carli had first started this part-time pet sitting gig, Queenie had been sulky, listless, and depressed, mourning her beloved human. Carli had yet to meet the dog's current owner, Mark Simpson, but she knew he'd taken over the dog's care when his grandmother passed away.

Carli worked at both a local veterinary clinic and the Furever Friends animal rescue in the quaint, bustling town of Magnolia, North Carolina.

After seeing a feature on Furever Friends while scrolling social media, she'd moved to Magnolia specifically to work with Meredith Ventner Sorensen, the rescue's talented and dedicated owner.

The segment had come at exactly the right time for Carli,

who'd been looking for an excuse to get out of Cleveland. Her goal was to start fresh someplace where she was only responsible for taking care of herself and any animals that needed her.

She'd left Ohio with little money and no savings but understood she would need to continue to send back part of her paycheck to help her father pay the bills.

She'd set things up so that instead of giving her dad cash, groceries were delivered to his ramshackle house each week and the rent and utilities were paid. She knew that if she gave William Connelly cash, no matter his best intentions, he'd more than likely end up gambling it away just like he did most of the paycheck from his job as an attendant at a downtown parking lot.

Carli had seen that outcome too many times to trust her dad's promises to go straight. He loved the racetrack as much as he loved his daughter.

So she did what she had to—working at both the rescue and the vet clinic plus her side hustle as a pet sitter/dog walker/poop scooper. Whatever it took to make enough to live on her own and still support her dad—from a distance.

Dr. Malack, her boss at the vet clinic, had recommended her for the job with Queenie, which was her most lucrative assignment to date. The mysterious Mark Simpson paid her an obscene amount of money to look after Queenie while he was at work.

And the man worked all the time. He did something for the athletic wear company that had recently moved to town, the Fit Collective. That much Carli had learned from the vet. Otherwise, she knew almost nothing about Queenie's mysterious owner, other than the dog seemed starved for affection.

Why keep an animal if you weren't going to love it? To

be fair, Mark Simpson might dote on the little mutt for all Carli knew, but when she'd arrived for her first visit, scheduled by a series of formal-sounding texts, she hadn't found one dog toy or a bed or any treats for the animal.

Queenie had been curled up in a rather pathetic-looking ball on the tile floor of the laundry room with only a pee pad to keep her company.

Carli wanted to believe Mark Simpson didn't know better when it came to taking care of an animal. But who didn't realize that dogs liked toys and needed mental stimulation if they were going to be left alone for long stretches?

Luckily, she had no issues with spoiling the tiny dog. In the past month, she'd been excited to see a change in Queenie. The dog came running when Carli entered the house, happy to see her babysitter and ready for whatever adventure she had planned for the day.

She'd bought Queenie the holiday sweater because the temperature in Magnolia, although temperate by Cleveland standards, was definitely chilly for a dog that had more bare patches than actual fur. Plus, Queenie had seemed shy and reticent meeting new people or other animals when they went on walks, a marked difference from the happy and loving dog Carli had come to know during their time together in the house.

Queenie didn't show signs of previous abuse that would explain her fear. On a whim, Carli borrowed a sweater donated to the rescue and put it on Queenie. The dog's whole demeanor changed like she was a runway model strutting through the neighborhood and happily displaying her fancy wardrobe to any passing animal or human they met.

Today, Carli was going to take Queenie downtown. She loved how Magnolia went all out on decorations and cheer for the holidays. Everyone seemed festive and friendly as they bustled along the crowded sidewalks to shop or enjoy the Christmas on the Coast festival events scheduled throughout the month.

Suddenly, a crash sounded from the back of the house. Carli went stock-still. A muttered curse followed, and she told herself to get up. No one other than her should be in this house today. She needed to grab the dog, escape out the front door, and call the police.

She wasn't sure what was going on, but it couldn't be good. Even though she knew what she should do, fear kept her rooted in place. There were so many times fear had paralyzed Carli, leaving her unable to take action. She hated herself for that weakness.

Queenie let out a low growl, showing more brainpower and gumption than Carli, but then the dog shocked her by moving toward the sound.

"Queenie," she said in a hopefully not so loud whisper. "Come."

The dog stopped and turned toward her for a moment, then faced the hallway again.

"Queenie, please come."

Carli was so consumed with the dog that it took a second for her to register the muscular, hairy legs that appeared in the doorway behind Queenie.

"Hello, mutt," a deep voice said, and Queenie wagged her tail. Maybe she wasn't any smarter than Carli after all. "Who are you?"

She realized with a shock that the question was directed at her. Carli's mouth had gone dry, and she slowly scrambled to her feet. She felt overwhelmed by a combination of adrenaline and her visceral reaction to the man standing on the other side of the room, wearing nothing but a bath towel wrapped around his waist.

"Don't come any closer," she said instead of answering. "I'm armed."

He gave her a skeptical once-over, maybe because she was now standing there in snowflake-patterned leggings and a sweatshirt that had no pockets. She looked around wildly and reached for the first thing she saw, which was a vase of dried flowers perched on an end table next to the sofa.

"I'm not kidding," she said.

"I doubt you are." He made eye contact with her for barely a second before looking at a space beyond her shoulder.

Oh, holy moly. Did he have an accomplice behind her? Was he trying to distract her so he could charge? If he was burglarizing the house, why was he doing it in a towel?

He continued to stare beyond her as he spoke. "But my renter's insurance doesn't cover tacky knickknacks, so I'll have to ask you to return the vase and dust-collecting flora to its rightful place. Miss Connelly, I assume?"

He looked at Queenie, who was now thoroughly cleaning her nether regions.

The man grimaced. "Is the sweater necessary?"

"Mark Simpson?" Carli let out a relieved sigh as annoyance spiked through her. Her uncommunicative client had practically scared the pants off her. Which reminded her...

"What are you doing here and why aren't you wearing clothes?"

That seemed to jar him into remembering that he was garbed in only a towel. Two bright blooms of pink appeared on his ruddy cheeks. The man looked nothing like she expected him to.

Carli had envisioned a thin, wiry, unattractive nerd. Not

this tall, handsome man—still somewhat nerdy but in a strangely appealing way—who stood in front of her.

He had a muscled chest and shoulders that looked like they could carry the weight of the world, which might not be too far of a stretch given his serious expression. He had striking blue eyes with enviable lashes framing them, but what Carli noticed was his mouth—full and soft but pulled into what looked like a permanent frown. It made her want to coax a smile from him.

"Right. I heard a noise out here, and I thought the dog had gotten into something. Give me a minute."

As soon as he disappeared, Carli glanced over her shoulder, still half expecting to see somebody behind her. It was just her and Queenie.

"You could have told me he was here," she whispered to the dog.

The animal's peanut-sized head popped up from taking care of business. She trotted toward Carli and sat on her foot. Either she was apologizing or drying her bum on Carli's fuzzy sock.

Carli preferred to believe it was an apology.

She placed the vase on the table and bent to scratch behind Queenie's floppy ear. "I almost forgot." She reached under her sweatshirt and undid the bow fastened to her bra strap, for lack of a better way to carry it. "I brought this to finish off your outfit."

She knelt once more, gathered a few wisps of dog fur, and clipped them together. Queenie loved bows, and the dog tried to stay still even though her tail wagged with joy. "Accessories are the exclamation point of a woman's outfit."

"The designer Michael Kors said that," Mark Simpson announced as he reappeared. At her befuddled look, he shrugged. "I work for a clothing company, so I pay attention to famous quotes about fashion."

"That makes sense in a weird sort of way. How did you get dressed so quickly?" Carli asked, standing once again and feeling foolish that she'd been caught talking to the dog, like Queenie could answer back. "For a man who seemed determined not to be seen or met, you make quite an entrance."

"I wasn't determined not to be met," he said, thick brows furrowing. Carli's stomach did an unwelcome dip in reaction. "I work a lot of hours, as I take it, do you. Texting seemed most efficient."

"I left you notes," she said, realizing the statement was out of the blue. "You didn't respond, even in text."

He ran a hand through thick black hair that curled around his ears. "There were no questions. Why would I respond?"

"Because it's the polite thing to do." She crossed her arms over her chest. "Just like it would have been responsible, not to mention considerate, to let me know you would be home today. I've been coming to spend time with Queenie five—sometimes six—days a week for the past month."

She gestured toward the neat-as-a-pin interior of the house. "I barely get the impression anyone lives here. I certainly didn't expect to see you."

He looked down at the floor and Carli mentally chided herself. He paid her double what any of her other regular clients did. She couldn't afford to lose this job.

Before he could speak, she stepped forward and stuck out her hand. "Let's start fresh. I'm Carli Connelly, Queenie's dog nanny. It's nice to meet you, Mark."

He stared at her hand like she'd just picked up a pile of dog yak with it. "I know who you are."

Embarrassment washed through her. Yes, this man with his expensive-looking jeans and black sweater that was probably made of cashmere or some other fancy fabric, clearly thought he was better than her. It was a point that could be argued in the affirmative on several levels. She had a high school diploma, average grades, and eked out a living with various low-paying jobs.

She didn't know what he did for the clothing company, but she knew she couldn't even afford to buy half of one of the leggings they produced and sold for exorbitant amounts of money.

She was about to take back her hand when it was suddenly engulfed in Mark's giant grasp. He shook hers quickly, and Carli would have sworn he was going to pull away.

Then he gave her hand a little squeeze and his thumb traced a circle along the inside of her palm. "You have soft skin."

He released her, and for a second, she thought she'd imagined his words. "I use a lot of lotion," she told him.

He nodded as if this were the most normal conversation in the world.

Carli swallowed and commanded her heart to stop flinging itself against her rib cage. She was being silly; it wasn't like meeting Mark Simpson had changed her world on some fundamental level. "So you're off work today?"

"Yes. Not really. I can't be in the office. My boss is forcing me to go to an event in town." She felt more than saw his revulsion. "Some sort of holiday celebration with music."

Carli grinned. "It's one of the Christmas on the Coast activities. That's where Queenie and I are headed. I'm staffing the booth for the rescue and figured she'd like seeing the other dogs and all the people. She likes attention."

"She's a dog," Mark said as if that weren't obvious.

"Man's best friend. You've heard the expression?"

"I never had a best friend," Mark said. "Until Alex. He's my boss. We were college roommates."

"Cool. I'm sure he'll love to meet Queenie."

"I won't be seen with a dog wearing a sweater. I'm not taking her anywhere. She barely weighs enough to be considered a proper canine."

"She's perfect," Carli countered. "I'll take Queenie. She's so excited." They both looked at the dog, who scratched her chin, and then let out a delicate fart—if farts could be delicate.

Mark started to shake his head then stopped. "You work with Meredith?"

"I do."

"She's friends with my boss's fiancée."

"Small world."

He studied her for a long moment. "We'll go together."

Carli grimaced. "Not necessary."

"You're my dog nanny," he reminded her with a grin that looked almost out of place on his stoic face. "I should get to know you better. I certainly pay you enough. We can discuss Queenie on the way downtown."

The dog gave a tiny yap and put her front paws on Carli's leg. "Fine," Carli agreed. "We'll discuss Queenie and some of the ideas for her care I left in the notes you never answered."

To his credit, Mark only nodded. "It's a deal."

CHAPTER TWO

"YOU CAN'T BE SERIOUS."

Mark forced his features to remain neutral as Carli studied him. He stared straight ahead but knew she must be looking at him like he'd taken leave of his senses. Perhaps that was true.

He'd come up with his odd proposition while she'd filled the silence inside his Mercedes sedan on the way into town. He couldn't decide if she'd been talking more than an average person because she was nervous or trying to distract him from his grandmother's mangy mutt drooling on the buttery leather of the console between the two front seats. Or maybe she just talked that much all the time.

Typically, people who talked incessantly made him want to shove cotton in his ears, but there was something about the lilt of Carli's soft voice and the way she didn't seem to expect him to respond that soothed his nerves.

Or maybe it was her creamy skin, maple syrup–colored hair, gentle curves, and ready smile. Carli Connelly beguiled him.

"I'm almost always serious," he said quickly.

"And now you want to become the life of the party?"

"Not being considered a party pooper would satisfy me." Carli giggled, and his gaze crashed into hers before he looked away. "Why is that funny?"

"You used the phrase party pooper," she explained. "It surprised me."

"My grandmother used to say that."

"It's cute."

"No one describes me as cute."

"Maybe they should." She smiled at Queenie, who trotted down the path like it was a fashion-week runway, but Mark had a feeling that smile was also for him.

Carli made him feel normal, a rarity in Mark's life, where despite his intellectual capacity and career success, he never quite fit in the way he wanted—and now needed—to with those around him.

Alex Ralsten, his boss and best friend, was different. They'd met freshman year at their Ivy League college and somehow forged a bond that lasted over a decade. Mark had been working as a partner and senior developer at a Silicon Valley startup when Alex reached out and asked him to join the staff of the Fit Collective, managing the tech department. He was tasked with finding new ways to connect with consumers across digital channels.

Mark had started packing his sparse condo that day. There was nothing he wouldn't do for Alex, even forcing himself to be friendly to his coworkers.

Although that initiative wasn't going as well as he'd hoped. He had trouble making small talk and didn't always get the jokes or cultural references other people made. He wasn't totally unaware of his deficiencies in the areas of people skills and social cues. He simply couldn't determine a way to make it so that his entry into a room wasn't greeted with all the enthusiasm of a burp in church.

He stopped and turned to look down into Carli's face. She was several inches shorter than him, and he forced the corners of his mouth to tip upward so it didn't look like he was scowling. He'd been accused of frowning far too often, and he'd worked hard to overcome his natural resting jerk face.

"I'll pay you well," he offered, knowing money was important to her. She'd enthusiastically agreed to every extra hour he asked her to watch his grandmother's dog while he spent long hours at the office.

Carli could help him. She was the type of person who got along with other people effortlessly, so her effervescent personality was exactly what Mark needed.

Perhaps not exactly. His brain might explode if he tried to be as cheery as the woman walking across Magnolia's town square next to him. She was an animated princess come to life. He almost expected to see her burst into song as tiny forest creatures followed in her wake.

But certainly someone with so much sparkle could teach him how to claim a tiny sliver of that. Enough to satisfy Alex and ensure that the staff working under Mark were willing to tolerate him.

"To teach you to be social?" Carli inclined her head as she stared at him, and he glanced away, focusing his attention on Queenie. The little dog tugged at the leash like she couldn't wait to join the throng of people gathered at the center of the town square.

They were announcing the finalists in a youth art contest with a short concert by the high school choir to celebrate. Since the Fit Collective was one of the major sponsors of the town's month-long holiday extravaganza this year, Alex had closed the office today so everyone could attend.

Even if, like Mark, they didn't want to be there.

"It doesn't come naturally to me," Mark admitted quietly.

"You don't say?"

His gaze darted to hers and then away again. She was

teasing him, her light brown eyes gentle. He knew more about Carli Connelly than he'd let on back at the house. It would have gone against his nature to allow someone into his life and home without proper vetting.

He knew she'd come to Magnolia from Cleveland to work for Meredith and had also taken a job as a vet technician along with her work pet sitting and dog walking. Queenie's veterinarian raved about her way with dogs, her dedication, and her sweet nature.

There were things that hadn't been said about why Carli had moved and what motivated her to work round-the-clock when she only had herself to support. It had been clear to Mark that the vet would have shared more, but Mark was an expert at shutting people down who wanted to talk to him.

Just not Carli, which was why he figured she could help him smooth things over with his employees. He didn't want to disappoint Alex or compromise the company's success with a dissatisfied staff.

He knew he was more intelligent than most people in any given room, so why couldn't he use that to his advantage?

"Have you tried being nice?" she asked, sounding generally curious.

"I was being nice to you back at my house."

She grimaced. "Then you do need help, no offense."

"Thank you for rubbing it in. That's a great comfort." He pressed two fingers against the vein that had throbbed in his temple. "Never mind. I can fake it."

"I'll help you make friends or fake it enough to get by at work." She placed a hand on his arm and squeezed, the touch comforting. "I want something from you in return."

"Name your price."

She bit down on her lip, and his heart seemed to stutter in his chest. "Well, I want two things. Money is the first."

"Are you saving for a house or a vacation or something? What do you do with the money you make now? Granted, you have crappy paying jobs, but still…the cost of living in Magnolia isn't—"

"First lesson," she said with a barely stifled laugh. "Do not make mention of other people's crappy paying jobs."

"Duly noted."

"As I said, there's a second thing I'd like to ask of you."

"What else could I possibly have to offer?"

Her pupils dilated almost instantly, and her soft mouth formed the shape of an adorable O. Although Mark had never been great at communication, he made it his mission in life to efficiently judge a person's body language and nonverbal signals for social cues.

If he weren't so good at assessing people, he would have thought he'd misread Carli's reaction to his question. But he trusted himself implicitly and felt a strange sort of primal satisfaction that she wasn't immune to him. Particularly because of his reaction to her, which seemed both unlike him and completely out of his control.

"I want you to go to a dog training class," she said. It took him a minute to register her words. "It would help you bond with Queenie. I'm sure that would have made your grandmother happy. There's a weekly agility class at Furever Friends. Meredith is donating a part of the profits to local charities. You and Queenie would be perfect. She'd have so much fun."

"I switched her to that expensive organic dog food you recommended, and I turn Animal Planet on when I leave for the day. It seems to me that is plenty of fun for a dog."

"She needs mental stimulation," Carli told him. "And you need to bond with her. That's an important part of being a pet owner."

"I'm a pet keeper. I'm keeping her because she was my grandma's dog, and I got her in the will. My grandma was her owner. They had the bond."

"That's not how it works with dogs. They have an infinite capacity for love."

"I don't need love," he said.

"Maybe not, but you need my help making the people you work with like you. This is my condition for our arrangement."

"What if I fire you from the pet nanny job if you don't do this?"

She arched an eyebrow. "Is that what you're saying?"

Smart woman to call him on the bluff before answering. "Fine."

They were almost to the center of the square, and he could see the group of his coworkers gathered before the small dais that had been set up in front of the town's Christmas tree.

"I'll do the class, but you have to come with me. It will undoubtedly be awful."

"My next tip is to refrain from channeling your inner Scrooge around people."

"You're not people. You're different."

Her eyes went wide, and he realized it was true. He couldn't explain why. He didn't even try. Before he knew what was happening, she transferred the dog's leash to his hand. "Queenie will help you make friends."

"She can't wear the sweater."

"Trust me," she said, her voice even softer.

It pacified something primitive in him, enough that he stopped arguing. "Would you go with me to where the Fit Collective staff are gathered for a couple of minutes? Please."

"Of course I will. I feel like we've already made progress." She patted his arm, and her pure pleasure elicited a grin from him.

She tucked her hand into the crook of his elbow, and he was unnerved by how right it felt. He realized he was actually happy as they drew closer to his coworkers.

He introduced Carli and while everyone, including Alex, looked surprised that Mark brought a friend with him, no one commented on it. As she'd predicted, several members of his staff fussed and exclaimed over the dog and her holiday sweater.

They were even more charmed to discover that Mark had adopted Queenie after his grandmother died.

Mimi would have loved the attention the snack-sized dog was garnering for him. His grandmother had been the one person who never acted like he needed to change. She'd loved and accepted him exactly as he was.

Adopting Mimi's high-strung mutt hadn't been part of his plan, but he'd do right by Queenie. He also couldn't deny that, as Carli predicted, the dog adored the attention.

She invited the Fit Collective employees to stop by the rescue's booth to meet their new forever friend. Chances were good that she'd entice a few people to open their hearts and homes to rescue animals before Christmas. How could anyone resist her?

After chatting with a few more of his coworkers, Carli gave him a quick hug then headed off to the booth.

Halfway through the concert, Mark found himself humming along while the choir harmonized to "Jingle Bell Rock." Alex, who was standing next to him, grinned broadly. "So our resident Scrooge has found his holiday spirit after all. It's a Christmas miracle."

Accustomed to Alex's gentle ribbing, Mark mumbled a

response, wondering exactly what sort of Christmas miracles Carli Connelly might be able to perform in his life if he let her.

CHAPTER THREE

ON SATURDAY AFTERNOON, Carli tapped her booted foot against the tile floor of the training room at Furever Friends, trying not to fidget as she and Meredith waited for the class participants and their dogs to arrive.

"I think this is going to be good. It isn't like I forced him, right? I would help him even if he weren't paying me, although the money is nice. I'm going to send it home to my dad. He's been doing really good in Gamblers Anonymous. I want him to have a little extra for the holidays. Am I babbling?"

Meredith looked up from her paperwork and snorted. "Yes on the babbling. You like this guy."

"I do not." Carli shook her head. "That is to say, I like him fine. I like a lot of people. But I don't like him like him. You know what I mean."

"Oh, this is going to be fun." Meredith reached down to absently pet the Labrador retriever lounging at her feet. She wore a flannel shirt, jeans, and had pulled her dark hair into a messy topknot. Her green eyes twinkled with amusement "You've had a goofy look on your face all week."

"Goofy? It's called lack of sleep. I've taken on more shifts at the clinic in addition to the hours here. And the pet sitting business has picked up with so many people traveling over the holidays."

"You've still found time to spend your evenings with

Mark Simpson," Meredith pointed out, unnecessarily in Carli's opinion.

"He's paying me," Carli reminded her boss.

"But you'd do it even if he wasn't," Meredith countered. "You're allowed to like a guy, Carli. Mariella told me he's hot."

"It doesn't matter whether he's hot or not. I don't need another man in my life. Men are trouble, and I have plenty already with my dad and brother, even from several states away."

Meredith stood and stepped closer. "I know what it's like to be responsible for your family, especially being the only girl growing up in a house of big and little boys. Just because your dad and your brother took advantage—and still take advantage, if you ask me—that doesn't mean you have to rule out men completely. There are good guys out there, Carli. It might not matter that Mark Simpson is easy on the eyes, but at least acknowledge it to yourself and me. You like him. Enjoy that feeling."

Carli's stomach swooped as she thought about Meredith's words, both regarding her dad and brother and Mark. She had enjoyed spending time with him this week, more than she would have thought. She was helping him, and he was paying her. That didn't exactly make them friends.

On the other hand, the arrangement didn't make her feel like he was taking advantage, the way it often did when her dad or brother asked for her help.

Caleb, who was a couple of years older than her own twenty-nine years, had many of the same issues with addiction as their father. He'd been just as unhappy when Carli announced on a whim she was moving to Magnolia to work with Meredith.

She'd made it easy on them for too many years. Neither

had to own up to being responsible for their lives. They preferred to let her bail them out when things got tough. She knew her dad gave a portion of any cash she sent home to Caleb, but she didn't like to think about that because it would make her too angry.

Her dad had physical issues brought on by decades of hard living, but Caleb was capable of working and being responsible for himself. He was too lazy and complacent to try.

She realized Meredith was waiting for an answer. Anxiety sizzled across Carli's skin like butter on a hot pan. "Fine. Mark Simpson is handsome. Gorgeous. I look at him, and my heart goes all haywire. But I'm trying not to react to him. I'm trying not to think about how hot he is and how I want him to kiss me. I'm trying not to make a fool of myself."

She'd closed her eyes about halfway through her rant but opened them again with a flicker of dread. Meredith had placed a hand on her arm at the same time Carli heard a muffled cough in a deep, familiar tone.

"He heard all of that?" she muttered. Was it possible for her face to literally catch on fire?

Meredith nodded. "I thought it was well done," she said with a wink. "It's certainly going to make this class interesting."

CHAPTER FOUR

CARLI ENTERED MARK'S house the following day with a tentative heart and little pride. She'd gone from abject mortification to a low-grade level of humiliation overnight, which seemed a step in the right direction. Her immediate inclination to realizing he'd overheard her comments to Meredith had been to bust a move out of the rescue and hide in her studio apartment until she could figure out a way to join the witness protection program.

Mark hadn't acknowledged what she'd said, although the tips of his ears had remained a stubborn shade of pink for most of the class.

In fact, she might have done him a favor by making such a fool of herself. He'd clearly been distracted, which seemed to prevent him from being uptight.

He and Queenie had been the stars of the agility class, the tiny dog a natural as she bounded around the course. There had been five other dog owners and their respective canines in attendance, and she'd noticed Mark hanging out in the larger group during one of the breaks.

She'd ignored the fact that he'd probably been trying to avoid her. Carli was dedicated to her goal. Despite her problematic feelings for Mark, the mission appeared to be working.

She tried not to feel disappointed that he'd resisted the potential urge to stride across the training room and take her in his arms while he exclaimed that he felt the same sort of driving, pounding, unnerving need for her.

Carli's recent binge of nineties romantic comedies was doing her no favors.

Queenie trotted forward to greet Carli after hopping off the new dog bed Mark had purchased. It was a tiny replica of a bright teal fainting sofa and absolutely perfect for the little dog.

In the span of a week, as Carli had given Mark tips on how to interact with Queenie, the mottled mutt's personality had bloomed even more. Carli had even noticed that Queenie's hair was starting to grow back in a couple of spots.

"Don't you look sassy," Carli said as the dog stepped closer to show off her rhinestone collar and the sparkly barrette in her fur. "You really are a little diva."

"She gets that from my grandmother."

Carli yelped as Mark appeared from the back of the house.

"What are you doing here?" she demanded.

He inclined his head. "I live here."

"I didn't realize you were going to be home," she told him. "Again." So much for low-level humiliation. Today he wore a tailored black sweater with ribbed cuffs and hem along with dark jeans and heavy boots. His man-in-black aesthetic was enough to send her pulse racing. The conflicting feelings of desire and wanting the ground to swallow her whole sent her anxiety into overdrive. "You could have texted me."

"I was…" He massaged a hand over the back of his neck. "You like Queenie's new collar?"

Carli transferred her gaze back to the dog, which calmed her nerves somewhat. "I do. More importantly, it's clear she does, too. Well done, Mark. Since you're here—"

"You've thought about kissing me?"

Carli rolled her lips together. "We're going to need to work on your conversation transitions. That wasn't exactly smooth."

"Is it true?"

He moved closer, just a few steps, but she would have sworn she could feel his heat radiating toward her. "I'm human, you know," she said by way of an answer.

He looked confused. "Were you just being polite when you said those things?"

"Nothing I said to Meredith," she answered with a laugh, "falls under the auspices of polite."

Carli sighed. Mark didn't play games. He might not be a whiz at the nuances of social interactions, but he wouldn't keep pushing if he had a clue how she truly felt about him. "Yes, I've thought about kissing you."

She waved a limp hand in his general direction. "I'm sure most creatures with a pulse look at you and imagine shoving their tongue your throat." He blanched, and she cringed. "Okay, maybe just kissing. Nothing so aggressive as shoving tongues. It's just that…well, you're quite handsome and a little mysterious with that sullen stare and how quiet you are. There are fantasies at play in the world, you know. Women have them. Men have them. Heck, dogs probably—"

"I think we can leave off at human desire," he said, taking another step toward her.

"As if I couldn't embarrass myself more. I'm sorry, Mark. If you want—"

"I want to kiss you, too." He was in front of her now, so close that she could see the golden flecks in his hazel eyes. "And definitely with tongue. Although I think we can do better than shoving, don't you?"

She felt her mouth drop open. "I'm not sure I can do anything or think or… I'm having trouble remembering to breathe at the moment."

"I know the feeling."

"You seem calm, unflappable. Annoyingly so."

He lifted her hand and placed it on his chest. She could feel the rapid beat of his heart. "I'm not calm. Not one bit."

"That's a comfort."

His lips twitched. "May I kiss you, Carli?"

"I think I've made it clear how I feel about that."

"It doesn't matter what you said before. In this moment, you get to choose."

"I choose you," she whispered and leaned in to press her mouth to his. Her nerves and adrenaline wanted to run the show, and they clinked teeth as they angled their heads in the same direction.

Oh, lord. She was ruining this moment. It had been years since Carli had kissed a man, especially one that meant anything to her, and now she was going to mess it up before she could truly enjoy it.

She felt Mark smile against her lips. He cupped her face between those massive hands and held her still, gentle but with an authority that made her knees go weak.

Then he traced his tongue across the seam of her lips and nipped at one corner. She sighed and he deepened the kiss, and it was everything she could have wanted and more.

When he finally pulled back, Carli resisted the urge to follow him like a lovesick puppy.

"Wow," she said on a shaky breath.

"Wow, indeed." Mark didn't look uptight or restrained. His lips were swollen from her kisses, color spiked high on his ruddy cheeks, and his gaze seemed lit from within. "That was unexpected."

Leave it to Mark to say what she thought but wouldn't have the nerve to voice out loud. Carli laughed, trying not to sound as shaken as she felt. "Maybe if you did that with people at the office, it would make you more popular."

His eyes cooled considerably. "Generally, kissing co-workers, particularly employees who are subordinate to me, is frowned upon at the office. HR might have something to say about that."

"I work for you," she said then wished she hadn't.

He retreated a step. "Should I apologize for the kiss?"

"It was mutual," she said, "but we shouldn't do it again. We need to stay focused on our objective. Making you more likable." She needed space to calm her pounding heart.

"Does a kiss make you like me more or less?"

"Irrelevant." Carli bent to scoop Queenie into her arms. She gave the dog a quick squeeze. "I came to walk her, but I should go since you're here. I won't charge you for today."

Mark blew out what seemed like a frustrated breath. "You stay. I need to get back to the office. I came here to see you…to discuss…never mind. I think we've worked it out. The kissing was wow, but you don't want to do it again."

"We have a professional relationship," Carli pointed out.

"That's funny because I thought we were friends," Mark said. "More of the social cues I'm missing. I'll work on it. Thanks for the clarification."

She'd never heard him string together so many words at one time and hated the resignation in his tone. She found it difficult to believe that she had the power to hurt Mark Simpson's feelings, but there was no denying his disappointment.

How could she explain that she couldn't be friends or anything more with him? She liked him too much to let him any closer. Near enough that he'd have the power to hurt her.

"The plan is working," he said as he ruffled Queenie's soft fur. "A few people from the office are going to Champions later to watch a football game. They invited me along."

"That's great." Carli ignored the way her smile wobbled at the corners. "By the time the holiday party rolls around next week, you'll be the life of it."

"I want to invite you to go with me tonight." He rubbed his hand over his jaw and looked past her shoulder again, reminding her of that first day they'd met. "But from a professional standpoint, I can probably handle the evening on my own."

"I have faith in you," she said with more enthusiasm than she felt. She would have loved to go with him.

"On a professional level," he said, seeming insistent on making that distinction clear. "Thanks for walking Queenie. Thanks for all of it. I'll see you at agility training."

And before she could protest—unsure if she even wanted to—he walked away.

CHAPTER FIVE

"WHO ARE YOU and what did you do with my friend Mark?"

Mark narrowed his eyes at Alex's amused tone. The Fit Collective CEO sat in the empty stool next to Mark at Champions, the popular watering hole in downtown Magnolia, as a trio of IT guys walked toward the pool tables in the back. "You'd better not complain that I'm being social," Mark told his friend and then took a long swig of beer. "You were the one who advised me to try harder with the workplace social scene. I'm trying so damn hard it's making my head pound."

"I'm impressed," Alex offered, then signaled the bartender for a beer. "This is a side of you I haven't seen before."

"I didn't have it before..." Mark trailed off. Before Carli, he wanted to say. What was the point? Typically, he wouldn't keep anything from Alex, but pride demanded he not reveal exactly how much of an effect his dog nanny and social-cues coach had already had on his life.

How he'd made the mistake of falling for her when she wanted to keep their relationship professional.

"I've been working on myself," he said instead, unconcerned that Alex would judge him. Alex was not only brilliant with business but also a first-class human, which was why Mark had wanted to make the effort in the first place.

"I should have known you'd succeed at anything you put

your mind to." Alex clapped him on the back. "I appreciate the effort. Tell me you're enjoying yourself a little bit."

"I like that people aren't actively trying to avoid me."

Alex laughed. "That's a start."

Mark placed his beer on the scuffed wood of the bar.
"Does this mean you'll give me the Chief Technology Officer position?"

"You don't need the money or the title. Hell, we both
know you could retire tomorrow with what you made when
your last company went public."

"I don't want to retire. I want to prove I can do this."

"Will the kinder, gentler Mark Simpson be heading up
the team?"

"It's not like I'm some green comic book hero with an
alter ego. I don't respond to 'Mark, smash.'"

"Did you just compare yourself to a superhero?" Alex
chuckled, and Mark growled low in his throat.

"You know what I mean."

"I do," his friend admitted, "but it's still fun to give you
grief. You're a good guy, Mark. I'm glad you're finally letting other people see what I've known since college."

Mark's heart thumped wildly. He didn't like the insinu-
ation that he'd been hiding something. He hadn't, at least
not on purpose. "I don't know why this is so important."

"Yes, you do. Otherwise, you wouldn't be making an
effort, which took you long enough. It's the dog woman,
right?"

"Excuse me?"

"You know who I mean. The one who's taking care of your
grandma's dog. She was with you at the event last week. Carla
or—"

"Carli," Mark said, trying not to grit his teeth.

"It's been a while since you've had a girlfriend."

"She isn't my girlfriend. She's my dog nanny."

"Whatever works."

"It's not like that. I hired her to help me."

Alex's eyes widened. "*Pretty Woman*–style?"

"Don't be ridiculous. She walks my dog, Alex. She's not a prostitute. I hired her to help me manage the social stuff better. She could talk to a brick wall like it was her best friend. She's coaching me."

"So you're not into her? I could have sworn you were into her. It would be just like you to make some weird arrangement with a woman you liked. Paying her to hang out with you would somehow make more sense in your brilliantly warped brain than asking her out."

"I had to pay her. She wouldn't hang out with me because I asked her."

"Why not? What's wrong with her?"

This was why Mark remained so dedicated to his friendship with Alex. Alex knew Mark was a social misfit who'd always struggled with making friends and having relationships with women. Still, Alex assumed the fault lay with Carli instead of understanding the issue originated with Mark.

"There's nothing wrong with her. She's perfect."

"Can I get either of you a refill?" the bartender asked.

"I think we're good," Alex told the tall, burly man wearing faded jeans and a grey Henley. "Are you the guy helping Bill get this place ready for sale? He said you were some kind of a bar genius."

The man made a noise that wasn't quite a laugh but still conveyed his amusement. "Genius is a generous description. I'm helping out over the holidays while I visit a friend in town. Name's Declan Murphy." He held out a hand first to Alex then Mark.

Mark didn't like shaking hands, but he'd practiced enough with Carli to know he could handle the brief contact without grimacing. In truth, he'd always known he could manage certain things about being social. He just hadn't cared enough to try. She made him care about a lot of things, as Alex had rightly pointed out.

"What's involved in fixing up a bar to make it ready to sell?" he asked and noticed Alex's raised brow.

Carli had also told him that asking people questions was an easy way to keep the conversation going. And he was curious to hear the bartender's answer.

"A few updates to the property, same as you do on a residential listing, and some equipment upgrades. Plus, the whole social media part needs to be enhanced. A necessary evil if you ask me."

Alex elbowed Mark. "My friend here would probably agree with you on the evil part. He handles the algorithms for our company."

"Algorithms are above my pay grade," Declan said with an actual laugh.

"Search engine optimization?" Mark raised a brow. The nuances of technology and how it could be used to improve a company's brand awareness and sales fascinated him.

Declan shook his head. "I can tell you the difference between most kinds of beer and what it takes to tap a keg, but the tech stuff is a mystery." He pulled a business card out of his back pocket. "If you're the expert and have ideas that apply to a local bar, I'd be happy to hear them. Give me a call."

"Unfortunately, we keep our tech wizard fairly busy," Alex said, ready with his usual excuse for Mark. "He couldn't—"

"I'll reach out next week," Mark offered before his friend could say more. "It'll be my good deed for the holidays."

"Thanks," the bartender told him. "I appreciate that. Drinks are on the house."

He moved away to wait on another customer, and Alex gaped at Mark. "Since when do you do good deeds?" Then a slow smile spread across his face. "I think the answer is heading this way."

Mark didn't need to turn to know what—or in this case who—Alex was talking about. Based on the way his body suddenly stood at attention, he knew exactly why Alex looked so smug. A moment later, Carli appeared at his side.

"Hi," she said with her now-familiar open smile then turned her attention to his boss. "Hi, Alex."

"Nice to see you again, Carli," Alex said before Mark could answer. "I thought you should know that after hearing you advocate for the animals waiting to be adopted, there has been a lot of talk at the Fit Collective office about the joys of pet ownership."

"So much joy," she agreed.

"Mark is proof," Alex told her with a wink. "I caught him scrolling online pet boutique sites the other day."

"Liar," Mark muttered even as the corner of his mouth twitched. He'd never minded Alex teasing him.

Carli moved close enough to place a hand on Mark's arm. The touch felt almost protective. "Mark is great with Queenie. She's lucky to have him."

Was she defending him in her gentle way? How odd. Other than his grandma and Alex, no one had ever acted like Mark was worth championing.

"We're all lucky to have him," Alex said, his tone sincere.

Carli nodded. "You might consider doing an adoption

event at your office," she suggested. "It could boost morale if you implement a new company policy that allows people to bring their dogs to work once a month or something like that. I can have Meredith give you a call to talk about it."

It was Mark's turn to grin as Alex blinked and then nodded. "Um… I hadn't considered that. But sure, have her call me."

Played by the princess, Mark thought and chuckled.

"I will," Carli agreed. "It will be great."

Declan approached again, and Carli ordered a margarita while Alex said goodbye, still appearing a bit shocked that he'd agreed to her recommendation.

"This is a nice surprise," Mark said as she took Alex's vacated school.

"Is it?" She seemed suddenly hesitant. "I don't want to infringe on your social time with your friends."

Mark darted a glance at her then looked back at his beer. "You're my friend and I made it clear I wanted you here."

"I'm sorry if I made things awkward earlier," she told him, then thanked Declan as he set the margarita in front of her. She twirled the straw in the liquid but didn't take a drink.

"I shouldn't have kissed you."

"I'm glad you did. We both know I wanted you to since I announced it to the world."

"Not to the world," he corrected gently. "But you don't want it to happen again."

He watched as her hand moved across the worn top of the bar to press against his. "I said it shouldn't happen, not that I didn't want to kiss you."

"Why?" The word came out more gruffly than he wanted, but he had trouble catching his breath as she linked her pinky finger with his. Damn, he had it bad for this woman.

"I don't have a great track record in my relationships with men and not just romantically."

Warning bells clanged in his head. "Did someone hurt you?"

He heard her sigh but continued staring at his beer, afraid of what he might see if he looked at her right now. "Not exactly," she said quietly. "I haven't allowed anyone to get that close. My mom died when I was three, so my dad raised my brother and me on his own."

"That must have been difficult."

"The hardest part is that I don't remember her. My dad has a good heart, but he's a gambler. My brother, too. It's put an emotional and financial strain on our family." She cleared her throat. "On *me*. Dad struggles to stay employed, and he tends to borrow money from shady people."

"Do you support him?" Mark thought about how much Carli worked, how hard she pushed herself to make money. A lot of things became clear to him.

"I don't typically give him cash, but I try to support him in other ways. Coming to Magnolia was my way of gaining literal distance. Boundaries are hard for me, so I don't let people get close."

He covered her hand with his and squeezed. "I understand that."

When she didn't answer, he glanced at her. His breath caught at the emotions he saw swirling in her honey-colored eyes. "I'd like to be close to you," she told him.

"I won't hurt you," he promised. It was a ridiculous pledge. He didn't have enough experience with women to make it, and there was nothing in his past to give him the confidence to believe he could offer Carli what she needed. All he knew was that he wanted to.

"I know," she whispered.

Her confidence humbled him, and he slid off the stool and wrapped his arms around her. "You're special to me, Carli. I'm not good with words or people, but you make me want to try."

She relaxed against him, then startled as a glass shattered a few tables over. He'd been so wrapped up in listening to her that he'd forgotten they were in a crowded bar.

He pulled back and cupped her face in his hands. "Can I take you home?" he asked, and when she nodded, it felt like the happiest moment of his life.

CHAPTER SIX

THE WEATHER TURNED gray and cold with sleet spitting from the heavy sky the following morning, but nothing could dampen Carli's spirits. She'd been brave last night with Mark, honest to the extent that she could, and he'd welcomed it.

He'd made her feel like he was a man who might keep her safe. Her heart, at least. She wasn't fool enough to believe she needed saving from a man. She'd given up the white-knight fantasy years ago.

Maybe Meredith had been right with the advice she'd given. There was a difference between men like her father and brother, who wanted to use her for their own means, and someone who would treat her with respect.

A man who cherished her in a way she might eventually believe she deserved. She believed in her heart that Mark could be that man. She'd come to Magnolia to start fresh. Allowing herself to be vulnerable was part of that.

Christmas was a time for miracles, and she would welcome one into her life. She would also welcome a cinnamon roll from Sunnyside Bakery, although she couldn't quite motivate herself to head out in the wet weather. She'd just poured a second cup of coffee when someone knocked at her apartment.

If Mark Simpson could read her mind enough to know that she was craving a pastry, then Carli knew he was a keeper. Only Mark wasn't the man who greeted her from the other side of the door.

"Caleb? What are you doing here?"

Her brother flashed his easy smile. Caleb was a natural-born charmer with boyish good looks and a jaunty twinkle in his eye that made him hard to resist. Women loved him. Men loved him. At least until he scammed them or left them heartbroken with an empty bank account.

Her brother was a charming devil in the most devious sense of the word.

His presence at Carli's door made her feel like Magnolia was somehow tainted. Now the weather made sense. How could it be sunny and blue skies with Caleb in town?

"Merry Christmas, sis. I brought you something." He picked up a wet lawn ornament that she hadn't previously noticed sitting next to him in the hallway.

"You stole this from one of my neighbors," she accused, glancing around as if she expected someone to come looking for it up the stairs to her second-floor apartment.

"Don't look a gift brother in the mouth, Car-Car. You hurt my feelings."

"You don't have feelings, Caleb. Take Santa back to wherever you found him."

"In a minute." He didn't seem concerned by her reaction, but Caleb had never cared one bit about Carli's feelings. "Aren't you going to invite me in? I drove all this way to see you."

"You weren't invited."

The smile never left his lips, but Carli could see annoyance flash in his steely gray gaze. Nothing good could come of angering her brother. She stepped back to allow him to enter.

"Interesting setup." He glanced around her studio apartment. "Kind of small. I expected more based on how you've been taking care of Dad."

She threw up her hands. "Duh, Caleb. I can't afford anything more because I'm supporting him. And you." She pointed a finger in his direction. "I know when I send money, he gives some of it to you. Or you steal from him. I don't know which it is but—"

"Don't get your granny panties in a bunch." He raised a brow. "I'd hoped your wardrobe and makeup choices might have improved when you moved away. How many times do I have to tell you? You could go far in the world if you played up your assets."

"I'm happy with my place in the world." She tried not to fidget under his stare. "Happier in this small corner of the world."

"About that." He moved into the kitchen space and began opening cabinets. "You got any Lucky Charms?"

"No." Carli felt like she was out of luck. "There are granola bars in the cabinet next to the refrigerator. You can have one of those."

He shuddered. "Granola sounds too healthy for my taste. Dad said you texted him that you'd be sending extra money for Christmas."

"It's for him, Caleb. He told me the car needed work. Dad can't get to his job without the car. I'm sending extra so he can get it fixed."

"Where are you getting that money?"

Her breath caught, and she did her best not to let Caleb see that he'd shocked her with his question. Showing weakness in front of her brother was like dropping a severed appendage into shark-infested waters.

"I got a raise," she said, which wasn't exactly a lie. "For your information, some people value me."

"Nice work. It's no wonder you're Dad's favorite."

Another knock sounded on her door.

"Annoying neighbor," she said in a hushed tone when Caleb glanced between the door and her. She kept her features neutral. "I'm going to ignore them."

An immediate gleam lit her brother's pale gray eyes. "Get the door, Carli. Unless you want me to—"

"Fine. I don't care." She said the words with conviction, hoping they would fool her brother but not feeling confident. As she guessed he would be, Mark stood on the other side, a bakery bag in his hands. Her streak of bad luck continued.

"This isn't a good time," she said before he could speak.

"Invite your friend in," Caleb called. "I hope he brought better breakfast offerings than what you have."

Mark frowned. "Not a good time," he repeated.

"My brother showed up," Carli explained. As much as she didn't want to introduce Mark to Caleb, she couldn't allow him to think she had another man at her apartment.

His face gentled. "It isn't a planned visit?"

She turned to lead him into the apartment. "Not at all."

Caleb ignored Mark's outstretched hand and took the white paper bag instead. Carli knew it wasn't easy for Mark to shake a stranger's hand, and she wanted to kick her brother in the shin for ignoring the gesture. She wanted to kick him for a lot of reasons.

"Mark, this is my brother, Caleb. Caleb, I work for Mark part-time."

"And your boss brought us breakfast? Good job, Car-Car. You learned from the best how to pick out a mark. Literally in this case. So what other perks does this job have?" Caleb laughed at his own stupid joke.

"I get to scoop a lot of dog poop," Carli said, speaking

around the choking anxiety that threatened to cut off her air. So much for wanting something good and pure.

She'd told Mark the bare minimum about her brother and dad and why she moved away from her family. Caleb's presence in her house was proof there was no way to run far or fast enough to get away from his hold.

"He thinks I'm grifting you," she said to Mark, squaring her shoulders. "That's what he taught me to do with men. You wouldn't have recognized me before."

"You probably would've liked her better," Caleb added. "Our little Carli was quite the party girl. She was fun and feisty and…" He made a point of giving her a once-over. "She dressed to entice a man so he would think of her as more than a poop scooper."

"I like Carli just as she is," Mark said, breaking her heart with his sincerity.

"I do think she's grifting you," Caleb chuckled. "I know my sister. Family is her number one priority. She says you're her boss, but there's always more with my sister. She's playing you, man."

Mark ignored Caleb and studied Carli. "Is that true?"

"I told you it was true," Caleb said. "I'm her brother. You think I don't know?"

Mark continued to search her face with his endearing, earnest gaze. He still struggled to make eye contact, but the way he looked at her made her feel special. She wasn't.

"Is it true?"

Carli felt her face grow hotter if that were possible. She thought about their connection and her friendship with him, unexpected and precious. She would cherish the one night when she'd been brave enough to share her feelings before her past showed up to ruin it.

Everything her brother said was true. She'd used men

for anything and everything in the past. In reality, her relationship with Mark wasn't so different, despite what she wanted it to be.

"You should leave," she told him instead of answering the question. "This is over. I don't think it ever really started."

Caleb gave a snort. "What a touching moment. Just a warning, she's a better actress than that Meryl Streep chick."

Carli let her eyes drift closed as she worked to control her emotions. She needed both Mark and Caleb gone before she allowed herself to break down. She could not show weakness in front of her brother. Even without Mark in the picture, he'd find a way to use it against her.

"Go," she whispered. "It wasn't real."

"It was real to me," he said.

She could feel her heart break inside her own chest. Splitting apart like her past and what she wanted for her future were pulling her in two different directions.

"You can deny it," he said in a softer voice, "but this was real for you, too."

Before she could respond, he walked out of her apartment and her life.

Caleb stepped into her line of vision, obnoxiously chewing the cinnamon roll. "You should have cut me in or let me figure out how we could keep your scheme going. There will always be car repairs and medical bills. What are the chances of Dad staying clean anyway? You'll have to bail him out and—"

"I'm done." She turned to her brother. "The money I'm giving him for the car is the last I'll send, Caleb."

"You don't mean that."

"I do, and I'll tell Dad myself. He can come down here

and beg me. You can push away everyone in my life. I'll leave and build a new one someplace else. I will keep rebuilding until you figure out I'm no longer your pawn."

"Dad needs you, Car-Car."

"I need me, Caleb. I hope Dad will understand. If he doesn't, that isn't my problem."

She went to the door and opened it. "You are no longer my problem either. Get out."

His features slipped into that charming mask again. "Come on, sis. Don't be mad. Mr. Stick-Up-His-Back-End was too fancy for you. It was never going to work. I did you a favor."

"Get out, Caleb."

"Where am I supposed to go? I drove through the night."

"You are *not* my problem."

"I'm your brother."

"I know." She nodded. "Despite everything, I love you, and I love Dad. But it's time to start learning how to love myself. Merry Christmas, Caleb. Now get out."

CHAPTER SEVEN

WAS IT PATHETIC to spend Christmas Eve bellied up to a bar? Mark realized he didn't care as he downed the scotch Declan Murphy placed in front of him.

The bartender shook his head as he watched. "Whoa there, big fella. Nobody likes to wake up with a holiday hangover."

Mark waved a hand at the half-full bar. "Your patrons would beg to differ."

"*You* don't seem like a guy who wants to wake up with a hangover," Declan amended.

Mark thought about arguing but why bother? "How did you draw the short end of the stick to be working tonight?"

"I wanted to give my friend some time alone with her sons. We're closing early, so when she gets them to bed, I'll get the gifts out of the shed where I hid them and get the tree ready."

"Is this friend your girlfriend?" Mark had spent some time with Declan after making good on his offer to assist with website updates and search engine optimization for Champions. He found that he genuinely liked the guy and enjoyed helping a local business.

"No, we grew up together. She had an accident, and I'm in town until she's back on her feet. Although, this is the kind of town that grows on you."

Mark nodded. "It does."

"What happened to the woman from the other night? You two seemed to have quite the connection."

Mark ran a hand through his hair. There were times his natural inclination not to make eye contact came in handy. "I've never been great at reading people. Apparently, she was no exception."

Declan frowned. "I'm good at reading people, and she liked you. A lot."

"I have money. It attracts women who wouldn't otherwise be interested in a guy like me."

"It makes you real interesting," a voice said from behind them.

Declan's frown deepened. "Hey, bud, this is a private conversation. Do you mind?"

"Mark and I are friends," Caleb Connelly told the bartender. "We're good, Road House."

Even though Mark despised Carli's brother after only a few minutes in his presence, a smile curved one side of his mouth. The Patrick Swayze–movie reference was perfect for Declan.

It shouldn't surprise him that Caleb could get a read on somebody so quickly. Wasn't that part of what made a good con man?

"It's okay," he said to Declan.

"Right." Caleb sidled closer. "It's fine. I'll have a beer."

Declan sniffed. "We're busy tonight. I'll see when I can get something to you." Then he walked to the other side of the bar and began slowly polishing glasses, definitely not looking busy.

"Customer service sucks around here," Caleb muttered.

"You should leave," Mark suggested.

"You really like my sister."

"I'm not discussing Carli with you."

"I have a lot of influence over her, you know. Big brother kind of stuff. She was harsh at the apartment, but I think we could get past that. If I talk to her and put in a good word—"

"You're going to put in a good word for me?"

"I don't understand the arrangement you and my sister had, but you could make it long-term. You keep paying her. She keeps sending money to my dad and me."

"You want me to pay your sister to date me so that she'll give you money. Were you dropped on your head as a baby?"

Caleb didn't flinch at the question. The guy was on a mission. "Let's look at it another way. My sister has made some bad choices in her life. She has a past. No arrest record or anything but some questionable behavior. Stuff she doesn't want to follow her into this shiny new life at the beach. You care about her and you got the money to help her out. Let's make a deal."

"That's a convoluted way of blackmailing both of us."

Caleb tapped the knuckles of one hand on the bar top, clearly agitated. The guy might be a smooth talker, but complex concepts obviously stumped him.

"All I'm saying is my sister has family she left behind. Responsibilities she doesn't just get to walk away from."

"That's where you're wrong." Mark turned in his seat to face the man. "Carli is smart, independent, and good-hearted. I don't care what you and your dad got her involved in back in Ohio. She's making a new life for herself. You need to let her go."

"Says who?"

"Me. I have a feeling you did your research after we met. You know I'm worth more than Carli realizes. But you don't know how much power I have and how much I'm willing to use it to protect the people I care about." He leaned closer.

"You were right. I like your sister. A lot. You need to leave, Caleb. Get out of Magnolia and Carli's life."

"I'm her brother."

"You don't act like it."

"Are you going to make it worth my while?"

"I'm going to let you go without taking you down."

"Merry damn Christmas," Caleb mumbled and pushed back from the bar. "You two deserve each other."

CARLI COULDN'T WRAP her mind around what she'd just heard. Neither Mark nor her brother had heard her approach. She held her breath as Caleb stalked past and out of the bar, not sparing her a glance.

"Did you mean it?" she asked Mark, her throat so dry she could barely manage to swallow.

Mark looked at her with an almost confused expression. "Which part?" He shook his head. "Yes, I meant it all, but what specifically are you talking about?"

"Your refusal to be blackmailed by my brother."

A shadow crossed his face. "That doesn't mean I don't care about you, Carli. The truth is, I'd do just about anything for you. I don't know how that happened so fast. I wasn't expecting it, but I can't let your brother—"

She threw herself forward and fused her mouth to his before he could say anything more.

"You believe," she said as she pulled back, grinning, "that I can handle Caleb on my own."

"Of course I do. And I support you but—"

She kissed him again and felt him smile against her mouth.

"Are you going to shut me up with a kiss every time I try to speak?"

"Maybe," she admitted. "No one has ever believed in

me. I've never believed in myself. I always thought other people had control. The men in my life, my dad and Caleb specifically. Even when it wasn't part of a scheme, I managed to pick guys who wanted to control me."

"You picked the wrong guys." He wrapped his arms around her waist and drew her closer. "I believe in you."

"And you like me," she said, letting her voice drop.

"More than I can tell you. I never thought I'd give credence to love at first sight, but you've changed a lot of things for me."

"You've done the same for me, Mark. I was lying earlier when I told you it wasn't real. Being with you is the best thing that's happened to me in forever, but we can't continue."

His head snapped back like she'd struck him.

"We can't continue pretending like our arrangement is anything but me falling for you. Head over heels. You don't need to change for me. I like who you are, and I like who I am when I'm with you."

He breathed out a relieved sigh and flashed an adorably rare grin. "I came to Magnolia to help my friend, but I'm the one who's been transformed. You make everything brighter, Carli. I've spent too long living in the shadows." He dropped a kiss on the top of her nose. "I want to live in the light with you."

"With me and Queenie."

He chuckled. "I can't help but think my grandmother had something to do with this. She would have loved you, just like I do. I know it's probably too soon. I can be intense, and I don't want to scare you off. But I love you, Carli."

Happiness burst through her like the brightest holiday lights, making her glow from within. "I love you, too, Mark. I wasn't sure I was even capable of it, but you make me feel safe and cherished. I want to do the same for you for a very long time."

"Let's go home," he told her. "You are the best gift I could imagine. I want to spend all night unwrapping you."

Her cheeks flushed as anticipation tingled along her spine. "I like the sound of that."

He took her hand and waved to Declan as they moved toward to the exit.

"Merry Christmas," the bartender called.

Carli grinned broadly. There was no doubt this would be the most amazing Christmas ever and the beginning of a wonderful new chapter in her life with this man at her side.

* * * * *